Claude Simon

THE GEORGICS

Translated by Beryl and John Fletcher

JOHN CALDER · LONDON
RIVERRUN PRESS · NEW YORK

First published in Great Britain in 1989 by
John Calder (Publishers) Ltd
18 Brewer Street, London W1R 4AS

and in the USA in 1989 by
Riverrun Press Inc
1170 Broadway, New York, NY 10001

Originally published as *Les Géorgiques* in 1981 by
Les Éditions de Minuit, Paris.

British Library Cataloguing in Publication Data
Simon, Claude, *1913—*
  The Georgics, Claude Simon
  I. Title
  843'.914   [F]

  ISBN 0-7145-4089-7
  ISBN 0-7145-3897-3 Pbk

Library of Congress Cataloging in Publication Data
Simon, Claude.
  [Géorgiques. English]
  The Georgics / Claude Simon : translated by John and Beryl S.
Fletcher.
      p.   cm.
  Translation of: Les Géorgiques.
  ISBN 0-7145-4089-7 : $19.95 (est.). — ISBN 0-7145-3897-3 (pbk.) :
$9.95 (est.)
  I. Title.
PQ2637.I547G413   1989   89-3483
843'.914—dc19   CIP

Typeset in 11 on 12 point Baskerville by Maggie Spooner Typesetting, London.
Printed in Great Britain by The Camelot Press Plc, Southampton.

To Réa

Climates and seasons, sounds and colours, darkness and light, elements and aliments, sound and silence, motion and rest, all act upon our machine and therefore upon our soul.

Rousseau, *The Confessions*

This is what we see: in a room of vast proportions a human figure is seated in front of a desk, with one of his legs tucked under his chair, the heel of the foot raised, the tibia makes with the horizontal thigh an angle of about forty-five degrees, while the right foot is outstretched and placed flat on the ground, and both his arms are propped on the edge of the desk, the hands holding up a sheet of paper (a letter?) on which his eyes are fixed. The figure is naked. Although we can tell that he is middle-aged by the fact that his features are thick set — his face has filled out and his cheeks have grown flabby — he has no doubt maintained, like certain horsemen or military men, a sound set of muscles on his body by regular physical exercise, and in spite of his plumpness those muscles can be seen bulging under the layer of fat; the very folds of his belly are powerfully stacked, like those of old wrestlers whose weight, far from detracting from their strength, adds to it. A second, younger figure — also naked — is standing on the other side of the desk in the classical pose of the athlete at rest, with the weight of his body thrown on to his left leg and with his right arm hanging down his side, his left arm crooked, clutching to his breast a rectangular portfolio which he grips in his hand. In his case constant physical exercise has also developed a strong set of muscles, so far free from blemish. The biceps of the folded arm bulges visibly. The torso, whose pectoral and abdominal muscles are boldly drawn, brings to mind those artistically moulded breastplates of Roman armour which reproduce with perfect academic accuracy in bronze the details of the male body. At the base of the abdomen, slightly swollen and without pubic hair, the short penis, ending in a kind of teat because of the bulge of the foreskin, lies on the full pouches of the testicles which thrust it slightly forward. Under the pellucid skin the network of veins is clearly discernible, attaining greatest prominence on the forearms, the backs of the hands, the shins and the feet which they enfold like the roots of a tree. The contrast between the nakedness of the two figures and the setting, the period furniture, gives the scene an unusual air,

7

accentuated further by the way in which the drawing has been executed, on a sheet of paper (or a finely-grained canvas), with a lead constantly, carefully, almost fussily resharpened by the artist in the course of his work. Just as the naked bodies are drawn with conscious detachment, in the manner of stereotyped anatomical drawing based on classical models, the objects surrounding them, the room in which the two figures stand, are depicted with the lack of emotion associated with the execution of architectural projects, which similarly offer the spectator not existing monuments but combinations and collections of forms that are purely imaginary, referring only to themselves, and the grey lines, incredibly fine, straight as a bowstring or rounded in perfect curves, mark the division not between solids (flesh, wood or marble) and the air around them, but between white surfaces that interlock as their inflexions or their angles dictate. It is obvious that the interpretation of such a drawing is possible only through the use of a representational code which is accepted in advance by each of the two parties, the draughtsman and the observer. Thus, just as in descriptive geometry it is agreed that two intersecting straight lines signify — rather than depict — the existence of a plane, the space enclosed by the walls is merely suggested by a few strokes indicating the edges of the dihedra which they form together or make with the ceiling, or even the tiled floor whose pattern shows up in strictly calculated perspective. Outside, through the tall rectangular windows, a long façade can be seen (no doubt that of some sort of palace) with three rows of windows capped by pediments (triangular on the first floor, arched on the second, and with a plain surround on the third and top floor) drawn likewise with the patient and meticulous precision of an elevation simply sketched in outline, the whole thing (as with the furniture, the desk, the armchair) not shaded, shading being reserved for the depiction of the muscles of the two naked bodies, which assume, in the context of this form of diagrammatic drawing, relief which is all the odder for the fact that no shading extends to their feet either, as if they were just there, embossed in marble like figures detached from a bas-relief and then stuck on to the sheet of paper, not sitting on a chair or standing on the tiled pavement with its coldly geometric design. It seems that the artist, faithful to a personal set of values, has sought in this particular scene to differentiate clearly between the various elements according to their increasing importance in his mind, as is revealed by the particular techniques he has used in treating them, that is, firstly: the inanimate objects (apart from the pavement, the walls, the furniture, the windows and the landscape outside, other items are also visible, represented in the same way, that is to say in simple outline: a large old map hanging on one of the panels, with its rose compass, its mountain ranges shaped like molehills, the jagged outlines of a coast with rocky headlands, its meandering and forking rivers — and also a large globe encircled at the equator by a zodiacal ring and mounted on a tripod); secondly: the flesh, the bodies with their muscles, veins and irregularities carefully drawn and shaded, the whole resembling greyish marble statuary; and then thirdly: the heads of the two figures which are no longer simply drawn and shaded but painted in oil colours just as if they were statues whose faces and hair some joker had taken upon himself to paint in such a way as to look like real flesh and hair. In the case of one of them, the man standing on the other side of the desk (despite the existence of a chair which seems to be there for the use of visitors), the layer of paint applied to the marble stops short a little below the chin. His very black hair twists in locks over his temples as if flattened there by a gust of wind which had caught him from behind. His face, its features looking hard already despite his youth, is impassive, concealing perhaps a hint of irony or mild disdain. His head is held back slightly, in a conventional posture whose stiffness he seems to be exaggerating deliberately. There radiates from him something at once servile and haughty, the instinctive reaction no doubt of a young man in the presence of an older and more important person. The colouring is more extensive on the man seated at the desk. Not content with painting the powerful, ruddy, somewhat flushed face, the heavy brown hair tinged with grey, the artist has proceeded to dress the shoulders in a royal blue tunic, with a high red collar over which falls the vigorous mane. The layer of blue paint (except for a few stray brushstrokes) stops short above the nipples, and the tunic is decorated with epaulettes and gold bullions which hang over the greyish flesh of the arms, bare to the hands which the colourist has as it were gloved in human skin, slightly reddish also, especially towards the tips of the

9

fingers which grip the sheet of yellowish white paper, painted in detailed trompe-l'œil, with faint shadows resulting from the folds of the paper and the lines of script written in a brownish ink. It is significant that the two faces are not merely sketched in, as a painter has the habit of doing when he starts a picture, putting down a few rapid strokes of colour here and there in order to establish an overall balance of form, leaving open the possibility of returning to a particular part, or even of reworking it entirely, depending on how the work in question turns out: on the contrary, the composition of both faces is characterised by a sense of completion down to the last detail (for example a wart on the edge of one of the nostrils of the seated figure), indicating that the artist will make no more changes. Moreover, although the sun enters the vast room only through the three tall windows ranged along the same wall, the diffused radiance (quite unlike, for instance, the natural light effects and sharp contrasts in the work of certain Dutch painters) contributes even more to the feeling of strangeness in the scene, directed as it is on the faces from all sides, like the artifically distributed illumination which falls from the glazed rooflights in artists' studios where, in silence, nude models pose on stands, their ribs moving almost imperceptibly as they breathe without disturbing their still poses, frozen in statuesque positions in front of screens draped in green serge. All this, added to the lack of any other colour (on the shaded bodies as much as on the background or the furniture) and to the fact that the artist has gone as far as he can in putting the finishing touches to the painted sections (only a light blue, a mere rubbing, more indicative than representative, has been applied above the meticulously detailed drawing of the buildings outside, without filling in the upper part of the windows which open onto them), seems to confirm that this is not an uncompleted canvas but a work deemed by its creator to be perfectly finished, in which, by virtue of the fact that they are coloured in, the two faces, the gold epaulettes, the hands of the seated figure and the letter he is reading are deliberately highlighted and picked out.

Still, a closer examination of the picture leads one to think that its author hesitated over when precisely the episode which he chose to portray takes place. Indeed, although it has been carefully rubbed out and now shows up only as a very pale, almost shadowy grey, the right hand of the seated figure was visibly drawn in a different position originally: not touching the letter which the other hand still holds, it is slightly raised and the fingers half fan out in a gesture both careless and commanding, as of someone who dismisses an underling or a pest, the forefinger pointing towards the door. The question still remains as to whether this gesture (this dismissal) occurs before the addressee has taken cognisance of the terms of the letter (which the other figure, the one with the slightly mocking expression in spite of his respectful attitude, seems to know already), or during his reading, or after it, so that he may safeguard his privacy in order to read the letter again since, while still limply waving his hand, the seated man does not raise his head, but keeps his gaze fixed, as if hypnotised, on the unfolded sheet of paper.

I

He is fifty. He is the general in overall command of the artillery with the French army in Italy. His residence is at Milan. He wears a high-collared tunic with a front embroidered in gold. He is sixty. He oversees the completion of the terrace of his chateau. He is shivering, wrapped in an old military cloak. He sees black spots. By evening he will be dead. He is thirty. He is a captain. He goes to the opera. He wears a three-cornered hat, a blue tunic gathered in at the waist, and a dress sword. Under the Directory he is ambassador to Naples. He marries his first wife, a young Dutch protestant, in 1781. At thirty-eight he is elected to the National Assembly as a member for the departments of both the Nord and the Tarn. During the winter of 1807 he is in command of the siege of Stralsund in Swedish Pomerania. He buys a horse at Friedland. He is a colossus. He writes jokingly to a friend that he has put on too much weight for his short height of five foot nine. In 1792 he is elected to the Convention. He writes to his steward Batti to be sure to plant the hawthorn hedges with fresh stock. When he is expelled from Naples he has hastily to commission a Genoese vessel to get him away. He goes into business with one Garrigou to mine iron ore in the Aveyron valley. He votes for the King's execution. He is a representative-at-large of the people. He wears a cocked hat with tricolour plumes, a uniform with red flashes, top boots and a cummerbund also in tricolour. On 16 Ventôse of Year III he joins the Committee of Public Safety. From Milan he directs the ceremonies marking the Emperor's visit to the Kingdom of Italy. At the height of the Terror he is elected secretary to the Convention and saves a royalist woman whom he will take to wife when he marries for a second time. He is stated in a report to have an iron constitution and boundless courage. For a whole year, with less than twelve hundred men, he holds out in Corsica against the Paolist rebels supported by the squadrons of Hood and Nelson. He is wounded in the leg at Farinole. The ship on which he embarked at Naples is captured on the high seas by a Turkish pirate. *He is retreating with his regiment across*

15

Belgium. For four days it is impossible to unsaddle the horses. In Pomerania he complains about the cold, his health and his wounds. He is a member of the first military committee of the Legislative Assembly. He votes for a decree which punishes with death those commanders under siege who surrender to the enemy. *They are harassed by air attacks and the regiment suffers heavy losses.* The Turkish pirate hands him over to the Bey of Tunis. He sits on the Council of Elders. He wears a sky blue toque, a heavy white cape, and a red belt with ends turned backwards, stockings and buckled shoes. He takes up the defence of the Babeuvists. He busies himself with the construction of the road from Cahors to Albi. *On Whit Sunday evening he crosses precipitiately back across the Meuse before the bridges are blown up.* Chief Inspector d'Orbey acknowledges his firmness, good education, sound morals and fine conduct. He is decorated with the cross of Saint Louis. He captures the leader of the Paolist troops and has him shot. In Tunis he buys an Arab stallion which he names Moustapha in memory of Sidi Moustapha, the Bey's brother-in-law, who made his captivity less unpleasant. He urges his steward to keep plenty of manure. With Carnot and Dubois-Crancé he gets the highest number of votes in the election for the second military committee. On his return from Prussia he points out to His Imperial Majesty that he has always served him faithfully and that he is the only general of the Grande Armée not to have been made a count or enriched. *The Meuse flows at the foot of an enclosed valley with escarped and wooded sides. A group of nuns in white butterfly hats, hampered by their long skirts, runs across the bridge at the same moment as the last of the retreating cavalrymen. He whips his exhausted horse with the sword-knot taken from the guard of his sabre.* His poor state of health enables him to avoid being appointed to command the artillery in an army in Spain. He writes to a friend that since not a single shot will be fired there is no glory to be had. He is a grand officer of the Legion of Honour. He gives his steward detailed instructions for the bottling of his wine. He is sent on a mission to the Army of the North. With his colleague Choudieu he spares the lives of the two thousand English troops in the Nieuport garrison. Robespierre and several members of the Committee of Public Safety accuse him of being too lenient. He is saved by Thermidor. *The oblique rays of the sun shine on the hand which leafs through the foolscap size notebooks covered with neat*

16

handwriting. He is the commander in chief of the artillery in the Army of the Rhine. He buys in Switzerland a mare he calls La Fribourgeoise. He carries out an inspection of the northern Italian bastions. He draws on the firm of Gerit Wanhorsgstraten and Son three bills of exchange, the first for 3,669 livres payable on 10 Ventôse Year 14, the second for 3,974 livres payable on 10 Ventôse Year 16, the third for 4,281 livres payable on 10 Ventôse Year 18. *The dry skin of the hand is pale ochre in colour, slightly pink at the knuckles and criss-crossed with hundreds of wrinkles, like crepe georgette.* In the name of the Committee of Public Safety he signs the order promoting Pichegru to the command of the combined Armies of the Rhine and the Moselle, and adds his personal congratulations to the decree. He exhorts the representatives to defend the Meuse without thought of retreat. *The horses' withers are soaked in sweat which sticks the auburn-coloured hairs down in dark patches. It collects in a grey froth where the reins rub and on the inside of the thighs.* In 1811 he is military governor of Barcelona. He writes that he has had an attack of apoplexy but that he has fully recovered. He writes poems to an actress. *Whit Sunday has been very sunny. When they cross the bridge the sunken floor of the valley is already filled with shadow.* His first wife dies after giving birth to a son at the chateau of Saint-M . . . When he arrives in Corsica he writes good-humouredly to the Convention I am going to Calvi, I am taking with me gridirons to heat the cannon balls, if our enemies come and attack us they won't take us, even if I have to blow the place up and myself with it. In Milan his second wife arranges to have herself followed everywhere by a black page called Salem whom she takes the trouble to dress in an oriental style with a turban and baggy trousers. She has her hair done in the Greek manner to imitate Josephine de Beauharnais whom she is said to resemble. *On his arrival in Barcelona he joins the militia. He fights on the Aragon front during the winter.* He takes part in the Belgian campaign. He takes part in the Dutch campaign. He takes part in the Swiss campaign. He takes part in two Italian campaigns. He takes part in the Prussian campaign. He is conducting the siege of Ostalrich in Spain when his declining health forces him to leave the service. *A black flight of crows wheels over the terrace, slowly beating its wings, and makes a harsh din with its cries. He is tired. He closes his eyes. The luminous imprint of the register, its pages brightened by sunlight, lingers on his retina. Under his closed eyelids*

17

he sees a pink rectangle on a purple ground. The rectangle moves slowly to the right. Kept away for more than two decades by his political duties, his special missions to the armies and by his own commands, he can make only rare, brief appearances at home, often separated by an interval of several years. The people's group at Bastia denounces him to the Committee of Public Safety, accusing him of having assembled troops at Calvi for his personal protection. In the name of the Committee of Public Safety he writes to generals Jourdan, Moreau, Lechère and Kellermann that it is virtually impossible for him to supply them with mules, horses, coin, rations, or fodder. He suggests they take what they need from the enemy. From wherever he finds himself he writes long letters to his steward Batti to prescribe in detail and according to the season the tasks to be performed on the land at his estate. He complains about the the state of the roads in Italy where he bruises both his back and his carriages. He is a knight of the order of the Iron Crown. He is delighted at the arrest of 'the infamous Pichegru'. He pursues an interminable lawsuit against his partner Garrigou. He draws up a schedule of his postal expenses which he sends to the ministry of war. There are 2 relays from Primaro to Ravenna, 5½ from Ravenna to Rimini, 8 relays from Rimini to Bologna, 3½ from Bologna to Modena, 3½ there and back from Modena to Spilimberto, 3¾ from Modena to Formigui, etc. Post horses cost 3 lire 10 schillings in Milanese currency. At the battle for Verona he is badly wounded in the leg at the crossing of the Adige. He votes for the death penalty against any emigré returning to France captured with firearms in his possession. *On the right bank of the Meuse the road runs down between rich villas surrounded by gardens in full bloom (clumps of hydrangeas with broad pale blue flowers, it seems to him) and gravel paths. Everything is deserted. One of the horses is lame. The breeches of one of the cavalrymen are ripped by a bullet on the side of the knee. From the tear a trail of brownish clotting blood runs down and disappears into the gaiter, constantly enlarged by fresh blood which flows in short red spurts.* On 17 Germinal he informs the army representatives of the arrest of the anarchist Choudieu and of the other conspirators. During one of his tours of inspection he gazes admiringly at Virgil's statue in Mantua and halts at the Trebbia to study the site of Hannibal's, Suvarov's and MacDonald's battles. He writes that the army which finds itself on the left bank will always be beaten if it doesn't attack from the right and vice-versa. He is a member of the Milanese Academy. He makes a speech in the Convention against those who resist new ideas. He writes to his father to inform him of his intention of marrying the young Dutch woman whose acquaintance he has made at the Besançon opera. In the hope of overcoming his opposition he stresses the size of her dowry. He is received in audience by the Bey of Tunis who holds court on a divan covered in green silk in a room the walls of which are decorated with weapons of all kinds. He has a south-facing terrace built on to his chateau. *He is eleven years old. He is sitting in the stalls next to his grandmother. Her gown is fastened with demure severity at the throat by a cameo brooch in which a Pompeian dancing-girl stands out against a violet background. Through a hole made in the stage curtain painted in trompe-l'œil, the stage-manager looks at the full house. The women are rapidly waving their fans.* To the question put, does Louis Capet deserve the death penalty, he answers YES. Ostracised by the Naples court he fills his time by visiting the ruins of Herculanum and Pompei. He writes If last year we had had to reckon on the basis of normal criteria in war our campaign would have ended at Brussels, whereas we got as far as Amsterdam. He writes to his friend General Miollis that stopping once at a coaching inn in Goro he spent the night with an Italian girl. He says that if the mosquitoes which infest the Po delta prick the girl he might as well do the same. He buys in Amsterdam a five year old mare with bay coat, mane and tail, measuring a full 4 feet 7 inches. On his arrival in Strasbourg he deals vigorously with the laisser-aller and disorder rife in the Rhine Army. In his stables he has thirty-four stallions, mares, mules, hinnies, and a donkey. He writes that at the crossing of the Tagliamento there was scope for everyone and that where others plucked the roses he only garnered thorns. He writes a diatribe against Masséna whose waggon-train is the talk of the whole army and who outraged everyone by lending a mere 25 louis to Soult who was left behind on the battlefield with a broken leg. He erects a tomb to his first wife in the park on his estate. *Between the heads of the two women sitting in front of him he can see the stage lit up by the footlights. The tenor strides on without looking back, holding the soprano by the hand. She is dressed in a flowing white robe and her head is crowned with flowers. The couple move slowly across the gap between the darkened heads of the two women. Their progress is broken by long pauses.* To the question put, should Louis Capet be reprieved, he answers that the execution should take place at once. He writes to the prefect of the Charente-Maritime that he has every reason to think that his brother was killed in the Rhine Army and that the prisoner can only be an imposter. He informs Hoche of the vote of censure passed on him by the Committee of Public Safety for having allowed a stage-coach to set out without escort in a region infested with Chouans. *He stops thumbing through the folios and looks at his hand. The sunshine highlights the thousands of wrinkles overlapping and criss-crossing, some deep and some shallow, but all running in the same direction, like folds in the ground. They run slantwise from the edge of the palm to the index-finger, rippling, moving together, breaking apart, vanishing between the roots of the fingers like the waters of a stream. Blurred black shapes pass before his eyes.* He writes a diatribe against Sieyès and the priests. He congratulates his friend Miollis who has just arrested the pope. He invites General Murat to come and stay with him at Piacenza, saying that his chef, flattered by the praise he has bestowed on his talents, wishes to allow him to sample them again. At Stralsund his old wound in the leg gives him great pain when he has to stay too long in the saddle. He writes to his steward that he has only four or five years left to live, that he wants to enjoy in peace the interval separating life from death and orders that the work on the terrace be pressed on with. After leaving the army he vegetates for another year, sick and alone, in retirement at his chateau at Saint-M . . . *Beyond the folio opened out on the table and through the ironwork scroll of the balcony he can see down below the courtyard of the calvary barracks where the horsemen come and go. They are dressed in black tunics. On the page of the register the name of Moustapha and three lines of description are struck through slantwise. The same thick pen has added underneath: Died at Saint-M . . . on 8 December 1811. He looks at the back of his hand on which two thick blue–grey veins bulge out over the tendons leading to third finger and forefinger. Between the stretched forefinger and thumb the skin forms two folds which intersect, like membranes, and is pinker. The folio lies at a slight angle on the table. The ivory-coloured paper of its leaves reflects the sunlight which lights up the wrinkled face from below. He screws up his eyes. The pages ruled in pencil are covered with the secretary's neat handwriting. In the margins are entered the names of the recipients of each letter: businessmen, ministers, tradesmen, friends, subordinates, colleagues, relations, generals, servants*. He orders twelve pairs of silk stockings and points out that he does not wear garters. He tries through his lawyer to recover part of his investment after the failure of the iron mines. Pestered for money by his second wife and by his son he replies that he only has his army pay to live on and that the income from the estate is swallowed up by his debts. At Bardo he is impressed by the Bey's aviary, full of birds of all kinds and colours. The noise they make is deafening. He says that the Naples court was plotting to have him murdered, as the Republic's envoys had been at Rastadt. He writes to his father: Our meeting happened by chance, there was even something romantic about it; for the present suffice it to say that it took place at the theatre. *The audience makes a confused murmuring noise. The orchestra tunes up. Above the mingled, ever-changing and frequently interrupted sounds the leader can be heard from time to time plucking the A string of his violin to give the pitch. Between the two headless towers all that remains of the terrace is a hump in the ground now laid out as a kitchen garden and beset by nettles. A few withered beds of tomatoes and staked runner beans lie side by side with cabbage gone to seed. Three or four hens and a cock wander about pecking the ground. In the pit and dress circle the fans in the women's hands quiver again like the wings of butterflies.* At the siege of Stralsund he has under his command more than four thousand artillerymen, Italians, Spaniards, Hamburgers, Wurtemburgers, Badeners, Hessians and Hollanders as well as Frenchmen. He is billeted with his general staff at Mittelhagen castle. He sleeps in palaces. He sleeps in cowsheds. He sleeps in woods. He sleeps in tents. *He sleeps in a gutted church. He sleeps on waste ground, hidden by high weeds, on a derelict building site, curled up on the stairs of an air-raid shelter, its bottom awash with stagnant water. During the daytime he evades his pursuers by frequenting expensive restaurants and the public baths. He sleeps on the bare ground wrapped up in his greatcoat. When he opens his eyes at dawn they are clogged with a gritty, crystalline, off-white, opaque substance. His face and cavalry greatcoat are covered in snow.* He recommends that particular care be taken with his campaign mattress in Barbary sheepskin. *The painted trompe-l'œil curtain rises on a darkened set representing grottoes. The wings of the fans stop beating.* On the evening of the Tenth of August a National Assembly decree sends him, together with Carnot the elder, Prieur, Gasparin, Antonelle and seven other representatives, to announce to the armies the deposition of the

King. The resistance of the Swiss Guards is almost at an end. From within the Assembly the dying echoes of the fusillade can be heard. *From his sentry post he can see the whole of the big city spread out between the hills and the sea which shimmers in the distance. Above the tiled roofs rise here and there domes and cupolas, with their heavy architectural features and the Gothic spires of the old town. The city is shaken by the explosion of bombs punctuated by the sound of the fusillade and by bursts of automatic fire. As no smoke drifts up he concludes that neither side has yet brought in the artillery.* He composes an epitaph for his first wife's tomb. *On the stage flats are represented in trompe-l'œil piled-up rocks, painted reddish-brown, as if oxidised by a subterranean fire, ferruginous. Orpheus is dressed in a short Grecian tunic. He stands with a dejected air. He has pink tights on.* By the terms of the decree he is given authority to suspend provisionally generals as well as all other public or military officers and functionaries and to place them under arrest if circumstances require it. He swears an oath to uphold liberty and equality and to defend the world against tyrants. After his stroke he suffers occasionally from giddiness. He sees black spots turning round and round. Indispositions of this kind become more and more frequent. The tomb which he erected in honour of his first wife stands at the foot of a dell, near the Callèpe stream, surrounded by an aspen wood. *From the terrace the tomb cannot be seen. All that is visible are the tops of the aspens whose leaves are shaken by a continual trembling, even when no breeze is blowing, as if they were moving ceaselessly of their own accord in a silent rustling.* He writes to the Committee of Public Safety that in the Army of the Western Pyrenees the dearth of shirts and shoes is appalling, that for lack of mules for the transports the attack on Bilbao has had to be postponed, that the Army of the Eastern Pyrenees is considerably weakened by mass desertion, with entire companies leaving the colours, taking their weapons with them as they go. *Below him he can see the pale green spring foliage on the plane trees on the avenue. The downy shoots at the ends of the branches are pale russet too. He is armed with two bombs clipped to his belt and a hand gun. The city shaken by explosions lies stretched out in the sunshine. The surface of the avenue is littered in places with boughs chopped off by bullets. The leaves are still green but are starting to curl. The tenor sings Euridice Euridice ombra cara ove sei?* At Calvi he manages to set fire to an English frigate which had ventured into the harbour and to sink it despite the intervention of other ships

of the squadron. He buys mules and horses in Turin which he
sends under military escort to his steward. He laments the fact
that the Piedmontese mule is not a patch on the Barbary variety.
At the Restoration his widow Adélaïde petitions Louis XVIII for
assistance, begging him to overlook the prejudice attaching to
the name she bears. She recalls that on the evening of the Tenth
of August she managed to get into the Convention as the last
defenders of the Tuileries were being put to death and to deliver
to the King a note from the Duc de Clermont-Tonnerre.
*Emerging from the nettles above the collapsed edge of the terrace the cock's
head appears. It moves circumspectly to right and left in sudden jerks which
make the comb (composed of a fleshy, grainy matter) wobble.* He writes to
Hoche to alert him to the possibility of a landing by English
forces at Belle-Isle once the equinox is passed. He carries out an
inspection of the defences on the Ligurian coast. He draws up a
plan of his estate which he sends to his steward. There are nine
sub-divisions in the yellow-coloured section of the walnut trees.
The first division begins at the elm on the plain of Change and
goes down as far as the enclosure. The section planted with
cherry trees runs the width of the field as far as the ditch. He has
a new gun-carriage adopted which seven men can easily
manoeuvre instead of twelve. *The hand's uneven shadow which,
pulled out of shape, extends along the upper part of the right-hand page of
the foolscap size notebook, masks the words:*

> night heard my complaints
> on a coffin when
> changed the face of Europe
> movement of the revolution
> run every kind of risk
> the greatest dangers I succeeded

*which end the first six lines written in a well-formed sloping hand, the quill
sometimes pressed down heavily and spluttering a little on the down
strokes.* The second division ends at the Caretal. The third which
follows on is the division of the large walnut-tree and is coloured
blue. The tomb is in the blue division. *The cock's neck is covered in
reddish feathers with glints of mauve and pink. Depending on the position of
the head the sun shines through the comb, illuminating it like a lantern with
a red transparent glow, then it seems to go out, leaving the comb purplish
and limp.* He arrives at daybreak at Peschiera arsenal. He has the
keys to the store rooms handed over to him and notices that they

contain artillery items which are not listed in the inventory. He writes to the minister that the stores of the French army are being pillaged with the complicity of the Italian officers. There are 2 relays from Borgo Buchiano to Lucca, 2 from Lucca to Viareggio, 1 from Viareggio to Pierro Santo, 1 from Pierro Santo to Massa, 1 from Massa to Lavenza, 17⅔ from Lavenza to Modena, etc. *Through the cast iron scroll and foliage of the balcony he continues to see indistinctly beneath him the dark shapes of the cavalrymen coming and going against the light. One after the other, leaving a gap of about fifteen yards between, they come out of one gateway in the outer wall, ride parallel to the central upright of the window, turn left and disappear under another porch. The horses' shoes ring out on the cobblestones. The noise reverberating off the walls is different when they enter the second gate. Their torsos clad in black tunics sway gently to the horses' movements. Their shadows, looking like those of equestrian statues, stretch along the cobblestones at the same angle as that cast by the hand on the folio. He screws up his eyes to read the words:*

> *a tomb; the*
> *dawn found me*
> *the event which*
> *the great*
> *led me to*
> *in the midst of*

by which the first six lines begin, written on the side of the page glaringly lit up by the sun. He turns over several leaves in one go: In 1792, after the destruction of the throne, when the French people called a national convention together, the army of the Coalition Powers was only 40 leagues from Paris, and men of courage were needed in a session which promised in every way to be stormy and so far as one could tell there was more likelihood against than for; ambitious people put themselves forward half-heartedly, but the people wanted to send men of character to the Convention: I was elected. *In the movement he makes to grip the top corner of the page between finger and thumb the wrinkles and the bulging veins are smoothed out and the skin is stretched over the back of the hand which then seems to be made of smooth pinkish marble shot through with a network of pale bluish lines. The younger of the two women has her hair coiled up in a bun. On the back of her slender neck a few short stray locks curl behind her ears. The light coming from the stage gives rise to pearly reflections on one side of the neck and on the cleavage revealed by the décolleté. The flight of crows moves away slowly. In fact it breaks up into a mass of whirling flights, without obvious connection, so that the black swarm is governed by a double movement: the one carrying it gradually away and, within it, that quantity of eddies, of turnings back, of loops inscribed in vertical or oblique planes creating an impression of chaos which however has no effect on the movement of the whole, the stragglers flying swiftly to catch up with the group while others start to wheel independently again, as in a relay race. The luminous imprint left on the retina by the rectangular open folio decreases in size and simultaneously changes colour, now a jade green against an umber ground.* He has his bust carved in grey–ochre marble lightly veined in darker grey. *He is forced to lean to one side to see the tenor and the soprano who have stopped again, at the extreme left of the gap between the two women's heads. From that angle he can see in semi-profile the delicate features of the younger woman. Orpheus turns his back on Eurydice who sings Che mai t'affanna in si lieto momento?* He converses with the Bey in Italian and requests him to order his release together with that of the Genoese vessel and its crew which the Bey stubbornly considers to be 'fair game'. *He observes that the wheeling of the crows inside the flock is always the work of two individuals, no doubt male and female, flying together and seeming to pursue some business of their own (a courtship ritual, an insect chase?) without however leaving the group or ceasing to follow its trajectory.* In the name of the Committee of Public Safety he informs representative Rittes, at Toulon, of the state of complete destitution in which the Army of Italy finds itself. In an address to the Convention he defends the new military arrangements. He says that when men are presented with great truths it is only to be expected that this will lead to great argument, that they will ridicule anyone who puts forward a new idea and label a wrecker anyone who is only trying to suggest a better way of doing things. *The crows have now gathered on three trees in the orchard which almost disappear under their black, funereal mass, like excrement. Under the closed eyelids the colours switch round. The jade green rectangle of the window divides into two cherry-cloured rectangles on an olive ground.*

For more than an hour before nightfall the three gun battery camouflaged on the other side of the forest track keeps up a continuous bombardment. The firing of each shell makes a

25

deafening noise, followed by a shrill moan which diminishes rapidly. There is a short silence, then the distant echo of the explosion. The horses are tethered together in a clearing some fifty yards from the battery. As daylight fades the more or less distant rumbling of the cannonade becomes gradually less frequent and then stops altogether. In the dusk and the recaptured silence the slowly darkening forest gives off a still damp smell of vegetation. The intermittent singing of a blackbird reverberates now and then under the high trees. The soft bluish mist oozing from the foliage gradually darkens and soon the leaves stand out black against the sky. The horses tethered together in the clearing make up a shadowy, sombre group. Light is dimly reflected off the polished leather of the saddles and off the cruppers. The relatively smart turn-out and the faces of the artillerymen contrast with the drawn features, the stubble and the dusty greatcoats of the cavalrymen. The troopers look at the gunners sitting on boxes eating hot soup. The last birds have long fallen silent when the hooting of an owl echoes through the woods. The men on sentry duty jump nervously. Despite their fatigue the soldiers lying wrapped up in their greatcoats on the ground turn restlessly without being able to get to sleep. In the end they get up one after another and wander aimlessly about, some of them milling around the gunners' radio vehicle talking things over with them. There is a rumour that enemy paratroops signal to each other to regroup by copying the cry of an owl. *He dictates to the secretary of the Committee of Public Safety a letter to the representatives attached to the Army of Sambre-et-Meuse. The secretary's handwriting is decorated with a mass of paraphs and flourishes. He writes And where will you go? You say yourselves that our positions on the Meuse would in the case of reversal offer only slight resistance. So we must be victorious.* The back door of the truck lets out a feeble glow which lights up the radio operator inside sitting in front of his set, from which pours a succession of crackling noises alternating with indistinct staccato voices. Sometimes the operator picks up a remote station and for a short while snatches of syncopated music, of symphonies or operas can be heard, tenuous, as if weakened by the distance, tepid and unreal in the vast gloomy forest. More or less close by the hooting of brown and white owls continues to arise from time to time. The soldiers stop talking and listen to the darkness.

As if coming through densities of time and space the fragile voice of the tenor sings *Che farò senza Euridice? Dove andrò senza il mio ben? Euri . . .*, then the instrument crackles once more. When the noise of frying ceases it gives way to the rhythmical sounds of a saxophone, these too almost imperceptible, as if the sounds themselves flickered a long way off in the darkness '. . . *courted by many gentlemen, I triumphed over them all, Miss H . . . r comes from one of the best families in Amsterdam, the tastes we share . . .' The tenor now stands on the far left of the stage (so that, leaning forward and to the right this time to glimpse him he can also see in profile the face of the young woman who has also turned her head to the left). Orpheus stands by a flat which runs from the ground up to the flies like a pillar made of heaped rocks, simplified by the set designer in geometric forms, with sharp edges dividing the planes to make triangles and trapezia painted red ochre, brick red, reddish brown and dark brown according to their situation in order to give an impression of relief. At the interval many young men in powdered wigs, frock coats, and tunics pinched in at the waist and flared out underneath like skirts, throng around the two women. The colours are: light blue, pale grey, pink, silver, pearl, royal blue lit up with red spots on the facings*. The decisions of the Committee of Public Safety are copied out in a register consisting of leaves sewn together without a cover. *The luminous rectangle clinging to the retina in the purple darkness of the sealed eyelids stretches sideways now, narrowing in the middle, making a sort of raspberry coloured horizontal sandglass, or rather a bobbin. It expands to fill the entire visible space in the middle of which appears a tiny mauve moon.* At about two in the morning a column of covered lorries halts on the forest road alongside the battery. Inside the lorries the men are sitting on parallel benches, facing each other, their rifles upright between their knees. In the darkness only the first in each row can be seen, those nearest to the backs of the vehicles. They do not speak. They do not answer when the troopers and artillerymen ask them if they belong to the division of reinforcements which is heralded. They look tired and frightened. *He feels a light touch on the back of his hand. He opens his eyes again. The diaphanous wings of the fly shine in the sun like mica. Its monstrous and transparent shadow stretched slantwise seems borne away on a static thrust, seems to be mounted on legs like long threads which describe an acute angle with the body while the folded wings stretch out behind it like a tail.* Inside the radio truck dance music is playing softly. The officers in charge of the convoy approach the artillery

27

NCOs to ask them the way and spread out a map on which they shine a couple of torches. After getting the information they seek they linger a while longer and talk softly away from the men. In the huddle someone says that the Germans have crossed the Meuse that evening on a dam which no one remembered to blow up. The worried voice of one of the officers says That'll cost us dear. *When the cock's neck retracts the feathers stick out horizontally and their coppery colour turns brown. When it stretches out they lie flat again, and are again pale bronze and glinting. In the movement the hand makes to chase the fly away the fingers stretch out and the skin creases again in innumerable wrinkles running in waves over the tendons and the prominent veins.* With his eyes closed he hears the horses' shoes striking the cobblestones. From the suddenly different sound reverberating under the vault he can tell at what moment each of the horsemen enters the gateway. The invoice is drawn up on greenish white handmade paper, the ink is dark brown, the writing is the well-shaped hand of an accountant: *Supplied to His Honour General L.S.M. By Richard Joallier no. 21 Cour de Harlay: A necklace of 63 diamonds mounted on claws weighing 21⁴/32 carats, fully made up: 4 300 francs; a tiara-shaped comb set with 109 diamonds mounted on claws weighing 17⅞ carats: 2 460 francs; a pair of ear-rings and ear-drops of 36 diamonds mounted on claws weighing 10/8⁹/32 carats, fully made up: 1 960 francs; a necklace, a pair of ear-rings, and a comb top in coral, the comb matching the diamond comb, with case: 225 francs, etc.* All that remains of the tomb is a rectangular stone in a tangle of briars, flaked by winter frosts, on which the inscription half-covered by lichens is hard to decipher. *The hum of conversation, the dazzle of chandeliers, the lustre of fabrics, music, everything blends in a sort of confused amalgam of soft colours and delicate sounds,* like a murmur, a distant flickering in the darkness, a tiny, unreal agitation somewhere at the bottom of the night. The hooting of the owl is heard twice, close at hand. *His constant visits to the armies keep him away from the events of the Terror. He returns to Paris only after the promulgation of the laws of Prairial. It is then that he is elected secretary of the Convention.* No one believes that the well-equipped troops which have suddenly appeared in the city and have started the shooting are acting on government orders. In fact no one knows precisely who is firing on whom. After the first ragged exchanges of gunfire a sort of tacit armistice seems to have been established in the sector. Supplies, and lack of sleep, constitute their main problem. *He has to wrestle with sleepiness and his eyelids burn. Even with his eyes closed he can feel on his face the gentle movement of the leaves of the plane tree which alternately shut off the sun's rays and let them through. The leaves are shaped like three-pronged stars. Under the eyelids the two parts of the horizontal sandglass separate to form two distinct spheres which melt into the brownish cloudiness. Only an indistinct flickering remains.* On the first night he is prevented from sleeping by the ceaseless crying of the baby and by the two bombs clipped to his belt which dig into his ribs. Taking advantage of the lull he slips into the streets one morning and manages to reach the food-market. Most of the stalls are closed except for a few which are besieged by customers. A shot is fired, shivering a pane in the glass roof, and panic breaks out. He makes good use of the opportunity to buy a piece of cheese which he cuts in two and tucks into his cartridge pouches next to the bombs. One evening the rumour goes round that their water supply is going to be cut off. They hurriedly fill up all the containers they can find and decide to storm over the roofs at dawn the next day the building occupied by the guards. He checks his bombs and his pistol. He thinks that he will be killed. *In June 1789 the 7th artillery regiment in which he serves is summoned to Paris. With several other officers he tells the colonel that he is resolved to desert if the government tries to use force against the people. The criss-cross branches of the plane tree leave on his retina an imprint which vaguely takes the shape of a 7 whose tips and apex are laden with little spheres, like nodules, as if the figure had been drawn in ink on blotting-paper, the pen hesitating, pausing at each change of direction, the blotting-paper absorbing the ink in round blots. The 7, at first turquoise blue on an orange ground, breaks up wavily, adding at the bottom a horizontal line to itself, like a Z; meanwhile it turns a dark blue, indigo haloed in black on a pale yellow ground. From Mittelhagen he informs his steward that he is taking advantage of a convoy to send her a white-faced chestnut mare, with white stockinged forelegs and offside back leg, a seven-year-old, full-grown, measuring 4 feet 9 inches high with flowing mane and tail, bought in the Mecklenburg Strelitz region and named by him Saléma.* The next episode takes place two days after the night spent alongside the gunners. Apart from its bloody character, its importance lies in the fact that it will mark for the survivors the end of the phase of the battle which could be called coherent, or more accurately from now on there will not be any kind of order, even a disastrous one. They will find themselves then between the Meuse and the Sambre outside all structured systems, individually or in very small groups completely astray, starved of news, guiding themselves by guesswork according to the sun's position, handicapped by their state of exhaustion and by lack of sleep. *And where will you go?* At about four in the morning the gunners are ordered to fall back. They have been gone a long time when the troopers remount at dawn and form up in columns. All day long they retreat along a road congested with military and civilian convoys of all kinds, with abandoned or burnt out vehicles (it seems that the most severe bombardments have taken place in their rear), with soldiers who have more or less broken into a disordered rout and refugees who ply the officers with questions as they pass but get no reply. Occasional shells, as if fired haphazardly, fall here and there in the fields. One of these, a huge calibre missile, spurts up into a massive pillar of black smoke which hangs upright for a long time in the still air. The weather stays fine. Formations of aircraft fly over them several times at high altitude without attacking them. About mid-afternoon the squadron takes a minor road and pulls up in a small village abandoned by its inhabitants which the troopers receive orders to prepare to defend. However their main concern is to find something to eat, but the retreating troops have already ransacked the houses and all they come across are cigars and jars of preserves which they empty directly by slipping the fruit into their mouths with their fingers. Towards dusk enemy reconnaissance units appear but fall back at once. At midnight the troopers are ordered to disengage in complete silence. They tear up all the material they can find (bedspreads, blankets, dusters) with which they wrap up the horses' hooves as best they can, and lead them by the bridle for about half a mile before getting into the saddle. They then ride along in darkness, their progress being often interrupted by long inexplicable halts during which they stand still, slumped on their mounts. *He writes to the Committee of Public Safety that attempts are being made on his life and that several of his officers who in the course of their duties went before him along paths he was to have taken himself have fallen into ambushes and been killed.* They jump now and then at the sudden woosh of a rocket which lifts off as they pass by, drawing a stream of sparks behind itself in the black sky. At one particular moment they pass a long column of burnt out lorries, some overturned in the ditch, which smoulder on, giving off a foul stench of scorched rubber and human flesh. They make out blackened corpses, some crouched over the trucks' steering wheels, others seated astride motorcycles lying flat on the verge. At a crossroads pockmarked with craters the ruins of a few dwellings are still burning, their fallen timbers licked by little silent flames which seem to chase each other lazily along the rafters, lighting up the dark silhouettes of men and women armed with buckets or carrying loads who stop for a moment to stare wildly at the troopers, then begin again scurrying to and fro. The troopers have now had no rest for more than forty-eight hours and they struggle as best they can against sleep, dozing off now and then, their bowed forms swaying backwards and forwards to the pace of their horses' movements. When dawn breaks once again they are riding upon a huge, almost bare plain, devoid of trees, scattered sparsely here and there with the odd clump of bushes, but offering no possibility of shelter. On the road they are following there are neither refugees, nor convoys, nor signs of any kind of combat. No sound of battle or bombardment can be heard, even in the distance. They nervously inspect the sky, which is cloudless except for a few thin horizontal bands in the east which the rising sun touches with pink. As it climbs higher in the sky it throws before them their pale, distended shadows, making them look like equestrian statues, or like giant insects on elongated legs which seem to retract and advance by turns without making any progress. The light is pearly-white, growing gradually yellower. The shadows are beginning to shorten when the first shots ring out. The horses rear and tumble and the men at the head of the squadron, which had turned right into a side road, fall back in disorder towards the road junction where they collide with the cavalrymen in the last troop who have been attacked from the rear and arrive at a gallop. They realise then that they have fallen into an ambush and that they are, almost all of them, going to die. As soon as he has written this sentence he sees that it is more or less incomprehensible for anyone who has not been in a similar situation and he raises his hand again. Between the root of the thumb and of the first finger the network of wrinkles, flaccid and then crimped, encircles the penholder in more or

31

less parallel curves. Raising his eyes he sees, one after the other, the top of the sheet of paper covered in erasures, the table edge, and then the ironwork scrolls and foliage of the balcony beyond which indistinct black shapes continue following each other. He takes off his glasses and can see clearly in the courtyard of the barracks the troopers, their upright forms clad in black tunics with red braid, their boots black and shining, their trousers royal blue and their képis cylindrical and black. The sun glints on shiny, mahogany-coloured cruppers.

fetné	*F*
Zobeide	*F*
Zizialé	*F*
négémet	*F*
giafar	*M*
abdelmelek	*M*
barmécide	*M*
Zoran	*M*
almakadan	*M*
Kalil	*M*
Karcas	*M*
némana	*F*
Simostafa	*M*
naraîs	*M*
nadam	*M*
dalhuc	*M*
Kallacahabalaba	*F*
Kokopilesobe	*M*
hicar	*M*
pharam	*M*
Xailoum	*M*

The list of horses' names stretches in a long column down the margin of one of the pages of a notebook whose leaves are also hand-sewn in simple fashion. On the flyleaf are scribbled with no concern for calligraphy the words Memoirs of my embassy in Naples and my captivity in Tunis. To protect the personal nature of these notes, or perhaps out of affectation, they are drafted in Italian: . . . *alcuni schiavi ricamente vestiti mi presentavano al Bey facendomi passare per une lunga oscura scala che termina sotto una grande uccelliera così piena di differenti uccelli che io ero stordito dal loro canto. Vidi il Bey sopra un soffa, di piccola statura, occhio vivo, sembianza viva. La sua camera contiente pochi mobili, ma molte armi. Vi ho contato 17 paia di pistole, 17 sciabole, piche e stili. Osservai una cosa sorprendente, ed è che il suo primo Ministro Jusuf non ha più di 22 anni, era un Georgiano grasso, fresco et polputo. Io ero un barbaro ma ...* Sometimes one of the young horses takes fright (at a sound, or just at a scrap of paper caught by the breeze) and shies. Mastered by its rider it bends on its hind legs, paws the ground, and its shoes clatter loudly on the cobblestones. One after the other, preceded by their shadows, they grow larger as they draw near, before turning at right angles, then are profiled an instant against the light, before disappearing under the porch. *He writes to General Mack, on the King of Naples' staff: ... it is one thing to be in one's study and draw up a plan of attack, and quite another to carry it out: working in the study one has time and leisure to reflect, nothing troubles the mind: in battle defeat or success depend on a single moment: noise, danger and smoke are all obstacles preventing one from seeing clearly and ...* The upright and two of the bars of the windows remain imprinted on his retina and form a cross making four turquoise squares which drift slowly towards the right against a dark red ground.... *in the midst of the greatest perils I have many times imagined I saw the shade of that adored wife covering me with a shield and clearing a path for me through dangers; every year I ...* Primly clasped at the neck by the Pompeian cameo the bodice-front of the old lady with the chalk-white face is embroidered with a multitude of black pearls shaped like tiny cylinders which glint discreetly in bronze-coloured, pink and turquoise flashes. She has difficulty breathing, and her open mouth sags at the corners like the downward-turned half-moon of painted clowns or of conventional tragic masks, podgy and limp, covered with a grey powder. The tenor now stands in silence at the foot of the heap of reddish boulders, holding an afflicted pose inspired by one of those paintings themselves inspired by antiquity and representing a funeral or some biblical catastrophe, plague, defeat, or massacre. He covers his lowered face with one hand, and stretching his left arm a little behind him, he holds his other hand palm open, as if he wished to hold at bay some vision or other, or fend off a busybody whom he refuses to listen to. From the girls' chorus massed on the right of the stage rises a concert of crystalline voices.

RECAPITULATION

	Saléma	
	odaïde	
mares	almaïde	greys
	palmire	
	zeraïde	
mare	fatmé	
colt	haraïs	bays
stallion	Zoran	
	abdelmelek	blacks
stallion	pharaon	grey

The stable roof is half fallen in and the wood of the roof timbers is bleached and worn by the weather. In the evening on the slope opposite the terrace, beyond the orchard, a dog gathers together the cows scattered over the meadow, running from one to the other and nipping their hind legs. The cows gallop in an ungainly fashion. The sound of the bells tied to their necks and the barking of the dog arrive weakened in volume and with a second's delay, as if they had to cross a thick layer of glass, a film at once transparent and opaque which isolates the face from the outside world. The autumn winds have stripped nearly all the foliage off the tops of the aspens which sway stiffly in their nakedness. In the account he gives of events, O. tells how as the first shots ring out a stranger grabs him by the arm and hauls him along. They cross the avenue in this fashion and take shelter from the bullets flying from the church tower. A motley crowd of passers-by caught up in the shooting, among them women and children, is seething in the building where they have found refuge. Nobody understands what is going on. A young man hands out rifles to the new arrivals. He manages to get one himself but has it stolen from him almost immediately. A baby cries ceaselessly. The brief skirmish at the ambush into which the squadron has fallen seems over. Everything is now quiet. After a moment he sees a mosaic of irregular polygons of different sizes, pale grey, blue grey, chalky, ochre and pink. He is on all fours on the ground. In the middle of the track, in the strip protected from the vehicle wheels, small tufts of grass and tiny plants with star-shaped serrated leaves grow between the

34

stones. He can no longer hear the machine-guns firing. His pale blue four-legged shadow stretches distendedly to his right. About two hours later he is mounted once again, riding beside another trooper behind the leader of the squadron and a lieutenant (he recounts in a novel the circumstances and the manner in which things happened in the interval: taking into account the weakening of his faculties through fatigue, lack of sleep, noise and danger, the inevitable lacunae and distortions of memory, this narrative can be considered a remarkably faithful account of events: the cross-roads and the fields littered with corpses, the wounded man covered in blood, the dead man stretched out on the edge of the ditch, his gradual recovery of consciousness, his sudden decision, his breathless run back up the hill through meadows divided by hawthorn hedges, his crossing over the road patrolled by enemy light armoured cars, his walk in the forest (*And where will you go?*), his thirst, the silence of the underwood, the cuckoo's song, the distant sound of bombardments, the unexpected meeting with the two officers who survived the ambush, the casual way he is ordered to mount one of the two horses led by the orderly, the crossing of the bombarded town, etc). The road which starts in Belgium and runs south of Maubeuge towards the Sambre stretches in a straight line roughly east to west between Solre-le-Château and Avesnes, lined with fruit trees, gently rising and falling with the slight folds in the ground. The verges and ditches are littered with wrecks of every kind, burnt out or abandoned lorries and cars, overturned carts, dead horses, etc., and above all an unbelievable amount of paper and cloth scattered about, harshly white against the green. He experiences the sensation of being separated from the outside world by the crackled and burning film formed on his face not only by dirt but also by his state of extreme exhaustion. Swaying forwards and backwards on the saddle to the pace of his horse's movements, he fights as best he can against the sleep which weighs down his eyelids. He dimly makes out the ramrod backs of the two officers silhouetted against a luminous background, swaying on their saddles without making any progress. At a crossroads he sees a road sign plate indicating: Wattignies-la-Victoire 7 km underlined by an arrow pointing to the right. Shortly after crossing the village of Sars-Poteries the two officers are shot down at almost pointblank range by an enemy paratrooper concealed behind a hedge. He and the orderly turn their horses' heads and gallop away under the paratrooper's fire. The orderly's thigh is grazed by a bullet. When they get back to the village they slow down, then stop. They stand there in the middle of the road (in fact the village seems to be made up of only two rows of low houses in dark red or purplish brick which stretch for about a mile on both sides of the dead straight road, interspersed occasionally with little gardens) littered with wreckage, not far from a dead horse almost completely covered over, although the weather is dry, with a wet layer of ochre mud. It must be about noon. The sun is high in the sky and their telescoped equestrian shadows make a black patch underneath them. *And where will you go?*

In September the big spiders appear. They weave their glittering, polygonal webs between the branches. One of them has fixed the axes between the laurel and one of the shoots on the trellis. The wind which sometimes bends the boughs makes the network stretch and quiver. In the middle of the glistening, geometrical structure of parallel threads the lurking spider waits, rising and falling elastically in tune with the gentle movements of the leaves. The hooked legs, spread out, are reddish brown, the heavy, dark, cone-shaped abdomen is dotted in yellow. Emerging quite suddenly from its motionless state it moves rapidly to mend a tear in the web or to seize a prey. The delicate design of threads made silvery by the sunlight stands out against the black background of the laurel. Its right-hand side, in shadow, is less visible where it gets lost on the trellis among the broad serrated leaves the edges of which autumn is starting to redden and curl, although their centre, where the ribs and their ramifications stand out clearly, is still green. The laurel leaves are oval, pointed, and have rippled edges, like flames. I intend to build a terrace above the cock-yard: you will see that trellises get planted along the wall which goes down to the river, you will prune the line of young elms, you will take a thorough look at the two lines of trellises which end in the laurel arbour, you will replace any that are missing, you will inspect all the water-meadows, you will replace any missing willows and poplars, you will replant the whole of the bank by the tomb, you will replant the poplars in the oval where the small fountain stands, you. Count Primoli has in his possession an album of drawings made by Vicar in Italy between 1800 and 1804. In this album are portraits of General and Mrs. L.S.M. during their residence in Milan in 1803. The colossus's face looks astonishingly young at this period: somewhat plump, clamped up to the ears in the embroidered collar of his uniform, his neck swathed in a high black cravat, he seems, under the heavy fold of skin which half covers his eyelid, to be keeping his quick, vigilant, reticent eye on the artist. There is a dimple on his chin, and his small, fleshy mouth, with the lower lip jutting forward, makes a kind of pout, the very high forehead is crowned by thick hair whose dishevelled locks frame the head and tumble about his ears and neck. His expression is that of someone who is careful not to be taken by surprise, at once impulsive and thoughtful, able to pass in an instant from reflection to action, from silence to vociferation. With his wild, leonine mathematician's shock of hair, his broad forehead, his tunic carelessly pulled on open to his shirt-front, the slight curl of the lips, the heavy jaw, the astute gaze, the look at once bold, circumspect, impenetrable and sarcastic, he reminds you of one of those corresponding members of a learned society who has at one and the same time something of the pamphleteer and of the horse-trader in him. The colours in sequence are these: cherry rectangle on plum ground, pink rectangle on purple ground, jade rectangle on scarlet ground, mauve rectangle on brown ground. The rectangle splits into two pale blue parts which slide together towards the right and the bottom. The background is colourless, simply dark. The rectangles grow slowly blacker whilst between them a luminous point appears which seems to get closer and gradually increase in size. On 8 Nivôse I received the order to besiege Peschiera: after having carried out all the works, after being riddled with shot, and with the investing batteries preparing to reveal their fire, the armistice came. With a siege no longer to be undertaken Brune, the general in chief, has given me the command of Piedmont and I need all my firmness not to fail in the preservation of the public order which I uphold, for people are in a constant frenzy about the future of this country. Will it be handed back to the King of Sardinia, will it be annexed to France? It is not for me to enter into political

37

arguments, as the head of the military authority I have only to carry out my orders. The bright lozenge stretches out, becomes an ellipse. The ellipse takes the geometrical form of a rhombus, bent to the right. The circumference of the rhombus is tinged with periwinkle blue whilst in the centre a second rhombus is formed, dark brown, increasing in size, and surrounded in the end by a thin sky-blue line. I am working on a project to set up a gunnery unit in Alexandria. At the moment I am having the plans drawn up and will send them to the Minister in a few days. I intend to get the draughtsman to do a bird's eye view which I will send direct to the First Consul. Meanwhile I am busy having seven fine mares covered here and will send them home if they are with foal. Farewell my dear friend. — P.S. Capt. Tridoulat of the 107th half-brigade is bringing a case of Turin liqueur, quite prized hereabouts which is a gift from my wife. The planes, flying no doubt just inside the low cloud cover, cannot be seen. Their path can be followed however by the bombs which explode one after another more or less parallel to the road ridden by the troopers as they make for the Meuse, but fairly far to their right. A second after hearing the explosions they see heavy smoke rising from point to point. Having used up all his munitions he manages to escape from Corsica under cover of darkness by foiling the surveillance of the English fleet. The countryside is empty and flat, greyish-green under a grey sky. Here and there a village steeple pokes up. From a distance the explosions have a grey sound. On the sixteenth day of October 1793, at noon, at the very moment when the Queen's head was falling in the Place de la Révolution, Carnot and Jourdan were marching in silence with half of the army, in the direction of the Wattignies plateau, leaving a vacuum behind them. Death has a dirty colour, iron grey, sooty and blackish in the soft green. He writes from Paris to a friend, on 24 Ventôse Year 3: I am very conscious that my election to the Committee of Government is a fresh mark of the Convention's confidence in me. Since I had the pleasure of seeing you I have had many adventures and I don't know how I'm still alive. I have formed fresh ties: I have remarried, this time to an old friend who is more a companion than. His loneliness. His arrival in Naples, at night, in the midst of bonfires celebrating Nelson's victory at Aboukir. Opening his windows the next morning he finds the English fleet lying at anchor in the harbour. The surface of the sea, its waves moving with a sluggish syrupy motion, pale, discoloured by too much light, as if covered with a film of tiny glittering flakes of marble (as if the winds were blowing across islands of whitened rocks, broken statues, columns, etc.). The sticky smell hanging in the heat of September, of the tail end of summer: rotten vegetables, melons, cabbages, rancid oil, excrement, black clouds of flies, detritus, refuse, pale underbellies of dead fish, garbage floating lazily up and down against the quayside. The heavy warships, black too, in the luminous haze, motionless, with their ranked gunports picked out in white. The same no doubt between which he slipped when escaping from Corsica. Their names taken from monsters, heroes, goddesses and muses of Antiquity (HMS Alexander, Goliath, Audacious, Minotaur, Colossus, Thetis, Terpsichora) like women's dress, the long gowns gathered up under the breasts and surmounted by the crackled rouged masks of old queens and old duchesses decked out in plumes and feathers and gazing bird-like, wide-eyed, as if their eyeballs had been peeled. Nelson who lost an eye before Calvi. Plus the rabble of émigrés, favourites, counsellors, uncouth generals. With himself in the middle. Talleyrand not answering his letters, lying low. His harangue to the King. Standing monumental in his blue uniform with its gunner's red facings, and that thick mane tossed back. He reads the clumsy sentences in which threats are wrapped up in high-flown phrases and which he has painstakingly rewritten and crossed out several times on the rough copy: the writing, impulsive, impetuous, the ink pale, transparent, rusty brown, almost pink: with their uneven festoons of down strokes, tracery, erasures, arabesques, the lines on the yellowed leaves look like thin shreds of torn, faded lace. People crane their necks to see him, elbowing each other. Sometimes they even snigger. Behind Ferdinand's throne the dusky shimmer of brightly-coloured or soft-shaded uniforms and court dress: ivory, plum, purple, green, almond, garnet, bronze, jonquil, hazel, azure. Chests studded with gold crosses and diamonds. The painter makes them sparkle by means of nervy, brief, casual impasto strokes. Queen Caroline is conspicuously absent. He writes good-humouredly to Minister Reinhardt in Florence that Marie-Antoinette's sister probably could not bear setting eyes on a regicide. He adds jokingly that

39

she was perhaps worn out by the high jinks at Pompei where the admiral was fêted like a new Octavian (he crosses out Octavian with a series of oblique strokes, then makes rhombuses and fills out every other one with hatching to create a chequered effect, putting a dot in the centre of the empty squares, and writes immediately after: Octavianus). For no obvious reason one crow, then another, then several fly away from the trees in the orchard. In the end the rest follow. Heavily beating their wings they come back towards the terrace, flying low, uttering their black, grating cries which get noisier all the time. Please tell the gardener to uproot the old fruit trees in the overgrown orchard and to plant them in staggered rows in the patch above the avenue not next to the orchard which was planted three years ago in the same enclosure at the foot of the hollow but to plant them so that in time the rows can link up with the existing orchard, restocking efficiently that side of the footpath wood which faces the rising sun in summer, the one which is below and to the left of the trellised walk which runs from the entrance to the laurel arbour above the newly-begun big terrace, and have a good look at those paths which are in that part of the wood lying between the two avenues which lead to the elm walk, and plant there as many cherry trees as you can lay your hands on, there is in the vicinity a circular area surrounded by paths, this circle must be properly levelled down, topped up with good soil brought in for the purpose, and planted with lilac clumps, cover the rest of the ground with rooted saplings such as oak, elm, maple, ash and put in hawthorn in clusters that are four or five bushes to a clump, you will look over the big field, you will replace all the dead trees and all the thorn bushes, you will look Falguières over too, you will replace the thorn trees and you will put in many chestnut trees, you . . . The riding drill is over now. The young horses are now tied up by their halters along the outer wall and their riders are busy taking off their saddles which they carry off holding them with both hands against their stomachs, and walking with their bodies arched backwards. Their spurs glint in the sun. On the bare backs of the horses a dark patch can be seen where the hairs of the coat are stuck down by sweat. He writes I recall the occasion when I was the object of my fellow citizens' preference: things were difficult: the first time I was appointed it was essential to follow on and defend if at all possible the solid achievements of the Constituent Assembly in the face of a monstrous Court which hoped to recover what it called its Rights by massacring the Legislative Assembly; the Tenth of August decided the matter otherwise. My second appointment came when the Prussians were in Champagne and marching towards Paris: it looked as if the pressure would be on and ambitious men then did not . . . In the midst of the deafening racket, of shouting and muddle, he tries vainly to resaddle his mare, with his forehead pressed against her flank and the vizor of his helmet pushed back. His nostrils are filled with the smell of ammonia from the hairs soaked in sweat. He sees a mauve sun against a brown background. The mauve fades, grows pale, like an indistinct moon gradually surrounded by a brighter halo which breaks up and divides into irregular mottled polygons. The night of the Tenth of August was a fine one, softly lit by the moon, and quiet until midnight. At that hour there was hardly anyone about yet in the streets. All the windows were lit up. So many lights for such a fine night, those solitary lights to light nobody's way, created an oddly sinister effect. The planes return and resume their attack, flying low this time, sweeping suddenly into view from behind the hill and machine-gunning as they go. He sees them (he hears someone scream) before he hears the noise they make. There are three of them. They sway slightly on their wings, rising and falling imperceptibly one in relation to the other. He hurriedly dismounts and throws himself into the ditch, burying his face in one arm and clinging on with the other to the mare's reins. He feels acutely how bare and exposed his back is. He is hauled up and dragged along the ground by the animal which rears at the roar of the engines and the din of the cannon, staggering on its hindlegs, its head held high, its rump pressed down as it picks its way backwards. Horses which have lost their riders gallop past along the road in an indistinct rumble of hooves, their empty stirrups clinking and sword-guards knocking together. The unexpectedly swift violence of the attack and the din accompanying it afford him no time to think of being afraid. O. tells how after hurling his first bomb he runs parallel to the line of fire to join the other men in the raiding party, one arm stupidly bent to protect his left cheek. In the darkness little blueish flames flare up and die down the

41

length of the enemy parapet. The noise of exploding bombs is unbearable. Only a little later does he realise that at that moment he was completely terrified. The sunlit zone, the edge of which has crept slowly towards the left, spreading out fan-like from the window, now covers more than half the table and the sun strikes his face, forcing him to screw up his eyes. When he closes them altogether luminous forms remain printed on his retina and give rise to a play of coloured lights. To General Dauthouard, aide-de-camp to H.I.H.: It would have given me great pleasure to have had you come to the siege of Stralsund; from what I had learnt from the Prince of Neuchâtel I had made arrangements to have you put up in my headquarters and as I had a quite satisfactory domestic establishment during that campaign with a pretty good table too you would have been able to dispense with the necessity of keeping one of your own; I am only sorry that . . . (Another portrait, in oils this time, painted probably shortly before this (that is at the time of his Italian command but some years after the drawing): the impetuous, caustic side of the man seems to have yielded to a sort of heaviness or placidity which the alertness of his gaze continues nevertheless to belie, an intensity held in check, as if, just like the body now severely buttoned up in a tunic stiff with embroidery and gold braid like those carapaces or corslets of coleoptera with bronze-coloured elytra, he were sheltering behind this solid mask, his skin tanned by the outdoor life and daily exercise on horseback contrasting with the still leonine but greying mass of hair, it too kept in order, at least for the occasion, that is the sittings in the painter's studio.) The table is laid in a meadow beside the road, covered with a white tablecloth, and it is surrounded by two high-backed armchairs and three ebony chairs upholstered in red velvet. The armchairs and upright chairs have been pushed back and turned to one side as if by guests who after a good meal make themselves comfortable, cross their legs and smoke a cigarette. He trudges in an endless column of men dressed in the dirty, untidy uniforms character-istic of every branch of the armed services. He is wearing his long cavalry greatcoat covered in dust; as he has removed the belt it flaps around his legs. The prisoners walk in silence, with exhausted faces covered in several days' growth of beard and vacant of expression, as if they were far away, absorbed in the sort of sullen concentration (or application) which is a sign of extreme fatigue, and their gaze is lustreless as if their very eyes were dirty, were also covered in a film of dust. The road winds through meadows covered in flowers and past woods and lakes. Sometimes at a corner, or reaching the top of a gradient, he can see the long column trailing like a streak of brown excrement through the dazzling green of the countryside. On the laid table there are a number of empty bottles and dirty plates in which half-smoked cigars are stubbed out. As they pass by they look at the armchairs, bottles and plates with a grey stare. The unremitting loneliness. The bitter taste left by the night spent with the young Italian girl: the strained note of levity in which he talks about it, the facetious and clumsy justification (his doing her less harm than the mosquitoes), his haste, his departure more in the nature of a flight, the curt brusqueness with which he changes the subject: I was eager to get away from Goro. I left at daybreak for Mantua which affords the visitor its Piazza Virgiliana. The place would be even more beautiful if . . . He sleeps on the asphalt in a school playground with his head propped up on his knapsack. He sleeps on the concrete floor of a factory shed. He flops down in a meadow and tries to nibble the grass. He is lying down on the boards of a cattle truck amongst bodies so crammed together that he cannot stretch out his legs. The truck is ventilated by two small rectangular apertures only. He can hardly breathe. The journey takes four days and four nights. He is plagued by hunger and thirst. There are 2 relays from Ponpone to Merola, 2 relays there and back from Merola to Goro, 4 from Merola to Magnasca, 3 from Magnasca to Ravenna, 5½ from Ravenna to Rimini, etc. He realises that he cannot go on much longer pretending to be a wealthy foreigner by day and hiding by night. Those who are arrested are crammed into the ground floors of shops with their steel blinds rolled down which are used as prisons. His main concern is to get some sleep. Gradually this preoccupation drives out all others and he gives up looking for political significance to events which are beginning to leave him cold. According to the precepts which he has been taught, he believes that one is safe so long as one respects the law. He discovers that in practice the law is what the police choose to make it. After the planes have disappeared there is great confusion. In groups or

43

by themselves riderless horses wander about, some galloping over the fields, wheeling round and round and changing direction for no reason, others standing stiff and motionless, and others calmly grazing. Cavalrymen without mounts try to catch them, running about clumsily in the light soil of the sown strips, or standing showily with outstretched arms in front of the bolting horses whose bridles they try to grab but who shy to avoid them. Helped by those who have remained in the saddle, they nevertheless gradually manage to recover most of them. As they adjust the reins and remount they can feel the muscles quivering in the horses whose flanks move up and down rapidly, and whose dilated nostrils are bloodshot, mottled with red veinlets. The limbs and the hands of the cavalrymen also shake with a slight trembling which they try to control. The sun starts sinking and shines through them at an angle, edging with gold the foliage of the trees lining the long paved gradient which the cavalry squadron were climbing when first they were dive-bombed. The sprouting corn, bright green in colour, bows before the evening breeze which shivers its surface into silvery wavelets. The sunlit area, the edge of which, starting from the west tower, has moved slowly round, swivelling like the side of a fan towards the left, cuts slantwise the ruined terrace, now touching only a thin triangle of the bean patch whilst the tomato plants are gradually being enveloped in shadow. In the skimming rays of the setting sun the delicate concentric polygons of glittering threads stand out clearly against the dark background of the laurel bushes. The day after the battles the local peasants and horse traders round up the horses which have run off into the countryside and sell them cheap. He buys a horse at Friedland. He arranges to have certified in Stettin by the two chief medical officers of the eighth corps of the Grande Armée that he bears: (1) in the lower front part of his left leg a wide, purple, poorly healed scar which reopens at the slightest exertion despite the application of a rolled bandage which he has to wear all the time, (2) another scar, somewhat better healed, on the lower part of the inside of the thigh on the same side; these two scars resulting from gunshot wounds, (3) that he presents a double hydrocele with such an infiltration of the scrotum that it is impossible to probe this voluminous tumour and establish with certainty the positive state of the testicles, that he is therefore unfit for active service and cannot undertake the military duties which are dependent upon riding on horseback as required by his rank. He wanders helplessly about on foot in the gathering darkness of the countryside. He is subject to hallucinations. He hears a tinkling sound of small bells growing louder and dives for cover behind a hedge. He sees in the dim light at nightfall a cavalryman riding past along the road wearing a round helmet from which a long bridal veil trails floating in the breeze. The horseman's face is a death's-head with empty eye-sockets. The trotting motion of the horse makes the bells shake and produce a silvery sound which rapidly dies away. He gets up and stares incredulously at the empty road. All around him hangs the unfamiliar, too quiet, melancholy silence of close of day after a battle. The end. The decrepitude, the decay even, of an old lion with no strength left in him, sick, almost infirm. His governorship of Barcelona, the corrupt police affair, ransom demands, and no doubt murder too, in all of which they try to pull the wool over his eyes. His very last ripostes, his very last roars, his haughty rejection of the reprimand handed down to him by MacDonald. He no longer buys horses. He strikes out one after the other the names and descriptions of his mares and stallions as they die off. He sends the resulting shortlist to the sub-prefect of Gaillac to underline the slenderness of his income and the sorry state of his finances. On the one hand it was inconceivable that it was the police since he was not aware of having committed any offence. On the other it was quite obvious, given the impunity which they enjoyed, the ease with which they let themselves into peoples houses at night or at daybreak, dragged them from their beds and made them disappear, that they were indeed a police of sorts. Autumn is the time for starlings. Gathered in their hundreds, they form pointed clouds in which, unlike crows, it is impossible to make out individual birds, and which first stretch and then shrink, being made up of an aggregate of dots appearing and disappearing to the rapid beating of wings. Again unlike crows, they all obey the same coherent movement, although with unforeseeable changes of direction, decelerations and accelerations of pace. The cloud is darkest where it is at its densest, almost black, growing paler where it stretches out; sometimes it heads in one direction or in another, sometimes it just hangs

45

motionless in one place, numberless and, as it were, flickering. By turns it decreases in volume, bunches up, gathers itself suddenly into a point, stretching out behind in streaks like iron filings drawn to a hidden magnet which moves across the sky, rising and falling, making large spirals, shifting with a minute unceasing internal motion. It is at Montmorency, on the estate purchased for his wife, that he takes advantage of a period of sick leave given as a result of the certificates issued by the medical service to have his bust carved by a sculptor. On the heavy-featured, slightly snub-nosed face the still firm flesh swells and bulges powerfully. The locks of the mass of hair grow in undiminished abundance and fall in artful disorder on the shoulders draped in an ancient toga. The cold even colouring of the stone used, the smooth sightless eyeballs half-hidden by the shaggy eyebrows, the two deep lines between these, the thick, ringed, naked bull's neck which projects the head forward in an oratorical or commanding gesture, the toga, all confer on the whole a solemn, timeless appearance. There arises a kind of contradiction from the contrast between the weight of the ton of polished marble and the ghostly greyness which merges the fleshy, hair-covered and clothed parts together, like the apparition of some spectre or other without real existence and yet somehow palpable. Now only one horse remains tied to one of the rings in the outer wall. Its rider uses a nozzle with which he spends some time hosing its legs down, moving round it in a circle to squirt at it from every angle. He has kept his képi on but taken off his black tunic and rolled up the sleeves of his bright blue shirt to the elbows. The jet of water sparkles like silver against the light of the setting sun. The increasingly pale shadows of horse and rider lengthen inordinately on the paving. The edges of the thick registers are faded pink in colour. The long olive green ribbons which serve to keep their covers fastened are untied. On the blue paper stuck over their stiff boards rubbing and scratching have resulted in a pattern of whitish fluffy constellations, looking like those wan, indistinct groupings of stars or nebulae, long extinguished perhaps but revealed by photographs taken in observatories. On their spines reinforced with vellum are inscribed in a careful roundhand the half-erased names of the months of the republican calendar and the words 'Army Business' or 'Private and Personal Matters'.

They contain the copies of hundreds of letters, reports, notes, dockets, domestic accounts, military projects, ordnance inventories, orders and instructions of every kind, and every so often travel diaries and drafts of speeches. The wrinkled hand which thumbs through the registers is now entirely in shadow and the diffused light shines weakly on the crumpled surface of the skin, the pale green knotty protruberances of the veins. He writes: Pilfering is still going on at Mantua, I have just been there about it. On my way through Pavia I noticed that cannon balls are being offered of a calibre which quite obviously do not come from the smithies. It is highly likely that the contractors have bought them from those who stole them from our positions before the handover. There is nothing we can now do about this piece of sharp practice but we must put a . . . He writes to the committee of representatives accompanying the Army of the North that he is informed by their colleagues of the Sambre-et-Meuse forces that the Austrians are on the move near Koblenz and Andernach and that the Sambre-et-Meuse right wing must be reinforced by restoring to it the two divisions transferred to the command of General Moreau. He lodges a claim with the burgomaster of Amsterdam, the brother of his first wife, in respect of certain items of plate and porcelain which formed part of the dowry. He writes to the minister of war, Gassendi, setting out the advantages of a new gun-carriage. He writes to his steward Batti asking whether La Fribourgeoise is in foal by Moustapha and requesting that her waters be closely inspected. He reminds his correspondent that the stockings of which he has ordered two dozen pairs must be loosely stitched because his arch is very high and his heel very long. He writes that one must be able to exercise clemency but must never fear to show oneself pitiless towards the foes of liberty. He writes that he has declined to use a carriage to which were harnessed two horses unworthy of his rank since he could not have ridden in it with decency in full uniform. He makes an inventory of his cellar: white wines, red wines, Cahors, Malmsey, Roussillon and brandies. At Calvi, to the two envoys sent to parley by Hood and Nelson, his reply is: We have no governor here, there are military commanders and in addition there is a representative of the people in overall authority. The French constitution forbids all dealings with the enemy while in occupation on the territory of the Republic; I refuse to accept your letter; you may retire. He writes to his steward to explain in detail the best method for growing potatoes. (The train comes to a standstill in open country and the guards open the sliding doors of the carriages. One after the other or in twos and threes they jump out and crouch down on the embankment to relieve themselves. Beneath the embankment stretches a meadow which dips at first and then rises to the edge of a dark green firwood. The sun has already set and the fresh smell of grass and damp earth rises from the ground. A woman dressed in a pale frock and a man walk slowly along the path at the edge of the wood. A small white dog and a little girl also dressed in pale colours run ahead of the couple. The eager yapping of the dog can be heard. Evening gently falls.) He puts in a claim to the Directory for an indemnity of 40,000 livres as compensation for his Naples adventure and captivity in Tunis. The last name on the list of horses, Xailoum, is written in letters twice as big as the others; the squashed pen has left thick downstrokes. After entering it the hand has moved back too precipitately and smeared the undried ink so that black wisps stretch leftwards from the heavy downstrokes of the letters, of the large capital X in particular, like the mane of a galloping horse floating in the wind. He writes: Since the geographical situation makes it necessary once the Adige has been crossed to move three divisions into the Tyrol or into the Trentino, either to block a corps which the enemy might throw on to this side, or to drop down into the Drave valley and join up in Carinthia with the rest of the army which will have crossed the Frioul, I have arranged to attach to this army a mountain team of 24 artillery pieces, this team . . . He writes to the admiralty minister to further the advancement of his son, a sublieutenant serving in the imperial navy. He writes: By the close of the Convention I had held eleven appointments; I have been a member of the Committee of Public Safety, member of the Council of Elders, prisoner in Barbary, and when after escaping so many dangers in stormy assemblies, on the battlefield, at sea and in captivity, I finally get home, just because three or four crates of porcelain are sent to me the rumour goes round that they are full of gold, as if anyone would despatch that metal by common carrier! Did anyone imagine that I would set off to take up my ambassadorship on horseback, with my portmanteau slung behind me? He writes: Would to heaven I had been less trusting with that scoundrel Garrigou, incidentally how do I stand with him, I put at M. Longairou's disposal about 14,000 francs in sound bills, if they were not paid at term I could not be expected from the depths of Pomerania to keep an eye on a debtor, if payment was not forthcoming he should have . . . (The surrounds are now deserted. Dressed in a coarse linen overall and wearing a forage-cap a man on fatigue duty is sweeping the paving stones and scooping up in a large shovel the droppings left by some of the horses. The paving is grey slightly tinged with mauve. Where the horse was washed down and on the wet meandering streaks of horses' urine the reflection from the sky makes golden puddles. The man disposes of the last scatterings of dirt with cursory sweeps of his broom which he then lays across his barrow. He picks the barrow up and moves off, pushing it in front of him.) He writes that on the question of whether the people ought to be asked to ratify the vote on the king's sentence his answer would be that the people should ratify the Constitution alone, he says that in his view the proposal to consult the people would be horrendous by reason of the civil war and the dissensions which it might provoke, that if they occurred he would be responsible, that he says NO. He writes to Citizen Deltet, battalion commander, on the latter's return from Egypt: My dear friend, I duly received the letter which you kindly wrote me; you were good enough to offer me a black slave, I learned that you were in Grenoble with your battalion, one of my friends was going there, I asked him to carry a letter for you in which I thanked you for the offer, he was to bring your negro over to me in Italy, not finding you in Grenoble he brought back my letter. I heard today that you are in Lyon. I repeat my warm thanks, my wife will in a few days pass through that city on her way to Paris, she will thank you in person and take charge of the negro which you are so kind as to give me, provided he is still in your possession. He writes to the minister of war in Paris: Citizen M., there has just been a theft of 70 bockses of copper wheels from the Pavia store. The thieves are known, and are being pursued. I have issued an instruction in accordance with the ordinance of 7 Nivôse Year 6 suspending pro tem the artillery commander of this place. With my respectful greetings. He writes: I have

49

noticed throughout Italy an air of discontent and a sullen attitude which suggest that the population fear us but hardly like us. In vain may we win battles, in vain carry the glory of French arms into regions where our nation's soldiers have never been seen, in vain: peoples will rise en masse to secure their repose, we will still encounter nothing but human slaughter, nothing but futile massacre as long as the French government tries to keep a hold over the republics which are established under its auspices, as long as it attempts to maintain this system of confront . . . He writes to MacDonald the minister of war asking him if the Emperor would be at all pleased to learn that two general officers are compromised in a shady police affair in Barcelona. He writes that his first attack of apoplexy not having given rise to any trace of paralysis leads him to hope that if he had a second attack it would be devastating and would carry him off. He writes to an old friend: For forty years I have been continuously on active service, but today my strength is ebbing and the last post will soon sound for me; I will go and spend my last days in my old chateau where I will be able to cast a final look back without regrets; I do so now, with great pleasure, recalling with you the moments spent together in our youth: the village fêtes in Flanders, the conquest of a country lass or of a nun being the most we ever yearned for, such happy times! With great affection, Farewell. As if coming from afar the voice of the soprano seems to swell gently, almost imperceptibly, mingled at first with the sound of the violins, then detaching itself, lifting, flowing, unfurling, tenderly, heartrendingly. She sings: Avvezzo al contento d'un placido oblio fra queste tempeste si perde il mio cor. Orpheus is about to turn round when he thinks better of it. He writes: As I approached the outskirts of Rome I was painfully struck by the poor cultivation of the countryside around, did this arid, fallow ground indicate that there were tombs nearby, did it proclaim that there reigned here too long a pope, a vice-deity of an absurd and contemptible religion? What can be expected of people imbued with the abominable principle that the most natural impulses must be stifled, that one must think only of. In the blue section where the tomb stands he orders the planting of Italian poplars, of beeches, of ashes, and above all of robinia. He uses oblique lines to strike from the register the description of his horse Le Superbe (15 Prairial Year

50

7, born at Saint-M . . . a bay foal, out of Mlle de Ferjus, a Normandy mare, black coat forward, height 4 feet 9 inches, nine years old, by Magnifique, a Normandy stallion, 4 feet 11 inches in height, aged 12 years in Year 6, bay coat). He writes underneath: Went lame after descending Mount Genèvre in Year 13, was sold for nothing in Turin. The last year. What he called several times in his letters 'the interval between life and death'. This last succession of the four seasons, of the twelve months named after frosts, flowers or fogs, which he spends alone at Saint-M . . ., looked after by an old woman steward, communing with his ghosts and his secrets. A black lead drawing by the architect Ledoux shows an inordinately enlarged eye, with the eyeball carefully shaded off, surmounted by the curve of the eyebrow, its curly hairs individually marked by the sharpened point of the pencil. In the iris, which a wandering spotlight has swept in part, sits the reflection of the interior of the Besançon opera house, the raked stalls and dress circle curving away in inverted arcs on each side of a horizontal median line. The ensemble is designed in a neo-classical style. The dress circle, decorated with columns, is separated from the stalls by a bas-relief frieze of figures clad in pepla. He writes that the year has been a fateful one in his family, that Monsieur de Pruyne has just recovered from a serious illness, that Monsieur de Loumet is dead, that the de Pruyne of Strasbourg has died at the age of thirty-five and that he too has peered into the jaws of death. When the registers are held up at an angle and the pages turned, fine rust-coloured particles, with glinting, golden facets like mica, fall from the letters and slide down the leaves. It is as if the assembled words, sentences and very marks left on the paper by the troop movements, battles, intrigues and speeches flake, crumble and fall into dust, leaving on one's hands nothing but an impalpable powder, the colour of dried blood. He writes What good have fortune and honours done me, when the most valued thing of all would have been to share them with that adored wife, consigned long ago to oblivion but whose memory, twenty years later, still breaks my heart.

II

It is so cold the wine freezes in the metal bottles. The liquid is purple, icy and bitter (as if the taste itself were purple, discoloured — like those faded stains, mauve turning to blue, which bad wines leave on tablecloths). The steely cold bringing out the metallic, chemical flavour. Iron making it go hard. They can feel tiny crystals on their tongue and against their palate which crunch under their teeth and melt straightaway. Their meals consist entirely of cold rations of corned beef and of camemberts, also frozen, which look and taste like plaster. They share them out and eat them without scraping the crust off. Under the knife the dry paste crumbles and breaks into debris which they try to gather up onto slices of bread.

Because of the cold, they have closed the sliding doors of the waggon. If you put your eye to the thin vertical slits which still show, you can see the monotonous and empty countryside under snow creeping slowly by. When they have eaten and drunk, they remain seated on the coarse wooden floor. What they have swallowed is like a lump of cold stone in their stomachs. They lean against the wall of the waggon, curled up in their greatcoats, silent and taciturn.

He experiences intensely (the cattletruck, the unknown destination, the violent thud of the wheels against the gaps in the rails, the enclosed, static cold, tight as a vice, the communal solitude) a feeling of aggression (not men, but war, things, existence). When he was a child in the lavatory of an express train he pressed on the pedal and through the open lid at the bottom of the WC bowl he saw the sleepers and the ballast stones rushing by with a violent noise of broken things. A stinking cold which seemed to be blown up from below. Streaks of shit, and soaked wrinkled tissue paper stuck to the sticky cylinder of the conduit. Almost thrown off balance by the sharp oscillations of the carriage in spite of having to stand with his hand against the partition and with his legs wide apart. A string of urine drops, trembling on the bottom rim before being torn off and swept rapidly and horizontally away.

Sometimes the train stops at a station, but far from the passengers' platforms, on a shunting line in the midst of lines of waggons carrying goods, ore or cattle. Lengthy and incomprehensible manoeuvres. Some of them slide the door wider open and try to see the name of the town, their limbs stiff, swapping vague guesses.

Their relationships: not true friendship — tolerance rather. With no animosity or hostility, but without any particular warmth either. A kind of secret society, implying no fellow-feeling, but a sort of tacit and spontaneous freemasonry, between those of peasant origin: the same behaviour which they displayed towards their horses, at once respectful (because of their commercial value) and marked by a kind of tenderness, complicity, even hereditary comradeship. The same attitude (the same ancestral familiarity) towards their tools (pitch forks and wheelbarrows), straw bedding, manure, hay, and oats. The heavy bails of pressed straw which they load to their backs without effort while those from the towns stagger under the same weight. The latter are in a minority, out of their depth in this anachronistic world of animals and weapons, protecting themselves by childishly creating a shell of raffish coarseness which is expressed in an excessively slang vocabulary. The few jockeys who have not been taken as batmen by higher ranking officers are being used in some way as a link between the two social groups. Close both to the countrymen (because of the horses) and to the city-dwellers. Apart, nevertheless. Aged before their time. Like people several years older than themselves. Not very talkative. Their eyes at once hard, thoughtful and weary. Like an indelible stain upon them. Stigmata of a world of easy money unknown to the others.

The brief battles will not have time to modify this state of affairs to any extent. First of all because of their violence: the cataclysmic speed with which everything will take place, the unparalleled aggression of the noise, the absence of orders, the way the commanders shirk their responsibilities, the lack of that minimum of cohesion which can unite the members of a group sharing the same dangers, the muddle, the disorder established right from the beginning, so that each person will from the outset have the impression of being alone, being lost, of not taking part in concerted, comprehensive manoeuvres but of

56

having been thrown in more or less at the deep end and left to one's own devices. Killed for no logical reason at the whim of pure chance, the platoons and sections being continually regrouped as well as can be managed with the accumulation of losses, so that, very soon, no personal link will remain, everyone increasingly having the feeling of being alone and cut off.

Night is beginning to fall when the train halts for good. That is, when they can hear stones dislodged by passing feet rolling down the embankment outside and the shouts of the NCOs. They realise then that they have arrived. They put on their equipment again, slowly, like sleepwalkers, and in silence, looking out all the while on the dead world framed in the opening made by the door which has now slid fully open. The stiff limbs, the awkward, heavy leap on to the ballast, the sharp shock that echoes painfully from the heels to the skull, the cold different from that which prevailed in the carriage, the tingling smell of ozone given off by the snow, etc.

Here it is perhaps necessary to digress for a moment to try and explain what will happen next, that is the despair which will grip them, the panic, the rout which nothing apparently seems adequately to justify: neither the natural circumstances (however severe the cold, they have become accustomed to it — it is now February — for some months past), nor the type of operation itself (perhaps the length of the day's march had been badly calculated and the command had not taken sufficient account of the combined effects of the low temperature and the physical effort required (quite considerable, certainly, but for all that not exceeding human strength, as events proved) — unless one supposes that the whole thing had been arranged as a kind of deliberate ordeal, like their departure from the quarters in which they have spent the first months of the winter and fallen into the habit of living in a certain way (similarly nuns in certain nursing orders are systematically transferred by their superiors as soon as the risk arises of a network of friendships or sympathies developing around them (or emanating from them) within the hospital service which employs them), although it is altogether more likely that this movement was ordered in a spirit of pure routine or in pursuance of instructions or regulations on the turnover of the first or second reserve army corps). And not because of any dramatic circumstance or accident, either of the kind which can normally be expected in war, such as, for example, an unexpected air attack, or an act of sabotage on the tracks (the only incident — but can that expression be used, although the event did undoubtedly have a morally traumatising effect? — having been a civilian passenger train passing through).

No: apart from the cold (still in an attempt to explain the rout which will take place during the march, foreshadowing the subsequent and final collapse under fire, one at every echelon, the officers themselves having seemed on that occasion to lose their heads, to forget the most basic principles, to have lost after a time all concern for what was happening in the rear, each one, officer or plain trooper, only thinking and acting as a mere individual — the fact that the affair gave rise to no sanction, no punishment, no reproof, was not, at the next roll call, two days later, in the new quarters, in any way referred to, confirming that officers and men will agree spontaneously that the whole shameful episode will not further be alluded to) . . . apart from the cold, then, it seems that the extreme banality and the ordinariness of the circumstances were working against each other, as reflected in the triteness of the spot where the train stopped, far from any town, far even from one of those goods stations situated on the outskirts of towns in which these kinds of operations usually take place, operations (such as the loading and unloading of troops, horses and equipment) with which they are familiar: one of those places where trains normally never stop, in open country, and which suddenly strikes them like a frozen emphatic fragment, one of those empty spaces without marked features made to look alike by the snow, glimpsed throughout the day through the vertical chink in the poorly fitting door. The fact too of suddenly being there, as if by surprise, and not having reached it by stages as they usually do on horseback, thus having the time to get used to the gradual changes — or to an absence of change — in the countryside. To which should be finally added the late hour, the short winter afternoon drawing to a close, the vague threat of approaching night.

They suddenly find themselves as if half-awake (although none of them has been asleep: but already diminished and made vulnerable by the hours of enforced idleness, the

58

numbness brought on by the cold, the unwarmed, indigestible food), and as it were expelled, torn from their shelter (the cattle trucks, full of draughts but still constituting an enclosed space), brutally thrown out, dumped as on the surface of a dead, uninhabited, frozen planet.

The long straight line of the parallel tracks which, in front of and behind the train, seem to stretch out to infinity on the snow-covered plain, only relieved here and there by the mauve patches of the thin copses (and not even copses: vague collections of bushes around a few trees), the sky leaden with snow darkened still further by the twilight, the silence, the emptiness, the long train of pinkish-brown wooden wagons pulled up on a siding, the three or four rusty hoppers (a factory, a gravel pit somewhere?), their peeling ochre paint (the patches of rust forming archipelagoes as it were, the faded paint becoming tinged with red and crumbling away around their jagged edges), the wide ditch of stagnant water between the embankment and the little wood which runs along the track, the thin triangles of ice, like ground, dirty, greyish glass on the surface of the black, opaque still water (something putrid, stinking, congealed by the cold), the thickets of brownish brambles with linings of wet snow caught in their tangles.

They become aware of that at once and yet in a detailed manner (or rather in a bare, elaborate way, like one of those precise drawings in blacklead) through the harsh and cold light of winter which (just like the long hours of jolting and bumping and the rumbling of the wheels on the lines suddenly giving way to motionlessness and silence), highlights the impression of desolation and abandonment.

At that moment (whilst they are stumbling towards the horses' cars) there occurs the incident of the passenger train which undoubtedly helps to sharpen their distress still further. First the preliminary sound, the distant rumble, then far away, at the end of the long straight line, a speck appearing, growing rapidly, then everything happening very quickly: the train hurtling at full speed along the main track in a thunderous metal catastrophe, the air violently shaken, the ground trembling under their feet, the swirling clouds of powdery snow stirred up by the wheels, and the men standing stock still, watching the long, green-sided carriages pass by one after another to the rapid rhythmic accompaniment of the syncopated jolts made by the gaps between the rails, their windows filled with curious or indifferent faces, pale, dingy, made to look unreal both by the speed at which they are swept along and by the fact that they seem (like fish behind the glass walls of an aquarium) to belong to a another world, as different from the one in which they find themselves as fire is from water (a woman gives a baby its bottle, a little girl with a bow in her hair waves to them — there is even a man in shirtsleeves), all that in a few seconds, the closeness and speed being such that it is impossible for them to read on the plates attached to the outside of the carriages the origin and destination of the express, then already the last carriage, the thunderous cataclysmic noise cut short, the rumbling dwindling rapidly, the red lantern lit already also moving very quickly away in the twilight, then no longer even visible, the rear of the train like a dark spot shrinking away there on the long straight line, as if sucked along, its cargo of babies on the bottle, of little girls with bows in their hair and of men in shirtsleeves sucked along too, then a speck, then nothing at all, the silence irremediable, definitive, the trail of black smoke left by the locomotive slightly to one side hanging for a moment longer, breaking up, sagging, dissolving in the still air, the sooty stench of the smoke dissolving too, diluted, absorbed in the white and metallic smell of the cold.

Until now, however, nothing irreparable has occurred, and the situation could no doubt still be saved by some easy diversion, such as for example a distribution of rum or something hot to drink, or even if there had been in the vicinity (as in those suburbs surrounding goods stations) some sort of dramshop where each squad could have delegated a man to go to and fro hiding under his greatcoat bottles of cheap rotgut (and perhaps in the latter case, less the beneficial warmth of the alcohol than the excitement, the charm, the always positive effect produced on the morale of a body of soldiers by the transgression of a taboo — the officers and NCOs being not only in the habit on such occasions of turning a blind eye but even of being able to look the other way so that appearances are not respected so much as the whole business of transgression and taboo, thereby securing at little cost (through the benefit of such minor infringements of the regulations functioning as a safety valve in a way) their authority.

Anyway nothing of the kind happened: neither the distribution nor the illicit supply of drink, nor even the hint (which may be bogus but is still of some comfort) of solidarity (if not of fellowship) in hardship, such as a military command can sometimes show.

Quite the reverse, and as frequently happens in such cases (that is when junior officers awake to the consciousness of a blunder committed by their superiors, of the issue of an ill-considered order, of the ill-judged nature of an exercise or a manoeuvre which they (the juniors) must see carried out), there arose among the NCOs (each modelling his conduct on that of his immediately senior officer) a kind of manifest hardening, either through embarrassment (the officers and NCOs travelled in a heated carriage at the front of the train, just behind the locomotive), or, as is more likely, because of the natural reflex of all authority being brought into play which amounts to nipping any show of protest or indiscipline in the bud by making the first move and entrenching itself behind an attitude of refusal and inaccessibility (another explanation of the aberrant conduct of the officers which had such a disastrous effect on the whole affair can more simply be found in their lack of personal commitment and their bad temper at the prospects of the hardships and the cold which they were themselves going to have to endure: very likely all three reasons played a role and cannot be separated).

And then this: the gigantic captain (his powerful blotchy face still rosy or rather purplish blue from the cold, his chin cut into and lifted up under his lower lip by the tightly adjusted strap of his helmet) striding up the column drawn up ready to leave, platoon after platoon, without a glance at the men or the horses, his head haught, thrust slightly forward, his shoulders high, his eyes stubbornly fixed on the ground a few yards in front of him, the flaps of his long greatcoat thrashing his huge legs, alternately covering and uncovering the bulbous leggings which encase his enormous calves, his heavy service spurs clanking at every step, the RSM walking slightly to the left behind him, the young lieutenants and second-lieutenants in ruinously expensive boots from the top makers, with their fine chromium-plated spurs, dropping one after another out of the group striding wildly, blindly on, each one placing himself at the head of his platoon, then, rather than an order, a hubbub, a commotion, the sound of stirrups, of clashing metal spreading by degrees down from the head of the column, and everyone on horseback, the squadron unstirring for a moment longer in the unstirring, icy air, the troopers now mounted noticing beyond the copse a few houses on a working-class estate: not a village, not even a hamlet: a dozen or so villas, all exactly alike, with dark pebbledash walls and roofs of dingy red, machine-made tiles, with the light already on in three or four windows, each one with its small garden of frozen, withered vegetables, of cabbages gone to seed, their leaves hanging limply under their caps of snow (and not even enough snow to cover everything over, to conceal the ringed and rotten stalks, the tops of the furrows, the blackish soil), and no one, not even a child, not even a dog to watch them as the squadron moves off, skirts the little gardens, no silhouette framed in the lit-up windows, and after that, once past the dismal row of houses and small gardens, nothing more, the bare plain, white or rather greyish–white, barely divided from the sky on the horizon by a narrow strip faintly tinged with pink towards the west.

And very soon night falls. They move forward in the faint light which seems to have been hoarded by the snow, and can already see only a few yards in front of them, and all they can make out on either side of the road are the snow-covered flat fields, and not even ditches (it is a country road or track, and if there are ditches the snow has filled them up, so that everywhere to right and left it is simply flat and white, or rather, in the twilight, flat and grey). At first, as long as a semblance of light persists, they cover a few miles at the trot in the usual quiet blend of sounds (the clanking of steel, of chewed bits and snaffles, of horseshoes sometimes knocking, the sound of the horses snorting, the stamping of hooves muffled by the snow), busts rising and falling mechanically on the saddles, and no warmth to speak of (the hands frozen, the fingers frozen, the nails like spikes of ice, the feet frozen in boots which are themselves like clamps of ice) but the blood nevertheless running more quickly, like something alive, something stirring inside the body, and then they can really see nothing at all and they are again at walking pace, and the ice begins to climb up from the feet along the legs, then they can no longer feel even their nails, and fortunately the captain orders the squadron to halt and dismount.

They set off again, walking beside their horses. They walk with a slight forward stoop, both hands in the pockets of their greatcoats, the horses' bridles merely slipped over their right arms. At the head the captain presses on alone, a few yards in front of his batman who holds both their horses' bridles. He treads the snow with large strides, without turning round, his head buried in his shoulders. Behind him no one turns round either, no one speaks.

Everyone's breathing becomes more rapid. The captain continues to march at the pace of his giant steps and the column behind him stretches out (although all that can be made out is the tail and rump of the horse in front, dark against the snowy background), and at one moment there is a helmeted silhouette, upright, motionless, at the side of the column, and from this silhouette emerges a voice which repeats (does not shout: which says): Come on close up, come on close up, and the silhouette and the voice disappear behind into the darkness, and a few troopers start to run (others not, going on walking at the same pace, in silence, not even articulating a protest or a curse between their teeth), their horse breaking into a trot beside them, the empty stirrups jumping and sometimes knocking against the sheath of the sabre, clinking, but not for long, and man and horse lapse again into a walking pace. That makes a series of metallic jingles which spread by degrees then stop, giving way once more to the quiet crunch of snow underfoot, and a little later the dark silhouette of the NCO is seen on the left running clumsily in the thick snow where it has not been trampled by the column, on the roadside or perhaps in the fields, how can anyone tell, since no trace of a ditch is visible, the NCO lifting his knees high, his shoes sinking to the ankle in the snow which they throw up at every stride and which is scattered behind his legs, and he does not make better progress than the men at walking pace but after all in the end he disappears towards the front and someone says without raising his voice as if simply talking to himself just look at the silly cunt.

At that moment the arrangement of the squadron must have changed significantly due to the fact that certain troopers have run to make up lost ground and others have not, and the NCO has no doubt alerted the captain, because shortly afterwards there is a halt (that is to say that each one, half asleep and numb with cold, nearly bumps into the hindquarters of the horse in front, which gives rise to a few bucks and curses but nothing serious, rather the horses lash out sideways without much conviction), and still nothing can be seen, all one knows is that the whole squadron comes slowly to a standstill because the crunching noise of trodden snow ceases gradually to be heard and finally there is silence from one end of the column to the other, and perhaps the order is going to arrive to remount, but from the tail of the column comes the instruction to pass the word forward that everybody has caught up or something of the sort, the order to mount is not given and they set off once more on foot.

That happens on three or four occasions, the halt getting a little longer each time before the NCO who brings up the rear informs those in the lead that the whole squadron is present and correct, the squadron moving off again almost at once, so that there is practically no respite for the stragglers obliged to start off again having hardly arrived. And to the right and to the left, behind and in front, always the same snow-covered bare plain, the road without a rise, without a fall, skirting or crossing sometimes an invisible wood (the noise, the crunching of the snow under the hooves then changing slightly, suggesting that it is thrown back by a wall of trunks and branches — and perhaps under the tangle of bushes and grasses scorched by the frost, those ponds or strips of water, dead and black, covered with a thin film of ice, and perhaps too, in the rushes, sleeping moorhens or wild ducks), everything quiet, and not a village, not a hamlet, only, every now and then, without it being possible to judge the distance, a lonely but very sporadic light (a farm?), and in that way an hour passed, and another hour, and another again with halts to regroup.

It should not be forgotten that they have been up since two in the morning, have covered a short stage of ten miles or so between their quarters and the station, have waited in the cold and darkness for dawn to break in order to load the horses (and that wait could no doubt have been avoided by fixing the squadron's reveille and muster two hours later), have spent the whole day in a frozen carriage, eaten frozen, drunk frozen, unloaded the horses in open country, and that they have now been marching for about three hours in the black cold, have no idea where they are, where they are going, nor how many hours more they still have to march.

And at a particular moment the snow begins to fall.

It is perhaps only eight or nine in the evening, hardly more, but what must be taken into consideration is that the winter night fell early and for the troopers walking in darkness time can no longer be measured. Unfortunately, whilst the advent of snow indicates a sudden milder turn in the temperature, the effects of the cold passively endured since the morning (that is before daybreak even) have at this moment so accrued no doubt as to reach a point of no return as it were (as if the cold had in a way been stockpiled within the organism after the fashion of heat in those radiators which store it during off-peak hours in order to release it afterwards), so that, far from mending matters, this fresh development (that is, in the more or less total darkness, the ghostly sensation of weightless touches dissolving on the face, clinging to eyelashes, melting on lips with a metallic taste, the soft whisper of invisible snowflakes enlarging at a stroke the space, the dimensions of the night), this advent of snow (inevitably accompanied in their minds too by the images of disasters which the word conjures up) will also have a decisive effect on men whose resistance has been worn down.

The affair (that is that disaggregation or perhaps better that complete disintegration of an officered and organised body of troops in a few hours of a night march, and without any important incident having occurred, the kind of panic, this distress, this abdication which spread and developed (in the same way as the news about the stragglers and dawdlers, conveyed during the early hours of the march during halts by the NCOs bringing up the rear, and which made their way by degrees up the column until they reached the captain), gaining ground by a sort of contagion, a sort of irresistible contamination, from the bottom to the top of the hierarchy, right to the highest level, to such an extent that, in the end, there were only isolated individuals, without distinction of rank, each one struggling on his own behalf against weariness, night and cold), the affair then (or the phenomenon) divisible into three phases, namely: the early hints of disaggregation, the threat of disaggregation (the first instances of break-up), and finally the disaggregation itself, consummated as it were, confirmed as an accomplished, irreversible fact, the ending of all cohesion, of all discipline (something almost inconceivable in a corps whose traditions were as stern and rigid as those of the cavalry), all notion of command and of obedience appearing to all and sundry without purpose, bereft of meaning, null and void.

The first phase comprises the unusual stop by the train in open country, the men clambering out of the icy carriages, the passing of the civilian train, the muster, the premonitory signs in the behaviour of the captain striding past the squadron drawn up in marching order, along the side of the train, with his closed, absent face, coloured by a redness which cannot be fully accounted for by the cold alone (flushed with anger?, the anger itself provoked by the absurdity of his orders?, or by a kind of shame, a presentiment of the inevitable, of the humiliation, of the loss of authority and prestige which will result? — how can it be explained?: his haste to reach his horse, his refusal to raise his eyes (or his reluctance to?), if only for a semblance of those inspections over which, before giving the order to mount, he would habitually linger with finicky attention, inspecting a pack, overlooking no detail of equipment or saddlery, punctilious on the subject of spit and polish (behaviour so unusual that it could only appear of ill omen, could only be interpreted more or less consciously by the troopers as both evidence of indifference and a sign of unusual distress), and later on, his haste in again ordering a trotting pace, in defiance of possible falls (the horses were not shod for ice), as if trying desperately to take advantage of the last moments of daylight, and, later again, his haste, at each halt, to give the signal for a new departure without allowing the laggards the time to get some of their strength back — all this to say that if the contamination, the dereliction did indeed spread, in the final phases, from bottom to top of the hierarchy, it was perhaps, at the outset, the result of what is legitimately called a real failure of command, sinning, as frequently happens, through an excess of severity, or rather of arrogance, which is then confusedly felt by the men as neglect of responsibility and, in some way, a desertion at the top justifying every individual act of desertion.

The second phase covers roughly the first three hours of the march (those during which, from time to time, the van of the column halts to allow the stragglers to catch up): although the undermining effects of fatigue are then being felt, there is still at this stage information, control, overall command.

The third phase (that of the disaggregation itself, the signal for which seems to have been given by the appearance of the snow — or rather in the dark, the touch of silent, woolly snowflakes, melting softly on their faces) can only be described in a fragmentary manner mirroring the phenomenon of fragmentation itself. To start with, and unlike what had happened before, there is a halt, at the end of which they set off again without having waited for news of the rear. From that point onwards (because when all is said and done, this resumption of the march before the squadron had regrouped makes acceptable what in normal circumstances no unit commander can allow: the destruction of its cohesion) it is necessary (since there is no organized unit any more) to pass from the plural to the individual. So, all at once, without understanding how, nor being able to say at what moment precisely it happened, nor for how long it had been going on, a trooper (one or another) realises suddenly that he longer has in front of him the hindquarters of the horse which was preceding him, and no horse nor any sound of hooves behind him either, and the only crunching of snow he hears is under his own feet and under the shoes of his own horse, and all he can see in front, behind, on the right, on the left, is black darkness, and only the vague greyish glimmer over which he walks, continuing mechanically to place one foot before the other in the same way as some animal instinct (his own or that of his horse?) keeps him on the track formed by the hard trodden snow, and no sound, except that kind of huge, quiet murmur of snowflakes continuing to fall — he cannot remember how long they have been falling — and at one moment he thinks he can discern in front of him a sort of motionless shape, black against the black, making it out indistinctly as it gets closer or rather as he gets closer to it, the stationary horse, planted on its four feet as on stilts, and the rider also stationary, his helmet propped against the horse's flank as if he were regirthing, or as if he were urinating, but neither is the case, and when he passes alongside he hears something like christ almighty oh christ almighty christ

67

almighty, but he does not stop, he goes on, and he hears the fellow and the horse walking now behind him, the sound of the snow crunching under four boots and eight horseshoes, and he walks, and the guy follows, and he hears him crying, and he does not turn round, he goes on, and then he cannot hear him any more, and he does not turn round, he goes on, and the snow is still falling, and it is not really cold any longer, but now it does not matter, and a moment later (but perhaps he is asleep?: he thinks that he has often been asleep on horseback, he thinks that one can perhaps also sleep and walk at the same time, and in that case what is before or after?) it starts again, that is to say another horse and another rider has halted (but perhaps it is the same person and the same horse, or perhaps the stationary rider is now himself, and that it is he too who, in his turn, utters strange, contemptible noises), and a horse and a rider pass by without stopping, and the stationary rider (perhaps himself after all?) sets off once more, continues for a while, still uttering these strange noises, then stops making any sound at all, and goes on like that several times in the night, except that this occurs at less and less frequent intervals, so that he walks (or stands still?) sometimes ten minutes or a quarter of an hour (at least so it seems to him) without seeing anyone, and sometimes there are (or it appears to him that there are) not one but three or four horses and their riders who have halted or who overtake him, or who walk in front of or behind him, then he finds himself alone again, he walks, he stops, he leans his head against the sweat-flap, after a while he feels his perspiration cooling on him, he moves off, he walks, he stops, he walks, the snow goes on falling, he stops, he walks, he walks, he makes out a point of light, he walks, he sees a helmeted man lit by a lantern dangling at the end of his arm, he gets nearer to the man, the man raises his lantern to see his face, then makes a sideways gesture with the lantern and says That way, he looks that way, he sees the faintly lit doorway of a stable or a cowshed, there is a lantern in the cowshed, there are already several horses there, the light of the lantern is reflected on the cruppers and the wet saddles, he pushes his horse in beside the others, he ties it up to the manger, he does not unsaddle it; in the light of the lantern he makes out a ladder at the back, he climbs up the ladder, at the top of the ladder there is something soft which he sinks into as he walks, there are bodies lying in the hay, he feels about until he finds an empty space, he takes off his carbine but not his other equipment, he stretches out full length, he falls asleep.

When he opens his eyes all is grey. He sees nothing. He rubs his eyes with his hand and the snow is falling. He is entirely covered with a layer of snow over an inch thick. He is not cold. He is lying against the openwork wall of the barn built of vertical planks separated by spaces. It is not snowing any longer. He sees outside another building made of mud or yellow clay supported on a frame of exposed wood. The wooden beams are grey. Because of the contrast with the snow the clay is bright yellow. Behind the building there is a half-flooded wood, or rather a thicket. Between the bushes, the black water is covered with slabs of grey ice. There is no ice in the middle of the stream. There are little birds (ducks?) sitting on the water, their breasts pointing into the current in which they remain motionless, sometime letting themselves drift slowly backwards, then returning back to their place.

They spent the winter in undulating country partly covered by dense forests. It was very cold that year. The snow began to fall around mid-December and only melted twice for a few days during which they floundered in an icy black mud. The horses suffered from a complaint of the hoof which was said to be characteristic to the region (some spoke of the particular composition of the soil) to which only the local breed was immune: squat, thick-set beasts with broad necks and withers, with russet coats and black manes and tails, resembling the sturdy mounts of the knights of yore, sufficiently strong to bear the weight of heavy suits of armour and whose full curves, cruppers, hocks and breasts match the geometric ornamentations of the saddles, the pink shafts of the lances, the caparisons decorated with triangles chequered red, white and black. Now there were only plough-horses to be seen, motionless, in pairs, or in threes or fours, in the snow-covered meadows against which, standing out as if ringed in charcoal and touched with black (manes, tails and thick tufts of hair on the posterns) the dark-yellow, clay-coloured shapes of their bodies free of harness and bridle, appeared like beasts of heraldic pride, gentle, thoughtful, fabulous and untamed.

Some of the troopers in the squadron, farmers or growers, and one of the officers, a big landowner, took advantage of these winter months to clinch bargains with the local peasants on favourable terms and send home (by heaven knows what subterfuges at a time when army convoys had priority and when, at least in the militarised zone, all transport was subject to the authority of rank) some of these animals reminiscent of chargers or palfreys. Sometimes, on the other side of a fence, one of them with flowing mane, with dancing airy trot as if filmed in slow motion, and with clumps of snow flying under its hooves, would follow, snorting, alongside a troop of cavalrymen with noses and ears red with cold, hunched up in their long greatcoats, their fingers numb and aching with cold, stooping forward as if curled up on their saddles, passing by to the accompaniment of the barbarous tinkling of clashing bits of steel in one of the country tracks with ruts and frozen puddles.

The horses had to be shod for ice every day, and the men blew on their fingers, cursing as they screwed broad-headed frost-bolts into the shoes. When they returned, the hardened snow and ice seemed to have as it were welded steel to steel and they toiled over wrenches to unscrew jammed nuts, tearing their hands on the toe of a shoe or the head of a nut. Although on their return to the stable the horses had trodden unclean litter and the dung had already caked hard with ice, the wounds did not fester. They even healed quickly and there were no cases of tetanus or other infection, however mild, as one might normally have expected. Were it not for the cold (it attained a quite frightening intensity, became something that one might call cosmic: implacable, alive, that is to say like a kind of wild force, too, like the strong, apocalyptic russet horses, at once placid and stubborn, inflexible, like a vice or rather like those cast-iron presses which can still be seen in bookbinderies, painted black (the sky was for most of the time of an iron grey hue, uniform and low) with a screw handle tipped with small balls at the end of each arm which had (most likely) been tightened once for all, compressing above the forests, the hills and the few scattered farms in the white countryside (or rather it, too, greyish) transparent matter, sharp as glass, at once compact and fluid since it penetrated everywhere: into the nostrils, the mouth, the

70

lungs, under one's clothes, through the smallest gaps, the tiniest crack, the very texture of the cloth, filtering through not only to the skin but to the internal organs, invading the body through the complicated networks of bronchi, bronchioles, vessels, dividing, branching out, thrusting spiky radicles into all the members, into fingers and toes, so that under the coarse cloth of the uniforms, under the leather straps and buckles, the bodies themselves seemed to take on the consistency of glass, and so that, were it not for the tunics, the greatcoats, the boots of hardened leather, varieties of mandrakes, webbing in the shape of rivers, streams, with their thorny tributaries, bristling on all sides with tearing barbs like fishhooks, with sharp, black points, could have been seen as if through one of those transparent fleshless and boneless dummies made for the use of medical students (or on those anatomical plates representing within diagrammatic outlines the vascular systems of man, of batrachia and of cold-blooded animals) . . .), apart from the cold, then, the service was not particularly arduous, reduced as it was to the indispensable minimum needed on the one hand to satisfy daily necessities (grooming and exercising the horses, the per-functory care of weapons, seeing to fodder and supplies) and, on the other, to carry out the directives that had been elaborated in far-off overheated offices by distant and invisible function-aries on the general staff, drawing with rulers on maps plans of battlefield fortifications or detailed schemes for repetitive, absurd manoeuvres, which provided the occasion for officers to make an appearance who, on ordinary days, were merely glimpsed in the morning at rollcall, stiff, bored and listless in their elegant uniforms, clumsily copied by young cavalry sergeants who came from approved schools, the dole queue or the farmyard: for a few minutes, the time needed to pose like a group of strange, polished and bow-legged birds, not apparently feeling the cold, behind the huge captain with the Teutonic knight's name, built like a Landesknecht, upright, a herculean figure, numb with cold, his nose and cheeks blotchy and blue, listening with barely-concealed impatience to the NCOs who, each in turn, totted up in front of their platoons the precise number of farm hands, salesmen and shop assistants (one after the other, during the early months of the war, the craftsmen, the miners, the metal workers, everyone who knew how to use a tool

71

or a machine, had been recalled to the rear) disguised as soldiers, forming up on the square with the fountain which was frozen in spite of being protected by straw, men who made up the squadron's strength; after which they (the officers) clicked their heels, raised their hand-sewn gloves to the peaks of their caps and disappeared, the others (the NCOs) merely swapping their képis for helmets, doing a rapid inspection of the men at attention, each holding his horse by its bridle, before leaping into the saddle and setting off without looking back, dragging at a fast trot behind them their jingling retinue of men and beasts through the snow-covered countryside until they reached some forest edge, hill, bend in the road where, on dismounting, they pretended to supervise the digging of trenches, listening to the clanking of pick and shovel on the frozen ground, their faces surly, blue with cold, standing there as if to satisfy some ritual emptied of all use and significance, as if the object of the exercise were not to find and build better entrenchments but to measure in the course of a tedious daily experiment (just as a scientist in a laboratory repeats tirelessly his observation of the same fluid or the same blend of acids) the capacity for survival of human beings let loose from a protective capsule into the lonely solitude of interstellar space.

The winter seemed never to need to come to an end; it seemed that it had always been there, would still be there when the lines struck through the days on the calendar reached May or July, that the spring and summer were part of the things abolished once and for all the day a minister shown by a chamberlain into drawing-rooms overladen with gilt or marble had handed another minister a document sealed with wax, bowed coldly (or exchanged a few polite remarks or comments) and turned on his heels. A document, a simple note or rather an announcement (like those pinned up in town halls or published in the newspapers to inform people that on such a day, at such time and for an indefinite period water or gas will be cut off), drawn up the night before (or three days earlier and kept in reserve) by five or six exhausted men more or less walking in their sleep to whom for some weeks coded despatches were being brought which they opened one after the other with the same downcast air, the same panic: the kind of badly-dressed men in the sort of trousers and waistcoats worn by former teaching assistants or schoolmasters, dignitaries of masonic lodges, sent or rather catapulted there (into palaces of stereotyped luxury, sculptured panelling, mahogany writing-desks and dull tapestries replete with heroes and foliage) by a series of accidents allied with a robust capacity of the stomach which had for years enabled them to absorb without turning a hair at bar counters on electoral tours innumerable little glasses at the same time as hearing endless complaints about poor prices offered for artichokes, melons or beef cattle, and opposite them, threatening and ranting, former NCOs, butchers, commercial travellers or decorators, their paunches and flabby muscles pulled in by Sam Brown belts, booted and helmeted, qualified at most to rear pigs or run slaughterhouses — and in the background, weighing up their chances, other people who looked like respectable clergymen, unfrocked seminarists or pawnbrokers, calculating, wily or slow-witted, but all more or less as bereft of imagination as dumb beasts and for all of whom the simplest solution to their problems, their ambitions or their fears could be summed up in one word: killing.

And now it was there. First of all there had been the autumn, the succession of endless night rides, the laggard, uncertain dawns, the days breaking slowly on landscapes of railway lines, blackish suburbs, chimneys, railway carriages, the cruppers of the horses, saddles soaked with rain, shining with pale reflections whilst they waited, dismounted, stealthily detailing one of their number who slipped off to some tavern or other and came back with (hidden under his greatcoat as in the skirts of an old woman) bottles of hollands which they held by the neck as they drank one after another, the liquid fire pouring down empty gullets whilst somewhere, emitting clouds of smoke, heavy and dirty as if it too were sodden, some wheezy locomotive was being shunted (meeting at crossroads, or by chance on embarcation platforms, artillery convoys, regiments of North Africans with grey faces, or infantry whose garbage they came across again in the billets — like an incomprehensible game, one of those ballets with complicated figures, which lead their participants to take up in succession, and in accordance with a carefully worked out pattern, the positions abandoned by the others): comings and goings, or marches, or rather pacings up and down whose only imaginable purpose (for there must after all have been a reason, a motive — unless it be thought, which was after all not impossible, that once the famous document sealed with wax had been exchanged between the two ministers a kind of mechanism was set in motion, a sort of machine obeying its own rules of gravitation and attraction, some higher law of physics and of migration which required no other justification than a cosmic one) was perhaps to acquaint them with the monotonous theatre of past and future butcheries, to impress on their minds by the repeated sight of the same roadsigns the greyish, ferruginous names which recur at every page in French history books: Bazeilles, Sedan, Mézières, Rocroy, Givet, Wattignies, Meuse, Moselle, Ardennes, Longwy (and beyond — beyond the last outposts, the last tanktraps blocking roads of shining asphalt or where no one any longer cleared the snow, Mons, Charleroi, Koblenz, Pirmasens, Trier, Mainz: not towns with trams, shops and cinemas, but simple assonances, letters which put together had no other meaning but siege, capitulation, conflagration or émigré balls. Then the cold had come. As if in itself it constituted, between two periods of action, part of the war proper, no doubt so that everything could be put in order, so that the phrases in the textbooks or the memories of the victors could be there too, in their appointed place, like a ritual, as if it were necessary for the brief mention of winter quarters, with their associated smells of rotten straw, their processions of shivering silhouettes around shivering campfires, stamping their feet, gummy-eyed, red-nosed, and the sentries' moustaches stiff with frost, to be made within the regular sequence of chapters between the proud accounts of campaigns and the lists of casualties through epidemic, fever and dysentry.

The frost, the dulled surface of frozen ponds, the wheeling, screeching flights of crows echoing in the silence as they landed on the snow-covered fields. On certain days, at certain dawns, with the return of a night patrol, after the hours spent without moving, huddled up in the cold (feeling this kind of invisible thing, impossible to touch yet of a presence, a substantiality as hard as steel, penetrating them slowly and inexorably — and the trees motionless around them, the white nocturnal silence only occasionally disturbed by the subdued thump of a load of snow slipping off a branch: but they had stopped jumping with fright, knew that they too were only there to satisfy yet again some useless ceremonial or other, had long understood that spies and bearers of defeatist tracts were crossing the frontiers comfortably installed in overheated Pullman carriages, breaking off, only to shake the ash from their cigars, their reading of magazines or the international prices of copper and mercury, and respectfully greeted (if not escorted) by customs and police officers) . . . on certain days then, at certain dawns, it suddenly seemed that at the same time as it hardened yet further the cold underwent a sort of transmutation, in the same way as fingers and limbs had stopped conveying pain signals, seemed now to have lost all feeling, they too having no doubt become of a different substance, beyond suffering, as if the winter had passed from the liquid state (the damp, the rain) to a solid state, then crystalline (it was no longer their flesh, their bones which registered it: only their nostrils, as if they had breathed in the frozen exhalations of some pharmaceutical phial such as ether), the cold now well beyond its earliest manifestations, as when from one of those rough, greyish and drab cocoons something winged, incredibly coloured and transient suddenly springs, without any more genuine existence than a flash of light, the men on the patrol as if drugged, drunk with sleepiness and exhaustion, only half-awake, making their way one behind the other amid the orchards of trees wrapped in sparkling crystal, speckled like chandeliers or candelabra, breaking down in their prisms the pink and jade lights of a northern sky washed of all cloud and petal-coloured, so that on pushing open the doors of their billets (the ill-lit houses smelling of mildew and bedbugs, from which the peasants had been driven away, and in which without undressing they slept three to a bed in bedsteads of dark oak or flat on the floor upon ripped mattresses, adding to the age-old smells of damp plaster and wet wood their stench not of animals (because the cows in the cowsheds, the horses in the stables and even the pigs in their sties exude only clean odours, so to speak, chemically identifiable and classifiable as simple organic compounds like ammonia or liquid manure) but of men, that is of the only animal species enclosed in garments, a thick, stale, intestinal smell), freeing themselves of their weapons with stiff movements, kneeling painfully in front of the frozen stove, they felt suddenly, coming in from the dazzling,

75

suave apotheosis of the adamantine dawn, an undefinable nausea, an indefinable disgust, whilst in order to try and rekindle the embers they screw up in little twists with their numb fingers pages torn from devotional handbooks or school textbooks swept from the shelves of a cupboard and scattered higgledy-piggledy on the floor with photographs torn from cheap illustrated magazines in which girls, half-naked or sporting suspender belts, held up their slips or went down on all fours to show off their rumps with gestures or sign language inviting the spectator not to an embrace, not even to a servicing, but to the gratification of some natural and evil-smelling need like those one satisfies in unbuttoning one's trousers in the stench of the latrine or the privy.

Some considerable time had by then elapsed (whilst the men back from patrol, kneeling before the stoves, still belted and buckled, stared swearing at the pale fat thighs of the knickerless skivvies) . . . some considerable time had elapsed since the billet had emptied down, since muster and the return of the officers to their well-heated rooms where, on the table, campaign service manuals and unfinished letters to aristocratic fiancées concealed the same enticing photos (although those reserved for the privates were printed on bad paper and used cheap sepia: those of the officers in technicolour and on art paper, their tanned nakedness nonchalantly reclining beside swimming pools or on Californian patios); some considerable time had elapsed too since, much earlier on, the warrant officer on duty, yawning and barely able to see in the frozen night, had left the empty schoolroom (empty, that is, except for a map of North Africa, coloured in green, ochre and pink, a blackboard and a stove which smelled of tar) to catch sight of a vague procession of fantastic black shadows moving in front of him, peddling their bicycles with the faint headlamps, dressed in black leather jackets, the earflaps of their caps pulled down to frame their waxen features: he knew them — not any particular one individually, but the same mask of fatigue, of wear, of passivity: once a fortnight (for upon them (those of the squadron, the troop, the peasants, the book-keepers or the shop assistants decked out in uniforms, armed, helmeted, booted and hoisted on the backs of warhorses) was lavished a care at once maternal, punctilious and barbaric, shielding them from the cold in

76

abandoned houses which nevertheless had their roofs and walls intact, feeding them on vile, unnamable, things (quarters of beef frozen ten years previously in Argentina dated with a purple stamp on their yellow fat, sticky rice) but nourishing for all that, injecting them with horse vaccines, nursing them even (with horse medicine again — but with medicines nonetheless) if the need arose, like those prisoners condemned to death who are the object of watchful solicitude on the part of their wardens and to whose bedside the leading medical authorities are summoned as occasion demands to keep them alive for the sole purpose of being able, on the appointed day, to lead them, dragged by two assistant executioners or on the backs of nags, in a grey dawn or on a radiant spring morning, to that for which they have been carefully kept able to breathe: to suffer and to bleed) . . . every fortnight, then, the squadron went to the baths, platoon by platoon: they entered a courtyard, stood waiting beside the horses stamping in the dirty snow, then in brick buildings with broken windows, going together into the tremendous metallic din where they had to shout to be heard, undressed, laying their dirty woollens, their dirty shirts, their dirty underpants in small piles on the wooden benches, soaping themselves as best they could between the walls of corregated iron under jets of scalding, almost boiling water, as if it (the water) had run beforehand over red hot plates, the snakes of iron which they watched leap and twist out of the rolling mills, grabbed in the air by the long pincers wielded by the cyclists now divested of their leather armour and whose exhausted and ageless faces they glimpsed by the light of the flares whilst they slipped back their clothes, stiff with dirt, on to still-wet limbs, wiping before putting on their socks and boots again the soles of their feet blackened by a fine sooty, rust coloured dust in which sometimes a splinter of filing shone diamond-like, turning round once more in their saddles to gaze behind them as they rode away at the mass of black buildings, of chimneys, of gangways, of travelling cranes and of warehouses, funereal in the blueish snowscape, whilst the dull rumbling which seemed to come from the depths of the earth gave way little by little to the stamping of hooves, and the sharp, keen, stinging, pure air drove from their lungs the miasmas reeking of bad eggs and carbonaceous gas; and, for the officer on guard duty, nothing

77

else: not a voice, not a word, merely a confused hubbub, a squeaking of brakes, the crunching of frozen snow underfoot when they dismounted in front of the zigzag roadblock, a clatter of pedals knocking against each other and of handlebars, of a bell touched off accidentally, and, in the niggardly light of the lantern held by the sentry, the procession not of faces but of empty masks with rheumy eyes, with sallow, flabby skin drawn taut by the cold, whilst the gloved hands held out one after the other in the circle of light the same printed pass, the same small rectangle covered in yellowish mica which he (the duty officer) barely glanced at, dazed by the dark, the cold, on leaving the schoolroom, concerned only to wonder, with on each occasion the same naîve and incredulous amazement, how it (the cold) could reach such a degree of (what exactly?: savagery? malevolence? — as if it had been an animal, a wolf, or a mad rabid dog), simply repeating, then, the same automatic gesture, the same horizontal swing to and fro of the forearm, as if to drive herded animals into a pen, his gloved hand despatching into the shadows one after the other the small grubby rectangles covered with signatures, with illegible rubber stamps overlapping the same illegible identity photographs showing the same Polish, Berber, Walloon or Croatian faces, weary and drawn (and amongst them, no doubt, one or two, or three, who carried nothing important enough for their employers to consider it necessary to pay for them to take a sleeper in a Pullman carriage, who probably did not even receive a wage or any kind of gratuity for smuggling in the saddlebags of their bicycles or fastened along with their lunch-box onto the carrier the defeatist tracts which the frozen patrols lying in wait on forest paths looked out for in vain . . .), then nothing more: the last small urine-coloured rectangle gone by, the man on guard kicking back into place the straw bales of the roadblock, the squeaking of some poorly-greased pedal crank dying away, the glint of the lantern dimly reflected in the last rearlights which cast in the frozen darkness fleeting ruby flashes, the whole confused metallic hubbub moving away, getting fainter and fainter, stopping altogether, and only the dark, the cold, the duty officer climbing up the steps, closing the door behind him once again, feeling his way in the darkened corridor, then once more in the schoolroom (or perhaps it was in the town hall, with a plaster

78

bust of the Republic on a wall console, her bulging breasts covered in a layer of dust and with the photograph of a moustachioed man in tails, the ribbon of a decoration round his neck and two fingers of one hand resting on a book?) and then standing there, in the miserly light, still enveloped in cold (like a sort of cope, or ogive, he himself gothic in his vast pleated greatcoat, or rather medieval, his face invisible under the visor of his helmet, bundled up in his frozen belts and buckles, in frozen cloth, looking just like a fortress, a war engine or an animal with carapace, a tortoise, an ordnance shell placed upright, numb, stiff, with, like a kind of phallic attribute (like those helmets boxers wear, except that he wore it on his side, as if at the same moment as he had been as it were castrated, deprived of his natural organs shrivelled with cold in his grubby drawers, he had, to compensate for it, been endowed with a supplementary organ, easy to get hold of without undoing his flies, of incomparable power and encased (testicles and penis) in a reddish leather which more or less, in a way at once modest and obscene, revealed its murderous shape), his revolver holster; then (just as a little earlier, assaulted outside by the cold, he had stood for a while motionless, winded and unable to stir), after a time (assaulted, assailed now if not by the warmth — the stove which gave off a tarry stench managing however to maintain in the premises a temperature slightly above zero — at least (how to put it? . . . by the habitability?) of the room — waiting, then, for the mass of frozen air which had come in with him to dissolve gradually), moving slowly forward, lifting with his thumb the strap wedged under his chin, taking off one after the other his helmet, his gloves, once again motionless, gazing with a meditative, dazed expression at the bare walls, the map of bland colours, the bare floor boards, the confused brown shapes of men asleep on the ground, and the mattress which he had left a little earlier, glancing finally at his watch and beginning without properly understanding what his eyes conveyed to him to turn over the well-thumbed pages of a picture paper showing the sooty photos of young princesses masquerading as women auxiliaries driving a lorry or stripping an engine, a half-sunk battleship lying on its side, its hull blackened by the flames, the clergyman and the former headmaster with the waiter's haircut reviewing troops dressed in tartan skirts, then (the duty officer) sniffing, wiping the snot off the back of his hand, then the back of his hand onto a tail of his greatcoat, slowly turning the pages of the magazine once more whilst as the blood began to flow through his veins again he read slowly the exotic-sounding names (Rio, Plata, Highlanders, Princess), then not throwing but dropping the magazine on to the grey floor (it (the picture paper) dating from two or three weeks before, forgotten there (as in dentists' waiting rooms) as a decorative accessory of the guard post no doubt, the cover half-torn and crumpled, the greyish folds in the art paper criss-crossing, covering like a spider's web the horsy faces of the two young princesses enlarged and coloured in afterwards, with their unnaturally red lips, their smears of grease and their made-to-measure uniforms in an unsightly yellowish colour), the duty officer still there, sitting without moving, his two red hands dangling between his parted thighs, listening to the sleepers' snores, looking once more at his wristwatch, moving aside the phallic holster in toughened leather, drawing from one of his greatcoat pockets a book, also dog-eared, with a yellow lozenge against which the purchase price stood out in black stuck onto its coloured cover, moving his chair nearer to the light, opening the book, thumbing through it to find the page with its corner turned down, and plunging into the reading of a story with anaemic titled characters holding impassioned conversations on the terraces of chateaux or grand hotels in a half incomprehensible language which however for the duty officer (he had been a butcher's apprentice before enlisting after sums of money kept disappearing from his employer's till) conjured up a fantastic empyrean inhabited by millionaires, counts and goddesses.

The guard was not changed until eleven o'clock. It had been already light for some time and the straw bales of the roadblock had been pushed to one side when the duty officer, intoxicated with dialogue full of unfamiliar expressions (now, having shaved, scraping his cheeks until they were raw, dipping his razor into the barely lukewarm water of a mess tin placed on the stove, he had reached the last chapter, the one in which the young rake reveals his tenderest feelings to the humble governess for whose sake he gives up his orgies, his hounds, his whips and his racing cars), watching through the window-panes rimmed with fan-like flowered patterns of hoar frost the fatigue party as it slowly passed by on its way to the forest: four men (or rather four shapeless lumps) with their forage-caps pulled down over their ears, their greatcoat collars raised, huddled in a cart followed by the corporal on horseback wearing a helmet rather than a forage cap, with his coat collar also raised, still half asleep, his hands thrust deep inside his pockets, the reins wrapped around his right forearm, letting himself be carried along by his mount, rocking back and forth to the same rhythm as the neck of the horse thrusting forward as if on the end of a pole its head with its nostrils bristling with tiny icicles and almost glued (as if it had been tied by an invisible rope) to the trail-ropes of the cart.

But the enchanting glitter, the icy, adamantine, almond-and-rose coloured glow, had been extinguished. Now the sky was merely blue, cloudless, without even those long, stagnant, hazy trails which sometimes look as if they have been left by a huge paintbrush, translucent and thin, without the slightest barrier against the sidereal, cerulean cold which poured densely down from the remotest interstellar space and fell with its whole incalculable weight on the hills and orchards covered in snow right up to the forest's purple edge.

To reach it, the fatigue party (the two draught horses, their heavy necks swaying, the four frozen men hunched in the cart, the corporal dozing on his mount) once clear of the guard post, followed the main road for a time, then, at a junction, veered left, taking a path which rose slightly as it went round a hill, dropped down into a valley bottom, rose again and finally entered the woods.

There was no wind either. As if on the spot the cold had frozen or rather solidified the air itself, as if through some chemical action its invisible component particles had amalgamated into one transparent, luminous block in which rose vertically, rapidly at first, then turning and twisting on itself, the smoke not of the fire but of the blazing mass from which the wild flames leapt up in a crackling roar, springing at first from a few twigs, a gathering of dead branches, then fed, fuelled by whole trees, young birches, beeches as thick as a man's arm, stacked and piled, their boughs crisscrossing in an enormous pyre as if they (the fatigue party) were taking their revenge or

81

throwing down a challenge, as if they were trying to compensate through a sort of mad bonfire for the madness of the cold itself, projected out of History as it were, or handed over to something which existed beyond all measure (just as the crimson column of the thermometer had long since fallen beneath the lowest marking (minus fifteen) devised for times, customs, a way of life if not civilised at least gaugeable): the state (time and space and cold) in which the world must have existed in the stone age, when mammoths, bison and other huge beasts were hunted in the depths of mighty, inexhaustible forests by giant men who wanted their skins to wear and their hot blood to drink.

This, then: the damp pale flesh of the young trees under the axe flying in chips which scatter over the snow, then the trunks breaking, tearing, their fractures bristling with sharp splinters, falling, dragged (they had to set about it all five together, urging each other on, swearing, driven by a kind of frenzy, of rage), cast into the flames, and the trunks at first as if insensible, then uttering a kind of feeble moan drowned by the wild, merry crackling, then exuding a giant snail's greyish slime whilst the fire consumed them and they snapped once again, toppling over in a shower of sparks, the flames redoubling in strength, leaping a dozen feet or so into the air (at present they (the fatigue party) could no longer stay even near the blaze, were forced back, retreating hurriedly each time they dragged a new tree up to it, grabbing hold of it all together and tossing it on as best they could), the flames snaking, whipping the air, their bifid tips vanishing in the thick smoke from the green timber which curled and tumbled, twisting upon itself and rising as if sucked upwards, and suddenly (up to a certain level there was the shadow of the clearing, the bluish snow, the dark straight trunks, the greyish swirls pierced by orange flames), suddenly, then, the sun, its beams still almost horizontal, sweeping the treetops, the column of smoke salmon-coloured all at once, pink, as if the substance had changed along a line cut by a knife, as if it were bursting through an invisible ceiling and entering a magical realm made up of enchantingly soft, iridescent colours normally found only on the petals of flowers, the rocks of Olympus and the bare bodies of women.

So that (standing there with flushed faces and frozen backs and shoulders, holding their ungloved hands to the blaze) they did not hear him come, jumped when one of them swore out loud, turned round guiltily, stiffened, raised their hands to their temples, whilst he emerged from a forest track, passed slowly by, his thin frame at once lithe and inflexible on his long-maned chestnut mare with its delicate legs and dainty hooves which trod the snow in silence, its powerful long neck, its fine headropes, its slender pointed head, its body so slimly built that beside their sturdy battle horses, tough Pyrenean halfbreeds, it seemed almost sickly, unreal in comparison, with its golden blondness, its narrow breast, its supple muscles under its bronze-coloured coat looking as if they were oiled, lubricated.

He was a very old general (or at least he seemed so to them), he too (like the elegant chestnut) without an atom of fat, dry, even desiccated, with his clean shaven, shrivelled, almost papery cheeks, as if he had been lifted for the occasion (the war) intact, ivory coloured and mummified, from an Egyptian tomb or had been kept perhaps by the cold (which he did not seem to feel, wearing only a light ratteen coat (a long jacket rather) slit up the back, that he might have put on for a morning ride in the Bois de Bologne, meeting in the Allée des Acacias ladies of fashion in carriages and victorias and the old upper class prostitutes he had known in his youth (for in the men's eyes he must have dated at least from that era, that is from the one preceding not this war but the first one — since it now seemed an established fact that History had to be divided not into centuries but into short periods of about twenty years or so, the time it took for couturiers of Babylonian splendour to stuff women into lamé cylinders, paint their eyes green, hang cubist pictures in their salons, then have the whole thing sold at auction before the bailiffs can move in, after which the normal state of affairs (war) could resume and old generals put away in the freezer reappear intact, fit once more for service, that is to wield the power of life and death, if necessary against themselves (this one was to put a bullet through his head), in return for which, during the months of forced inaction, they were assigned a pedigree Anglo-Arab to enable them to perform not inspections but the few hours' daily exercise in the fresh air which, no doubt, mummies cannot do without).

But they had no need to get alarmed: he did not even glance at them, but passed by as if lost in his general's solitude, perhaps inwardly debating not the future disposition of the line of battle, of fortified positions for which they (the fatigue party) were supposed to saw off and transport logs, but only the best way of pointing a pistol barrel at his temple in order to blow his brains out decorously without running the risk of remaining still alive but blind. And perhaps (since apparently the cold had, from one war to the next, kept him so well preserved, while couturiers were being ruined, bankers were throwing themselves out of the window, fashion models were losing their looks, art dealers were suffering agonies of uncertainty, surrealist painters were selling their works to millionaires and millionaires exchanging whole populations of the jobless at the stock exchange), perhaps, right enough, all he was doing there (on this early morning ride in the frozen forest) was properly fulfilling some military duty, or some medical prescription with the force of an order aimed at delaying until the right moment the time when he would start to decompose (and after all they (the doctors) were not all that mistaken in their diagnosis that he would not outlast the coming of warmer weather: in fact he did not even make it to the second half of May).

Emerging then from the thickets covered in hoar frost like a messenger from the kingdom of the dead, Elysian, meditative and princely (he who commanded a whole string of colonel-counts, of marquis and baron captains and lieutenants, and whose own name was simply Charbonnier, Ducourneau or Lacombe), passing by, absent-minded, distant, to the imperial stride of his chestnut mare, followed by another thoroughbred (a bay with an auburn coat as glossy, as shimmering, as a boot in a tradesman's window), on which was perched, not astride but squatting, like a kind of small monkey, or dwarf (it was a jockey already well-known in civilian life who, standing up and booted, chin up, four-square on his short bow legs, and drawn up to his full height, measured no more than five foot one), huddled up under or rather inside (as if in a habitation, like those creatures with retractible extremities retreating into their shell or carapace) the huge cavalry greatcoat from under whose folded-back skirt-like flaps peeped out the doll's feet hauled up by the stirrups, as did the tiny sapajou monkey hands in black leather and as, from the too-wide collar, did also a pallid little guttersnipe's mug, no bigger than a fist, with its hatchet mouth,

84

broken nose and two small black hard ferrety eyes with no more life or expression than agate marbles — the midget did not turn his gaze aside either, both of them (the one pharaohish and desiccated, the other ape-like, microcephalic and dangerous) resembling an apparition, at once terrifying and burlesque, engendered by the cold, by the war or by the morbid genius of some fantastic engraver conjuring up on the whiteness of paper the spiky lace work of the bare trees, the cold glint of arms and allegorical characters of legend or nightmare.

And for a time they (the four men and the corporal) remained there, unmindful of the cold, of the neolithic blaze crackling behind them, turned towards the path, half incredulous, continuing to stare at the now deserted thickets where the two horsemen had disappeared or rather had vanished, noiselessly, the elegant hooves of their mounts silently treading the snow in the same fashion as they had materialised a moment earlier, out of nothing, like a hallucination, until one of them recovered himself, uttered an oath or one of those handy phrases which serve to express in one go amazement, dread and reverence, the corporal pulling himself together then, as if he were waking up, and starting suddenly to tell them off, bawling and gesticulating, peppering his orders with filthy words.

Not that they had never seen him, although his existence had something so to speak mythical about it (knowing that above the colonel upon whom they clapped eyes on occasion — but hardly ever, to tell the truth, since on mobilisation the regiment had left the quarters in which it was stationed — there existed a whole complicated hierarchy of brigadiers, major-generals, lieutenant-generals, generals and the rest, higher and higher up, right up to the former headmaster and the melancholy moustachioed character dressed like a head-waiter to whom (from the plain trooper to the commander in chief) they were all answerable): he (the general) had appeared to them once before, not on that occasion in the shape of a zombie, of an unreal personage engendered by an apocalypse of cold, but expected, heralded from afar by the string of commands, bellowed out nearer and nearer and louder and louder that made them stiffen, go through a sequence of short jerky movements and then freeze, one arm placed across their chest, the other hand holding against their thigh the butt of their cavalry rifle, whilst in the distance, on the road, at the far end of the water-logged meadow where they had been waiting in the rain for over an hour, a procession of motor cars stopped to let out a cluster of tiny shapes which gathered together in accordance with a ceremonial interspersed with short pauses, moments of immobility, facing each other, saluting stiffly, then stirring again, moving apart, always with the same attitudes, the same abrupt robot gestures, coming together finally in a kind of indistinct, brownish aggregate against which, as he approached skirting the front of the line of the troops, they saw his spindley silhouette gradually outlined, walking slightly ahead of the others at a pace which (either from the effect of his tall stature, his slender shape, or rather his thinness (and perhaps indeed he was not so tall, perhaps it was only the result of some optical illusion produced by this assemblage of bones set end to end and covered with stretched skin, polished like ivory and itself so to speak bony, incorruptible), or from the effect of a kind of boredom, of disillusionment, of weary authority which emanated from him) which seemed (his pace) based on a form of parade step, slow and stately.

Indeed, they realised that he was moving forward very fast. The officers a little to the fore of the line of the troops, their sabres (for they had been issued with sabres: not only the officers but the plain troopers, as if in mockery, like those convicted prisoners who in a refinement of parodic cruelty are decked out for the scaffold with marks of rank or grotesque crowns: they formed part of their equipment, placed under the left quarter of the saddle, the copper handguard near the pommel, the gleam of the scabbard concealed by a brown canvas sheath; they had even been taught how to use them, or at least how to wield them — always doubtless in the same spirit of mockery, parody and masquerade) . . . the officers, then (and the NCOs slightly to the rear) holding their sabres upright, the handguard touching their lips, the sabres forming a sort of railing whose bars, the sharp cutting blades, blurred in the distance by the perspective, shone dully in the rain with a cool, deadly, cruel glitter (as if their designation, cold steel, applied not so much to their appearance, their material, but to their function — that of plunging into living flesh (in the same way as the lily-cold whiteness of bridal veils heralds a bloody deflowering, or even like hospital sheets) in the sudden pallor of a face beneath which, like a blackjack, a body suddenly empties itself of its blood), the sabres, then, like the bars of a railing, the gap between them gradually widening, the front of each platoon sporting only three blades (that of the lieutenant and of the two section leaders) behind which they (the men drawn up in line) could see approaching, passing in front of them, their own death: not he (the general) exhumed and lifted from his cold room, ivory coloured and, so to speak, under stay of execution (or perhaps already dead, as if touched by a sort of premonition, a man distant, absent), not even the colonel or the captains who, abandoning their place, accompanied him, walking at his side the full length of each of their squadrons, but the nondescript group which followed him (or rather pursued him) out of breath, stumbling in the spongy grass, the strange cohort, or herd, of individuals, accountants or commercial travellers in appearance, whose helmets concealed (invisible, but complementing the flabby midriffs, the stumpy legs and the narrow shoulders) the prematurely bald heads of sedentary office dwellers whose supportive attributes consisted not of the four feet of a mount but of a chair: waddling hurriedly now like a flock of ducks trailing behind a marshwader, chosen (or perhaps one should say: selected — if indeed he (the general) had chosen them, had not (how to put it?) simply noted their existence (eyeing the newcomer for a moment with characteristic indifference and disenchantment, then putting him out of his mind) on the recommendation of a cousin, of a former mistress from the Bois de Boulogne, or of a principal private secretary hand-in-glove with the Jesuits or the Freemasons, watching over the fate (the career?) of a relation or rather, if their appearance was anything to go by, of someone related to their dairywoman or their concierge), chosen, then, not by virtue of special knowledge in matters of strategy or tactics but of specific talents such as for example the ability to sharpen different coloured pencils and line them up in good order beside a desk pad or, using small pink, pale blue or almond green cards, to keep up to date wall panels listing men and munitions.

As they passed by, hurrying in the cold rain, without a glance at the men lined up, mindful only of not falling too far behind him and of where they were placing their feet while abiding by a mysterious code of precedence and hierarchy, twisting their ankles on the uneven ground, the elegant mapcases tossing about below their belts, their faces stamped with that particular hardness and show of importance habitual with cowards and slaughterhouse workers, their thick calves encased in shiny black leggings, overbearing, as if they were already speaking in their excessively high pitched, peremptory voices into telephones which they would hang up with a curt gesture, drawing with a soft pencil angles of advance, inflexible lines of resistance on maps which, as far as they were concerned, were only plain paper surfaces to stick pins with coloured heads into and not this sort of (how to put it again?: not field of battle or manoeuvres but, to anyone who could see it as a whole, a kind of enclosure) corral in which like panic-stricken herds they (the regiments, the squadrons, the platoons, the sections or at least what remained of them) would wheel and gallop in all directions, bumping into each other, moving off again in another direction, harried and hustled by the bellowing drovers, veering away only to come up against another fence, another wall of fire, retracing their steps, each time somewhat fewer, their faces a little more drawn and exhausted, their eyes a little redder from lack of sleep, a little crazier through no longer being able in the end even to tell their right hand from their left, through living in fear of the sky, the woods, a bend in a road, a farm, a simple hedge, and somewhere, in a villa, a chateau, the pitiless wielders of pencils barking again into their handsets, hanging up, grumbling as they moved the pins, then when, one after another, the telephones began failing to answer and the dispatch-riders to return, gradually losing their haughtiness, becoming jittery, dabbing the sweat on their brows, getting into a huddle together and muttering in corners before knocking with ever-increasing diffidence on the door behind which he (the general) would be pacing up and down or standing still with his hands behind his back looking out of the window through which he could see the comings and goings of the dusty motorcyclists and on the road, beyond the flowerbeds and the well-trimmed hedge, dazed and mingling with the refugees, the first deserters, singly at the beginning, then in groups, then on bicycles, then whole lorries full of them, and they (the fierce cousins of concierges or the masonic protégés) now increasingly drawn, sweaty and haggard themselves, picking up and putting down one after another the dead telephones, until they hear from the other side of the door a sharp noise, only one, then nothing more, and on hurrying in they find him, slumped in his chair behind his desk with half his head missing, and they then, losing all self-control, beginning in their turn to panic, rushing up and down the stairs, scooping up their shirts, their drawers, their toothbrushes and the petty cash, hurling murderous blows with their accountants' and penpushers' fists at each other as they ran, before squeezing into three or four cars and scurrying off without bothering even to burn the archives, or the maps still stuck here and there with pins.

But that hour had not yet struck. It was necessary first no doubt that they (the men, the troopers) went through (as during the initiation rituals practised by orders and secret guilds) a series of ordeals long hallowed by custom (the rain in the autumn, the cold next, boredom) before reaching spring, and the supreme and final consecration: that of fire, sudden, violent, short, just long enough to learn what (by regulation orders and the metaphors of poets) had been kept from them, namely that what was called fire really was fire, and it burned, that the ruins, the dirty piles of bricks, of rubble with beams still smoking sticking out of them to which what had been a house, a barn, a crossroads tavern could suddenly be reduced, or else the scrawny carcases of lorries, of motorcycles, of cars (and of their drivers) which were still burning, licked by little tongues of flame, and which were strewn here and there, stinking, over the green countryside in bloom (and they (the men) exhausted, dazed on their broken-down horses, the platoons getting thinner in number every day, then regrouping, thinning again, regrouping a second, then a third time, until all that remained of the entire regiment was two officers, two troopers and two cyclists, then the two officers and the two troopers, then only the two troopers), that they (the ruins) had been attacked, disintegrated by a dense flame in a fraction of a second, shaking the air, the whole countryside, like a vulgar canvas set, leaving behind its sooty mark, the uniform layer of ferruginous grey which covered the bricks, the slates, the dead indiscriminately, and long blackish streaks, as prosaically dirty as a badly-swept chimney or the bottom of a frying pan.

89

Those times, then, had not yet arrived, things (that is to say what was decided — or not decided — in their overheated offices by the school headmasters raised to the rank of masonic dignitaries, the worthy clergymen, the crafty millionaires, the former seminarist, the old American actor and the butchers strapped about in leather) were probably not yet ripe. Perhaps laws (an order or rather an ordinance which it was impossible to detect but which was just as imprescriptible, as mathematical in nature as those that govern the spirals of shells, that shape snow crystals into stars, or that structure the most minute living particles) laid it down that the different phases, the different stages of the process (or of the ritual) which had been set in train should be observed. Or perhaps, having struck a first blow, and appalled herself, History had given herself a respite, had put off (like feeble murderers, drinking and dawdling to pluck up courage) the moment after which the din of thousands of houses crashing down, the deaths of children by the thousand (and by the thousand thousands), the screaming of thousands upon thousands of men and women under torture, would count for no more than the daily ration of news items, road accidents and hooligan killings. Perhaps it was the last stage: not a respite but the final period, the ultimate phase of the process (or the first of another): that in which in the silence of the night the sound of trains rumbling interminably could be heard on and off in the distance, as if the mysterious mechanisms which had been set in motion took advantage of the cold, of the darkness, to hasten to carry, to get into position their loads of iron, machined or not, of ore, of missiles, of things made to tear and mangle flesh, the frozen still air continuing, it seemed, to reverberate for a long time after they had passed by, like the booming echo of a bell, as if everything it contained, trees, hedges, houses, animals, men, could from one moment to the next shatter, crumble to dust thanks to a mere vibration spreading by degrees in a catastrophic jangling of broken metal and glass, the night itself comparable to a black diamond, embracing the somnambulistic, petrified sentries and the odd sick man driven by the gripes from the stinking bedrooms, crouching over the trench latrine above a pile of frozen excrement, his trousers round his ankles and the most intimate and delicate parts of his body defenceless and exposed to this cold darkness which seemed as if to assault

90

him, to lash him, as if, feeble and wretched, he had been mounted by a monstrous divinity, whilst he listened, in a sort of calm despair, to his tortured entrails emptying themselves in the sealed and terrifying silence.

Then a new day broke, crystalline once again, iridescent and boreal during the period in which the cold seemed to stabilize, as if having attained its proper limits and as if expelling from itself by its density alone whatever (clouds,fogs) might stand in its way: and then, only the greyish, dull dawns, in which, slowly emerging from the night, there stood out, took shape, the confused masses of the woods, the trees in the orchards, the houses, the silent white countryside with its belt of forests, mauve, lilac, slate, brown or only black like a dreary horizon in mourning, depending on the hours, the skies, the dusks. Sometimes migrating flocks of wild geese passed in triangular formation, under the low ceiling of clouds laden with snow, flying over the hills with slow wing-beats, vanishing in the distance above the horizon on which stood out here and there the steeples of the deserted, abandoned hamlets. Raising their heads the men would follow them avidly with their eyes (some, cunning peasant poachers, weighing up the possibilities of catching one or two, plotting a nocturnal, clandestine expedition to some lake or pond from which they would not return before daybreak, frozen, half drunk on alcohol they had gulped down to stave off death, empty handed and boastful), quickly taking their picks and shovels up again, called to order not by the NCO supervising the digging of trenches (he himself, unmindful of his position, his indolence, rediscovering his plebeian instinct of self-preservation, would spit on his hands and dig frenziedly) but by the unbearable vigilance of the cold.

A truce then, a breathing space, not a ceasefire but as if the frost had gripped in a sort of metallic immobility the cogs of the huge machine which in the early stages had ground into motion, then had stopped, abruptly, like a piece of machinery suddenly seizing up, or as if the mechanics had suddenly noticed an oversight, checking every part one last time, the rods, the piping, the gears, everything which was going, at a given signal, to burst, to explode with the force of a cataclysm, but waiting still, making way temporarily for the cataclysm of another kind which was also holding in its grip the hills, the

91

bluish horizon of the woods, the snow-covered countryside under the bilious sky in which the same flocks of crows wheeled ceaselessly, screeching discordantly, veering as they banked, swooping and settling, dotting with black the snow against which showed up, as if drawn in graphite, the sturdy little horses with their bushy pasterns, their powerful withers, shaking their wild manes, snorting as the platoons went by at a fast trot in a muffled clatter of hooves, the men with reddened faces, set, weepy eyes, struck dumb by cold (with only the occasional sneeze of a horse, the clink of a shoe, an oath to be heard) the air spurting from nostrils together with the steam rising from sweaty flanks and rumps drifting away in bluish streaks, shrouding in a thin cloud smelling of ammonia the cavalry in double file escorted for a moment (the length of the meadow, of the paddock which held the little horses as if they were kinds of fabulous creatures, of the species that unicorns or double-headed eagles belong to, apparently unaffected by cold or hunger (feeding on snow perhaps?) and asexual, with their large almehs' eyes and long eyelashes, at once gentle, languid, and shy) . . . escorted, then, by these heraldic beasts which seemed to go at a silent, airy trot, without apparent effort, as if they were floating under water or moving in a slow-motion film, the muscles of their lumpy chests, of their powerful thighs, surging, contracting and relaxing at every stride with springy slowness, the unreal silence of their stealthy progress through the thick snow contrasting with the jerky pace of the armed horses, the savage cacophony of clashing metal, of hoofbeats, of panting breath which, like the misty steam making haloes around the small troop in the icy air, moved with it — until on reaching the corner of the meadow, they (the graceful and powerful cobs) came to a halt, their chests against the barbed wire fence, their sturdy legs firmly planted in the snow, their rounded flanks rising and falling as they watched the jolting silhouettes moving away, growing smaller, vanishing in the distance, becoming lost, absorbed in the silent, abandoned vastness, with every now and then a farm from which there rose a stubborn thread of smoke, or one of those tapering and anonymous slate-covered steeples driven like nails into the winter sky.

They too, were sad constructions, characterless, almost soulless: they had burned down so often (on certain occasions for the pleasure of it, such as when armed brigands or armies of brigands after dismounting from their emblazoned horses were holding the feet of peasants over the flames, digging up their gold and ripping open their women, on other occasions under bombardment or a hail of fire), they had been rebuilt so often over the centuries (and the last time barely a few years earlier) that unlike those provinces whose past can be read in the antiquity of their churches and façades, the age of timbers, the elongated faces of saints decorating a porch, what bore witness here to the tumultuous burden of History was not old stones or an ancient date on a door lintel, but the trite ordinarinesss of machine-made tiles, of tin gutters, of drab cement renderings, and inside these churches with their monotonously similar steeples, the statues of saints with their pink cheeks, painted lips and insipid wishy-washy smiles. But it was the same roads, the same frozen ponds, the same silent forests crossed and recrossed by successive hordes of pillagers, firebrands and murderers, first those originating from the depths of Asia, then of red-bearded men wrapped round with iron, mounted on horses also wrapped round with iron, like crustaceans, carrying banners depicting feral or fantastic beasts, wild boar, bears, salamanders spitting tongues of fire, all bearing spurs, talons, sharp beaks, and later of armies shod only in bundled twisted rags, and afterwards of others again, and still the same valleys, the slopes of the same hills climbed, crossed, laid waste, recrossed, laid waste again, merely because it was the best route leading from the East to the West, the villages, the towns invaded, plundered and burned for the hundredth time which seemed, in the anonymity of their cement, haunted by the ghosts of mercenary footsoldiers and medieval horsemen, of princes with lace cuffs, with soldiers trained by the cudgel and with courts of musicians: the same skies of limpid glass, icy, or rubbed with charcoal, the same undulating hills, the same thickets ideal for laying an ambush . . .

And now, sitting in their distant offices set up in palaces, in austere brick buildings or in marble-walled chancelleries, the former headmaster, the respectable clergyman or the painter decked out in Gauleiter's uniform had succeeded in what, in one way or another, constituted an apotheosis in the career of a headmaster, a clergyman or a Gauleiter. So that they (they, that

93

is to say the few million peasants, clerks and shop assistants who had been registered, called up and vaccinated) were there, rigged out in mud- or sludge-coloured uniforms, dejected, stupefied, docilely gulping down their ration of frozen Argentine beef, of sticky rice, of photos of princesses, battleships or bare-bottomed chambermaids. They slept in cowsheds or stables, taking advantage of the animals' warmth, in abandoned houses smelling of damp, in evacuated schools, changing once a month the shirts, black and stiff with dirt, which they never took off even in bed, merely buttoning up again clumsily every morning the greasy collar under their illshaven chins, their eyes puffy with sleep, shivering with cold by the dead stove in the stinking bedrooms in which they were packed ten at a time, after, every morning, the duty trumpeter stumbling in the dark and in the deep ruts of frozen mud had gone round the village and blown reveille.

Beyond the panes whitened by hoar frost a greyish, waxy light could just about be made out. Through the petals of the geometric, silvery flowers the sky and rooftops could be seen. Sometimes, though, the upper pane was tinged with a pale bluish colour, and whilst bending down to lace their boots, pull on their leggings and buckle their spurs, they swore softly or argued viciously, surly, frozen in advance by the deepening cold heralded by the pitiless and dazzling limpidity of sapphire.

At the same hour the old general, his lean-flanked thorough-bred carcase dressed only in a vest, was lathering his wizened cheeks with cold soap and water. Already one of the two jockeys with pale gutter-snipe faces whom he had made his batmen had brought and served the coffee which was steaming in the cup while, crouching in front of the stove, he endeavoured to relight the fire. At the same time the other batman with his impassive features, lipless mouth, pale complexion, tiny hard eyes and little monkey's hands, was finishing saddling the first of the two chestnut mares which the general mounted every morning. At the same time, too, the delicately refined lieutenants were dipping their shaving brushes in lukewarm water as they totted up their overnight losses at bridge before slipping on their boots and their handsewn gloves. In the room in which the troopers were finishing dressing the fatigue man came in carrying canteens of boiling coffee, bringing with him from outside like an aura the surplice of icy air which radiated from him whilst, pouring out a stream of swear words, railing against the stench of the place, he moved vindictively to the window and despite angry protestations opened it violently, the terrifying winter rushing inside, sparkling, black and white, like the contents of one of those dark leather boxes which a jeweller opens, suddenly laying bare the cruel, icy glitter of the stones, like a mineral apotheosis, the ultimate triumphant manifestation of carbon, of forests submerged thousands upon thousands of years ago, spreading its sharp smell of ether, of ozone, like the heady, costly perfumes given off by flowers and sprays piled up in burial rooms which seem the very emanations, subtle and macabre, of those blocks of dry ice placed against the bodies of the dead, keeping them preserved for a few hours longer before they are handed over to the worms, to rot.

III

And once a month, the old lady (the old widow, always dressed in black, with her waxen face perpetually stained by the tears which sprang so easily, with her dark bodices closing over the old tendons beneath the flabby folds of old skin, fastened by the same oval cameo from which stood out against a violet background the flowing robes, in drapery as white as a shroud or bones, ectoplasmic and frothy, depicting some Pompeian tambourine player, which she seemed to wear faithfully as a kind of profane relic handed down from generation to generation, perhaps even dating from before the Empire, hanging paradoxically in the place of the traditional cross of garnets at the withered throats of successive ancestors, the equivocal and Aeolian evocation of hetairai or dancers, their bodies thinly veiled and engraved: although she had no doubt long ceased to see it (the cameo) or even to think about it, her fumbling fingers piercing each morning the severe military collar of her long dresses with the long golden pin of the brooch given as a birthday present at the time when as a young girl she still bore that name now extinguished which she had been the last to use on the fly-leaf of her books (books won as prizes in the strict institutions with religious or military names, with the romantic lilac or royal blue bindings, embossed with gothic scenes, or even that 'Journal des Demoiselles' in which the illustrations showed ladies in bustles, children in sailor suits and little girls with belts of reseda green bows, perched on high heeled boots of yellow glacé kid): then nothing further, from the day of her marriage: a sound, a simple grouping of letters which on a map or a crossroad sign now meant nothing more than the site of a hamlet and of the ruined chateau long since sold (the old lady, even her father, had never lived in it), a large farmhouse, in fact, with decapitated towers of which only the body of the main building remained, although it was itself half in ruins, the left-hand side, between the West Tower and the almost intact wing, having been replaced by a shed with a corrugated roof under which were piled bales of straw next to a tangle of rusty mowing machines, harrows, disused carts, bean poles, bundles of sticks, old barrels, mildewed harnesses, all tossed together in an inextricable tangle of wheels, broken axles and ploughshafts between which one glimpsed the russet feathers of some scrawny hens pecking around as they wandered about: all this and, immobilised in the yard, the gaudy orange of its paintwork half obscured by patches of dusty grease and mud, like a sort of dead shellfish (as if the cracked buildings or the ruins exuded a sort of malevolence, as if some spirit, some curse, attached to the place, bearing desolation, still held sway after having brought down the roofs and the Italian arch of the main door and was pursuing its course to the bitter end, eating away the fabric, corroding and destroying), the wreck of a tractor, itself already anachronistic, in this décor, amongst these broken remnants of a glorious past (of these there remained only the proud coat of arms, the escutcheon in the colours of steel, plumes and blood which in her particular combination of besottedness, affronted dignity and affliction she (the old lady) had piously kept, placing it as a sign of mourning on one of those little ebony frames normally used to hold family miniatures themselves also framed in gold and ebony), as if it (the tractor) itself dated from an era almost as distant as that of the dog-tooth moulding of the arch, as if as soon as the dealer from the nearby town had delivered it, as soon as it touched the ground of the yard, it had fallen under the spell of this same malevolent spirit and had remained immobile, since then, a heap of disjointed metal sheets and seized-up gears, unused and unusable, slowly rusting, its only rôle that of offering a perch for the russet hens, tipping lop-sidedly on one of its missing wheels, hideous and at the same time pathetic, as if, like the truncated towers, the crumbling wing and the remains of the façade, its facing under attack from the weeds and nettles, it was only there to bear witness to the insatiable vindictiveness with which, regardless of time, people, successive sales and mechanical progress, the headless ghost of a decapitated king, ignoring years, lustra, decades, people and owners, took revenge without distinction upon the ancestral home of the judge who condemned him and the very spirit of that century of the enlightenment with its inventiveness and sacrilege, which was guilty both of his death and of having

100

engendered the line of foul machines a final incarnation of which had come to rest there in the metallic hulk of an oily, impotent Massey Ferguson tractor.

So there was an owner, and occupants. It was not one of those obviously crumbling ruins, overrun by brambles, flamboyantly exhibiting their old stumps and jagged walls, in some way virginal, that is abandoned, inviolable, saved by its very ruined state from future injury, improper, as it were, for profanation: not ruined enough, therefore, to be beyond habitation, not preserved enough to be considered a place to live: merely a squat: on a larger scale but rather like those old holed drums that people use to make shacks and shelters, the only difference being that here the drum had two floors, the walls are a metre thick and the holes are stuffed not with cardboard or roofing felt but with bricks and rubble, the whole group of buildings, some abandoned without hope, others patched up as best possible (the stumps of towers, the barn, the shed, the stable that had once sheltered up to thirty five horses, stallions, mares, foals, mules, hinnies, the cow-shed, the lofts, the outhouses), reminding one of those houses whose impoverished occupants, unable to maintain them, close down the living rooms and the bedrooms one after the other, finally taking refuge in a single room which acts as kitchen, dining-room, living room and bedroom, and leave the other parts to the wind and the rain, the doors, the corridors without exit, hurriedly walled up, sealed off by unplastered walls with the mortar oozing out of the seams in hardened cushions, not so much to bar the way inside of leaking water or the squalls of storms as to erect a barrier against emptiness, nothingness and the ultimate finality.

And there it stood, on the windy plateau, still towering over the houses of the hamlet in its great bulk, clinging to life minus its superstructures, stubbornly intent on surviving, cut in two (from afar the low shed (which served as a dump for all scrap material) lying between the extant wing and the half tower, could not be seen, and one had the impression of a half-submerged wrecked ship whose forecastle and bridge-house alone stood out), having reached this state of indestructibility, guaranteed not only by its foundations anchored to a rocky base, covered with poor soil, the stony fields, divided by low walls, undulating feebly towards the bluish horizon, dotted here and there with wooded valleys, but also by the sort of basic, obstinate life which seemed to protect it at the same time as it was protected by it, the life to which it gave shelter (which inhabited it, was sheltered by it: there were geraniums at one of the windows, and as if to hide a wound, someone had planted a laurel bush against the jamb of the door with the broken arch, the old main entrance opening today (or rather yawning wide) onto a pile of logs and rabbit hutches, the broken staircase having been replaced with a flight of concrete steps set obliquely against the façade like a patch), the old, crumbling masonry bathed in or rather exuding an aura of silence around itself like a cape, of past centuries, outraged, abandoned, amputated and split open, determined to remain standing as a sort of reproach, silently accusing the descendants of those who had sold and denied it, those who had got rid of it, not out of necessity or penury but quite the reverse, out of a sort of disdain, or scorn, a desire for gain, for money acquired later by means of a series of clever marriages not contracted but arranged (as are business affairs) firstly by the son of the man who spent his last winter there, his last spring, his last autumn and then by successive generations, each one continuing to grow richer, the family fortune which had carried away with it at the same time as the money from the sale the name that was wrongly embellished with the tatters of past glory (the solemn figures with severe high collars and ties, trimmed side whiskers, then photographed, stiff, formal, idle, submerged in a uniform and a yellowish sodium tint, standing beside their wives with their fortunate inheritances, their hair dressed with head-bands, wearing stiff bodices and wide moiré skirts, bearing one after the other, with that insolent and morose haughtiness of renegades, the name that was itself in some way amputated, altered, perverted, that is (in the same way as they had sold the chateau, the meagre lands in favour of town residences and fertile domains) reduced, shortened by them to the only syllables that seemed har-monious in their evocation of power, of battles and gilt decorations, thus obliterating, effacing, or rather blanking out (as in noble families the daughter who loses her honour is hidden way in the depths of a convent) everything that to their stiff sense of decency seemed to be a blot, a disgrace, in their minds reducing to the same dimensions as inadmissable

102

youthful follies and gambling debts the colossal exploit of bringing about a new world and of killing a king), their fortunes, then, continuing to grow, the family continuing to prosper, to grow stronger in their armour of pride and respectability until the phylloxera epidemic brought it all crashing down, bringing in its wake that succession of ills which inevitably accompanies all disasters, the long list of funerals and early widowhood which had little by little given rise to the grief-stricken face of the old lady which she revealed as she wandered from room to room of the overlarge and ambitious house: two wrecks, then, the abandoned château, or rather farmhouse, the monumental, indefinable pile of stone which, in spite of everything, clung on, arid, eroded, its windows unseeing, continuing to raise its head like a symbol above the lands that had also been rejected, vaguely frightening, like the visible part of a deceptive iceberg, infinitesimal, in spite of its size, when seen against the substructure of history on which it rested, with its truncated wing, its worn-away tower, like those strange architectures with overhanging walls, indicating beneath them the hidden threatening presence of tons of ice which suddenly break away with a bang like thunder or cannon fire (or the deafening salvo of a firing squad) from the ice-cap covering some dead continent, buried beneath thick layers of cold and time.

For there was something hidden there. Something had closed over it, which had at one and the same time struck it down and kept it standing like a tomb, a mutilated guardian of that to which it bore witness and for which it paid: not the mere crime of cutting off a king's head (although she (the plump, limp, soft-fleshed old lady, always in mourning, condemned for ever, it seemed, to this jingling walking about, opening and closing in turn the doors and cupboards whose keys she looks for on her bunch) would sometimes allude, in a kind of sad complaint, which seemed blurred by tears, to the majority of one that had decided the death sentence, uttering a sort of moan, the living image of desolation or rather of expiation, as if one alone of these three hundred and sixty one sacrilegious votes assumed the stain of the spilt blood, as if the death of the martyr-king was brought about by one will alone, that of a lone assassin who not only bore her name but had even fathered her father's father . . .), nor the denial by the last but one member of the

103

dynasty to which he belonged, but something else (what to call it? the event, the tragedy, the secret? it was never spoken of in the family) which had shaken it (the family) to the marrow and afterwards it (the chateau) had itself been condemned, abandoned to die (as if it had been fled from precipitately, as if the spirit of greed and gain had found its justification in horror and loathing to get rid of them) destined to subsist only in this derisory form, chipped away, amputated by half, engulfed like a tomb (it looked as though the walls and the mended roofs were lined or rather contained by a larger transparent construction whose walls were soundproof) by this cape of silence which seemed to secrete or distil it: this silence could be felt some distance from the walls, it became evident at a certain moment when, as one was going through, not exactly the gate (one of the heavy, rusty double gates had been forced inwards, only held upright by one of its hinges and by the way in which its weight had pushed it askew into the ground — the other gate had disappeared, sold for scrap perhaps, or stolen . . .) but an invisible threshold (the rustling of the breeze in the dwarf oaks, the twittering of the birds, the harsh sound of corn leaves rubbing against each other) which seemed to cease, denied, cancelled, leaving the way clear for that quality of silence which is only found in cemeteries and only disturbed (or made even more palpable) by the infrequent, ridiculous cackling of hens, with gawky, bright pink necks, which seemed to penetrate it with raucous, wild, sacrilegious cackling like the harsh screeching of some stupid funereal bird, evil and incapable of flight; the visitor (the old lady had already been dead for a long time and her children as well and the illustrious name, the coat of arms, the escutcheon now enjoying only a derisory existence, improperly used on the label of a cheap aperitif sold in groceries . . .), the visitor, then, coming to a halt, uneasy, almost frightened, letting his incredulous, questioning gaze wander over the peeling façade, the window with its potted geraniums, the corrugated-iron shed, the stranded tractor suddenly jumping, making out a strange being moving towards him, funereal himself, dressed in a kind of black cloth jacket and corduroy trousers, a strange person (thinking (the visitor): 'The keeper, the man with the keys to the vault, who no doubt waters the flowers, keeps intruders out . . .'), a man still young, overweight, staring at him with a kind of quiet fury and humble indignation, standing still, mumbling something (a question, command?) then falling silent, standing there, like a bear, a clockwork toy, his arms dangling, at once aggressive and pitiful, the visitor hastening to excuse himself, justify himself, indicating the courtyard around them, the desolate buildings, the ruined tower, the face of the man who has just appeared, of the appearance of a bear or rather baboon, or giant baby, hardening, contracting, the voice raised, coming from lips moving rapidly, saying in a flash, swallowing or rather choking the syllables in a tone of defiance, threat and complaint: 'It's not my fault!', the visitor repeating his excuses, trying to explain (curiosity, or rather interest, the distant relationship . . .) the baboon man continuing to watch him in this same suspicious, threatening but humble way until, hearing the name the face relaxes, suddenly lightening, brightening, the thick lips moving again, the strange person saying: 'It's me!', repeating with a sort of pride and defiance the name, that is the second of the three, in fact that which, deprived of its final half (that of the fief) and the ancestral patronym, became a name commonly heard in the region, as widespread as Fabre or Roques, then, without transition, without discernible warning, the features hardening again, threatening, aggressive, the body moving forwards a step as if he were going to hit out, his voice equally threatening, saying: 'A stag! You don't know what a stag is?', the visitor disconcerted, alarmed, lowering the finger he has pointed at the carved stone above the door of what may have been a kennel, may have given shelter to a pack of hounds, hastening to say: 'But of course, of course . . . I was just asking . . . I . . .', then falling silent (or perhaps continuing without realising it to mumble vague excuses, vague conciliatory words), trying to smile, backing away slowly, still apologizing, smiling, moving his hands in a conciliatory gesture, in acquiescence while the baboon (the madman?), moving in step, his podgy face indecisive, painfully strained, his thick lips moving, now saying: 'But do stay, of course, look around, I beg you, there's no harm done, anyone c . . . ,' at this moment his expression changing again, his features hardening as his gaze alights on something beyond and behind the shoulder of the visitor, his face suddenly stamped with anguish, the visitor turning round, both of them

105

standing still now, he and the baboon man watching a dark person with a moustache, covered in grease, emerging from beneath the tractor (the visitor getting the feeling of a farce, of one of those cinema or music-hall effects, where an empty scene suddenly fills with people and becomes animated as if by magic, wonders whether the window will not suddenly open and a soprano start to sing, whether a troop of Tyrolean dancers will not come down the staircase . . . But apparently that was all): the three of them, then, now standing in the middle of the yard with its wild plants in the autumn light, he slightly to one side, the baboon man near to the broken-down tractor, as if on the point of tears, listening to the account of the little man covered with grease, as he chatters and gesticulates, a monkey wrench in his hand, and suddenly moves towards a van, also broken down, leaning to one side (he (the visitor) hadn't noticed it: perhaps because it was painted in dull grey and also because of its state of dilapidation which linked it, matched it rather to the other useless machines), throwing (the little man) the wrench inside, grabbing a cloth, coming back, still talking, towards the tractor and its owner, indicating from time to time with a gesture of his arm the kind of metallic crustacean, ailing and muddy, never ceasing to wipe his black hands, finger by finger, with the equally black cloth, the visitor fascinated, watching the scene which seems to him to continue in silence like a silent film or, what amounted to the same, in a foreign language, the sequence of words that poured from the mechanic being so loaded with incomprehensible technical terms that they were devoid of meaning for anyone but himself, as he must have realised in the end, his face also splattered with streaks of grease, taking on an expression of disgust as if he were insulted whilst, renouncing words, he shrugged his shoulders several times, opening his arms, raising and lowering his bent elbows (both his hands still joined together, the one continuing to wipe the other with the black rag the wiping of which brought to light however, here and there on the salient parts, patches of pink skin as on the palm of a negro), looking like a sort of winged penguin or auk, then suddenly turning on his heels (still flapping his wings) going towards the van, throwing the cloth into it, sitting behind the wheel, slamming the door and moving off, shouting something incomprehensible through the window whilst he

106

turned, making the jolting van describe a semi-circle in the bare yard, and disappearing through the gateless gateway leaving imprinted on the retina the word BREAKDOWN painted in sky-blue on the rear doors of the van, leaving objects and people still in this atmosphere of irreality and incoherence, so that later, when he (the visitor) tried in vain to remember, he could not say how he suddenly found himself in a vast room (the one with the geraniums at the window) in which everything — the walls, the ceiling, the floor, the furniture (dresser, bed, chairs, table, sideboard, chest, bench, even the set of tins decorated with a pattern of ribbons and forget-me-nots, and printed in rococo lettering with the words 'Coffee', 'Sugar', 'Flour', 'Salt', 'Pepper', etc., arranged in descending order of size on the mantelpiece) seemed to have been gone over with or soaked in or uniformly daubed with a tobacco-brown stain through which could faintly be seen the periwinkle blue (in fact turning to green) of the Louis XV bows surrounding the names of the spices and condiments on an ochre background speckled with rust . . .

Paris, 9 Germinal, Year 3 of the Republic — to General in Command Moreau: The Committee of Public Safety, my dear General, sends to the Army of the North the position that it must hold until further order, and I am taking advantage of the same post to write to you in confidence and to make a few observations. It seems to me that the left wing of your army is slightly too far advanced to the north, it would be dangerous to allow your lines to be cut by letting them become too stretched. Moreover what should be your aim? . . . That of providing cover for Holland in order to protect it from invasion, to contain the Stathouderian party and to keep your right flank up against the left of Sambre and Meuse, and to watch Molendorff's army. I am sure that the King of Prussia acts in good faith but it is sensible to have a sense of mistrust and it is necessary to keep a careful watch over the Rhine and the Ijsel, even if you had to withdraw your left wing. A failure in this area would be less important than on the Rhine. The intention of the Committee is not to give you a fixed position and this order is purely indicative. Depending on the circumstances, the essential thing is to vanquish the enemy, to live at his expense and to maintain at all costs good order between our various armies. Moreover my letter is confidential and is not binding: I am merely setting out for you my ideas and it is for you in your wisdom and with your skill to consider them and to use them as a basis for your plans; I can assure you that the Committee of Public Safety knows your ability and places the greatest trust in you.

107

The Army of Sambre and Meuse is going to replace the troops blockading Luxemburg and will keep watch over the Rhine for the present from Gelderland to Renfelsh and will not cross the river until the army of the Moselle and Rhine has gained some ground. This latter army will join up with the troops from Mayenne now at Huningue and those which are now at Luxemburg, will cross the Rhine at two points, will sweep across the Margraviate, the Brilgass, will go on to attack the left wing of the exhausted Imperial forces on the Neckar, will take Philippsburg, Mannheim, and will sweep down the right bank of the Rhine: at this point the Army of Sambre and Meuse will cross the river to take up a position over Frankfurt which will cover the siege of Mainz.

These are the present orders which will vary according to circumstance.

As for you, General, you are engaged in an active defence and you know that in order to defend themselves well the French need to be permanently on the attack.

Farewell, I shall write to you often personally, and I urge you to do the same.

. . . on a background speckled with rust, in the same way as the light fitting, the faded gilt frames of the chromos losing their gilt (there was a Christ with a blond beard pulling apart the folds of his robe (this also had been Prussian blue but had become spinach coloured) to indicate with his finger his bleeding heart, pale pink and surrounded by rays of light) and (the) two sepia enlargements depicting, within a surround of artistically shaded sepia a man and woman, stiff, rigid in clothes which are themselves stiff and rigid , both man and woman already ageless (although the photos had obviously been taken on the occasion of a marriage), everything then yellowish or rather earth-coloured as if (although the room was immaculately clean), the dust, the the earth from the ploughing, the mud from the paths with which the inhabitants came home impregnated or encrusted each evening, had little by little taken possession of the place, the furniture, impregnating even the paint on the walls, allowing only a range of browns and ochres, like a cameo from which stood out, amid this earthy uniformity, a sky-blue enamel stove, an old alabaster water urn with a copper tap, hanging with its bowl to the left of the window, and one of those chairs known as deck-chairs, brand-new, bought no doubt some market day on the square of the nearby town, aggressive in orangish stained wood, with its canvas striped lengthways in all

108

the colours of the rainbow, and its narrow arm-rests gripped by
the trembling wrinkled and deformed hands of a fragile old lady
(or rather an object: a thin small bundle, a weightless faggot of
bones, of twigs, on the point of snapping, but held together by a
network of ligaments, of tendons threatening at every moment
to break, a problematic assembly of calcium and shrivelled
tissues which seemed like a parodic version, a parodic
transformation on the human scale, yellowish, dried out and
plucked, of the skinny chickens wandering around under the
lean-to — and yet it was a woman all the same: a human being,
an envelope within which circulated the blue–green blood
which coursed in, swelled the veins or rather the thick ramified
tubes which could be seen bifurcating, winding and twisting
beneath the transparent membrane of skin but which was still
irrigated or rather animated by this secret flux, imperceptible to
the eye, this permanent series of actions and reactions of acids,
bases and salts, those relays, those signals of fantastic com-
plexity and lightening rapidity which produce reason, sadness,
joy, memory and speech): the object, then, the fragile,
ephemeral and prodigious system of conduits, fluids, articula-
tions, tissues, secretions, worn and even exhausted organs (the
visitor thinking: 'That's it: matchsticks: something that can flare
up and burn itself out in a few seconds', the effort that she was
making to get herself up was such that, leaning on her arms, her
back hunched, the slender arm-rests of the gaudy deck-chair on
which she was leaning were trembling as well, moving in and
out), this object raising itself slowly, despite the entreaties of the
visitor, onto its thin legs clad in black, her face jutting forward at
an angle to her scrawny neck (as the two men came in she had
stopped reading the paper, now lying at her feet and where her
glasses had been pressed were two pink indented marks,
framing the bone of her nose), her voice broken, fragile and thin
as well, reciting (with that sort of enthusiasm and laborious
concentration common to children), the words which had no
meaning for her, remembered by heart, like a prayer in Latin or
a fable, at any rate something that one must stand to recite and
which (between the dirty, yellowed walls, in the room decorated
with the furnishings of a grocer's shop and a sacristy, with the
urine-coloured oil-cloth on the table, the chairs with greying
straw seats and the two solemn enlargements of people in their

109

Sunday best, one of which was no doubt her own portrait made fifty years earlier) seemed (the words that is that emerged from the toothless mouth, the rhythm of the lines, the epitaph) to be a simple sequence of absurd sounds, invented to speak of things with no real existence such as marble columns, the foam and the indigo tones of the sea — and later (he (the idiot) now seemed to be seized by a sort of frenzy, as if in ecstasy, guiding him, leading him through narrow corridors, narrow doors through which, aping the colossus whose shoulder span he depicted with his hands, he slipped crablike to one side, naming one after the other (baptising them with the names of drawing room, library) rooms with nailed up shutters, with mildewed panelling once painted pale grey, in which piles of sprouting potatoes were heaped on the floor, showing him, on the other façade between the two stumps of the towers, the broken-down terrace, without either balustrade or steps, reduced to a plain hump in the earth where tomato seedlings and withered beans did battle with the nettles), later, then, the baboon-man running along the path that led down the wooded slope where the visitor slipped on the clay, recovered himself, feeling the cold mud gradually penetrating his thin town shoes, stopping, trying to suggest going back, saying: 'No, it doesn't matter . . . There's too much . . . Another day . . . I'll come back another . . .', the idiot turning back, climbing back up the slippery path with big strides, legs apart, feet sliding to right and left, like a skater (or rather a monkey, a quadruped: bent double, leaning one arm on the ground when he nearly fell, straightening up immediately, relentless), with his face ready at any moment to darken, to become menacing, taking the visitor by the arm, saying: 'We're on top of it . . . It's over there . . . very near . . .' forcing the stranger to continue, his enormous grasp like a vice, with that Cyclopean strength which seems to characterise the innocent, the angry and the mad, on the arm which was trying to get away, voluble, inflexible, reassuring, half carrying the other man, almost forcing him to run, both of them floundering up to the ankles in puddles made by the last rainfall, slipping together, regaining their balance, the freezing wet mixture of water and mud squelching in their shoes at each step, the idiot shouting: Whoa! Heigh! Hoy! Whoa! in the difficult places, in the way in which one speaks to animals, as one encourages a restive or a frightened horse, the two men as one, like a sort of four-legged animal, the visitor with his resistance overcome, giving up, allowing himself to be dragged along, able as it were, to see himself, or rather the two of them, as if he were a spectator: both grotesque, he in his town suit, his trousers bespattered to mid-calf, the other man almost carrying him, thinking (the visitor) in a sort of ironical rage, bursting at one and the same time with fury and laughter: 'Two drunks . . . Or rather a dog, a big dog trying to urge ahead an animal from a flock, driving it where he wants to,' thinking again later on: 'A dog, I had the right idea . . . a dog, precisely . . .' standing upright now in the damp meadow looking down at the idiot kneeling on the ground at his feet this time (there had been heavy rain in the previous days: it was autumn and tufts of strange tender green grass were sticking through the thick carpet of dead leaves, brown, rusty or ochre, some of them black and slimy, already starting to rot, with the lines of their veins still visible, clear, sometimes surrounded by an olive fringe, their ramifications star-like against the dark, velvety background, the layer of leaves so thick in places that his feet seemed to sink into something like silence itself, walking on silence which not only, in the bottom of this valley, was noticeable to the ear (that is to say that one could hear the slightest noise, the silent crushing beneath the soles of decaying vegetable matter, sodden with water, spongy, the least rustle of a leaf, detaching itself, slithering down from branch to branch, dangling in the still air, like a tarnished gold feather, weightless, ephemeral, finally subsiding without sound, indistinguishable from the others on the variegated red and brown carpet and starting at once to rot), but also distinguishable (the silence) by something that one could breathe in, the damp, cold air, laden with a subtle, deleterious odour, not of death or its agony, nor of putrefaction, but rather (how to put it?) of transmutation: the rich earth, the soil, taking back to itself what it had produced, nourishing itself in turn, swelling with it, in mellowness, and suddenly the rain began to fall, peacefully, giving rise to a different sort of silence, diffuse, a silent murmur spreading slowly by degrees over the wooded slopes of the valley, eventually surrounding the two men on all sides and punctuated at intervals by the plop of bigger drops from the last leaves, which sometimes near, falling

111

down onto the rotting carpet with a dull sound, or sometimes more distant, enlarging the space as it were by the repetition of the same distinct plops, separated, as in a scansion like the beating of an invisible time-keeping system patiently and indifferently meting out the successive units of time), the idiot, then, kneeling in the wet grass, not noticing the rain, the mud, his face glowing, radiant, pointing his finger at the rough-grained eroded stone, the inscription, the epitaph, the visitor bending down to read (or rather guessing at the shallow hollows in the stone amongst the lichen — their orange marks sticking together, spreading gradually like blotches on blotting paper) the words that the old woman, clutching the arms of the chair, had risen to pronounce and of which again the first (Greece, Sparta) there, in the gentle rain, amid the peaceful, fresh smell of decomposing leaves, the smell of rain, sodden earth, seemed even stranger, more unexpected, saying (the idiot) very quickly (and once again more in this same mumbling, broken, brutal delivery in which he had shouted: 'It's not my fault!'): 'You see? You see? . . .', reading, slowly, as his finger traced the line of letters MARIE ANNE . . . then scraping the stone with his nail, crumbling the yellow scales of lichen, saying HASSEL . . ., the end of the name being completely effaced, the stone having disintegrated at this point, the letters becoming more legible a little further on IN THE DAYS OF GREECE'S GREATNESS, then the hand with fingers square as shovels and with black nails, going down a line, moving again from left to right, from one word to another IN SPARTA (the rain was still falling, a little heavier perhaps, the drops more numerous, always enduring, infinite, the sides of the valley, beyond the nearly leafless branches of the aspens, now veiled in grey, seeming more distant, even disappearing, as if they were in the midst of a limitless space without contours) WOULD HAVE BEEN CITED WITH PRIDE, the finger moving down another line, quickly knocking down a patch of moss (the stone underneath brown, incrusted with soil), the voice spelling out again SHE WOULD HAVE (and still the rain all around, infinite, a tiny nibbling, like the materialization, the bringing to sound, so to speak, of millions and millions of numbers of decimals contained by the sonorous rhythmic plopping of large drops, of drops becoming more and more

112

frequent, the time divided into millions and millions of infinitesimal fractions, seconds, years, centuries... IN ANY COUNTRY, WHETHER AS SHEPHERDESS OR PRINCESS ..., the idiot still on his knees, straightening up, turning round, staring at the visitor, repeating with a sort of violence, a sort of fervour: PRINCESS! then saying again or rather growling twice (and now in his voice there was a touch of defiance, of exaltation, of anger): 'See? See?', leaning forward again, his finger brushing the stone again, continued in brief jerks DRAWN EVERY GA ... (and no doubt he knew by heart too what these slight lines cut into the stone allowed one to guess, like ghost letters, words, the worn remains of grief, GAZE, of a tear) AND WOULD HAVE BEEN GIVEN THE SAME WELCOME, after which there was an empty space, the space of a line with no trace of an engraved letter, nothing but the grey stone, cold and naked, the idiot pausing a moment, motionless, silent as if his eyes, travelling across the blank stone, could make out what only silence and grief were saying, then his finger, the nail with its black edging, beginning again to follow the line of almost eroded letters which could just be made out a little lower down, his voice pronouncing at the same time SHE CAME TO THE CALLEPE, pausing, straightening up a second time, his vacant eyes gazing with pain on the invisible countryside, the valley drowned in rain, the tears, melting away, his hoarse voice (like that of an animal or a deaf mute who had been taught to speak) repeating CALLEPE!, his head tipped backwards, jerking his chin towards the stream a little further down, the flooded meadow, the water as still as if lacquered, on its surface the closely spaced drops described silver circles, and finally the torso bending over again, the square finger climbing slowly from one dot to the next, then moving rapidly, violently, up to the last word, the voice now become desperate, heavy with real despair, real distress, saying (but less rapidly than the finger, or perhaps the visitor had already let his eyes slide towards the end of the inscription — not read: recognised, without even needing to see the, the words that he had already heard issuing from the old toothless mouth a little before:) ... AND HERE IS HER SARCOPHAGUS!, the rain which was now falling heavily, trickling down the face turned up towards him, a face soft and yet bestial, distorted, pained (and at the same time radiant, as if illuminated by a kind of pride or bliss), the rain snaking down the cheeks in long trickles like tears, gathering in shining drops, hanging for a moment from the stubbly chin, quivering, before they fell, the shoulders of the black jacket now coloured steel-grey, soaked, shining, the visitor watching him get up, mechanically wiping (with the same absurd conscientious care as the mechanic had used earlier on for his hands covered with grease) the dark, wet stains which marked the knees of his corduroy trousers; the visitor again letting his gaze drift around them, seeing the bottom of the valley, the river, the square clump of aspens, the fields still green stippled with the gold of the dead leaves deposited by the wind at the foot of the hawthorn hedges (the small leaves shaped like a three-fingered glove, like tiny hands, also on the point of dying, pink, saffron and coral red) instinctively seeking with his eyes . . .

Milan, 17 Nivôse Year 9 — to Citizen Batti: Dear Mistress Batti, here we are in the month of February; you must tell Louis Cotais to inspect all the trellises both those at the wood with paths and those at the North house. He must turn over the earth at the roots so that the new spring shoots will be that much better. Now is also the moment to plant the muscatel vines that I want to put into the walled orchard: if the servants do not have the time to do this, hire someone else at a fixed price, making sure you choose someone who will do it both well and promptly: don't forget that I want only muscatel. Have some ivy planted around the walls of the spring and around the poplar opposite; make sure that it is planted carefully because nothing takes so easily as ivy and if it does not take I can assume that you had been negligent: do not forget to have a check made on the vines that are planted around the trellis-work of the spring and replace any missing stocks with muscatel. I had told Blanchard to have the willows replaced, both in the river and on the side of it and to plant them thickly. You will have those at Bournazel cut back and plenty of others planted in all the ditches around the meadow where they will take root. You tell me that you have made thirty five ells of oakum and twelve of linen. That is very little: a house needs so much linen; I am not pleased that you have made so little, you ought to make five hundred ells of each per year: you ought to use all the flax, have it spun, either paying for it with money if the spinning is cheap or paying for it in kind if it is expensive; I don't refuse to pay for the making up. Since your arrival I should have acquired a wardrobe full of linen and I have very little.

Have all the dead hedges and little trees been replaced?

114

Leaf mould, leaf mould, manure and plenty of it.

Plant the small orchard of the North house, all with muscatel, and have an alleyway left in the middle of the orchard six feet wide in the direction of Ligne and another of the same width along the wall which goes from the Mercader road towards Strebola. Make sure the vines are planted with a good ditch between them and not as that rascal Turlan did it.

My wife sends her regards, my son is well, affectionately yours.

. . . instinctively seeking with his eyes the other stone that should have been there, the other monument, (for it wouldn't have been called a tomb, at least not as is usually seen: there was no cross, no angel, no cherub in tears: it looked more like a fountain or rather one of those profane tombs of antiquity, something austere, classical, like the altars of Pompeii, dedicated to some household God or to Venus, the vertical stone, where the epitaph could be divined, surmounted by a triangular pediment on which, under the overhang of the cracked cornice, stood only a date, four figures: 1, 7, 9 and 0, and nothing else), and no doubt, without a word being spoken, the idiot understood the question, speaking again very quickly in that way peculiar to him; as if out of breath, panting, the visitor following the direction of the pointed finger, looking up above them at the chateau (from where they were it was grey upon grey against the turbulent sky, rising solitary on the crest, obscuring the hamlet: it seemed quite different, jagged, emphatic and theatrical like a shape cut from a sheet of metal), the stone cross of the church emerging from behind a neighbouring clump of trees, the visitor thinking: 'What? A cross? . . . Him! . . . A cross! . . .' but saying aloud 'The cross of his grave? But wh . . .' the other explaining then: the new road, the reduced cemetery, the desecrated grave, the cross alone hoisted then up to the top of the bell tower, the visitor fighting against incredulity, bewilderment, saying: 'Well then, where . . .,' the idiot making a vague gesture of ignorance, impotence, his lips moving silently, his face suddenly hostile, threatening, as if he was repeating in a sort of dark despair the few words that absolved him, the sort of magic formula by means of which he cleansed himself of all sin, forestalled, resisted any reproach: 'It's not my fault!,' the bewildered visitor, as a short while before, half-way between stupefaction and laughter, thinking: 'It isn't true. It's not possible!,' as if the whole matter was at one and the same time

115

too unjust and too feasible, as if everything (the desecrated tomb, the bones dispersed or thrown without thought by the jaws of a roaring bulldozer, pell-mell along with those of former serfs and old servants, into the common grave), as if everything, then, had been ordered, decided, programmed by a force that was neither mocking nor facetious but logical, rational, in order to perfect things beyond death, beyond putrefaction, a fate out of the ordinary, at the same time violent, sacrilegious and intractable or rather indomitable (thinking: 'But not only that: something else as well, something more relentless, more powerful than the ghost of a beheaded king, more powerful even than that of a dead young woman, the Huguenot lady who had been refused the right of a Christian burial, for whom he had had built, apart, in the sodden valley, the solitary mausoleum, and from whom he had been separated against his will in death. She had been won, that night at the opera, seduced, brought here from her flat nordic land, carried away from her town of canals, diamond merchants, ship-owners, cloth-merchants, and confined in a distant chateau, built in a far-off country hundreds of kilometres from any sea, imposed, in spite of the hostility of half-savage locals, upon a family of peasants decked out with titles, with their tarnished double-barrelled name, fecundated by a stud, then abandoned, left alone, surrounded by those hostile, bigoted rustics, forsaken not for a rival, a mere woman, but for a thing which no woman could resist, nor even any man, something that for many years was going to crush children as well as adults, turn everything topsy-turvey, a city first of all, then a kingdom, then a whole continent . . .), dusk falling rapidly (or the clouds thickening again), the rain beginning to fall heavily, comfortably settled as one might say, the chateau (the ruin) completely black at that moment at the top of the hill, the church cross black as well, the idiot (whilst they were both climbing back up the sodden path, slipping and skidding in the mud, holding on to each other, a grey vapour escaping from their lips at each exhalation) become voluble again, enumerating in a broken voice, made jerky by the shortness of breath occasioned by the climb, listing (perhaps in order to clear himself of blame for the desecration of the remains but, it rather seemed, more with a kind of negligence and disdain, to make it clear that it was a question of distant

116

relations, of collateral branches, unimportant ones, with no rights to enforce) all those in the surrounding hamlets and farms that bore the same name: a café owner, a tenant farmer, a blacksmith, a cattle-dealer, a garage owner in the town (perhaps the breakdown man with the van), and others still, as if the colossus had left behind two lines of descendants, one bastard line, illegal, with rights to only a third of the name (or rather to one of the three), which had remained there, like the serfs of former ages, bonded to the land (or rather hanging on, rooted (this family line), made up of artisans, farm labourers and all those who have nowadays replaced the grooms and coachmen, no longer equipped that is with curry combs, brushes and pitch forks, but with monkey wrenches, grease guns and jacks, the other (the other line), that of the heirs in direct line of descent, by right as it were and which, if one considers only the male line able to pass on the blood-stock, was to see itself extinguished (indeed was already extinguished) with the old lady 300 kilometres away leaving no other trace than the proud series of portraits or photographs of people posing stiffly, an estate mortgaged down to the last brick and, as the derisory remains of a century of pride, opulence and stilted display, the too spacious house acquired in defiance (or as a repudiation, an execration?) of the ruin, with its entrance court, its garden, its cellar which was also now too large, its empty stables, its paved coach-house where the place of the landaus and brakes was now taken by the solitary and incongrous old Ford of Uncle Charles, perched high on its wheels, in a state of decline itself, resembling (with its canvas hood, its protruding lights, its mudguards, its dull grey paintwork and its snout of a radiator) some monstrous insect, and the twenty odd rooms, the two drawing rooms, the terrace, the verandah on which the last male to bear the name (the name that had swayed the fatal vote, that had subsequently done the Grand Tour on horseback and whose initials featured now only branded on the apricot pickers' ladders or stencilled on tubs for the grape harvest and on wine casks) had allowed himself to be photographed, posing seated at an angle on a chair, lean, haughty, a shawl thrown around his shoulders against the cold, an astrakhan hat on his head and casually holding his cane with its silver head knob, with his narrow mandarin's beard, his aquiline nose, his high cheek bones, looking severe, haughty

117

and stiff like a slave owner, a baptist pastor or a Cossack hetman, surrounded by his grandchildren and his daughters one of whose number could be recognised as (hardly any younger, as if she had always been old, as if she was already all tears, alarmed by a premonition of ills to come), the old lady whose destiny it was to wander endlessly, vague and dream-like as if sleep-walking, in the corridors with their permanently damp walls, in summer as in winter, decorated with old wallpaper with faded colours, dank, hardened and peeling . . .

Once a month, then, the old lady gathered around her family (or rather the remains of her family) a few collateral relatives or some more or less intimate acquaintances, and for the occasion opened up the large drawing room, closed and double-locked on the other days, out of bounds except on these rare occasions, lit up then, with its gilding, its silks, its glazed cabinets filled with precious trinkets brought out or rather exhumed for one evening from the sepulchral existence that they led the rest of the time at the heart of the house, behind the coffin-varnished door with its dark ebony handle, lit up then by the grey light meanly filtered through the bay windows which opened onto the verandah, hanging there stagnant during the day as if within some sanctuary, revealing the two rows of armchairs covered with white drapes (or rather grey like the grey light which revealed them) and looking like a gathering of ghosts seated face to face, their skinny bones, their fleshless hands resting on the arms and lifting the shrouds which were draped over them, solemn, faceless, and towering above them from the top of the plinth on which it was placed, behind the sofa set in one of the corners, the shadowy bulk, ill-defined and colourless, of the monumental bust, its shoulders covered with a marble toga, its visage powerful, depicting at one and the same time the serenity and cunning of the man who was surrounded by a mysterious aura of glory, of execration and of respect, periodically dusted on the orders of an old limping servant by the feather duster of a cleaner, hired specially for these receptions, the memory of which would, in the minds of the children (or rather of those who had been the children); remain indissolubly associated with a persistent and vaguely funereal smell of furniture polish, sweat and raised dust.

The covers were removed, the carpets were beaten, hanging

over the verandah, exhaling a sort of subtle, faint perfume of faded things (bunches of pale roses, discoloured garlands mixed with washed out decorative scrolls) whilst the pendants of the chandelier, abruptly disturbed, moved by the draughts, knocking against one another in a wave of light, crystalline tinklings, like the high-pitched music to the sound of which mannequins in the costume of a marquis or a shepherdess move, similar to those that are to be seen, graceful and melancholy, in the shape of Dresden china or painted in water colours in the middle of arabesques on fans with ivory frames opened out in the cabinets filled with those tiny precious objects (pistols with mother of pearl grips, purses embroidered with pearls, Florentine daggers and bottles of smelling salts) the grouping of which on the brocade covered shelves always seemed like the inventory, the panoply of miniature symbols, elegant and costly, of basic and brutal acts like murder, barter or copulation, incongruous, almost unseemly, kept under lock and key, put out of harm's way, placed there as if out of some kind of superstition, of fearful respect, like those familiar or precious objects themselves, those weapons, those jewels, those cups destined to serve some dead potentate in the life to come, the colossal ancestor, always present, sculpted from 200 kilos of marble, brought one hundred years earlier by cart from the distant chateau and installed (deported), foreign, in the heart of the ambitious and over-large house to which, when the body had hardly become cold, the renegade son went, this son who was shown painted in a miniature which formed the lid of a tortoise-shell snuff box, pink cheeked, sulky and chubby with his mop of blond hair inherited, no doubt, from the Dutch woman and styled like a poodle's, and having sold off everything of value, fleeing the old ancestral pile at the same time as he cast off, threw to the four winds his ensign's tunic, inaugurating that opulent and idle decay over which the bust of the formidable frowning progenitor seemed to have watched with malign patience, that type of lethargic disaster in the likeness of the century which emerged exhausted from a bloody confinement, eager for respectability and gain, stumbling into unsuccessful revolutions, undertaking rapacious colonial conquests and leaving as an official souvenir, bought from year to year by the false baptist pastor (the renegade's son, the father of the old lady), the complete series of that gallery review whose name (l'artiste) could be read in gold letters on the spine of the red leather bindings which held the issues arranged in date order which were placed on one of the shelves of the large ebony bookcase with its glazed panels where she (the old lady) kept them in the same spirit of filial piety worthy of a character in a tragedy by Corneille, as if they were sacred relics, they too kept under lock and key, less out of fear of burglars no doubt, than to hide from the eyes of the children (they discovered them later at the time of the inventory, the sharing out) the pale nudity of an Andromeda or of odalesques with hairless vulvas, in rapture, plump and uniformly glabrous, like pale temptresses inhabiting oriental and libinous empyreans, reappearing slyly at the mere turn of a page, between the 'Assassination of the Duc de Guise', some chlorotic allegorical figure, or some twilight homecoming of the flock.

As if, on certain dates (rendered by age into a kind of sterile virginity, a mourning vestal, responsible for maintaining not a flame but something extinguished, long since forgotten), she felt herself obliged to make a sacrifice to a ceremonial which, once the invitations had been sent out, the menu decided on, the wines chosen and the house plants arranged, she felt herself to have satisfied that from which she then seemed to detach herself, being content to be quite simply present, resembling, with her half-opened mouth, her plaster complexion, her eyes underlined with bluish bags, one of those asphyxiated fish, those bream with their glassy look and mother-of-pearl scaly cheeks, tortured, presiding hierarchical and woe-begone over these interminable dinners, staring into space before her, sending away with a wave of the hand the dishes that she barely touched, occasionally nodding agreement (that is when she was no longer listening, alerted, exhumed by the silence of that beyond in which she seemed to be lost) to the words of her neighbour, that other elderly person (but to the children — the grandchildren of the old lady — they all seemed very old, equally solemn, severe and vaguely frightening) whom for obscure reasons of relationship or of protocol she always seated on her right, a sort of dwarf, who only just came up to her shoulder, like a person brought out himself, so to speak, in the same way as the blouses of the old lady, from some box or from some cupboard smelling of camphor, making up with her a macabre caricature of a duo in which he took the vocal part . . .

The first aircraft attack. These (three) are flying horizontally and quite slowly, heading eastwards (returning from a mission?), their flightpath cutting obliquely across the long straight road lined with ash trees, on one side of which, going in the opposite direction to the cavalry, the trail of refugees slowly moves. At the sight of the planes they abandon their carts and their belongings, run away from the road or lie down in the ditch. The three planes continue their straight flight at a medium height (one can easily make out the black crosses on their fuselage), seemingly taking no notice of the road (after all the congestion on it cannot easily be seen through the thick foliage of the trees that shade it). The first cluster of bombs explodes suddenly to the rear and to the left in the meadow (or rather field of green wheat), there is a burst of smoke and dust, a series of rapid cracklings rather than an explosion, as if the bomb or bombs were breaking up into a multitude of little bombs, exploding one after the other very quickly, rather like the final bursts and flourishes of a firework-display.

Indeed everything happens in a few seconds, almost simultaneously and it will be impossible for him to say with any certainty in what order the various phases of the action followed upon each other (whether for example: the noise of the plane engines, then the dispersal and the terrified cries of the refugees, the noise of the explosion, when he turned his head and saw the burst of grey smoke (grey–brown) studded with sparks and glowing points of light — or whether, on the other hand, the refugees first began to run before he understood the reason for it, whether he saw the planes before he heard them, whether it was the panic-stricken shouts of the refugees, before they began to run and be scattered, which sounded the alarm, or whether the first cluster of bombs fell before the engines were heard and whether it was the explosion that gave rise to the flight and dispersal of the refugees, or yet another order of events.

The flight path of the three planes having at that moment already crossed the axis of the road, the planes disappeared into the distance, indifferent, so to speak, as if they had simply jettisoned the remains of their load on their return journey.

It was then (then: whilst they were moving away) that the second bomb exploded — or the second cluster (still this impression of multiplicity because of the crackling, the secondary explosions which seemed to come from within the first), again behind and to the left, but this time very close to the road, so deafening that he thinks he has been hit, knocked by the blast no doubt, perceived as well (the blast) as a rapid succession of blows all over the body, like violent punches, at the same time as if blinded (unless he instinctively closed his eyes?): something obscure, brown, shattering into pieces, a rush of triangles, like infinite fragments of flying glass exploding (although it all takes place in the middle of the countryside with no house in the vicinity), the edges of the triangles luminous, dazzling, the noise (no longer that of the explosion but of what?) like the din of breaking glass whilst an odd smell of ether stings his nostrils. He experiences all this however in one instant, feeling his mare beneath him throw herself forward, or rather the powerful structure of muscles and bones contract and relax between his thighs, and when he re-opens his eyes (or rather when he is able to see again) he is galloping (or rather his mare is galloping) alongside other horses — some of them riderless), already almost at the top of the long road which they had started to climb only moments before. He pulls violently on the reins, sawing at the horse's mouth in order to regain control of the animal. All this still in a state of confusion and semi-consciousness, still convinced he is injured although he feels no pain (he only keeps his seat and pulls on the reins by means of mechanical reflex movements). Just as he manages to get the mare back to a trot he has reached the very top of the hill. At this point the road is no longer lined with trees and the ground is completely open. He then sees the three planes which have turned coming (slowly) towards him, flying low this time, rocking slightly on their wings like planes preparing to land. They rapidly become bigger and he hears the crackle of the machine guns getting louder. Then he throws his mare into a cross road to the left.

. . . holding forth (the dwarf, the guest of honour) or rather soliloquizing in a thin, nasal voice and in a sententious tone beneath which could be discerned an insolence as of someone who had strayed into an unsavoury gathering, who had come out of condescension not only because there existed between the old lady and himself an enormous difference in fortune (he had remained, in spite of the phylloxera, immensely rich) but (at least from his point of view) because of an impassable gulf the existence of which he sought to emphasize as much by his behaviour, his constrained manner, his ill concealed aggressiveness (or rather beneath his apparent urbanity which he flaunted maliciously) as by his constant reminders, in relation to everything and to nothing, of his uncompromising royalist convictions, either because he considered them inseparable from his aristocratic name of which he was very proud or because he felt himself connected by an instinct of solidarity to

122

the hapless locksmith king whose passion for tinkering about he shared, as if his millions, his life of leisure and his extreme opinions placed him in a separate category, absolving him from the need to renew his wardrobe (he always wore, like a miser, the same worn jacket) and imposing upon him an obligation to invent a series of ingenious accessories which he showed off by indicating their excellence, from the clip-on tie to the special knife for peeling oranges, the children watching him awe-struck, fascinated, as he produced from his breast pocket a case out of which he pulled something that resembled a bandage or a gag and then having raised it to the light, with a look of satisfaction on his face, in the manner of one of those street salesmen, extolling their vegetable mills and potato mashers, he fastened it (each movement always being accompanied by a commentary) behind his head with two cords, the protuberant moustache disappearing into a kind of long pouch, then lifting his head . . .

This time again it was one of those sheets of paper, firm to the touch, creamy and slightly rippled, on which the hand press had printed in hollows as on imperishable material (one could feel them as one ran one's finger over it) engraved characters traced by hand, not absolutely regular and with some slight smudges in the downstrokes, square, categorical.

The whole did not quite take up four sheets of octavo, sewn together with a plain thread with a knot, the first of which bore at its head in small capitals the words:

NATIONAL CONVENTION

bordered by two horizontal lines, the following:

OPINION
OF
J.P. L.S.M.
DEPUTY FOR THE TARN
On the Trial of Louis Hugues
Printed by order of The Convention

——————

I have put my name down to speak on several important questions; and although I made my request at the opening of the session, I found myself the hundredth or even later. I have without complaint sacrificed my opinion several times: I do not have the pretension to instruct my fellow citizens: but on this over-long question, where everything, even silence, will be misinterpreted, since I could not be heard, I wished to record my opinion in

123

writing, so that if I am worthy of blame in my treatment of kings, I should be seen to be entirely so.

Is Louis guilty? . . . Nearly everyone agrees . . . Well then! If he is guilty either we must tear up the declaration of rights or he must be punished. What reason then is there to stay your judgement? . . . Justice? . . . To delay the punishment of a guilty man is an outrage against the law . . . Politics? Let us consider. Do you expect, by such timorous behaviour, to influence foreign Powers? . . . Do you think you will be held less responsible if you evade this judgement? . . . What pusillanimity has seized hold of the Convention? . . . Is this how a republic is founded? . . . Is this the way to sustain the energies that our constituents displayed during the revolution of 1792? . . . You swore to live free in liberty or to die: then what do Foreign Powers matter? Do you not think that if they were to gain the upper hand you would all pay with your lives for having pronounced the word republic? . . . Why should we refer back to the primary assemblies? . . . How could that elucidate a matter that we have been debating here for months? . . . Do the primary assemblies know . . .

. . . then raising his head, exhibiting then (the dwarf) a mongoloid appearance, horribly cut in two by a bandage, as if to hide a horrible wound, a wound from a sabre that had sliced him across beneath the nose, blowing noisily on each spoonful of soup, all his movements observed closely with the same dumb fascination by the children whose eyes were now contemplating, etched by the light from the ceiling lamp, his withered face, divided by this sort of yellowish leather bandage, as if it were a macabre apparition, like those Indian heads, shrivelled by some clever treatment to the size of a fist, a sort of maleficent being whose presence by the side of the old lady (although the children would not have been able to say quite why, being incapable of establishing a connection between what the bust in the drawing room stood for and the poisonous behaviour of the dwarf) was confusedly perceived by them as an insult, a sort of sacrilege, as if the old lady was inflicting upon herself some unknown penance, sitting there, with in front of her those plates which she barely tasted, lost in the contemplation of a succession of disasters amongst which the phylloxera epidemic must have seemed obscurely to be the final blow, along with the series of deaths that had occurred in the family, like a vengeance exacted by fate, the inescapable and distant punishment for a fortune amassed amidst tumult and

124

violence which she seemed to consider herself condemned to expiate for ever and even to show herself responsible for it (in the same way as she kept the indecent collections of THE ARTIST) by wearing the ever present cameo which, on those evenings, fastened the collar of those blouses or rather of that blouse (whether through a wish to save money (living as she did, in spite of the vast house, her still comfortable income, in spite of her land, her furniture, her jewellery, her cupboards overflowing with linen, her silver, in perpetual fear of social decline and poverty), whether then out of desire to save money she put it away somewhere, wrapped in tissue paper and once a month unfolded it, brushed it and wore it — or whether out of an obstinate attachment to her status as a widow, to past times and old styles, she had the same model made again and again by her dress maker) that Victorian blouse with vertical pleats, embroidered with coal-black, sooty stones which at the slightest movement or sigh which sometimes made her flabby breast swell, sparkled like the corselets of those large blind flies which butt into walls, their bodies dark blue, sparkling with unhealthy green and bronze hues.

On the one hand, then, the chateau (or rather the ruin: he (the renegade son, the ex-ensign) had made it over to a quarry owner who immediately undertook its demolition in order to sell the stones and then, once he had knocked down the left wing, finding the undertaking worthless, sold it off at a loss in his turn at the best price he could get, doubtless to the great grandfather of the idiot) replastered then, or rather (like the tractor later stranded in the yard) patched up as best it could be, used as a farm — on the other hand the vast mausoleum at the heart of which the drawing room sparkled with its myriad lights once a month (the antithesis, the derisive counterpart to that single, smoke-ridden room which served as both kitchen and bedroom — the idiot slept somewhere no doubt with the animals, in the cow shed or in a corridor, or on the pile of sprouting potatoes in what had once been the library), the tall, lighted French windows, through which one could see from outside the crystals of the chandeliers glittering like diamonds and the imitation candles shining amongst the pointed fan leaves of the dwarf palms and the decorative plants arranged on the verandah, the ostentatious display corresponding to the dim light, which at the same moment, in the darkness covering the mean, stony plateau, flickered no doubt, yellowish and oily, behind the shadow theatre of the three pots of geraniums — or had long since been snuffed out: the formidable ruin completely black in the dark night, solitary and sinister, like a mere pile of stones kept upright by some unknown obstinacy of stone, irrecusable, gaunt and broken down.

Two ruins in spite of appearances. The one resigned to (or rather proclaiming proudly) its status (or its identity) as a ruin, the other so to say preserved, or rather prolonged (in the same way as one puts off the final moment of a dying man with the use of serums, oxygen bags and injections), and this formal room, flaking away, wearing threadbare in spite of its gilding, its crystal candelabra, its plenitude of light surrounding the occupants, gathered together there after the ceremonial dinners, like a vast backdrop set round the old lady, the old bundle of moiré tissue, iridescent and black, her eyes set, wandering, settled against the corner of the fireside opposite one of her friends or some distant relation, bending from time to time to poke at the embers, deaf to the indistinct, genteel murmur of the conversations as well as to the silvery tinkle of the glasses on the tray which the lame servant distributed, both of which were dominated by the nasal voice of the dwarf, now without his moustache protector, invariably sitting at the bridge table in such a way as to turn his back ostentatiously to the marble bust, holding forth, commenting on the progress of play, sarcastically triumphant, lecturing his partners, handling the cards with the dexterity of an old club-man, shuffling them with his wrinkled hands, the two halves of the pack placed opposite each other blending with a sound like the crackling of sparks, then straightening himself (the dwarf), dealing them again, his horn cigarette-holder (also made especially for him) held between the fingers of his left hand, whilst onto the green cloth there followed, fell, arranged themselves, allying, rescinding, destroying each other in their turn the motley figures of kings, queens, knaves with their brilliant doublets, with enigmatic, impassive porcelain faces, holders of obscure power, scattered onto the derisory battle field, gathered up, mixed again, ready once more to confront each other in random encounters and conspiracies of an ephemeral nature.

Then she died. The children were ushered in and made to kneel down . . .

Milan, 20 Ventôse Year 12: Soon now, my dear Batti, is the moment when the grasses will start to grow. It is imperative to have all the stones cleared from the alfalfa fields, the meadows and the fields of clover: have the stones from the Main Field carried to the road that I've had made to give access to the elm; those from Falguières should be carried to the path.

It is two months since you wrote to me that Numide, Emerode, Mignonne and Ferjus were in foal and since then it must have become evident that others are in the same way; keep a careful watch on Normande, Carthage and Topaze who were put to Moustapha last year, and Margot, La Cauchoise and Cap-de-More who were serviced by the animal: tell Blanchard to watch carefully when they drink and tell me about them in each letter.

Moustapha must have some oats, he must be well fed for a month before the breeding season and now is the time to start.

Build up my dung heaps! We now need some at the château for the hemp and the potatoes. Each time you add to the dung heaps in the fields you should have them covered with an inch of good soil so that the sun will not dry them out.

My wife sends her greetings, my son is well; our regards to Blanchard. Farewell, I send affectionate greetings.

29 Ventôse Year 3 — To the Representatives of the People with the army of the Sambre and Meuse: It is not within our capacity, my dear Colleagues, to create resources as we see fit. We have, as much as you, urged our Colleagues in Holland; to supply you with food and fodder; after all we have already written you that we hoped that the artillery horse contractors should make a successful effort to restore the numbers to full strength. But in the meantime, my dear Colleagues, whence this lack of heart? Are the roads any better for the enemy than for you? Can a large river be crossed by an army in so short a space of time that you should not yet have been informed of it? And if you have received the information, would you be in so bad a state as to be incapable of opposition? Do not our soldiers have arms strong enough any longer to position 4, 8 and even 12 pound cannon which could be used on a day of battle? Have our divisional generals no reserve horses? And do we no longer even have even bayonets? Of course one must not neglect any major means of defence when one can get them but when one cannot must one then always withdraw? And where will you go with the army of Sambre and Meuse? You say yourselves that our strongholds on the Meuse are short of all kinds of supplies and that in the event of a reverse

127

would put up little resistance. You must therefore win, otherwise where would you retreat to? Do you hope to find better supplied strongholds? You see from these questions, dear Colleagues, that when ordinary means are lacking one can only follow the counsel of one's own courage and count on that of the republican soldier who is accustomed to triumphs. If one were to suppose that the enemy could succeed in crossing the Rhine without resistance, they would have to carry food and forage with them, since you agree that the country offers no such resources: could you not then take these resources from them? Cut off their means of communications and retreat.

We do not doubt, dear Colleagues, that after you have thought over all these reflexions and pondered all these ideas with the generals, we shall receive from you more reassuring dispatches by the first post.

1 Pluviose, Year 13

On my arrival in Turin, dear Batti, I received four letters from you. I shall reply to all of them. You see you are very punctual when you want to be. So I tell you that I am pleased and warn you that each time you do not write to me punctually every 10 days and reply to all my letters, I shall scold you like a child, so beware.

I told you to kill two pigs instead of one because I shall be home this summer, but since Mr Chaffort told you sell them, if they have been sold so much the better.

I am pleased to hear that the alfalfa are sprouting. In March you should not forget to sow with oats and alfalfa all the Francinan hollow from the path that divides it from Falguières up to the paddock and the entire hollow on the path to Vaour and also to La Gamasse.

I am delighted to learn that my Mignonne is with foal by Moustapha and not by the donkey. She should not be put to the latter again. Has Epine Blanche been covered successfully?

Now is the time to sell the wheat at the going price,, but you must only sell it for cash.

I want some boards made from the wood at Vaour. The trees elsewhere are not large enough. Since the wood belongs to M Garrigou I do not wish to bargain with him any more: tell him my price from the start.

Are the mares and Moustapha in particular being carefully curried each day? I met an officer who saw him at Gaillac when he was taken there and he told me he was then in a sorry state.

Make sure that all the passage ways on the side of the road to Le Guillard and up the slope by the elm drive are properly closed off so that the flocks cannot get in. Make sure that the meadow by the river is well enclosed, and take care to plant there some new thorn-bushes to protect in spring the young thorn planted around the big field. Plant at the bottom of the garden a nursery bed of Italian poplars. If anyone asks to use Moustapha as a stud only agree to five or six requests at the most, and allow him to cover only fine mares.

I have had sent to you from Toulouse a large plough with an extra extension. I have sent you three barometers in crates, do not unpack them. I have sent you 8 pounds of chocolate and have left you two sugar loaves and 2 pounds of coffee, which is enough, for at a time when colonial products are so expensive and so rare. one should only use them in the case of illness.

My wife and son send you their regards; yours affectionately, farewell.

5 Germinal, Year 3 — to General Hoche:

The departments of Mayenne and Sarthe and a part of the Orne are heavily overrun by Chouans. And yet in our letter of the 27 Ventôse we impressed upon you the need to station along the frontiers of the departments which are not yet overrun a force large enough to prevent contagion. According to the letters that the deputies from these departments are receiving, far from being drafted to these places, forces are being withdrawn from them each day.

Without indicating any precise destination for these troops since we cannot judge from here the respective localities, we impress upon you once more the urgent need to send to these 3 departments an imposing force with the combined object of putting an end to the ravages of the Chouans and to be ready if necessary to advance by forced marches to the Channel beaches and to defend this peninsular against any invasion.

The state of affairs that your army is in and the difficult task which is the reason for it provoke frequently repeated complaints. We only accept these with a sense of measure and justice, but when we notice some evident negligence in the service we must register our discontent. Thus we wish to express to you our complete surprise at the event of the 19 Ventôse: should a stage coach ever proceed without escort through a country rendered so unfortunate by the ravages of Civil War?

We urge you to issue a general order that all Official transport should be escorted and conveyed by an armed contingent; please inform us what punishment has been meted out to the guilty commander. Fraternally yours.

9 Germinal — To the representatives of the people serving with the Army of the Alps and Italy.

We have just received, dear Colleagues, your letter of the first of this month. It was written to The Commission for Supplies to request the supply of the shoes that you lack. You will see from the enclosed decree that the Army of Italy should maintain until further order an offensive attitude, but we do not have it in our power at the moment to give you all the necessary means to invade Piedmont. First and foremost we must supply the Armies of the Rhine with all the materials that they lack. The consumption of twelve armies is enormous, and although during the early years we used extreme means with profusion, we are now forced to institute extreme economy in supplies, and even then we shall not be able to supply all the armies at the same time.

We shall send back to the Supplies Commission your request for cash for supplies. We can merely point out that cash is very rare. The orders have been given to send to the Army of Italy one hundred thousand measures of gunpowder as soon as circumstances allow us to give you the order to advance into Piedmont.

We are counting on you, dear Colleagues, since you are on the spot, to provide from local sources what we are unable to send you: we know you to be zealous. You can count on our good will, but when the means are not available one has to make the best of what one has and, last year, our armies often put this principle into practice. Greetings and fraternal wishes.

The same day — L.S.M. to the Supplies Commission.

Citizens, the people's representative Sanies, with the army of the Alps, complains of the lack of shoes for his soldiers. I urge you in the name of the Committee to comply with his request.

. . . the children were ushered in and made to kneel down in the bedroom which looked out onto the terrace, sunlit in winter, and in which they saw for the last time the greyish features lying back on or rather in the pillow, the bags under the eyes the colour of wine dregs, the closed lids not even moving, the half-opened lips slowly allowing something grey and grainy, almost furry, to slip out, on which the priest laid the wafer, then the thing (like an animal, a worm, a sort of underground creature retreating into its hole) retired, disappearing into the inside of the mouth, and that was all: the grey strands of hair in the lace, the bulge of the sheet over the laid-out body, the ivory Christ framed against a background of garnet-red velvet with its eternal sprig of dried box-wood threaded through the arms of the cross, and after that they (the children) were never to see her again except dressed up once more in one of her moiré dresses, serene perhaps for the first time in her existence, her mouth now closed by a bandeau, limp and worn like an empty water skin, but retaining a certain hint of something grandiose and impressive, her head framed by two candles, the running wax merging into grainy lumps, and surrounded (her head) by those pot plants the arrangement of which were the object of interminable arguments between herself and the lame maid on the evenings when there were receptions, but this time the old limping servant placed them as she pleased, giving orders to the floor polisher, carrying out what she no doubt saw as her last duties to the old lady whose well-being she had jealously guarded until the end (and during the few days that she took to die this was the only person that she spoke to: once only: the old servant seated at the bedside, her eyes never leaving the dying woman, suddenly noticing a feeble trembling of the blue lips, starting up, trying hard to guess, already looking for the glass of water or the spoon, then realizing, leaning over further, listening to the weak voice, the indistinct murmur which made her the recipient of the last thought, the last piercing worry, as if in the obscure darkness into which she was sinking, the old lady equipped with her ever present bunch of keys and accompanied by the lame maid, having gone down once more into the three-quarter empty cellar was contemplating with sad eyes the only bin still containing a few precious bottles, anxious, seized again no doubt in a final flash of consciousness by those fears, that constant worry, that constant preoccupation about proprieties, calculating, evaluating the number of relatives and friends who were preparing to flock together, some from afar, in order to follow her procession, concerned not with her sufferings or the approach of death but with the arrangement of the last meal which she would give (would preside over, albeit from the depth of the family vault), saying with a sort of despair in a final effort and a final feeble breath (using that word ('one') by which she linked to herself, as if to a double, the faithful lame maid, like the confidants, the ageless nurses in classical tragedies): 'All those people! . . . What are we going to give them to drink? . . .,' then never speaking again), lying now in the middle of these display plants, this exotic salon vegetation with leaves shaped like fans, sabres, jets of water which, around the recumbent figure, seemed to be mounting a final guard so that, having

131

found peace at last, she might take with her to the tomb the memory of that immutable order of things in which she had lived, carrying away with her at the same time the secret (out of loyalty to the bloody name which she had borne) of which she felt no right to relieve herself or to destroy the traces (not in this instance sheltered by the glass doors of a bookcase fastened with a key but hidden, at least as long as she should live, as long as she should be there to stop anyone changing the wallpaper (of the well of the monumental staircase) that concealed the door of the cupboard in which the heap of old archives was stacked, old letters and old registers over which had gathered a crunchy dust of mouldy plaster, believing perhaps, as Uncle Charles was later to say (or trying not to think about it), that once she was dead, once the last being to carry that name in the flesh had disappeared, it would no longer have any importance . . .): like a corpse buried behind the tangles of faded red leaves recurring symmetrically, blistered by the pervading damp, coming away from the wall, stuck back every so often, the torn parts concealed by strips cut from the inexhaustible reserve of decorated rolls in the same antiquated pattern which she (the old lady) kept no doubt for this purpose alone, not allowing anyone else the job of supervising the floor polisher and the lame maid who, under her direction, tried after a fashion to match up to the faded garlands the squares and rectangles cut so meanly not so much through avarice or a desire to economise as from the effect of anguish she felt each time she saw the rolls diminish and the reserve dwindle, fearful of the time when the last roll would have to be started, when the ephemeral screen of glue and paper would rot irremediably, would finally come unstuck, leaving visible beneath its bulges and through a tear the damp dark tomb in which lay decomposing like a decaying corpse (perhaps she hoped —although perhaps without precise knowledge — that the sodden plaster, the dampness would get the upper hand) the evidence of something inexplicable (something monstrous?) which had taken place more than a century before and which for her at any rate must remain forgotten, denied.

As if (although Uncle Charles also said later that she had no doubt really forgotten it — she who sometimes confused the names of her own grandchildren —, even supposing she ever

132

knew much more than the contents of this letter folded into four (even perhaps forgotten itself) in the false bottom of her jewellery box, contents that were themselves an unanswered question, and that these makeshift repaperings meant nothing more in her life than an old person's obstinate determination to keep everything as she has always known) . . . as if, then, she saw herself as interdependent, bound to an obligation even stronger than her moral convictions, a sort of nutritious umbilical cord (of which the three orgasms, the three ejaculations of male seed as a result of which the name had carried down to her, constituted the stages) to the man in whose memory she sported, like a seal or a relic, the immodest Pompeian dancer, that intrusive ancester for whom she wore mourning (or shame) not only on her account but on behalf of the whole family, as if at the age of nearly eighty, she lived so to speak as an orphan, the family itself somehow orphaned for more than a century, since that day when a final attack of apoplexy had felled the giant, prolonging a sort of posthumous existence drowned in grey shadows in which, for the old lady, were confused in a single perspective past or imminent catastrophes, the most minute and the most painful events in life, conferring the same apocalyptic dimension on all that could be seen as reason or pretext for worry, for alarm, in such a way that she placed indifferently on to the same level the children's colds, the breakdown of a boiler, a friend's illness, her estate-manager's accounts, the trimming back of the ivy, the execution of the Russian imperial family, the disappearance of a pillow-slip or the composition of a menu for the following day, not interrupting this sort of calm; resigned lament except to stand there, immobile, forgetful of the world surrounding her as if in her contemplation of emptiness she was seeking to fill in the void with some other object for her anxiety and grief, with those rheumy eyes underlined with bags, that mouth of which the drooping corners were prolonged by two traceries of wrinkles on each side of the chin which itself fell loosely in folds onto the cameo with the violet background which was removed each evening by those wrinkled hands and put in its place on the dressing table amongst those pathetic accessories not for beauty but — how can one put it? — to keep up the decencies, those dull powders, those creams to combat chapping, those discreet

perfumes such as old ladies use, the cameo put back in place
each morning however great her feelings of revulsion for what,
over and above its commercial value (if one prefers it that way)
by its very commercial value, it stood for, this jewel acquired by
an ancestor besmirched by a crime which, in her mind, she
must have considered (like the execution of the Tsar) as the
worst possible: a parricide; defiantly parading a filial piety
stronger than all else (like those kinswomen, both wives and
daughters of executed criminals who, scorning their own
feelings of horror, even having perhaps approved of the
punishment themselves, go, in defiance of public opinion, to
ask the executioner for the corpse or secretly remove it from the
paupers' grave in order to bury it with their own hands), making
her point (it was of little importance that for a long time she may
well have pinned it under her old folds merely mechanically,
once the habit had set in) with that pride which in spite of the
bemoaning within herself, she had inherited from the distant
ancestor, the distant sire whose bust she still kept in the same
spirit, the giant bust which, although it had been sculpted after
his return from the campaign in Prussia, showed him not
dressed in his general's uniform with the heavy gold trimmings
but with his shoulders already draped in a classical toga from
which emerged, naked, the bull neck jutting slightly forward,
surrounded by the untidy crop of hair, the powerful face
stamped with an expression at one and the same time ironical
and severe, as if when ordering this effigy of a Roman tribune
from the sculptor he had wished that it should bear witness for
posterity of the act of defiance which he had embodied, the
calm determination derived from the reading of those Roman
authors, whose works bound in calf, with yellowing spines and
engraved titles, were now relegated to the higher shelves of the
sombre, ebony bookcase, displaced by the collections of
CHARIVARI, of LA VIE PARISIENNE and of L'ARTISTE kept under
lock and key in the same nether region in which the strict and
timid old lady put away indiscriminately as so many scandalous
objects the plump bodies of the smooth-skinned odalisques,
the tarts in their crinolines and the austere or bucolic Romans
invoked in order to demand the head of a King or to compose
the clumsy yet heartrending epitaph that was destined to be
made out word after word by an idiot against the melancholy

and soundless rustle of autumn rain.

And with her it was as if all that remained of an obscure past, of a slice of History (even if in the uncertain memory of an aged brain), had been wiped out, abolished, the immense house larger than ever, even more empty, so that now, deprived of the woman in whose presence it found some justification, and although its walls were still standing, its roofs almost weather-proof, its furniture not yet dispersed, it seemed to be already linking up in a vanished world with the old abandoned stone stumps as if being sucked along at high speed, shrinking dizzily, sliding along invisible lines of retreat, the resplendent salon was disappearing into the distance, the salon with its threadbare brocades, its yellowing paper, its damp stained walls, lit up once a month, gathering together the survivors mourning some collective catastrophe, like those figures on an improperly reduced scale which one can see depicted at the foot of ancient buildings, growing smaller all the time: the shapeless black bundle of moiré huddled at the side of the fire, her guests, the bridge players, the silent children watched over by the ancestors immobile in their sculpted gold frames, as if on the other side of the walls there processed across a sort of daîs or gallery, the crowd of numerous dead the silent hum of whose conversation one seemed to hear, the swish of satin, the rustling of skirts, of fans, the countless cohort of male and female begetters long since eaten by the worms, their skeletons with empty sockets lying in the dark, resuscitated, called together for one evening, like the guests at a costume ball, disguised as coquettes, as deer hunters, as poets like Victor Hugo or as stern old men with goatee beards, pausing, contemplating beneath them, vaguely surprised, vaguely offended (or simply expressionless) the latest products of their couplings and of their unions gathered around the last to inherit the name now written only on the façade of a vault with half empty vats and in the registers of the mortgage registry. Even though for a long time it seemed that she (the old lady) continued to haunt this Pharaoh-like tomb in which she behaved as if buried alive, not leaving it, in summer, except to go to the house near the sea from which on fine days the old Ford took her to the beach, spending there her afternoons consumed with anxiety, disdaining the shelter of the canvas to remain uncomfortably installed in a deck-chair at the very edge

135

of the water, hat on her head, buttoned into one of her long dresses right up to the neck, her face protected from the wind and the sand by a veil knotted under her chin, formidable also in her way, pyramidal, topped by a puce-coloured sunshade, rising on the foundations of her spread-out skirt, enduring the fire of the sun, fatigue, to watch with alarm in her eyes the games of her grandchildren as they disported themselves in the narrow rolls of the waves, then after the grape-harvest, at All Saints (as if the day of the Dead called for a return to this sort of confinement, of voluntary seclusion), coming back to shut herself up for nine months in this maze of corridors and over-large rooms which in winter (in spite of the fires which seemed themselves to shiver in the hearths), contained a static glaciation to which the old lady seemed indifferent as to the torrid heat of summer, only breaking this seclusion two or three times a year, regretfully no doubt, not for her pleasure (this word had probably long since lost all meaning for her) but, as with these receptions that she gave, out of habit, to conform to a ritual, when there appeared in town one of those companies or singers on tour, persuaded when they were old enough and she judged them to be sufficiently mature, that following a tradition which was both educational and recreational, which she had always observed, it fell to her lot to take her grand-children to these concerts or these performances, incapable as she was of imagining (time had stopped for her even before she was born) that once grown up these children could savour other distractions, that for years now the little girl (who was no longer a little girl) had been coming back later and later from her music lessons and that the elder of the boys spent his Sunday afternoons shut up in the smoky stench of a cinema auditorium.

As if to isolate her even more . . .

Do the primary assemblies know the facts as well as we know them? . . . I maintain that this is a trap that has been laid for them. You will hand the gentle and peace-loving inhabitants of the countryside, the useful citizen who cultivates the arts, over to the cunning intrigues of a few; you will sow discord throughout the republic; you are laying up for it misfortune without number which you alone can shield it from. The people are just; they have invested you with their full powers; it would be cowardice on your part to cast on the mass of the nation a responsibility which diminishes your own. This appeal to its sovereignty will be to open up Pandora's box so far as it is concerned. No single one of us underrates the people's sovereignty; we did homage to it at our first meeting; but why are you so scrupulous today, when it is a question of a guilty man, whereas you were not in the least perturbed when you decreed the indivisible republic, before you even knew whether this form of government suited the country? You nevertheless then did precisely the right thing, because you had regard for the salvation of France. Well! have due regard again for it now, and you will have as a guarantor for its approval the good deed which you have done.

Lawmakers, forget the individual ego; remember that each one of us represents the whole of France; make yourselves worthy of the full majesty of your office; then every petty intrigue will evaporate. Through the storms which envelop you, behold the fine days which you are laying up for the future generations who will honour your name; the freedom of the whole world will be your reward. Be just, be stern, do not bow down any more to superstitious notions. The road you have trodden has sunk beneath your feet: this is no time to . . .

They ride all morning through a gently undulating, almost flat region, grey–green under the grey sky. It is an area of crops and meadows, interspersed with woods. Parallel to the road they are following they can see a monotonous line of trees jagged against the horizon, no doubt flanking another road, running, more or less straight, from west to east. Now and then, long tapering belfries draw attention to the existence of villages or hamlets hidden by dips in the terrain. The landscape is utterly bare and silent. No vehicles are to be seen in the lanes or on the road running parallel to the horizon, no peasants, teams or machinery in the fields. They have been on the move for about two hours when they hear at intervals the dull rumble of explosions. The planes, flying no doubt at the boundary of the low flight ceiling, are not visible. However, their path can be traced by the successive sounds of detonations. Soon afterwards they see dark columns of smoke rising one after the other above the plain. However, they themselves are not attacked. The sun makes its appearance towards midday. At that moment, the road curves downwards, along a small wooded valley. Suddenly, round a bend, they can see the river Meuse, sparkling beneath them through the trunks of the trees. The hillside opposite rises steeply, also seemingly deserted, peaceful, dangerous. A little later they cross the river, troop after troop, at a fast trot. The sky is completely clear now. As they go over the bridge, they hear the echoes of massive explosions, very near now, and they can see the planes wheeling in the sky, like insects, over a spot a little further downstream, round a bend in the river, hidden by a projection of the hill. Immediately afterwards the road reascends the steep valley, under cover of the trees once

137

more. The bombing has ceased. All is still and silent again. Too silent. Too
still. By turning in their saddles they can see, to the left and slightly behind
them, the bridge that they have just crossed. The river flows peacefully along
the bottom of the deep, narrow valley. Seen from where they are now, the
water reflects the blue sky. They feel a sort of uneasiness, a muddled distress.
No-one speaks. It is as if the door of a trap had just closed behind
them.

. . . as if to isolate her even more, they had, when the false
baptist minister died (the artistic review collector), sold the part
of the house overlooking the street and the heavy panel of the
main door that had once closed with a clunk like an anvil,
thrusting back behind it, annihilating the echoes of the town,
thinning them down, reducing them to the distant rasping of
the tram on a bend, the feeble sound of a car horn, as if the high
walls around the courtyard, the garden, formed an insuperable,
blind impenetrable barrier around this sort of fortress in the
depths of which there lay (survived) something uncompromising, something invincible in the double incarnation of a
groaning old woman and that of an impassive man of stone with
an impassive gaze showing no pupils, condemned to silence
and obscurity from which he was only snatched to be thrust
straight back into it by the dreary festivities of one evening (she
— the old lady — no longer opened up the salon to receive her
guests, when it was her 'day', a few friends, other old ladies like
herself, disappearing, being snuffed out one after the other,
until there only remained about two or three to whom she
offered tea in the little salon), the four hundred pounds of
marble as if encysted, like a foreign body, a sort of meteorite
detached from some lost world millions of light years away and
of which the flashing, ephemeral trajectory had happened to
abort there, in that constant semi-darkness where the ectoplasmic flaccid Cassandra held sway, making despotic use of her
very fragility (against which, guided by the infallible instinct of
weak people, she guessed no doubt that no-one (except perhaps
the lame maid) could fight) in order to impose on her circle
through the suspended threat of muffled lamentations (or, even
worse, of those silences in which she so theatrically enfolded
herself) a confinement that seemed to push back millions of
light years the world outside into which the children were only
reluctantly allowed to venture when weighed down by endless

138

advice deemed able, in the same way as the woollies that they were wrapped in at the slightest drop in temperature, to protect them against the countless dangers among which the old lady ranked indiscriminately microbes, violent games and evil acquaintances, as if there existed side by side two irreconcilable universes, which never communicated, as hostile the one to the other as the decrepit Municipal Theatre where there appeared in classical repertoire the prima donnas and soloists on tour, and on the other hand, what seemed to the young boy to be the exciting opposite the stern and deadly silence from which (himself making use of that endless ingenuity of weak people, that genius for dissimulation and lies which all authority inspires in those over which it has power, even the authority of an old woman) he managed to slip away, containing himself, keeping himself under control (already, as he gently wound round his neck the inevitable muffler, listened patiently yet again to the endless plaintive litany of advice, he seemed to hear, at once imperative and throbbing, the jingling of that bell whose continuous stupid sound was for him like the call itself of that forbidden universe towards which, within himself, something was running already, indeed was rushing), forcing himself to go slowly down the stairs, crossing the courtyard, followed from the verandah by the anxious stare of the old lady, sometimes called back (halting, turning, his heart suddenly ceasing to beat) to hear a final solemn entreaty, a final caution, then hardly through the gate, hurling himself forward, running normally now through still dormant streets in the Sunday torpor, tearing off the muffler without slowing down, stuffing it anyhow into a pocket of his coat, unbuttoning this, his head only filled, ringing (and not only his head: his muscles, his whole body, his legs that were moving beneath him) with that harsh ringing, obstinate, fateful, still inaudible in fact, beginning really to sense it, becoming more precise, ever more imperative, harassing, as he gradually drew nearer, skidding round the bends, picking up speed again, rushing out at last (or rather surging), still running, onto the esplanade, the deafening, touting ringing dominating everything now, louder than the noisy beating of the blood in his head, the precipitate storminess of his breath in his lungs while crimson, breathless, trying to regain his breath, he fumbled feverishly in his pockets, exchanging on the grooves of

the copper plate of the kiosk his week's savings for the little
rectangle of pink furry cardboard whose acquisition gave him
the right to slip in, his heart still beating (but not only because of
the running) through the crack contrived between the two leaves
of a dirty velvet door watched over by a person with occult
powers (a small, greying old man of cantankerous disposition
with a greyish and very dirty cap) who ripped the tickets as he
counted with suspicious eyes the small group of schoolboys
entering, once having passed the obstacle, into the uncouth din
which echoed round the vast, bare hall, painted mustard yellow,
with bolted metal rafters and meanly lit by festoons of yellow
bulbs: like a rumbling, like the noisy incoherent prelude to the
celebration of some barbaric worship, growing louder (the
noise) by degrees, banging against the curtain divided into
garishly coloured squares on which were inscribed the merits of
the principal shops of the town and their trade names (they
knew them off by heart, no longer even saw them, recorded
unconsciously the names of the hairdressing salons, sellers of
saucepans, of wedding rings, of alarm clocks, of passementerie
or of ironmongery which, for them (underlined with flourishes,
diagonally written in ornamental lettering or even set in
imitation engraving in capitals, playing on the contrast of
clashing colours, blue on yellow, or black on orange, or green
on pink) had ended up by becoming an integral part of the show
itself, the painted canvas rippling occasionally under the
influence of some flow of air, feeble undulations spreading
across its surface, deforming as if through moving water the
advertisements whose loud panegyrics, whose static insistence,
seemed to flout the anticipation of the spectators, to interpose
between them and their hoped for enchantments the prosaic
obstacle of everyday mendacious commercialism, themselves
invested however with some sort of magic function, their
irritating and interminable presence (indifferent to the catcalls,
the stamping of feet) forming an obligatory preamble which
conferred on them (and indirectly on the traders themselves) a
sort of aura, the curtain of gaudy advertisements rediscovered
each time with the same impatience and the same lulling
satisfaction, for if it interposed its presence, it stood as an
obstacle, delayed the pleasure, it was at the same time the
guarantee, the promise that, behind its dense opaqueness, there

140

lay somewhere, ready from one moment to the next to flicker in the spluttering of the projector, the long awaited visions of gallops, kisses and battles which seemed, in order to start, to be awaiting only the permission of 'Sam', of the 'Three Niggers' and of 'The Golden Ring' promoted (like a numerical code allowing one to open the door of a safe) to the role of all powerful keepers of an inexhaustible treasure house of emotions and spells, until the moment when, with a noise of rusty crank-handle, gears and pulleys accompanied by a long purring sound, the long sigh of deliverance which ran along the surface of the rows of seats, the multicoloured advertisements slowly began to roll up on themselves, rising by degrees (the movement sometimes punctuated by pauses as the mechanism jammed, the spectators holding their breath), revealing finally (surrounded by black hangings like the scene of a mysterious and lugubrious ceremony) the magic rectangle of the screen, virginal and unpolluted: they (the schoolboys) had taken their places some time before, sitting in the front stalls (they were the seats then considered 'popular', the only ones they could afford) in one of the spans of tip-up chairs, with reddish wooden seats pierced with little holes, with metal feet screwed into the constellated floor or rather in which there seemed to be permanently incrusted yellowing fag-ends, their paper crumpled and soaked with saliva, wrappers of acid drops and those peanut shells with mother-of-pearl insides, with twin protuberances, pale-ochre coloured, dotted lengthways with minute indentations (everything — the dirty wooden slats, the fag-ends, the peanuts, the purplish red socks darned in blue or pink, the stockings slipped into espadrilles or old shoes with inturned heels suddenly revealed in close-up to one or other of the schoolboys bending to pick up, groping around in the spittle, a beret or a muffler which had fallen to the ground — inseparable, in the same way as the annoying, aggressive publicity curtain, from the fascinating mirages in black and white), seated then (the schoolboys) or rather transported as if by magic for the price of the pink cardboard ticket (although absorbed as they were in their excitement they were incapable of realizing it) into something much more fabulous than the chases or the insipid love stories whose images giving way one to the other on the screen seized their attention whereas it was open to them to sense in their flesh (that is inciting — or assailing — in addition to their sight, their other senses: of smell, hearing, touch) the sort of heavy muddle, tepid, stinking, as if palpable, made heavier by the inhalations and exhalations of hundreds of unwashed bodies that surrounded them (the boy leaning instinctively away from the neighbouring seat, retreating to one side, inhibited in spite of himself by the assertion heard a thousand times (not from the mouth of the old lady who never went there, who had no doubt never set foot in a cinema in her life, except perhaps, out of a so-called scientific curiosity, on the occasion of a visit to the Universal Exhibition — but considered unquestionable) that not only was what one saw there staggeringly stupid but even more that the gypsies who piled into the 'popular' seats were crawling with lice): something like the perpetuation, the living delegates of primordial man, unchanged, the unvarying and unvariable specimens, resistant to the centuries, to progress, to successive civilizations and to soap, having come straight from the depths of Asia, of the ages, arisen just so from the entrails of the earth or rather (they, their stench, their sticky damp heat, their inexhaustible fecundity, their elemental quality) like its bowels themselves, spread out, still steaming, more or less contained . . .

and this: in the stifling dusk of a Saxon summer, the stench of ammonia, thick, stinging the eyes, from the choked latrines that open onto the narrow lobby of the prisoners' hut, where each evening, after the doors are closed, six or seven thin dirty men, dressed in dirty uniforms (or rather what remained of uniforms), themselves stinking, are standing, leaning against the board walls, drawing on fag-ends sticky with saliva, waiting until the glowing tobacco burns their lips before carefully putting out these fag-ends made from fag-ends on the holed soles of their shoes, managing yet again to peel them off, to retain the tiny pinch of unburnt tobacco, to put it into a tin or a bag hidden right at the bottom of their pockets in which are accumulating some threads not full of, impregnated with nicotine, but brought, (transmuted) to the state of nearly pure nicotine, because two cigarettes are negotiable here for a can of soup, if however one could still call soup the warm cloudy water, with a fer:..ented, bitter smell, in which there float vegetable peelings, waste, no doubt what the pigs would not eat, what would normally be thrown into the dustbins. The five or six men (who were only a few months before young men, and even youths) now like hungry beasts, with greyish faces, with watchful eyes, uneasy, swindling, pitiless

*(because vigilance, cheating, hardness are the only means of survival here),
with heads like thieves or rather (worse than thieves) of beaten men (some
moreover professional thieves, small time criminals, or pimps representing
(how should one say?) the cream, the aristocracy of the hut), retaining
enough strength in the evenings to gather together and palaver in the
stinking hallway along which floats as well, indelible, the sickening smell of
rotten potatoes mixed with that of the latrines, that of the stacks of bodies
piled into the narrow, superimposed bunks, like coffins, their straw infested
with lice, putting off the moment when stifled, stretched out in the semi-
darkness, each alone, they would feel them over them, countless, like a
minute and light swarming, as if time, History, were themselves decaying,
were rotting, were being reduced to this invisible, foul and voracious
swarming which was attacking their living flesh, lying there, impotent and
soaked in sweat: six or seven, then, dressed in torn uniforms splattered with
stains, bargaining under their breath, teeth clenched, as thieves speak, their
derisory treasures, vindictive, embittered, boasting of achievements, of their
war time exploits, accusing their leaders, cursing those, whoever they were,
(statesmen, generals, politicians, journalists) who had put them there,
thrown them in, covered with vermin and starving, into this filthy hole, the
oppressive summer night slowly falling, the light of the day decreasing,
imperceptibly replaced by that of the searchlights of the watch towers lighting
up the deserted streets of the camp, the huts the rows of which they can see
through the dirty windows, all the same, with their roofs of tarred felt, their
brown walls, exactly like the one they are shut up in, the windows tightly
closed over this infection, this warmth as it were intestinal, all fronted by the
same narrow hall in which at the same hour, other spectres gather, argue,
boast, barter, draw avidly on their fag-ends, standing aside sometimes,
making way for some man with dystentry, his cadaverous face haggard,
bent double, terrified, whom they listen to as he relieves himself noisily
behind the thin plywood door, indifferent to the moans, the death rattles,
sometimes the sobs, the fetid odour which intensifies that permanent one of
human excrement, urine, dirt and nicotine: wild, humiliated, looking, with
the protruding tendons of their skinny napes, like those animals that one sees
in zoos, captive birds with featherless necks behind their bars, outraged,
hanging with their talons onto dead branches whitened with crusts of dung,
treading their own excrement, in a smell of wild beasts and animal
dejection.*

. . . the very bowels of the world spread out, still steaming, more
or less contained in the narrow tip-up seats whose creakings,
mixed with those of the peanut shells, with the wailing of young

143

babies and the high-pitched sound of the piano, provided equally a background noise for the silent dialogues and endless clinches, the dense cloud of coagulated smoke floating like a canopy above the heads of the spectators, undulating, rippling gently, crossed by slow syrupy swirls, twisting and untwisting with reptilian sloth, its curls pierced by the bluish beam shooting from the projection room which revealed its slow drifts like a sort of roe, of placenta, appearing and disappearing in the oblique, pyramidal shaft of light, rigid, manifold, changing brusquely, moving from silver to grey, striped, dividing, mixing, splitting at the whim of the images whose alterations, modifications, seemed to be dictated, above the sputtering of the machinery by a series of clicks which provoked the succession on the screen of chases, facetious jokes by obese comedians, duels, or the face of that actress with the chalky mask or rather (in the jerky fuzziness of the poor projection, the shakiness of the sooty and sharply contrasted images) sooty (evocative of those photographs of nebulae in which against a background of impenetrable darkness there appears, with blurred contours, terrifying and vertiginous, the glow of millions of gaseous and agglutinated suns), stained by the dark fruit of her painted lips, her eyes enlarged by fear, whilst she moved around, unreal and ghostlike in semi-darkness, as if the projector in the cabin had pinned her against the brick wall, was tracking her down as she fled bewildered, beset, crouching behind a row of dull metal dustbins, wildly followed by the anthracite eyes, glowing in the dark, of the primitive tribes occupying in clans, in whole families, the rows of seats and who seemed like so many living repudiations of the fake princesses and fake Hollywood rajahs got up in glass trinkets, appearing (or rather materialising from out of the darkness; it was like a sort of chaotic swarming, the chaotic awakening, the chaotic hubbub of a barbarian, infinite horde) when the screen dimmed and there reappeared the mean light from the clusters of bulbs, resembling (the tribes) what they were like at the beginning of time, they, their skeletal or enormous women, sometimes even deformed, elephantine, as if the immemorial laws of wandering and pillage had fashioned them once and for all in the sole images of famine and feasting, as impassive, as insensible, one would have said, in either of the two states, with

144

their taut profiles of birds of prey or, on the contrary, their wide thick-featured faces like those of Hindu gods, with thick lips, flat noses, cheeks pitted with smallpox scars, their oily black hair drawn back into chignons, wrapped up in their rags which occasionally revealed a full swarthy breast, its plum-coloured nipple smeared with milk, sticky, from which they pulled the lips of their new-born ginger-bread babies, with their closed eyes, their minute and tragic clenched hands, like little dead things which, whilst they buttoned themselves up, they put into the arms of their companions with their assassins heads biblically surrounded by biblical swarms of shaggy children covered in filth, with their tousled mops and shiny teeth beneath the thick filaments of snot hanging from their upper lips; after which (after having, against the background of clattering tip-up seats, crushed under foot the peanut shells and skins scattered over the floor) they (the schoolboys) found themselves outside again, their ears buzzing, their cheeks alight and their heads heavy, flushed, blinking in the blinding afternoon light, expelled from the fallacious warm shelter where for three hours they had lived an existence of pretence through pretend adventures, finding themselves once again on the pavement amongst the matriarchal and malodorous bronze deities, undaunted, their swarms of brats, their men equally emaciated or obese, prolific, invested with occult powers which allowed them the gift not of casting spells or of predicting the future but in some manner foreshadowing it, that is of speeding up time, blending past present and future in one melting pot, assimilating, transforming into archaic, primitive, broken up objects all that they came near to or touched, returning to chaos, to original matter (rust, mud, rot — in the same way they could indiscriminantly reduce to the same common denominator of filth, foul odours, rivers of excrement, wrecks or pigsty, any dwelling, whether it was made of reeds, oil drums or concrete) the most robust and sophisticated products in the world that surrounded them: bicycles, sewing machines, screeching radios or those old American cars, battered, flaking, both skeletal and huge, into which one could see them, at last in breathable air, clambering in hordes, wild, lousy and disdainful, the old bangers moving off in jerks amid a protest of tortured gears (the rigid scarecrow busts tipping backwards with one movement, then as if corrected by an invisible spring, brought to the vertical again, stiff, as if carved in wood, sinister) and disappearing, their loads carried off again or rather carried back to those depths, that beyond (or that within) where they seemed to be kept in reserve, only brought out for a brief appearance, like the reminder, the Mane-Thecel-Pharès, the unchallengeable categoric conservation in human form of violence in its pure state: then he was (the boy — that is no longer a boy then, grown into a man by a brusque change in the space of a fraction of a second, projected as defenceless as a newborn baby into what one might call the hidden face of things, so much so that he was to ask himself whether the years that had passed, in the meantime had not had, in fact, even less reality, even less stability, than the illusory fictions in which the black and white two dimensional characters moved, loved, confronted one another in the heart of a fourth dimension, time subjected to terrifying compressions, staggering cancellations or regressions, that is where two scenes, two tableaux, two episodes which followed each other immediately on the screen were separated only by the brief appearance of a board on which sparkled (the shaking contours of the letters edged with smudges, excrescences that stuck out and then disappeared, like the bubbling of fusing and phosphorescent matter) short notices such as: 'And the following day . . .,' or: 'Fifteen years later . . .,' or even: 'Some years earlier . . .'), savagely assailed there as when leaving the cinema, whose lights the little old man with the cap shut off one after the other and then closed the doors, incredulous, too bewildered, too indignant for the moment to be capable of fear, deafened (so that the spluttering of the explosions in the cloud of dust — the sort of burning bush, dirty brown and dotted with sparks, suddenly materializing in the field next to the road — seemed to reach him as if attenuated, like the crackling sound of matches) by the cluster of bombs dropped with the indifference of birds defecating in full flight by three lazy planes which, by complete chance, as they passed over, in the declining light of a late afternoon, tried, casually as one might say, to kill him . . .

It was spring: now, and for a month since, the motorbike dispatch rider who brought from the neighbouring town papers and pornographic magazines, took money and gave back change on the tank of his machine,

146

his legs spread out as props, his feet no longer resting on the frozen ground of the winter quarters but in the thick mud of the undergrowth trodden by the hooves of the horses and in which the tyres of the motorbike skidded, between the tents under which they slept with their saddles as pillows on a litter of young criss-crossed branches, discovering each morning around them slightly more opened out the fragile shoots of the hornbeams and the beeches, the thorny wood with its claws, the brownish thickets which surrounded them gradually becoming stippled with minute green dots growing more numerous, opening out, growing, finally joining up into high arches, filtering the warm rays of the sun, giving weight to branches loosely swaying in the air suddenly become mild, as if the whole of nature were awakening, were preparing for some festival, some millennial, propitiatory sacrifice, an immolation to some imperturbable and voracious divinity of flocks of beasts, men and machines crowned with leafiness.

It was a long time since the old lady had died, since the haggard old face . . .

Perpignan, 5 April 1809. Spring is coming, my dear Batti: I forgot to tell you in my last letter to have some wood cut before the 15th of April: if there is still at Laussière some that is not thriving, cut that for preference, but still at Beltal, if not cut some at La Gamasse in the same area as it has been cut in the past two years but whatever happens have enough cut to make 1000– 1200 bundles not counting the pieces of wood that may be amongst those cut which can be taken to St M . . . uncut to make logs if they cannot be used for other purposes. Recommend to Tabouret that he should have the sheep watched. My dear Batti, now is the moment to secure my hedges and make sure that the herds do not eat my willows by the river. You will need several pairs of legs, watch the flocks as the grass grows because without that I shall lose a year's crop and I cannot afford to lose a year. In each letter tell me about the progress of my fields, write a lot.

Here are my instructions for the coming month. I am giving them to you in advance because you will only half read my letter and each time I have to repeat the same things two or three times: you must be sure to harvest the alfalfa seed, I want to have a lot of it this autumn. As soon as the clover has grown and is beginning to bud, you should give it to the cattle whilst still green; you should have it mown from the top to the bottom by furrows starting at the Le Four ridge and making sure that you have put away in the barn each evening what you will give as fodder the next day and in the morning the feed for the evening; right from the start you must mix clover with straw, when the animals are used to it you can give them as much as they can eat; if I can judge from the clover that I planted some twenty or so

147

years ago in the same place, the clover that is in the field should provide green fodder for all the animals in my stable for about two months, you can bring in the rest as ordinary hay. I send you my greetings.

. . . since the haggard old face had ceased to wander or rather to float in the semi-darkness of the damp corridors with the mouldy paper, the old lady reduced now in the underground darkness to a few bones . . .

Perpignan 8 May 1809. I had hoped, dear Mother, to come and see you in May but it will be a month yet at the earliest: those wretched English are threatening to effect a landing on our coasts and I must be there to receive them: I am preparing for them as personnel several thousand good cooks and as equipment 52 well harnessed and well munitioned cannon in order to render them military honours and in order to be able to correspond more quickly with them with bullets and cannon-balls. If I leave my hat there, which could well be, I shall go in peace because I shall leave no-one in distress and you will see that I have not forgotten you. I send my love.

. . . a few bones: later, when the vault was opened for another burial, the grave diggers said that she lay there, visible in her coffin which was falling apart next to that of her father, her face reduced to hard folds of shrivelled parchment crowned with grey hair — and they told how when, to make some space, they embarked on moving the coffins, the oldest had, as it were, disintegrated, had only left in their hands a little dust, with the result that they transferred as best they could the fake baptist pastor (the one with the taste for pulpy Andromedas) or at least what remained of him (his frock-coat intact, so they said, and his pearl-grey trousers with under-straps) into that of the old lady, tying it up with rope, so that the father and daughter were finally reunited in a sort of incestuous and macabre coupling in the form of two skulls and a few sticks or half hoops of calcium contained (gathered up, put together in the same way as one tidies a house, stuffed haphazardly) in their ceremonial cast-offs made of rot-proof silk like that of that dress with the bodice embroidered with little tubular pearls, black ones as well, which twinkled darkly, which she wore to preside when in the middle of her family, with her unchanging face with her creased eyelids and soft flesh, made from a substance that seemed already lifeless, like a sodden cloth hanging symmetrically from each side of the nose-bone, this tragedian's mask with a mouth in the shape of a haricot bean, always open with some silent

148

Aeschylean protestation, its staring eyes, its blue-veined hands, taken straight, one would have said, from one of those operas that she felt herself constrained to take her grandchildren to, installed (slumped over like some very old dying queen kept as it were by force in this life that would not let her go) in the third or fourth row of the front stalls, the only seats she seemed to know (either still out of habit, or because a sort of obligation that she considered due to her birth and past fortune did not allow her to reserve anything cheaper, or perhaps again, simply, because of her slight deafness), like some mythical incarnation, as if she were only there to give the cue to those characters from a time and place equally mythical whose appearance in flesh and blood produced, for the first time, on the boy used to flat adventures of luminous flat shadows which moved about a screen an uneasiness or rather a shock for which nothing had prepared him before he entered that Municipal Theatre which was closed for most of the year (to such an extent that he — the boy — had ended up by placing the dilapidated façade amongst those historic buildings, those remains of a past time, slowly flaking, relegated by the cinema with its gaudy coloured advertisements to an oblivion in which, he thought, it should slowly decay, eaten by worms, something almost as outdated as the shabby ostentation of the family mausoleum of which it seemed at first to form as it were an annexe, the dreary replica, so inseparable for him was any notion of pleasure from the lie, the forbidden and the clandestine, crossing in the wake of the old lady not the narrow slit between two dirty curtains but the upholstered leaves of the folding door that led to that auditorium with old-fashioned décor as different from the tumultuous noisy cavern held up with rivetted joists and reverberating with wild echoes as a salon can be from a station entrance hall and which seemed to him, with its reduced dimensions, its crackled painting, not only exiguous but derisory, at the same time, paradoxically (dressed in his best suit, with clean nails, his hair neatly combed, politely greeting other old ladies decked out in jade, to some extent deprived of that protective cuirasse of the bohemian and of vulgarity that the small band of schoolboys flaunted, exaggerated out of bravado), he felt himself at every step overcome by a vague uneasiness even more accentuated when, seated in his place,

149

bending to pick up the programme that had slipped from his hands, he discovered instead of the floor littered with spit, peanut shells, and instead of the forest of dirty feet in espadrilles or shoes with inturned heels, lines of well-polished court shoes, well-pressed trousers and silk stockings, sitting up again, even more ill at ease, to contemplate again not the loud chess-board of advertisements but, painted in trompe-l'œil, looped to one side by a cord with heavy gold acorns also painted in trompe-l'œil, majestically draped, the immense crimson curtain which (although — or perhaps because — greyed by mould, faded and even repaired in places by means of patches, repainted parts) seemed wretchedly ostentatious, touched up as best possible like the fake moiré with silvery glints lining the salon of the old lady, as contemptuous of the outrages of time, fashion or of reverses of fortune as the orchestra stalls of the old queens assembled there in their sombre dresses, sporting their old family jewels (which for certain of them were reduced to one alone, a single brooch of diamonds, a garnet cross saved through disasters, the richest (for the town still numbered several families with ancient and considerable fortunes) covered with sparkles, ill-concealing beneath their august and senile serenity what everyone knew, why for the most part they were only accompanied by their daughters, their daughters-in-law or their grandchildren: that is that at that very moment at that Club of which the monarchist dwarf was one of the pillars, their husbands and sons were occupied in ruining them), and only a murmur, a discreet well-mannered whisper running along the surface of the rows of heads, grey, brown and blond, the unusual mix of old faded faces, hollowed out, with cheek bones inexpertly rouged or purplish, dark bodices plum coloured or anthracite or midnight blue, and of flower coloured dresses, delicate profiles of young girls like flowers themselves or like fruit above their modest necklines, their slender thin arms naked . . .

living in a Milan where his duties make him one of the top people as they would in any provincial military headquarters, Dunkirk, Mainz or Toulouse. He has just participated in the greatest revolution in history and believes in nothing any more, serves with docility the despot whose maintenance in power alone protects him now from Bourbon vengeance, limits himself to carrying out each day the boring work for which he is paid,

*checking the accounts of army suppliers, going on exhausting tours of
inspection, denouncing cheating in the foundries and thefts in the arsenals.
He deplores the mediocrity of the plays put on there and which, he says, 'you
have to close your ears and sometimes your eyes against,' complaining that
famous Parisian actors like Talma or Mrs George ('those stars,' he writes)
only come on tour there infrequently, not impressed it seems by the pomp of
La Scala where his position obliges him to show himself, accompanied (or
rather dragged) by the fake Josephine followed by her black page. He gazes
with indifference at the brilliant gathering, the bare shoulders of the
dazzling Italian countesses who fascinate the young Stendhal newly posted
there too, totting up in his mind the value (in terms of steel deliveries, forge
contracts and adulterated supplies) of the diadems and necklaces paid for by
their aged husbands with interminable aristocratic titles, taken up with
petty political and commercial intrigues. Apart from Batti's letters, his
money problems and the military career of his son, the only news which
seems to interest him is that of the near-certainty of approaching war. He
spends in this way seven years in that gilded exile made exciting only by the
campaign in which he is wounded at Verona, until he is posted to the
Grande Armée in Prussia. He is bored.*

. . . their slender thin arms naked, their cheeks delicately
tinged by fever, an equally well-mannered excitement infecting
one and then the next, the discreet hum of the voices blending
with the timid attempts of the orchestra trying to tune up, to the
anarchic disorder of plucked strings, crochet rests, brief
arpeggios, heralding (or forming part of) a ceremonial of a
totally different nature from the plays waited for amid the foot
stampings, the stench and the howling of the newborn and
which, confusedly, seemed to him to have its origin in a
clandestinity so much the more protected in that there did not
seem to be anything forbidden, hidden, that he was there not
out of deceit or ruse, but sitting next to his grandmother,
amongst people many of whom were relations or friends of his
family but whom he had the impression of seeing for the first
time, metamorphosed, young women and girls partly bared,
embellished, the members of the public united, like the initiates
of a secret society, by a sort of complicity betrayed by their
whispering, their strict and studied bearing, assembled there to
participate in one of those rituals at one and the same time
sacred and barbaric of which, when after the performance of the
overture the impressive curtain had been raised, the officiants

suddenly materialised on the stage, so close to his seat that he could almost have touched them, evoked at first irresistibly for the boy by those mysterious creatures not outrageously but exhuberantly painted, hideous, stuck on walls, or on the threshold of mysterious houses in that street of the upper town, near the ancient ramparts, where with two or three of his classmates he ventured sometimes, scarcely daring to cast furtive glances, immediately deflected, towards those motionless figures, nothing feminine about them (at least with nothing of what characterised or symbolised femininity for him at that time) or even human, posted there like some sort of minor deity whose function could only be that of go-between, as if for the price of some disgusting and formidable test they were able to usher one behind the closed façades to the presence of one whose keys they held and who was in defiance of all logic, all desire and all reason, eluding all explanation, like what happened when in the heavy odour of incense, the flickerings of candles, the profusion of lights, embroidered vestments and surplices, the choirs of crystalline voices, the thunder of organs was suddenly interrupted and when, stretching his neck and cocking his ear, he managed to make out to the left of the altar the old bishop, covered in gold, seated or rather huddled under his crimson canopy, raising amid a sparkling of stones his hand gloved in fuchsia at the same moment as the quavering voice could just be made out, worn out, so weak, so thin in the monumental silence that it seemed certain at any moment to break, vacillating, fading, picking up again, managing as one might say to reach, stumbling, the end of the short sentence modulated rather than sung, the short blessing, then ceasing, whilst spent, exhausted, the inhabitant of the golden pyramid threw himself back, huddled a little more onto his throne, and there surged, unleashed, rose with joy towards the high vaulting the multiple voices of the celestial choirs and the rumbling of the bellows of . . .

For a long time he will remain marked by the proximity of Spain, of those barbarous and funereal stagings, the traditions left by her in that province which once belonged to her: for a long time, too, the idea of death will remain associated in his mind with the scent of eau de cologne soaking the sponges which were put into their hands when as children, during Holy Week, dressed as penitents, they were led beside those gaunt Christs laid out on beds of flowers and whose toes they wiped before setting their lips on them. Mothers lift in their arms the smallest children so that they may kiss the wounds. Close to, the huge nail driven into the feet with their bulging tendons, sculpted in an earthy wood and polished by the kisses, the head of the nail in the form of an elongated cone with sides. The heady, cadaverous and peppery smell of those heaps of flowers in which lilies and carnations predominated. At the moment when his lips brush the brownish wood, he sees close up the painted fringes of the drops of blood in relief as they flow from the wound itself like a mouth with swollen lips. The robes of the penitents are black, with a white lace collar, and they reach to the ground. The children wear on their heads a black skullcap trimmed with a narrow green border. They are wearing white socks and patent black leather shoes with round toecaps and with toggles. An element of coquetry brought to this pious disguise which takes place shortly after Carnival. The sponges are genuine sea-sponges, orangy–brown in colour and of a lacey, frothy, honey-combed substance.

Later on the idea of death will be associated in his mind with the sickening smell of hot rancid oil which saturated the food served to the foreign volunteers in the big dining room of the requisitioned grand hotel in Barcelona. In the glass of the large bay windows the marks can be seen of bullets fired during the recent street clashes. The cracks in the glass fan out from the bullet holes like stars with angular and irregular branches. In the clatter of plates and cutlery there mingles the deafening chatter of voices speaking every European language. On leaving the dining room one enters the hall where, to the left of the lift cage, a stair leads down to the basement and to a former night club which now serves as a gaol. It seems that the place remains decorated with large paper fishes hanging from the ceiling. The militiamen tell with amazement the story of how one of the prisoners remained sitting there for twenty-four hours on a chair, his arms and legs crossed, as in a drawing room, refusing to eat or to lie down, until they took him away to shoot him.

Later still and for many years afterwards the same idea of death will be for him inseparable from the names of a succession of hamlets or villages strung out between the Meuse and the Sambre, deserted in the deserted countryside shaken from time to time by the thudding echo of explosions: Lez Fontaine, Profondeville, Saint-Gérard, Mettet, Morialmé, Beaumont, Cousolre, Anor, names half-seen (or remaining in the memory) as through a fog at once luminous and dirty (the eyes scorched by sleeplessness, exhaustion, as if dirtied, as if the sun, which had not stopped shining for ten days on the fields, the glistening meadows, the woods, the gleaming slate

153

roofs, was itself somewhat dusty, eerie), the last (Anor) with its sombre connotations (as if a contraction of Anubis, Nord, Noir (black), Mort (death) echoing like a knell, reappearing obsessively on the signposts (Anor 7 km, Anor 3 km, Anor 12 km) at the crossroads of the route ridden over twice from west to east, the first time on horseback, the second as a prisoner, exhausted, stunned and dying of hunger, the interminable herd of the vanquished pursued for many a mile by the fateful repetition of the two syllables plodding on in a winding column in the blossom-covered landscape.

. . . whilst there rose with joy towards the high vaulting the multiple voices of the choirs and the rumble of the bellows of hundreds of pipes: bewildered, then, watching moving forward only a few yards from him on the stage those real people who yet had nothing human about them, dressed in peplums or armour, their violently made-up faces lit from beneath by the footlights inverting the shadows, covered, one would have thought, on their protruding bones with a thick layer of black dust like that which accumulates on the seldom-dusted rafters of a drawing-class studio, as though they had themselves been brought down from those cupboards or shelves where there were kept the bloodless busts of Caesar, Antinous or Poppea, the heavy statues moving around with the slowness of a sleep walker, lifting an arm, taking a step, then falling back into immobility, remaining thus a long time before moving off again, adopting another pose, the heroes and the maidens moving from one attitude to another, going away, confronting each other, blending their flexible voices modulated like the calls of injured birds, the roar of beasts, in turn violent, plaintive, groaning, tender, as if before the public with bated breath, petrified in the rows of seats covered with crimson worn velvet, there was enacted not as at the cinema a show in trompe-l'œil, but spread, unfurled without restraint between the cardboard rocks and the trees of painted canvas something at once immodest and terrible in which the words had no more importance than those of the bishop's blessing rising, hardly audible, from the golden pile sunk beneath its crimson canopy, just as Eurydice or Norma could well be these imposing singers, rigid, with their make-up running with sweat, their tired faces and their drapes in attitudes of eternal passion, eternal anguish, only there, like the bishop and the enigmatic painted idols of the red-light street, as intercessors, delegates with hideous exteriors, derisory or pitiful to enable one to communicate with some world possessing no common measure with that of appearance, kept carefully hidden, revealed, glimpsed on rare occasions, and later, after the old lady had disappeared, some days, returning home from school, the heavy door closed behind him on the noises of the street (what were once only sporadic echoes changing over the years into an enveloping din, the last horses who still pulled vehicles now replaced by machines, the central corridor of crushed brick made in sloping streets for shod hooves now cobbled like the rest of the road, then the cobbles themselves disappeared, the roads uniformly macadamed, uniformly covered with a greyish lava, the whole town engulfed in an aggressve, discordant chaos), he (the boy) stopping, standing still a moment in the courtyard, listening, as if the big house was resisting, obstinate, preserving itself intact, not so much through the enormous pile of masonry as through the stubborn will of the old lady who had so long lived there, an inviolable retreat in which the noise of the piano which came dimly through from the salon separated from the courtyard by the conservatory seemed to be part of the silence, to be there only to make it more noticeable, the notes now scattered, falling slowly one by one, now hurried, gathering together, scolding, then again disjointed, articulated, and one day he took a decision, turned the handle (the door was no longer locked now), standing then in the window recess, directly assailed, enveloped by the harmonious noise, as if within the music now, and without interrupting his playing, Uncle Charles said: 'In or out, but close the door: your mother is resting . . ,' so that often, afterwards, he went there, sat down, placed his worn leather satchel against the foot of the chair, and they remained there, both of them, in the great icy drawing-room, Uncle Charles dressed in his usual greenish velvet jacket, such as hunters wear (he who, all his life, had never been able to understand how people can shoot animals), his shoulders snugly wrapped in a cashmere shawl, the boy in his unbuttoned coat, his beret in his hand, then, overcome by the cold, buttoning up his coat, putting his beret on again, motionless, trying not to draw attention to himself, to put off the moment when, still continuing to play, Uncle Charles would raise his voice again to

155

say in the same calm neutral tone: 'Don't you have a translation or an essay to do? It's perhaps time to go and get down to it now . . . Or at least to pretend to. You still have an hour before dinner to bring me the nonsense you'll have managed to write. But try to get Cicero to speak in a slightly less odd manner than the last time . . .'; but it was not yet time: it would be the right moment when it was completely dark: as if the darkness woke him up, brought to him a consciousness of the external world (he was neither old nor young, his face not emaciated, merely bony, usually wearing an absent expression, distant, his head covered with thick grey hair, silky, brushed slightly back, now bending forwards slightly, straightening himself, his long fine fingers running across the ivory keys as if alone, playing from memory, without a score on the stand, or improvising, drawing from chords struck with the left hand a slow melody of which the other hand detached the notes), the boy as if numbed, his bare thighs purple with cold, amidst the unchanging decor, the pistols, the Dresden china, the fans, the furniture with its more or less precise contours still towered over by the marble colossus in the corner, as if the huge dark room contained a third person, outside that time which the struck notes, jostling each other, overlapping and separating in turn, seemed now to rush, now to slow down, to divide up . . .

Between the 10th and the 12th of May the horses covered about a hundred and sixty kilometres, and to get back across the Meuse before the bridges were blown up they still had fifteen more to go, sometimes at a gallop and across impossible terrain such as, at this point, the ballast of a railway track, the stone chippings of which made deep cuts in the soles of their hooves. When they were able to unsaddle them for the first time, the evening of Whit Sunday, most of them had large raw patches on their backs. Curiously, there were many more men killed and wounded than horses. Relieved of their riders, they galloped wildly, bolting, their heads high and turned slightly to one side, with wild eyes, stopping only when out of breath, one of them occasionally standing athwart the road or path, wretched, exhausted and confused.

Several of them reduced to a state of exhaustion so great that they could not carry a rider or even stand had simply to be left behind. So it is that he is forced to abandon his own mare on the eve of the Saint-Gérard business. It is the Tuesday after Whit. They spend the whole of Monday on reserve, in a forest, listening to the sounds of the bombardment, which never lets up,

156

coming from the direction of the Meuse. In the evening, the order arrives to move on. They resaddle the horses, straight onto the open sores, and begin to advance southwards (the squadron now consists only of three troops made up of survivors), parallel to the river, then turn left, going towards it again. Although they progress at a walking pace, towards the end he feels the mare sinking several times beneath him, as if her legs were giving way, and he has to use his spurs to get her up again. They spend the night in another wood, a fairly sparsely planted one. At daybreak the Meuse bombardment starts up again, very near now, and around midday they begin to see moving along the road that skirts the wood, in small groups or singly, infantrymen who in reply to the questions of the officers give them a stunned look without stopping, turning their heads away and continuing their journey towards the rear. Some have no weapons. Some still drag their rifles along unthinkingly, holding them by the barrel, the butt scraping along the ground. Small white clouds, lazy and still, hang in the sky. In the wood and the thickets the sun dapples the leaves of the trees with pale yellow.

A little later, helped by the sergeant and a man from the squadron, he manages to get his mare onto her feet (to do this he has to kick her) and to get her into a meadow on the other side of the road. At each step it seems that she will collapse. The sergeant and the other man hit her with heavy sticks on her rump and in the back of the knees each time they appear to be giving way. In this fashion they take her as far as possible into a meadow which slopes gently down towards a stream. About ten yards from the water they are unable to prevent the mare from sinking down. He then takes off her bridle and goes back to the wood (he is exhausted himself, as much from fatigue and the lack of sleep as from the shocks his nerves have suffered, and even walking requires a considerable effort), takes from his equipment a canvas bucket, goes back to the stream, fills it and takes it to the mare whose head is resting on the grass, flat on its side (her body is lying on its flank, the four legs slightly folded under her). The mare does not lift her head to drink. Slowly he pours the contents of the bucket over her lips. He goes on pouring until there is nothing left in the bucket. The lips of the mare do not move. Her flank rises and falls very fast. The only visible eye is open and is watching him from under its fringe of long black lashes.

. . . the drawing-room growing slowly darker, the stern enigmatic portraits of dead ancestors merging little by little into the semi-darkness, first their costumes, the dark velvet jackets, the sumptuous faille bodices, the frock coats of men of means, their faces, their hands, showing still as light patches, with no clear outline, growing more and more indistinct, disappearing by degrees, and finally, in the dying light filtered by the conservatory, only a few glints from the barrel of a gun, the gilt of a frame, the row of ivory piano keys weakly phosphorescent and the polished relief of the bust shining blurred in the dark, revealing in ghostly outline the folds of the Roman toga, the excrescences of the battered face . . .

others, on the contrary, trotting peacefully, alone, making their way westwards, as if guided by a sixth sense, like those animals who are able, they say, to cover incredible distances to get back to their stable, their nest or their master, using the right-hand side of the road out of habit, not hurrying, as though lost in thought, keeping up a steady pace, the empty stirrups rising and falling in turn against their flanks, sometimes swerving abruptly with two fast steps, with a sort of sleepy disdain, to avoid a retreating infantryman trying to grab their bridle, and then falling back once more into their calm trot, the peaceful lozenges of sunlight filtered by the spring foliage playing on their necks, the gleaming saddles, their dusty rumps, as they moved away along the endless straight lines, of the road lined with trees and wrecked vehicles, getting smaller and smaller and then disappearing.

. . . the excrescences of the battered face, mineral and yet possessed, one might say, of a secret life, as if the drapes of the marble, the muscley chest continued to rise and fall imperceptibly, a bluish vein beating in the bull's neck, massive, placid, as if caught, preserved, in this sort of glaciation, with his mane of stone, the blank gaze of stone, and years later still . . .

. . . path you have trodden has sunk under your feet as you have walked: this is no time to retrace your steps; every obstacle must be overcome, or you must die of weariness. Courage, citizens! The Convention has little enough; it's unfortunately true: it has little, since it is afraid of braving petty passions; it has little, since it is not strong enough to ignore personalities; it has little, since it is unable to sacrifice to the important tasks for which it was summoned the disdain with which it is surrounded and the slanders heaped upon it.

Citizens, that is the true courage of lawgivers, instead of insulting each other, to the great scandal of the whole nation, or adjourning to the Bois de Bologne, for the Cazales and the Lameths have been there too.

Lawmakers, let us put an end to this protracted business: the Convention decrees in its wisdom the option which should be taken up. If you are united, all options are valid. It will not be the alliance of all the European Powers which will destroy the French Republic; it will be divisions between the members of the National Convention: it is at the present time the only place

158

where all France comes together. What possible confidence can their constituents have in representatives divided amongst themselves? Europe is amazed to see in this assembly a crowd of good men and true; she sees in them great talents, but she seeks a statesman amongst them: let him show himself therefore; let him take upon himself the predominance owed to genius; let us rally to him to attack tyrants and our own prejudices. Can we doubt of our success? All France would back you. My conclusion is that Louis XVI should be found guilty and punished as such without delay.

. . . years later still, he (the one who had been the boy, was now in his turn an old man) wanted to see again, if only to take a photograph of it, the sort of colossal and quizzical marble divinity which had for more than a century reigned over the drawing-room with the worn brocade, and after many steps, questions (there had been apportionments, lots drawn, then sharing of apportionments, removals, displacements: the family virtually bloodless for a while, reduced to almost nothing by bereavements, widowings, exploding so to speak, as if by a sudden change of fate, a balance of matter too long compressed suddenly dilating, multiplying from the last shoot, the youngest of the three children who, before killing himself at the wheel of his car, had had time to leave behind him a host of children and grandchildren reproducing in their turn, marrying, divorcing, remarrying, divorcing a second time), he managed (the old man) by dint of explanations, justifications received with distrust, begun again, listened to or eluded with an uncomprehending air, through determination, to obtain the address or rather the telephone number of a defensive and so to speak meditative voice, leaving time for long silences during which there seemed to be reflection on the part of the person who, having agreed on a time for a visit, opened the door to his importunate visitor (or rather half-opened it, slid into the opened crack a glance like that of a small cornered animal), then when he (the visitor) had given his name, closed the door (the time it took to undo the chain), opened it again, appeared entire this time, looking like a ferret, with a little blond moustache, a pointed face, with a preoccupied expression, and as he went into the appartment he (the visitor) wondered whatever the occupant could be worrying about (hearing him close the sophisticated security system behind him, with its chains, three locks and vertical bar), what could he imagine people would want to steal, the rooms having already been emptied of everything that could possibly be carried away except for a mattress on the floor, a table on which lay uncleared away the remains of a cold meal, a chair, three stacks of files against the wall and, of course, the indispensable telephone with whose help the person conducted the lucrative business which brought the bailiffs to his home: it was, in a luxury block with a marble entrance hall and lift with polished steel doors, an apartment of which he did the honours, explaining that the seizure had been due to a simple misunderstanding with his partners complicated by the stupidity of a bank manager and the falling due of an unfortunate bill, but that all had been settled and the furniture, the Shiraz, the Chinese vases, the screens in the style of Coromandel (or the bear skins, the white leather sofas, the moulded plastic tables) were going, in the days to come, to be replaced: 'As in the movies,' thought the visitor, 'as in advertising films where with a stroke of a wand a fairy with pointed bonnet fills a room from one frame to the next with divan beds, armchairs and potted plants . . .' 'But perhaps it's his job; a producer or something like that . . .,' then re-membering: 'No, a promoter, someone in property . . . since as far as furniture goes . . .,' not wanting to laugh even, looking at his host with incredulity, the flat as if emptied by some giant vacuum cleaner: on the walls the pictures had left pale rectangles, in a corner the fitted carpet still retained the imprint of a square where the flattened pile no longer stood up, and as he spoke, explained once more the reason for his visit (which he had already done on the telephone, getting only confused and evasive replies), he could see the suspicious person gradually regaining his assurance, retrieving his flow of words, saying as he indicated in a nonchalant fashion, at once fatalistic and amused, the bare room with its dirty carpet: 'D'you see? I didn't tell you any fibs on the phone, more's the pity . . . Cleaned right out! What more can I say? I didn't go to the sale. I . . .'

Briançon, 2 Floreal Year 8. Citizen Minister: I got here on 1 Floreal and I have undertaken without delay the checking of the siege provisions. I will send you shortly an account of the state of the fortress both as regards its fortifications and its armament, but the situation concerning victuals is so critical in my view that it constitutes a danger to the Republic, so I cannot delay acquainting you with the details: the enemy seized Mont Cenis, he has been driven from it but he can retake it with reinforcements; General Tureau, in command of the left wing of the Army of Italy has 6000 mouths to feed but only 2000 men to attack the enemy who make feint attacks every day, but everything points to the fact that he intends to launch a real one on the Tournoux camp where we have only 300 men, so he does not bother to beseige Briançon or Mont Lion; he need only move 200 men on to Savine, he covers Embrun, Mont Lion and Briançon; if he moves at the same time via Mont Cenis to Le Galibier he will cut communications between our fortress and the 7th division; and since he knows as well as I do that the three fortresses have less than eight days' supplies he is of course certain to take them without firing a shot. General Tureau told me that the enemy had 20 thousand men in reserve in Piedmont. I implore you, Citizen Minister, to have shown to you the letter I wrote from Grenoble to your predecessor, I have for a long time now . . . The following day, at dawn, the squadron moves to take up a position at Saint-Gérard. He mounts the horse of a trooper who has gone missing and, whilst they ride alongside the meadow, he can see the mare trying hard to get up again. She thrusts her head forward and up and down, using her neck as a balance, managing in this way to place her two front hooves on the ground and to lift her fore-quarters slightly (reminding him of an injured horse that he saw during a corrida which was trying convulsively to get to its feet, its head also moving up and down, but with its hindquarters seemingly paralysed, the two buttocks together and almost extended, while the pool of blood grew beneath it). Finally she managed somehow to get on her legs and to take a few steps in the direction of the road along which the squadron is moving. Almost immediately her legs bend and she sinks back into the grass. He turns round several times in the saddle and sees the dark heap she makes in the dawn, at the foot of the meadow whose grass is now grey (he imagines he can see her long, yellow teeth, the black lips crumpled or rather puckered, like glove leather, on which he poured the contents of the bucket, the long sparse hairs that grew under her chin). The grey dawn, the sky growing pale, periwinkle, before becoming pink, silence still for a few seconds (a skylark very high up climbing swiftly, its song in the grey emptiness like a little rusty pulley turning very fast) before the battle starts up afresh, the tanks lined up along the side of the road, their crews sitting in the open turrets or leaning against the tracks, sometimes chewing something or with a bottle in their hand, their empty staring eyes expressionless in their terribly pale faces, watching the cavalry go past, staring at each other silently, distantly, each man alone with his own fear, without sympathy, simply dumb, the whole like the wings in a theatre, an opera house, where the crowd of players silently take their

161

places before the rise of the curtain and the glare of the footlights. Turin, 28 Brumaire: Dear Batti, I got your letter of 14 Vendémiaire and that of the 22nd on the same day: the proof that I'm right when I say that you haven't a good head on your shoulders is that in spite of my advice to acknowledge the date of my letters you never do. You address your letters to Embrun whilst mine are dated from Turin. By sending your letters to Embrun you delayed them by fifteen days. You did not write to me for 37 days whereas you should write to me at ten-day intervals. I am not pleased with this negligence. I can see that you do not re-read my letters when you write to me since in this one you say that you have followed my instructions to plant oats at Falguières whereas I never told you to put them there since it has just had a crop of it; Falguières should be sown with wheat and alfalfa above it; there should be some alfalfa in the cleft of the field up to the Gindarme road. How can you expect me to deal with everything when I'm not there and when I'm preoccupied with military matters? Eight days after Mignonne, Numide and Emerald have had their foals, put them to Moustapha, so that one or other of them has a chance of conceiving. It seems that Cap de More is barren; don't put her to Moustapha; I intend to have her sent here with Superb and Salema. Ask Monsieur Delteil to supply you with all the corks and bottles you need and to bottle last year's white wine. Reread my letter of 3 Vendémiaire and reply to it point by point, I don't like you to pretend to be deaf. You must keep on the go, making sure that no damage is done, seeing to it that all the gates are properly closed, seeing to it that all the servants do the work according to my instructions and how much time it takes them: I only ask you to use your legs and your eyes and to keep me posted. I have more than enough work here for one man and I should at least be able to rely on you because if . . .

. . . the visitor realising that the voice had not stopped, wondering how long he had ceased to hear it, then realising that he had perhaps only just missed one sentence and perhaps not even that: a silence, the short space of time during which the ferret had remained watching him, or perhaps he had spoken himself, hearing again the thin voice, now ironical, almost aggressive: 'The name of the purchaser? But I keep telling you I don't have to . . . I mean: if she didn't let you have it, it's not for me . . . I mean: after all, that's her business . . . Ultimately mine as well, of course, since we were married under . . . But the purchaser, well, the purchaser . . . And who is to say that he himself won't want to . . . You know: one of those people who like to acquire ancestors . . . There are people like that . . . A general, after all! . . . Although that particular general didn't leave us much to remember him by, it seems to me . . . She herself never managed to tell me precisely what it was he . . .,' the tone of voice becoming impertinent, saying spitefully: 'Well after all, if only for the weight of the marble . . . Just think!: it took at least three men to lift it, and they were hard put to it! . . . So, the marble alone . . .,' the visitor not listening any longer, turning his back, already moving away, crossing the empty room, the entrance hall, waiting whilst the person slid open the complicated lock, then, the door shut to behind him, standing now on the landing, still imagining he could hear on the other side of the wooden panel, whilst the lift climbed towards him with a soft swishing sound, the laugh, the amused suave voice, repeating: 'Just the weight of the marble alone! . . . three men . . .,' the dirty bare carpet still flattened in the place where the plinth had stood (the lift stopping with a click, the luminous arrow going off, his hand mechanically pushing the door, as if there could be nothing left of the formidable mass other than the empty imprint, like the prints of giant feet that people pretend are left in a rock by some fabulous creature, imagining the three removal men bent under their inert and impassive burden, puffing, staggering and swearing . . . — the piano still playing, the shadowy figure of Uncle Charles standing out darkly against the window of the conservatory, with his romantic mop of hair, his eagle nose, uniformly flat, like those figures that skilful street hawkers rapidly cut out of black paper, the boy as still as the furniture, as if he was trying to put off not so much the moment when he would have to get up, go to his room and pore over the enigmatic periods of Cicero or the commentaries of Caesar, as the moment whose approach he sensed with foreboding, when this period of his life would soon end, because he knew that his mother was not 'resting', as Uncle Charles said, but that she was going to die in her turn, as if she had waited to do it with decency until the old lady had gone, that he was soon to leave the big house himself never to return except as a stranger, at long intervals, in the holidays, the marble ghost almost invisible now, keeping in the background, as if it had never been there, forgotten, stored in that drawing-room between two removals, two stages of that interminable wandering which would bring it later, incongruous, still

163

imperturbable, Olympian, to the anonymous flat of the bankrupt financier, and even later into other drawing-rooms, unknown houses, as if it were fated to be trundled endlessly (as one sends on their way from a pillaged temple to the places where they will be newly erected those huge, monumental statues, laid in cradles, staring at the sky with their blind eyes, anchored on to pads and bound with ropes by a host of Lilliputians in the middle of complicated scaffolding and lifting gear, dragged along paths by long lines of draught horses), as he had been from one corner of that Europe to the other which he had challenged, which he had crossed and recrossed in all directions back and forth in journeys always renewed which took him back time and again to the same places, to the same shores, to the same fortresses, to the same rivers, under the same ramparts, from Artois to the Alps, from the Alps to Corsica, from Corsica to Flanders, then from Flanders to the Rhine, then from the Rhine to Vesuvius, then from there to the ruins of Carthage, then back to the Rhine, then to the Po, then from the Po to the Baltic, then from the Baltic to the Ebro, like a labour of Sisyphus, always travelling back to the same crossroads (that city which was not only the capital of a nation but the thinking head, the terror of a continent), the time it took to dance attendance (to be left) in the hall of some committee or ministry, then shown in, borne in to an office in which stood before a spread map one or more of those men with the same wooden or marble faces (and for some time he had been one of them himself, sending couriers, deciding on manoeuvres, requisitioning horses, provisions, equipment — or rather not requisitioning, not sending horses, nor provisions, nor equipment, but only letters in which he said (as people also said to him) that they must fight without horses, without provisions and without weapons), severely dressed or even ridiculously pomaded, all alike covering themselves through the course of time with braid, gold decorations, diamonds, and who turned round as he was introduced, lifted their head, their anxious brows looked at him with an incredulous air, slightly reproving (he there again, indestructible, colossal, with his lion's mane of hair, his muscular neck, the smooth folds of his Roman toga), then contented themselves (by chance, it seemed, without even bothering to look where they were placing their forefinger) with

164

indicating a point on the map, and he (or rather the bust, the two hundred kilos of polished marble) moving off again, sent away once more, pressing ahead, pulled at full gallop by the indefatigable and apocalyptic teams of draught horses in the wake of cracking whips and oaths, with his clanking escort of armed cavalry (less to protect him perhaps than to stop him being stolen, to stop the enemy seizing him and erecting him in a place other than the intended one, sealed once and for all on a plinth), bouncing in the ruts, held in place by his harnesses, his apparatus of ropes, pulleys and winches, crossing mountains, getting bogged down in the black mud of Holland, skidding on the icy roads, sent from one end to the other of that map with its soft colours of pink, green, yellow, like those he assigned to various sections of his estate, the old world parcelled out, reshaped, criss-crossed by the sinuous lines of rivers, the frontiers, and once even hurled (as if continuing in his projection, borne by his mass) beyond the limits of the continent, touching the coast of Africa, then as if sucked up again, returned (in the manner of those balls or toys fastened with elastic) he, his mane, his two hundred pounds of bone and horsemeat bundled into the between-decks of a ship thrown on her beam-ends by a storm, rising and falling in the hollow of the waves, the man of marble and the stallion of bronze carried off in concert, sliding helter-skelter on the sloping floor in a thunderous crash of clinking stone and metal, rebounding against the hull, the ribs, moving back again in the other direction with the rise of the wave, until someone managed to capture them, between two slides, as in a lasso, to rope them, stow them away securely with the help of solid hawsers, then, once in port, once certain that the stallion had no broken bones, taking again that road from Genoa to Paris which he had followed six years earlier (overwhelmed by two naval squadrons, escaping from ambushes mounted by assassins, from denun-ciations drawn up no doubt by the same assassins), ushered in this time by lackeys in breeches and silk stockings bending beneath his weight into a drawing-room or drawing-rooms fitted like aviaries with half-naked women, with men of fashion looking like spaniels with their dressed hair, hovering over the powdered décolletés at the gaming tables, and examined there with an ironical eye by a big man covered from head to foot in

165

braid, ribbons and lace, with thick hands, carefully manicured, decked with rings (and perhaps, on one of his fingers, one of those little cameos depicting against a blood-red background of cornelian a simple head in profile, its neck cut off in an elegant curved line), his eyes shining with malice and greed examining him from top to toe, searching the marble for a crack, a split, until the hand heavy with precious stones picked up a card at random on one of the felt mats, turning it in his hand, hardly looking at it (it was perhaps the knave of hearts), then observing him again (and an imperceptible nudge of the elbow perhaps to someone standing nearby, to some courtier), watching for the sudden start, the jump, whilst the mouth with thick lips opened, let drop at last another name of another city where people were fighting, dying (since they had not managed to break him, rid themselves of him, kill him, even by making him a general at a time when, as some person of the time said, that type of appointment was just about the equivalent of a warrant for the gallows, or even, between two wars, in a short interval of peace during which they could not get rid of him to any battlefield, by sending him to Naples, as they had sent others to Rastadt — or perhaps it was pure fluke, simply so that he would no longer clutter the drawing-room, because he had to be put somewhere where there were guns and danger), the motionless marble countenance . . .

The weather remains desperately fine and the sun, already hot during the day (they are still wearing their long cavalry greatcoats in spite of which, however, they shiver at night) hangs over the still woods with their blue shadows, the meadows divided by hedges, the gently undulating countryside. The planes rise unexpectedly from behind a hill, or rather materialize suddenly, with no warning sound, are suddenly upon them, flying generally in threes and quite low, their line of flight indolent, undulating lifelessly, in such a way that they rise and fall in relation to each other, like long fish gliding with no apparent movement at a certain depth. In one of the endless retreats the troop is assembled, already on horseback, in an orchard, the first section beginning to move off, when several appear, coming towards them. The order is given straight away to regroup under the apple trees and to stand completely still. Through the gaps in the foliage they watch the planes in triangular formation at a middling height, like grey crosses in the white morning sky as they continue to fly straight on. All heads are raised and they hold their breath, jumping nervously at the neighing or sudden movement of a horse reprimanded by its rider with a stifled oath. The planes seem to be moving in slow motion. The sun plays on the tender green foliage and turns it into a transparent lemon. Two birds have just settled chirping on one of the trees. They chase each other, quarrelling, invisible, and one can follow their movements through the sudden rustling of leaves, the rapid sound of wings. They move in jerks, leaping and tumbling unexpectedly from one branch to another and the tips of the branches are shaken with their little tremors. The planes pass overhead with a deafening roar and continue their flight.

. . . the motionless head of marble not even quivering, the motionless marble lips hardly parted (only perhaps the marble a little paler), the marble voice itself saying: 'Strasbourg!,' then almost immediately, very fast, even more like marble: 'All right. Strasbourg,' the two Zeus-like furrows carved between the brows not even moving, the face as impassive as when he stood on the rostrum or commanded his men to fire, the lackeys bending, lifting again the block of marble with the Heave! of porters, carrying him out of the drawing-room, away from the chirpings, the cackles of the aviary, the scented warmth of naked flesh, stumbling in the staircase, swearing, beneath the weight, stuffing him into the cabriolet already prepared, harnessed with horses already pawing the ground, closing the door, as they returned rubbing their bruised hands to mount guard in the antechambers, to serve refreshments to the Phrynes in transparent dresses, the postilion cracking his whip, the horses springing forward, the carriage jolting for a moment on the cobbles, then travelling through the suburbs, then surging along the open road, by ways that were no longer anything but quagmires, crossing without stopping (just the time it took to harness new horses at the stages), the towns which he had already crossed so many times, travelling again the immemorial itinerary marked out with names like armour, crenelated, emblazoned, smelling of iron, gunpowder, camps (Bar-le-Duc, Epernay, Chalons, Toul, Lunéville, Baccarat), the bust, in the icy interior of the carriage, swung wildly around, jolted, but still as colossal, not even chipped, when the door was opened at the end, staring, taking stock with his marble eyes, at the staff of general officers and aides de camp who were watching him (probably slyly beneath the feigned obsequiousness, ill concealing their insolence, probably nudging each other with their

167

elbows, whispering the name in each other's ears), except that it was not a bust that they saw, a ghost which they had probably expected, but a giant, even if a marble one, under whose weight the man who held his knee to help him mount his horse nearly gave way, never taking their eyes off him, their mouths wide open, staggered, while he rode off without looking back, the carriage itself not even unhitched, riding straight out to the outposts; silent, observing everything, indifferent to the icy wind, crossing the river with its swirling eddies, letting his gaze travel over the redoubts, the entrenchments, the muddy breastworks, the men taken by surprise, ill-kempt, dirty, continuing on his way without a word, then, still without saying anything, having himself taken to headquarters, going up the staircase, passing in front of the orderlies without seeing them, scorning the meal prepared for him, entering the office he was shown into, seating himself heavily (and in the icy drawing-room, now almost dark, where the mass of the bust was growing dimmer and dimmer, the boy felt he could see him: the powerful body, muscular, beginning to thicken out, naked, like those drawings copied from the antique which painters of the time traced onto canvas and then clothed with drapes or uniforms painted onto the skin from the collar, the epaulettes downwards, the body disappearing little by little beneath the layers of paint, red, gold, blue, leaning forward, one of his legs bent back slightly under the chair, itself copied from the antique), turning over slowly by the light of the candlestick the pages of registers, states of forces' strengths which he had brought to him, asking a question sometimes, listening in silence to the answer, plunging back into the registers, and at the end closing them, straightening up, tipping backwards, leaning against the back of the chair, remaining silent a moment, his eyes staring ahead into the void, with no glance at the one or many elegant staff officers standing at the side of the desk, then, with a single gesture, dismissing them, not even taking any notice of the clicking of heels, the chink of spurs, calling the aide-de-camp, telling him to sit down, then starting, calm, exhausted, to dictate: 'Strasbourg, 3rd successive day. To Battalion Commander Legros, Head of the Artillery School in Strasbourg: I would be grateful, citizen, if you would give the order to citizen Balure, captain in the third regiment of foot artillery, to go within 24 hours to rejoin his company *bivouacked at the moment in the fortifications before Kell. The administrative council of this regiment will appoint if it thinks fit an officer of a lower rank to replace him in the duties he performs at the moment. I would be grateful if you would order citizen Friess, 1st captain of the 17th company of the 3rd regiment of foot artillery, to go within 24 hours to his company presently manning the forward positions at Kell. Be so good as to give the same order to citizen Lebart, 2nd captain in the same regiment. The depot of the 5th regiment will have citizen Friess replaced on the administrative council. I am informing the Minister of the order I am giving you and my reasons for doing so. Please see to its prompt execution,'* the secretary's pen squeaking in the icy silence, the colossus looking calmly ahead, waiting, the quill ceasing to rasp (the piano playing as if silently as well, in the distance, muted — indeed, now, the boy no longer heard it), the marble voice raised again, dictating: *'To the Minister of War'*, the pen beginning to squeak again: *'Citizen Minister, my appointment as commander-in-chief of the artillery in the army affords me the freedom to deploy the troops in the district which you have allocated to me, from Brisach to Dusseldorf. On my arrival in Strasbourg I went to visit the artillery attached to General Le Grand's division which occupies the Kell bridgehead; I found one of the forward positions occupied by the 9th company of the 5th regiment of foot artillery and not a single officer in sight; a unit had been detached, so that there should have been four officers left, two captains, and two lieutenants. Citizen Minister, I never give the same order twice; on the second occasion, I hand out punishment. The artillery has always served with distinction, and I will not allow a few officers in my command to blot its escutcheon. I think it is the height of indecency for officers to try to avoid confronting the enemy by taking easy jobs which can be carried out by wounded officers. I pay no attention to the representations made to me by the administrative council of this regiment's depot, by which it is claimed that these officers, the one employed on the armament of the Vauban fort, the other in the regimental clothing store, were the only ones to enjoy the council's confidence. I am sure that they will write to you in this regard to explain to you the special talents which they discern in these officers for these functions, but I have the honour to assure you that wherever I find evidence of slackness I will see that good order is upheld . . .,'* the painter now reaching the legs (the body contained, buttoned up, in the blue tunic with red facings, covering the dressing of the wound that never healed, the broad feet with their knotty veins, supple boots, adding the spurs, making them glint with a thick layer of titanium . . .

169

'Because they . . . I mean Barras and the others . . . didn't choose Strasbourg at random,' said Uncle Charles. 'Whence this tone, this strength of feeling. He who normally hid it beneath an apparent bonhomie . . . Like a challenge. To men who could have his head chopped off,' the boy saying: 'Chopped his h . . .' (it was summer, or rather the beginning of autumn, and no longer the icy drawing-room, the piano, but the little office with its shutters always three-quarters closed for protection from the sun and where, during the grape-harvest, on the estate where, although no one bears the name any longer, the casks, the carts and the ladders continued to be marked with the three initials, Uncle Charles weighed the musts into the copper kettles of old Dujardin-Salleron, the whole room filled with the sweetish odour of the alcohol and the sugar, the velvety flames flickering at the slightest draught under the kettles, the tiny vibrations of the liquid inside making a continuous sound, monotonous, the drops of alcohol falling one by one into the little flasks that Uncle Charles watched from out of the corner of his eye), and the boy who now wore long trousers, had been using a razor for several years, repeating: 'Chopped his head off?' — 'Or shot him,' said Uncle Charles. 'Little more was required at that. And their police work was efficient . . .,' ceasing to observe the quivering drops falling into the flasks, looking at the boy over his glasses: 'Because for a man who had been a representative on mission, secretary of the Convention, member of the Committee of Public Safety, president of something which in those days was like what the Senate now is, an ambassador, the title of General in Chief of the army artillery, even if it was an important command, did not exactly constitute promotion. Have you ever thought of that? As for the precise choice of that army and of Strasbourg . . .,' he leaned towards one of the flasks and said: 'It's almost ready,' continued speaking without turning his eyes away from the end of the rubber tube: 'Yes, their police work was efficient. Or rather it worked by itself. I suppose as always it was enough to have sufficient patience to go through the piles of denunciations. And then no doubt they found the flaw, the chink in the armour . . . And I think I've found it as well: he didn't return directly from Genoa to Paris when he came back from Tunis, he . . . Mind! . . .': he bent over, nimbly withdrew one of the

170

little flasks with long necks, lifted it up to the light to check that the liquid level had indeed reached the correct mark, put his hand over the opening, turned the bottle upside down and back again several times, then emptied its contents into a test-tube in which, as it filled up, there rose myriads of silvery bubbles, saying at last: 'Would you pass me the thermometer? Thanks,' leaning forward a moment, then writing a figure on the sheet of paper on which the bottom of the test tube had left a damp, swollen mark, then plunging carefully into the clear liquid the alcoholmeter which rose and fell for a short while before stabilising, turning slightly on itself, Uncle Charles observing it intently, referring to a table pinned on the wall and saying: 'Eleven two. Good. There's still time,' then whilst he unscrewed, blowing on his fingers, the top of the kettle, rinsed it, poured the residue into another test tube, saying: 'He had made a detour to the chateau . . . Yes: which is no more today than a big farmhouse half in ruins . . . And he hadn't just come to leave the stallion there which the brother-in-law of the Bey had presented him with, or o enjoy the local air . . . Unless he didn't know what was awaiting him there . . . or was perhaps not awaiting him: the telephone didn't exist in those days . . . In any case he had apparently found there something other than the country air, or rather someone . . .,' and the boy: 'Someone . . . But who? What's . . .', and his uncle: 'I'll show you. Your grandmother never told anyone about it. Neither me nor anyone else. She always kept this piece of paper more carefully than her jewellery, at the bottom of that small box which she kept locked in the bottom of a locked drawer in the writing-desk which was also always kept locked . . .'; he jotted down another figure, poured the contents of the test tube into a grape-pail at the side of his desk, saying: 'Now if you'd like to pass me the sample I took a while ago at the 4? There: against the wall . . .,' refilling the kettle, screwing the lid back firmly, relighting the small lamp, saying: 'Naturally it may seem silly to you. In fact it does to me. Something that happened over a hundred years ago . . . Only for her it was not so distant. And it was her name. And after all it was her great-grandfather and her great-great-uncle . . .,' and the boy: 'Uncle? But what . . .,' Uncle Charles tapping the tobacco into the bowl of his pipe, lighting it, taking several puffs, then raising his eyes: 'Because he had a brother . . .,' and the

171

boy: 'A br . . . What brother?,' and Uncle Charles: 'Legally and biologically. Yes. Since it is usual to give that name to the products of two embryos issued from the same male glands and which grow in the same womb. Except that they resembled each other almost as a negative of a photograph resembles the print. That is to say exactly similar and exactly opposite . . .,' and the boy: 'So he had a brother? But why . . .,' and Uncle Charles: 'You mean: why has no one ever spoken of him? Well, there you are: that's just it!'

IV

The side of a railway carriage, photographed at a slight angle, occupies the whole length of the picture. It is one of those massive cars, of Belgian make, which travelled on the wide-gauge tracks of the companies set up with foreign capital in Spain at the turn of the century. Even in peacetime these trains had something sad about them which was not due solely to their dirtiness. The carriages and their windows were indeed always thickly coated with a greasy soot which came off on one's hands, and the locomotive whistles made a sound at once plaintive and lugubrious, with a double note which recalled those trains of the wild west slowly pushing their way through herds of bison as they crossed vast distances as arid and barren as the plateaux of Aragon or Castille.

Of course these foreign companies had been nationalised along with all the others, and clearly visible on the side of the carriage, written in chalk or white paint, are the initials of the two main trade unions, the UGT and CNT, as well as inscriptions glorifying the Iberian Anarchist Federation.

Strangely, the black and white snapshot gives a better idea than a colour photograph could of the greyish, remarkably dusty appearance of these carriages, although, in fact, they were not exactly greyish but a muddy brown. The impression conveyed by the mournful wailing of the locomotive and this unusual dirtiness was reinforced by the perfunctory, brutal nature of their construction, a utilitarian, robust quality, conforming no doubt to the directives of the Belgian bankers, and the profusion of bolts, screws and rivets which nothing had been done to conceal, as well as the solid girders of their underframes, gave them, like certain monastic or military vehicles, something that was at once penitentiary, metallurgical, funereal and barbaric.

From the narrow windows sealed in thick bands of copper (soot does not cling to it as it does to the paintwork of the carriages but deposits itself on it in the form of fine granules under which the yellow metal can be seen, and a quick wipe is enough to make it shine, as happens where the fingermarks are edged by black streaks of soot crushed and dampened by sweat from sticky hands — in other places, where a finger has simply touched it, there is a fingerprint with its concentric, graphite rings) . . . from the narrow windows, then, the torsos of young men lean out, in shirtsleeves or overalls, remininiscent of those rowdy groups such as sports teams seen returning from a match on a Sunday evening, standing in train doorways and bellowing victory slogans and bawdy songs punctuated by animal cries. Despite its narrowness three of them are pressed together in one of the rectangles from which the slimmest seems to be squeezed out as far as his waist, with his head raised and thrown back, his arm raised too, as if he were brandishing at head height a flask or other object (a weapon? a posy?) which cannot be seen because the right hand side of the photograph cuts off his arm just below the wrist.

Most of the carriage's occupants look at the camera and two of them show off their rifles, which they hold at a sloping angle, the barrels pointing skywards out of the windows. They all have thick, black, shiny, oily hair combed backwards, except for one, prematurely balding, who has only two tufts on the sides and a quiff in the middle, his high clear forehead visible above a shy, gentle, almost childlike face which could be that of a restaurant waiter or barber's assistant. The webbing straps of his cartridge pouches stand out against the white shirt he is wearing. There is also something vulnerable and childlike in the way he brandishes his rifle and raises his fist, which instead of presenting it with the palm forwards he shakes in a boyishly threatening gesture.

The window next to his is occupied only by a single militiaman whose head and shoulders are all that are visible, perhaps because he is kneeling or crouching on the floor of the compartment, with his body concealed by the side of the carriage as if he were shielding behind armour plating. He is older than his companions and indifferent to the general excitement; he shows no interest in the photographer but stares at a point on the platform in front and slightly to the left of himself. In his right hand he is holding one of those heavy, flat, shiny black pistols seen in gangster films. It is almost as if he has just pressed the trigger on which his forefinger is still bent and that he is watching carefully the enemy he has just shot. The

176

breech and barrel of the weapon hide the lower part of his face seen in semi-profile and bar it with a thick black line running from slightly under the ear and ending up like a sort of moustache on the upper lip. To the right of the barrel's mouth a cloud of smoke curls away in a whitish blur in front of the militiaman standing at the next window. In fact, it drifts up from the end of a lighted cigarette held between the index and middle fingers of the left hand which the man dangles outside the door. This individual has thick crinkly hair which looks as if it has been piled up in dense waves above his low forehead. His features are of a mediterranean type, sharp, hard and regular with a straight nose, and his eyes are hidden by the patches of shadow cast by his eyebrows; he has a concentrated, grim, even slightly histrionic expression, no doubt exaggerated for the benefit of the photographer (that is of the public who will eventually see the photograph) engaged in taking the picture. No friends or relatives seem to have come to see the men off. Above the top of the carriage the iron vaulting supporting the sooty glass roof can be seen, its massive beams studded with rivets.

Fortunately, so his account goes, it was June, and although the nights were sometimes chilly, especially just before dawn, they were never really cold, but at the same time, again because it was June, the sun rose early, so that in the morning he or rather they (he and two others like him) were forced to remain hidden for a long while yet in the shelter (the gutted church, the derelict building site, the ditch in the tall grass of a patch of waste ground) where they had if not slept, at least dozed for a few hours, if at least even that word was not an optimistic description of something which was the opposite of relaxation and rest, not only because of the discomfort of the places and of their positions (curled up or somehow or other stretched out amid the rubble or on the earth itself) but also because of the permanent state of alert in which they lived even when asleep, although one or the other stayed awake to keep watch, so that they were ready to get up and take off at the slightest suspicious noise, and perhaps they could have gone into some brothel or other — since these were open again — and pass themselves off as rich foreign tourists (or journalists), except that it was very likely that they (that is to say those who were looking for them) were also watching those sorts of places (or the prostitute with whom they might have spent the night), not to mention the fact that what they would have had to do there to justify their presence was undoubtedly the last thing not only that they cared about at that time but probably that their bodies felt any desire for, the reflexes of rutting being replaced (or wiped out, although they were all equally young and vigorous) in their flesh, their muscles, by those other emerging reflexes, no less bestial, such as vigilance, instinctive fear, brought back to the stage of being wild beasts (or even domestic, like the cat for instance, capable at any moment of switching suddenly from motionlessness, whether of watching, stalking, or the deepest of sleeps, to a dazzling rapidity which makes leaping, clawing or escaping, even though three different words are needed to describe it, a single action, governed (the flesh, the muscles) no longer, as he described it, by a brain subject to bewilderment or despair (they had not, or rather had no longer, any time for that) but preoccupied solely with the means of survival, postponing until later all questioning (that is debating good and evil, examining, weighing the whys and the wherefores, that is to say why and how all that, which had brought them or rather made them regress to this situation of animals hunted like game, had come about), trusting now only to their continually alert senses. Whatever the truth of the matter they had to spend the hours which separated them from those during which the city would awake in its turn, warm (or rather damp) and heavy, and in which the cafés and the barber shops would open their doors, and even then they would have attracted suspicion if they had rushed in as soon as the barbers took down their shutters or the waiters swept up the sawdust and set out the tables, so they had to wait and warm themselves up slowly, hidden from public gaze by a fence or following on the flagstones of a church the slow progression of the sunbeams shining, horizontal at first, then at more and more of an angle, through a rose window with all its glass smashed glass and the tracery of the blackened arches, watching out for the last motorcars returning along the deserted boulevards from their nocturnal or early morning expeditions with their night's prey, that is those who hadn't become primitive enough to escape the hunters, sitting motionless on the back seat between two guards, their eyes fixed, empty, with that air of having been freed of a burden, a care, as if relieved in a way, or else (the cars) with only those passengers who had got in in the middle of the night or at daybreak cleaning their guns carefully by blowing through the breech, closing one eye to look with the other down the still-warm barrel, the whole thing (the slanting sunlight, the empty avenues, the cars or vans (which were not delivering milk) passing infrequently by, the façades with their windows still closed, the pavements not yet swept by the concierges — then, later, the same avenues, the same façades with their windows now open, the concierges swabbing out the doorways, the café terraces where the waiters were setting out chairs and tables once again) suffused with the sort of unreality, of incredibility which the external world offers to the reddened eyes of the traveller who has come off the morning train after a night spent on a badly upholstered seat, stiff all over, standing on the forecourt steps, insulated from the station square, the buses, the very sounds, by a sheet of glass as it were, a film of weariness, like wax or vaseline which he can feel cracking over his face, splitting long the lines of his wrinkles, like a mark, as if he were covered with a second skin sealing him off from the cool air and the morning in which the rest of his body shivers, realising then that he has envisaged his journey in terms of distances whereas it has been a question of an internal transformation of his own being because it is not only the places which have changed but he himself, his substance: for now, evidently, it (the substance) which constituted them was no longer the same since they could feel more or less what a rabbit feels when it is pursued by hunters or rather (because it happened in a town) what a rat must feel or some animal of the same kind which firms of exterminators or specialised teams undertake to clear from cellars and lofts: a metamorphosis which he (the one who later told the whole story) suddenly realised, as if he had been able to feel his body getting covered with fur and his tail growing, hearing with his own ears the woman who was his own wife telling him to go away (and he: What? — and she: Get out. — and he: What? — and she: At once. — and he: Why?) and which (when she had rejoined him again a little later, in a quiet café in a side street, away from prying eyes, so that already then and even before she

179

had explained to him the whys and wherefores he knew that all problems, philosophical or other, were wiped out at a stroke, and even resolved, except one: running and hiding, alone, still convalescing from a wound, in a foreign town in which those who could have helped him also had to hide), and which, then (the metamorphosis) rendered all notion of legality and illegality futile (as someone to whom, in other circumstances, the thing had happened, had told him: that is the irruption — the intrusion — into the place where he lived of men who, without bothering even to show what they carried in a holster on their hip, had simply conveyed to him the order to clear out, without even bothering either to laugh when he had asked the same question, the same ludicrous why — after which he (the one they had driven out of the house) had understood what usually people have some difficulty in accepting, namely that the law is not a question of morality or justice cogitated over by philosophers and applied by parliaments and assemblies but, in fact, a simple matter of conventions and that the only legality in conformity with the nature of things consists in owning a revolver when the man opposite you has not got one), so that again it seemed to him that he was living out (but the other way round) the famous joke (which one of them reminded him of — one of the others living through the same adventure with him — one morning when they were waiting for the moment in which they could without too much danger slip out of their hiding-place) of the chap who takes himself for a grain of millet seed and whom the doctor succeeds by dint of patient explanation in persuading that he is a man and not a millet seed, but who, on the doorstep, suddenly draws back, telling the doctor that he is now quite sure that he is a man and not a millet seed but that nothing can convince him that the hens think the same way — and also if he (the one who told the story later) was quite sure that he was a man it seemed to him that those who were hunting him down did not know it and indeed considered him no more than a rat, for she (the woman) told him that they (that is five or six of those characters who, whether they wear a uniform or not, reveal their social function pretty clearly: a bit too well fed, a bit too polite (or brutal, depending on the circumstances), their eyes looking a bit like dirty water), had pounded on the door one morning, and without waiting for a reply (being no doubt equipped with one of those instruments which allow you to get in to people's houses and open locked doors without leave) had rushed into the room according to the rules of a tried and trusted strategy, if not of taking prisoners, at least (since they had not found him at home) of disinfection (preventive, in a way — he had not yet been able to decide what exactly they were: it was hard for him to believe that they were policemen because so far as he knew he had broken no law and that, normally, you are safe as long as you obey the law: still, it seemed clear that the word (security) must have had a double meaning because it was that very word which the expedition's leader had uttered when announcing himself as he entered the room, dignifying it — although it was not written down only spoken — with a capital, which appeared to alter its meaning, security with a big S turning out to be the opposite of the one in lower case), the whole operation carried out in any case according to the most minute rules of hygiene, for as soon as they were in they began with great thoroughness to search for every trace of harmful germs which might be lurking there, invisible but without a shadow of doubt virulent, seizing every scrap of paper, newspapers, books, press cuttings, private correspondence, dirty linen, rummaging through every drawer and suitcase, the waste paper basket, the bathroom, sounding the walls, taking up the mats, feeling the curtains, probing under the bath and the radiator, feeling every garment and holding it up to the light, picking every packet of cigarette paper to pieces and examining each paper separately, all of which — although there were six of them — took nearly two hours, yet all this time they never searched the bed in which the woman was lying with the sheets drawn right up to her chin, gazing silently on their comings and goings, a detail which (or so he wished to believe, could not bring himself to think otherwise) made him feel that they were not real professionals, attributing that omission (not having searched the bed) to the survival among the visitors (or rather the intruders) of a vague feeling of shame or of honour and not to mere stupidity: in any case, now (as they had not kicked the woman out of bed and had not taken her away with them, it was fairly obvious that they hoped to use her as a decoy duck) the only solution open to him was to hide while waiting to find a way of escape, the paradoxical thing being that searches (tracking down, running to earth) only took place at night, so that when they considered it sufficiently late in the day (that is when the life of the streets had resumed its normal pace) they would slip out of their shelter, but only after meticulously inspecting each other, after picking off the blades of grass, the specks of mud or bits of rubble from their backs, after lengthily brushing down and as far as possible smoothing out their clothes until with their flannel trousers and tweed sports coats which they had put on instead of the dangerous corduroy breeches and dangerous leather jackets they looked more or less like harmless tourists — or newspaper correspondents — their faces perhaps a little too tanned and their hands perhaps too calloused to be taken for genuine tourists (although they could just about hope to pass off their tan as due to sunbathing on one of the nearby beaches) strolling with a nonchalant air to the first barber shop where they would explain, by knowing winks and ribald hints, their eyes reddened by lack of sleep and their drawn features, their stiff limbs enjoying the chairs upholstered in imitation leather, surrendering themselves to diligent hands which smothered their emaciated cheeks in soap, sinking into a kind of confused torpor made all the deeper by the stale heavy smell of cheap perfumes, of lavender and toilet water, gazing at the advertisements for shampoos and hair lotion stuck between the mirrors with their glossy frames, posters in which, touched up in soft shades, impossible faces smiled, powdered in pink, the faces of gawdy women with heavy blond wavy hair, with prominent bosoms, half-clad or dressed in pale green shifts offering or holding under their ecstatic nostrils some magic bottle or other of French perfume: but you had to be careful not to doze off, just as you had to ignore the bombastic poster stuck on one of the mirrors with strips of paper which printed in garish colours announced the end of the age of slavery and of the humiliation symbolised by tipping, a bit of progress which, given a poor grasp of the language that they were in a position to claim as foreigners, they could claim to be unaware of, the barber himself no doubt (perhaps because he was illiterate?) incapable of grasping the meaning and appreciating the liberative powers of the little bill, so that everything went well even in the luxury restaurants which it was wise for them to frequent, and there again (in fact they were the only places where they could go

182

without too great a risk, and even without much danger at all, thanks to that immemorial and international way of guaranteeing feelings of respect, even of sympathy, which are prompted by an adequate supply of coins — or of notes (that is to say the tattered bits of paper coloured a pinkish or greenish brown, which did service as such) slipped carelessly into the hand of a waiter whether freed from slavery or not), there again, then, as long as they took care not to throw themselves on the food like starving people and even to leave some uneaten or, better still, to order unnecessarily dishes which they hardly touched, they could enjoy relative peace and security (without the capital S), there being no philosophy or metaphysical prescription in any country, under any regime, against customers dressed in flannel trousers and tweed sports jackets, well off into the bargain, enjoying, even where the rest of the population lives in squalor, the privileges conferred by money liberally spent, whatever its source and smell. Unfortunately, even dragging things out, it was difficult to spend whole days at the barber's, in a café or sitting in expensive restaurants: there were of course also the public baths, with their sweating walls of glazed brick, their stale smells of lechery and that vague, emollient and libidinous atmosphere which pervades those sorts of places, the weary bodies floating milky and weightless in oyster-coloured transparencies from which impalpable and convulsive vapours arise like grey smoke creeping and twisting along the surface of the scalding water, like the ectoplasmic venal ejaculations of innumerable catamites: it was one of these no doubt (or perhaps the bath attendant frustrated of his usual tips) who alerted those who were searching for them, for soon they (the rats) learned that they (their pursuers) were beginning to make raids there, taking away with them one or other of the imprudent customers and taking them away dressed only in a towel or even not dressed at all (which after all did not matter much in view of what they proposed doing to him — that is to say to convey him to a place where, or to reduce him to a state in which, he would not even need any kind of garment, not even a towel), so that, like the brothels at night, they had to give up such places, not to mention the fact that (since it daily became clearer that they (the hunters) were not acting as a result of an error or misunderstanding, but by virtue of instructions and of powers given if not by the legal authorities at least by an authority for whom legality was a small worry since it conferred its own legality), not to mention, then, that hiding led in fact to nothing else than continuing to hide and that as a result it became more urgent to acquire the means to escape, not only from the city but from the country itself, and for that purpose the consul offered the only chance of safety provided that it was first possible to contact him and secondly that he was willing to undertake the business of getting the necessary rubber stamps applied to passports (which without visas and stamps were just the same as warrants for their arrest) and by the legal authorities (or by those at least who claimed still to be the legal authorities): it was the woman who contacted him (through intermediaries no doubt or in a discreet place: it being out of the question to take the risk of going up to the building on the entrance to which hung the sign with its coat of arms, since it (the building) was discreetly watched by several facsimile reproductions (that is the same overfed appearance, the same eyes looking like dirty water, the same sly, insolent and ignominious bearing) of the six who had carried out the room search, idling there or planted on the pavement opposite without even taking the trouble of appearing any different from what they were), a race against time involving on the one hand the consul and on the other the kind of gangrene whose propagation in the offices where the official stamps were kept was fortunately slowed down by its very nature, coming up, although progressing inexorably, against that laziness and those vices (confusion, inertia, incompetence) which are as it were the corollaries of ignominy, making up its weak as well as its strong side: but no doubt something still remained (whatever name it is called by: soul, spirit, reason, honour . . .) if not to convince at least to redeem, even at the risk of that life which the consul was working to save (he had put it on the line some months earlier when he had become involved in this affair, knowing that he was probably going to lose it, had even acquiesced in the loss of it — only not in this manner . . .) so that throwing discretion to the winds (although after all with the barber shops, the cafés, the posh restaurants and the public baths, a prison was perhaps the safest refuge for a hunted animal) he rushed into it of his own accord, mingling at the visiting hour with relatives, with families carrying packets of food, and with weeping women: not one of

184

those buildings surrounded by high blackened walls (here yellowish, as almost everywhere in that country), built in star shapes or pentagons, studded with barred windows, but (the prison — or at least what did office as one — or rather (because there were several in the town) one of the places requisitioned for this purpose) a more or less clandestine place (just as the rat-hunting only took place at night, in a clandestine fashion — although they were beginning also, as was happening in the public baths, to arrest people in broad daylight but still in a way clandestinely, the passers-by, the witnesses to the scene, continuing on their way, as if seeing nothing, without stopping or gathering, not even turning their heads, deaf and blind you might say, in the same way as one passes by on a pavement beside a drunk or indifferent to a prostitute's leer or the displays of an exhibitionist, continuing their way with at the most, if necessary, a slight movement to one side to avoid, to bypass, the invisible car or the invisible van parked there and the group of its invisible occupants around the invisible prisoner they were pushing inside), in the same way as there exist brothels and gaming clubs which the police are supposed to know nothing about but which operate all right: a mere shop, then, whose sign still bore the name of the tailor or the grocer who had run his business there, but whose corrugated steel shutters were almost three quarters fully lowered so that once inside he needed time to get used to the murky light, not to mention the deafening racket and the beastly stench you always get when crowds of people are penned together (there were even children; two prisoners also with amputated legs, one of whom had been brought to prison without his crutches and was hopping about on one foot) and among whom he recognised at last the one he was looking for (one of those who had not had his luck, had been arrested a few days earlier, dressed in his uniform (with the badges of his rank of major) which he had kept neat, waving to him, elbowing his way through the sobbing, swearing crowd, joining him at last, embracing him, holding him at arm's length to gaze at the familiar face, smiling, clean-shaven as usual, as if nothing were amiss, hearing the familiar voice, cheerful, even gay, speak the words, the phrase (or rather, in the double meaning of the word, the sentence) which offered a reply to the question asked not even by his own voice but no doubt by his

185

gaze, the look of amazed incredulity which showed on his face, the battalion commander saying in a light, casual way, 'Well, I suppose we shall all be shot,' and then, as at the moment when the bullet had entered his own body, the blow, the jolt, the bang, tapping instinctively with his sound hand the poorly-healed wound, saying 'Sho . . . sh . . .,' then rushing out again, running (or rather hurrying, clumsily holding on to his painful arm) under the pretty dappled sunlight, between the pretty flower and odds-and-ends stalls, turning round every now and then without stopping running, then, as soon as he saw one, hailing a taxi, tossing the address to the driver, sitting now on the edge of the seat, head forward, pestering the driver, pointing out the streets, tossing a note into his hand, slamming the door behind him, rushing on, leaping up the steps four at a time over which he saw, flapping gently, in the glowing light of the late afternoon, the flag in the exotic colours of boiled sweets, cigar boxes and candied fruits (purple, yellow, red — or, as some people were now putting it, permanganate, urine and blood), the bringing together of which had meant to him — still meant, in spite of everything — justice, liberty, courage, in the same way as the sentry (the guard under whose nose he waved a piece of paper which, if the man had been able to read, would immediately have led to his arrest) seemed, with his peasant's face, his grubby hands, his illiterate's blank, pathetic look, to personify, to justify by his mere existence that which was proclaimed with pride by the three colours, fluttering in the clear blue sky in which the tops of the high palms waved, then sent up these stairs, down those, along interminable passages, from one floor to another, from one office to another, in the din of clicking typewriters, pursuing on his part another race in which he came up against not, as he might have expected, hostility of some kind, but a succession of polite, even affable faces, a shade surprised, indolent only, who looked at him in astonishment while he carelessly repeated the name of the battalion commander, stammering, getting muddled up, watching on the faces of each successive, inexorable clock the hands marking five o'clock, then a quarter past five, then half-past five, then a quarter to six, and now the secretaries were putting the covers over their typewriters, and now, in the absence of the unlocatable general, he began again to pour forth his story to a little slip of an officer in smart uniform, with large and squinting eyes, his legs encased in highly-polished boots, courteous and even attentive, frowning slightly, not from irritation (except perhaps a vague impatience at being detained at a time when the offices were closing) but from the effort of following the incoherent words of his interlocuter, trying with a will to understand, glancing at the clock, saying gently, 'Tomorrow,' and he insisting, protesting vehemently, imploringly, although he tried to keep calm, to remain clear, calling desperately to his assistance once again reason, justice, human rights, until the frail young man started, gave a sudden jump, choked, opened his eyes with disbelief (his voice rising, high-pitched at first, almost a scream, shocked and alarmed, then dropping, and stifling or gagging itself), repeating with a sort of terror the number of the regiment, of the division which it had been decided not to disarm, nor even to decimate, but to exterminate, to wipe off the face of the earth, and not again for any refusal to obey, any act of insubordination, poor conduct under fire, but simply because it existed, and then both of them (the two men) standing there a moment looking each other in the eyes, he in his elegant jacket as if he were a nonchalant tourist, his nonchalant flannel trousers, his eternal student appearance, his reddened eyelids, his hands, damaged by frostbite and injured by abscesses, which were not those of a tourist, the imperfectly healed scar on his neck, the other stiff in his well-cut, crisp uniform, his boots, his malaise, both breathing only, although perhaps a little more rapidly, he from having run, having spoken too long, too passionately, the other nonplussed, pensive, uncertain, and not a word more, only their eyes, their two looks, their two immobilities, their two silences, then suddenly both of them outside again, the one following the other (they did not find a taxi — no doubt the little officer had not a sufficient number of years of office work behind him to entitle him to an official car — one thing balancing the other however since if he had had sufficient office experience he would not have bestirred himself, car or no car . . .), or rather the second man following the military step of those sparkling polished boots, following again the avenue planted with palms, passing again under the plane trees in the fading light and in the deafening twitter of the sparrows in front

187

of the heaps of flowers, the cafés, the stalls selling headscarves, ex-votive photographs and effigies over which now proudly reigned, smiling indefatigably, fatherly, moustachioed, haunting and reticent, dressed in a cap or with his stubby hair uncovered, the inevitable and ubiquitous face of steel, then (the prison (the former shop) being in a sense the stomach of the beast) in the very lion's mouth, pacing (up and down) another corridor, alone this time, occasionally meeting the eyes (stared upon, peered at) of one of those men with the dismal look of dirty water, at once penetrating and distant, which he had now learned to recognise, whilst on the other side of the door through which the little officer had disappeared he could hear a long, heated conversation, bangings on the table, voices furiously raised, the frequently repeated name of the battalion commander, the door opening suddenly, the little officer emerging again, red and flushed, stiffer than ever, holding a piece of paper in his hand (something with a letter-head, impress and scribbled signature), grabbing his arm, pulling him quickly away — and of course it made not the slightest difference, since the battalion commander was later placed incommunicado (or perhaps shot that very evening — in any event he was never seen again), and that night they (that is to say he and the two others who had resolved like him to trust their animal instincts) slept in an abandoned building lot, shivering again although it was June and unable to sleep, curled up in a ball, their coat collars turned up, trembling in silence until the sun was high enough for them to resume their life as tourists, go and get shaved, have their shoes polished, take lunch in an expensive restaurant, all the while with the feeling of having been beaten black and blue, and having sand under their eyelids. Heaven knows how the consul had managed to get the necessary stamps: the train was due to leave at half past seven in the evening, but the engine-driver changed his mind as usual and it left at seven so that they missed it, had to wait until the next morning again, but this time it was all right, and as they took the precaution of travelling first class and eating in the dining-car they were taken once more for tourists travelling deluxe, and those who searched them from head to foot at the frontier did not apparently know (had apparently not been told — no doubt the beast moved more slowly than a train) what the

188

29th Division was. The first station after the frontier was a little fishing-town which in summer filled up with bathers. But it was still too early, the holiday-makers had not yet arrived, the café waiters were ill-tempered and rude because the four travellers (the woman was with them) were no longer obliged now to order the *menu gastronomique* or give huge tips. It was chilly weather, the water was dull and choppy. They bought newspapers and read an announcement that one of them had been arrested (this time the beast had surpassed itself), then they stopped reading the papers, they stopped talking even, they sat on the pebble beach and watched the water bobbing under a thin grey scum of sardine-heads, ashes, vegetables peelings, fish-guts, small bits of seaweed and cork.

There were no aeroplanes in that war, at least on that part of the front, and they only saw any once: a single plane, flying very high, whose fuselage could be seen glinting on and off in the sunlight in the wintry sky, of a pale and icy blue, but which seemed as if astray there, since they had not any weapon capable of bringing it down, although it moved very slowly, almost motionless, as if hung on an invisible wire, and which, after a moment or two, no doubt through boredom, out of range of the bursts from the old machine-gun and the rifle-fire crackling at the same time, at last turned lazily round, as if disgusted, contemptuous, dropping, as a mark of supreme disdain, supreme derision, like a bird on the wing relieving itself, a thin turd, a tiny, white explosion which remained floating behind it, filling out bit by bit, unfurling in the air, glittering as it broke up into a myriad of tiny particles which began tumbling with the same indolent slowness, turning over and over, whilst they grew bit by bit until the pages (defeatist tracts, incitements to desertion) fluttered and fell softly to the ground, dotting with clear patches the expanse of the stony hills against which stood out, coloured yellow (or rather that dirty ochre which is the colour of muddy water mixed with filth and stagnation in the bottoms of trenches), the lines broken and discontinuous which, from fortlet to fortlet, from ridge to ridge (that is to say what seemed in the pilot's eyes scarcely more than little bumps in the ground), vaguely indicated the positions occupied by the two enemy armies confronting each other, both equally chilled to the marrow, crawling with lice, and having absolutely nothing to do.

Although you died as well (or as badly) there as anywhere. For apart from the major hazard of pneumonia, against which they (the men in the trenches) struggled with the help of sodden woollens, there was also the danger of stray bullets, let off here and there quite haphazardly (that is, given the distance between the two lines and the antiquity of the weapons they had at their disposal, without the slightest chance of hitting the target) as a way of lessening their boredom (or perhaps also to convince themselves that the abominations they were enduring could justify being called war), but which (the bullets) ricocheting simply by chance had still enough strength to pierce a ribcage, smash a jaw or an arm (or else, for those unfortunate enough to be hit in the lower abdomen, to award them, by slicing off their sexual organs, what in army slang the English call with grim humour a 'D.S.O.', meaning thereby not the glorious 'Distinguished Service Order' but the unenviable 'Dickie Shot Off', which turns a warrior into a eunuch without supplying him with feminine graces in return), the main (and the most dangerous) field of confrontation (or, if you prefer, theatre of operations) in this sector being marked out by the four sides of an abandoned potato patch in which the two enemy camps came to forage in turn, the lifting of the potatoes being complicated by the fact that it had to be done in the position — fatiguing and especially awkward from the point of view of filling a sack — of a prostate target, under fire from a machine-gun which although of a model long obsolete still cut up the clods more or less all around (and fortunately more behind, the tendency of every gunman being always to aim too high) the harvester flat on his belly in the furrows.

However, in spite of these two hazards (pneumonia and spent bullets — there was also from time to time of course firing not exactly from artillery but from isolated guns which had it seemed been brought up and aimed at them in a haphazard fashion, no doubt so that all this should seem like real war, that is with the use of different combat units (infantry, artillery and aircraft) prescribed in the regulations, guns and ammunition of a type again so obsolete that they (the shells) plunged one time in three into the ground (or bounced off the stones) without going off, so that as the weapons of the two armies were of the same make and calibre you could, after reconditioning them, return the projectiles to their sender, and all along the front ran the legend of the old shell (it had even been given a nickname of its own) which travelled daily to and fro in this way, never exploding); so it was, then, that, in spite of these two hazards he (the volunteer) had after three months still not been given the impression that he was taking part in a war, he, the exterminating angel or archangel who had come a long way not only in order to redeem centuries of iniquity and debauch, as it was written in the Book which has nourished his childhood, but also to obey the other Bible which had in turn fed his adolescence, the work of another Moses, just as heavily bearded, lacking horns though and dressed in a lounge suit, sprung nevertheless from the same ancient people as his predecessors, updating as it were the stern exacting legislatorial god which they had made for themselves. As for him (the archangel) he calculated now, not without sadness, that in three months of this ordeal by frozen mud, filth and sleepless nights, he had enjoyed, in all, only three opportunities to fire his rifle (and then he seriously doubted when he could possibly have hit anyone) conscientiously nevertheless playing his part in what one of them (one of the other volunteers) called a bloody pantomime, gazing at the horizon on his night of sentry duty during which he felt himself slowly changing into a block of frozen meat and at the pink flashes of distant gunfire, the stars immovable in the black sky, listening to a chorus of frogs rising from the irrigation ditches, trying on his return to get warm by dipping into steaming tea — sent by the poor old Army and Navy Stores — biscuits which had also come from the shelves of that venerable emporium and, as a crowning humiliation, during the only mildly violent action he had been lucky enough to take part in (outside, that is, the patient extermination of lice which crawled over his testicles (he told how, close up, they looked like tiny lobsters) and the exploit (carried out on his own initiative and for his own personal satisfaction) of having crawled one night close enough to the forward positions occupied by the enemy sentries to hear them distinctly talking amongst themselves), finding himself, thanks to an inglorious abscess resulting from an inglorious scratch, with his arm in a sling, forced to huddle up in the trench bottom, plunged into a detective story called *The Missing Money-Lender* (the only personal item left in his possession after the hospital assistants had stolen everything else) and concerned only to shift his legs constantly out of the way as his comrades hurried stooping down the trench, flinging themselves on their knees and frantically digging, deepening the trench around him and scooping out small shelters to hide in.

So that (spring was upon them already, the crocuses and wild irises were already beginning to come through), when the battalion commander announced that he wanted fifteen volunteers for a raid he was the first to come forward, or rather leap forward, being anxious not to miss the opportunity (that is the opportunity which he was beginning to believe would be denied him, to really do battle at last for that to which he had dedicated his life, and for which he was going perhaps in a few hours to cease living, or to go on living henceforth with an arm, a leg, or half a face, or even his genitals blown away): a surprise attack as the battalion commander explained, at night (in virtue of the elementary principle expounded in campaign service manuals that in trench warfare it is extremely difficult and even impossible, if artillery is not available, to hazard an action in broad daylight without courting disaster), on the corner of the L-shaped salient formed by the enemy lines which they would seize under cover of darkness (because neither of the two armies had flares, any more than they had artillery). So the salient, the night attack, the tiny banal episode which, in the next day's communique would, depending on space available and on other needs, either quite simply be passed over in silence, or, if no other action was reported, be given exaggerated importance as a titanesque exploit, but which, whatever happened, was after all going to be for him a bit more than the monotonous 'bloody pantomime' which he had known up till then. And not fear — or at least fear seemed to him so indecent that it was incumbent upon him not only to betray none but even to devote no more attention to it than to one of those inescapable and unsavoury physical contingencies to which the body is subjected —, so taking steps to hide (and to hide even from himself) all manner of feeling (excitement, or a strange and suspicious joy) under which it (fear) could try to masquerade, concentrating in the hours which preceded the action all his mental capacities on the meticulous material preparations for the task he would have to carry out, getting totally absorbed in it like a mechanic or rather as a racing driver checks for the nth time his machine, the stationary mass of inert steel and piping which a few moments later will with a savage roar precipitate him (or rather precipitate towards him) victory, glory or death, with nonetheless this difference that when he would come to fling himself, to leap forward, he would not have before him an asphalt ribbon lined with bales of straw and thin fences bending under the weight of spectators dressed in caps advertising a brand of anisette but rather Corruption and Wickedness personified, his heart beating only perhaps a little faster, his voice perhaps only a little calmer and a little more level than usual whilst he busied himself conscientiously dirtying his bayonet, oiling his cart-ridges, and checking the pins on his grenades (that is those projectiles hastily put together, made out of a piece of tubing stuffed with explosive, fitted with a dangerous detonator and graced with the name of bombs), packing up a hunk of bread, three inches of red sausage (the kind which gives you the runs) and the cigar (he had received it in a parcel after he'd had everything filched in hospital) which he had been hoarding for this long-awaited day. Then it was time (a little after midnight) and pitch dark, and in theory the orders were that to prevent them from shooting each other by mistake white armlets would be worn, but there were no armlets — and one joker asked whether they could not arrange for the other side to wear them instead — and naturally the rain was pelting down, one of those torrential rains which fell without a break from the clouds rolling in off the sea to bump, pile up and burst against the mountains, so that before the men had barely started and had not even got to the place where they were to leave their own parapet they were already wallowing about in the sodden beet-fields, slipping sometimes up to the waist in an irrigation ditch, the cold mud and the water smelling foully of rotten reeds oozing gurgling over their boot-tops, making all together, or so it seemed to him (fifteen volunteers from another company had joined them and there were now about thirty of them) as much noise as a herd of elephants splashing about in a swamp or rather, he thought a little later raising his head and looking

193

behind him (but with a violent thump the battalion commander made him lower it again), as a bunch of tortoises (for they were not going very much faster) whose round and humped shapes bobbed heavily along as if, so to say, they had sprung from the very ground, as if the mud, the earth over which they were now crawling was silently heaving and seething — at least he hoped very much it was so, kicking himself (with a hunter's automatic instinct) that they had not taken the trouble beforehand of checking the wind's direction so as to approach at the right angle, then noticing that if the rain was still falling the wind had dropped, then realising that from whichever direction the wind might have come, had it been blowing, they were left no choice in the matter and that there was only one way of approaching the enemy lines, and that was unfortunately ahead: and still not fear (at least he was unaware that it bore that name: jumpy nervousness at the terrifying sound of the smallest stone rolling under someone's foot, the slightest rattle of a tin can, the impression of frightening slowness with time and distance multiplied, interminable, the endless progression, one minute an hour, a hundred metres several kilometres, his heart thumping more and more violently (breathlessness, he simply thought, the effort), progress becoming slower and slower so that before long he had the feeling that the world, the night, the whole earth had stopped moving and they were only crawling about on the same spot like worms without doing other than wait, terrified and wriggling in the dark and without moving an inch forward, for that which could not fail to happen, that is to say that a bullet would traverse their body, and then suddenly however he saw it (the enemy parapet), very high, it seemed to him, above them, and black against black (like spiky, threatening sentences written on the night), the barbed wire: unfortunately the battalion had only one pair of wire-cutters between them and of course that (the metallic grating, the click of the jaws of the pincers closing, the soft hiss of wire slackened, freed, whipping through the air) made another horrible noise in the silence, but still nothing except the monotonous pitter-patter of rain in the puddles, the unbelievable racket of his heart beating in his chest, and they were at the inner wire, and naturally they (the enemy) had heard them, let them approach to a fair distance, for before they had even had time to deploy after getting through the narrow gap in the wire, everything suddenly exploded together, that is to say there was a first shot and almost immediately, whilst in quick reply the first bomb was going off, a serried crackling, a line of little blue sparks lighting up and going out without a break, and so close that he could see and hear at the same time the flashes, the detonations and the snapping of the bullets, but above all the whole crazy inhuman racket of the bombs, that din (and more than din: the air, the earth shaken and ripped apart) which, even if one has experienced it already, . strikes whomever it deafens with something far stronger than fear: horror, amazement, shock, the sudden revelation that it is no longer something which man has any part in but matter only, unleashed, wild, furious, indecent (the mix, the combination of a few inert dusts, of ores, of things extracted from the earth and spontaneously catching fire, as it were, with the usual extreme violence of natural elements, bursting, breaking free as if to settle a score with or get even with man, in blind, insane vengeance), and he, flat on his face, crushed in this kind of cataclysm, of apocalypse, his eardrums shattered by the din, wrestling feverishly with the pin of his first bomb, cursing, realising after a while that he was twisting it in the wrong direction, then rising to his knees, tossing his arm briskly forward, throwing himself down again, flattening himself out, digging his face into the mud, then lifted bodily from the ground, blinded, enveloped in a blazing red blast, struck violently on the jaw, thinking 'This is it!' then realising that he had hit his own neck, rising to his knees again, flinging his second bomb, then everything pêle-mêle in a black and fiery muddle, a cacophany of shouts, orders, screams of pain: he running (that is, as a man mudded from head to foot can still run with his boots full of water, weighed down with rifle and a hundred and fifty cartridges, that is, in fact, walking rapidly, at most trotting along), his left arm bent idiotically over his left cheek (he was moving parallel to the line of fire) as if an arm had ever shielded anyone from a bullet, then his third bomb (and screams once more, and then delirium, barbarous, primitive, bloodthirsty joy, ecstasy, triumph) then the shattered enemy parapet, trench and dugout, the stench of cordite, then he, the exterminating angel, limping now along the embanked earth, chasing and lunging with his bayonet at the shadowy

195

form of a half-naked man, his shoulders covered in a dark blanket, bent double beneath him, scampering along the communication-trench, while he tried to remember the lessons of the boxing instructor in the aristocratic public school where he had received his education, gripping his rifle clumsily by the butt, kicking out clumsily, lunging, prodding the steel point which he was trying to ram between the shoulder blades of Iniquity in flight (a poor devil, quite obviously, who had been press-ganged into fighting), missing him, stumbling in his haste, picking himself up again, Iniquity gaining ground, vanishing into the darkness, leaving him behind, foiled, frustrated, breathless — and no longer afraid, although from the enemy's other posts a concentrated fire was now being directed at them in a way that made for an unbroken drum-like roar, stabbing the darkness with innumerable greenish flashes, but at too great a range, and especially no more bombs, so that there was a period of relative calm, most of their rifles being jammed with mud, those with weapons which still worked firing more or less at random, even at their own medical orderlies, the confusion still more or less absolute until they managed to build a barricade to protect their rear with the help of sandbags dragged from the parapet and dumped into a rough heap: so no longer feeling afraid, feeling indeed nothing any longer except horror at the darkness, the chaos, the din, the mud, the sandbags, as heavy as donkeys, the rotten sacking which was splitting open, the damp earth dribbling down his neck, up his sleeves, thinking: 'This is war! Isn't it bloody? Isn't it bloody!' then realising that he was talking to himself, shouting out loud in the midst of the din, and addressing not the others, but the night, the noise, the bullets which passed over their heads, then when the barricade was high enough another respite of which he took advantage to ask himself calmly whether he was afraid, coming to the conclusion that he was not since he could now ponder the issue and no longer, as a short while before, feel sick with terror, but it did not last, not the absence of fear but the respite, and once more he succeeded in lobbing his bomb in the right place, throwing himself flat on his face, shaken as before by the explosion, and then instantly afterwards the howling, the screams of pain, until the thing, the horror, became as it were familiar to him, lobbing his bombs methodically now, protected by the parapet, calmly, in the continuing din, but now there were only eight or nine of them, and not even a light submachine-gun, and no reinforcements, and obviously the attack on the other salient had failed, because the order came to retire, which was no easy matter, loaded down as they were with their loot, the clutch of rifles, and taking it in turns to haul along the ammunition-box weighing fifty kilos, wandering in the dark and in the mud, slithering about, falling down and picking themselves up again, with bullets now coming at them from every angle, including from their own side, but still, in the end, after changing their direction a couple of times, they made it: day was starting to break, the sky was growing a little lighter in the east, the landscape was emerging slowly from the night, getting clearer, the tall weeds, first grey then white, shining with moisture, metallic in that light which is not exactly light, that is, not yet capable of colour, then, above the hills the sky suddenly became pale yellow, changing to orange (a narrow strip), then pink, then grey again, although the rain had stopped, then it was fully light, a few shots still cracking out snapping here and there like the last fireworks at a fête, everything gradually getting quiet then stopping altogether, and in the bottom of the trench into which one after the other they jumped (dropped) the stagnant water was still the same dirty yellow, the earth greyish round about, desolate, the poplars still bare, they too shining with rain, and he re-emerged almost at once from the stinking dug-out in which not having had the energy even to take their equipment off his companions had fallen asleep: so he remained squatting on the firestep, his feet drawn up in the dry underneath him, reaching into his pocket for the cigar. By pure chance it had not broken: he lit it.

The snag with those bombs, which were more or less home made (although it was the government which was now supplying them — which gave rise to their thought that they were dealing with a government which was itself more or less home made), was that they were just as liable to fail to explode when they were hurled, as go off of their own accord or as a result of a wrong movement as one carried them about one's person, so that, not to speak of the discomfort they caused a

197

sleeper — or at least for someone who was trying to get to sleep — by digging into his ribs (he had hooked them on to his belt), the dread of setting them off as he rolled over, in those sudden fits and starts which dreams sometimes give rise to, was sufficient by itself to keep you awake, or at least to act as an alarm signal whenever you felt the least bit inclined to doze off.

Not to mention the fact that the baby was crying ceaselessly. Not to mention the fact that a dusty curtain or a torn, stiff, brittle, harsh piece of stage canvas, like the material which he had rolled himself up in (all the while taking care that he was treating the bombs with due respect), hardly made either for a particularly comfortable form of bedding. Not to mention also that the attics and passageways of a cinema (or of a music hall: he did not know exactly: seemingly both at once: at that period cinemas used, between two houses, to put on stage various turns, arcobats, tightrope walkers or jugglers) offered nothing very comfortable themselves, or only an old mattress on which two huge women were sleeping (singers, perhaps?) and a baby, silent this one, which was not without its unusual, even disturbing side.

Not to mention, on top of everything else (as is always the case in that kind of situation), that no one really had much idea what was going on, except perhaps the baby which was crying ceaselessly, red in the face, with its fists clenched and its eyes closed, with that dogged despair, that stubborn dread, the obstinate premonition of wailing creatures (or lowing: like those oxen, at night, shut up in wagons standing on the tracks of a marshalling yard and bellowing dolefully) not yet gifted with speech but perhaps with some clairvoyant ability which enables them to see in reduced form the terrifying sum of suffering and misery which will be their lot, and which disappears (the gift, the clairvoyance) as soon as the comforting use of words is substituted for it, strangled until then in tears and protestations.

As for explaining what women and babies were doing there, and why women and babies were mixed up with men (and boys) armed with all manner of nondescript weapons (and who morever tried to steal them from each other — the boys especially), wandering in the rambling, dirty, dusty building, filled with broken furniture, between cabaret decors still upright (on one of the stages — there seemed to be several theatres — a

198

grand piano, strangely intact, was still in place), was no doubt once again another question as vain and irrelevant as persisting stubbornly (he tried for a time, then gave up) in learning, in going through every ill-lit nook and cranny, the complicated layout of a building normally used for the projection of westerns and love stories, alternating with acts by conjurors, contortionists or by dancers with clacking heels, seen through the bluish haze of the acrid smoke of cheap cigars and the soft rustling of bags of sweets.

Just in case, an armed lookout had been posted at each window and down below, in the street, a small group of trusted reliable men stopped and questioned — also just in case — the few passers-by who were hurrying home. What one was sure of (insofar as one could be sure of anything) was that the government (the homemade government) had nothing to do with any of it. One knew only that the telephone exchange had stopped working (at least one thought one knew — few people at that time being on the telephone, at least the sort of people who were gathered there: in fact calls were interrupted only for a couple of hours). The fact remains that beside the shooting which had broken out here and there during the afternoon, something must have happened over that way, which (so far as the telephone exchange was concerned) means, in a modern city, near the site of an organ corresponding more or less to the equivalent of the brain in the human body.

That was how the first night passed — that is the first slice of darkness (about eight hours, it being May); in any case it could hardly have been called a night's rest, because at three in the morning he was shaken awake (if, that is, one can wake someone from somnolence: a sleep likewise homemade as it were, or, in other words, a knocked-together sort of sleep) so that he was at once in a state to undertake historic actions, that is to say in that semi-consciousness and that sottishness thanks to which the fatigue of the body and the mind, the diminution of intelligence and of the faculties of perception, make bearable what under other circumstances (that is with a sated and rested body) it (the mind) would never accept without revolt — or at least without indignation, or at least complaint. Particularly since there was no light outside: no doubt the telephone exchange should not alone have been thought to have ceased functioning —

199

although he had succeeded the day before (but was it the day before? in any case it was dark then too) in digging out in an office (the impresario's, no doubt, or the cinema manager's) an old directory and had been able to get in touch with a friend who had assured him that all was well and, to prove it, had brought two packets of Lucky Strike: a real lucky strike, as the name implied, through dark streets patrolled by men with their finger on the trigger who were only too keen to open fire, if only to make a noise (people for whom killing a man was of no more consequence — although infinitely more pleasurable — than killing a rabbit), which raised the act of heroism to the level of the weight of a few grams of tobacco, or, through combustion, about two milligrams of nicotine and three of tar for the two packets, making in all several kilotons of courage which, at the price courage (physical at least) fetched in times such as those, did not amount to much, except that the brand of cigarettes could only be found on the black market, an aspect which, after all, increased the quoted odds somewhat.

And three o'clock in the morning, then, and at least, at the window where he had been posted (not by the battalion commander: by the man whom he did not know but who seemed to be in charge, about whom all he says is that he was young and handsome) he could no longer hear the baby crying (or not so loud, anyway: in the building's lower depths, as it were, heard only as a stifled lamentation, from within the womb, so to speak, complaining in anticipation at the subsequent ineluctable replacement of darkness by light, and at what would then result), while in the half-light (that is in what was no longer night and was not yet day) he was looking out of his window at the swarming mass of men and women — and even of small children, he wrote later — working frantically (although half, even all of them (and not only the small children) would have been incapable of saying what it was all in aid of, did not even wish to know) to build a barricade to protect the cinema entrance behind a wall of ripped-up cobblestones and of sandbags filled with shingle taken from under the cobblestones (so that things were now, literally, upside down). So that when it was quite day and whilst there came to him, louder and louder, the sounds of rifle-fire and detonations which were shaking the town, growing in intensity and increasing in volume at the same rate as the light (as if it too were endowed with explosive power), he (the lookout posted at the window) was able to form a more precise picture of the situation, at least in so far as it existed on a purely local level: on the one hand the two barricades protecting the entrance to the premises (as he called the cinema and hotel next door which served as headquarters to the adepts of his philosophical sect), on the other a café filled with uniformed men (who perhaps were not too sure either what it was all in aid of, except that they were being fired upon because they were in uniform — just as those who were firing at them were doing it for no better reason) occupied, for the moment (and perhaps also quite at random), at taking pot-shots themselves at a head which, he said, was sticking up for all the world like a coconut at a fair, coming and going as the bullets snapped around it behind the shelter of a newspaper kiosk (closed, naturally), an entertainment which the occupants of the premises soon put an end to (but without warning him, so that he jumped, his eardrums shattered by the violence of the explosion, his eyes searching for the field-gun, then realising that they (the hand-grenades) made here (that is in town, the sound reverberating between stone buildings) double the noise they would produce in open country) by bowling down the pavement cylindrical devices which, carried by the slope of the avenue, ended up exploding in front of the café situated a little further down, the amusing game of skittles in danger of continuing indefinitely when the battalion commander (he had suddenly appeared and he (the lookout relieved of his duty) was now talking to him, both of them, although their eyes were red with lack of sleep and their features drawn by fatigue, speaking with that kind of tranquil detachment inculcated by familiarity with danger, or perhaps by exhaustion — or perhaps, simply, by disgust) decided to intervene, thereby accomplishing what, he related, even after a sleepless night lying on two bombs, rolled up in a stage curtain, even in that state (one conducive to historic deeds) and even after having had a quick wash in cold water, he could never have accomplished by himself, even, he said, for his weight in gold, ordering (the battalion commander) the bomb-throwers to get back inside the building, after which he moved forward, casually brandishing his stick (as when he was inspecting trenches), in a silence suddenly more terrifying

201

than the din (that is to say the sounds near or distant of gunfire and explosions seemed all at once to have become inaudible, to such an extent that one could hear at every step the click of his heels and of the metal tip at the end of his stick), alone, without cover, on the central pavement of the avenue, in front of rifles pointing at him from inside the café which, either from deep-rooted respect for authority (although the battalion commander was not wearing any uniform, unless his kind of gentleman farmer's get-up — the stick, the leggings, the drab corduroy breeches and the dull jacket unmarked by any distinctive badges of rank — could be considered a uniform, a battledress of sorts), or out of amazement, remained (the pointing rifles) silent, halting (the battalion commander) in the middle of the carriageway, tucking his stick under his arm like a riding-whip to keep his hands free, calmly drawing his revolver from its holster, bending down, ostentatiously laying it at his feet on the asphalt, straightening up again, grasping hold of his stick once more, and waiting, until one of the occupants of the café came out in his turn, without a jacket, in shirtsleeves but decked out in well-cut breeches and boots shining with spit-and-polish, the battalion commander and the newcomer parleying, the battalion commander still motionless, leaning on his stick, the man with the gleaming boots gesticulating vehemently until they parted, the battalion commander picking up his revolver again, putting it unhurriedly back in its holster, his stick once more under his arm, then coming back to the barricade and ordering one of his men, pointing out the target with his stick, to touch off two bombs which had rolled without exploding a short distance beyond the café; after which a sort of armistice, or armed truce, was established, at least in that sector, the avenue remaining deserted however, all the corrugated steel shutters pulled down over the shop windows, two trams immobilised at the spot where their drivers had abandoned them precipitately the day before when the first shots had rung out, and two cars, one of them the battalion commander's, riddled with bullets, their tyres burst, their windscreens smashed, as if sunk on their bellies amidst the broken glass, covering the pavement of the café windows shattered by bursting bombs.

On top of the cinema roof were two more or less ornamental cupolas built in that iced-cake heavily decorated style, at once

202

medieval, moorish and Bavarian, in line with the taste of the bankers and building societies by whose efforts that huge town had grown, which during his long hours of duty he (the lookout again on guard) observed with its vast expanse of tiled roofs above which rose here and there (like pustules or blisters) slated domes sparkling in the sun and a few Gothic spires beyond which he discerned the glittering, calm, motionless sea. Just short of the roof the topmost branches of the plane trees of the avenue reached, with their delicate spring shoots, their foliage of a still uncertain green, just beginning to take a shine, topped by the pale ochre of the young leaves trimming the tips of the boughs with a light dusting in the soft May light, and which he (the lookout) could see each morning a fraction more unfurled, as if the buds were taking advantage of the darkness, of the truce brought by the nights, the cessation of the din of bombs and gunfire, to get free, to extricate themselves a little further from their sheath, and to unfold, like a delicate russet down, the tender and fragile blossoming, the tender, irrepressible renewal, faithful to the rhythm of the seasons, blind, formidable, patient, above the roadway strewn with broken glass and branches chopped off by gunfire, like the débris of some festival, the litter of some triumphal procession, curling and slowly shrivelling.

So that, as long as he did not lean out of the window (from further down the street, from the building occupied by the Youth League, a stubborn and alert sniper, moved no doubt by some morbid obsession or other (perhaps only of adding to the noise himself, since he regularly missed him) let fly at him with his rifle whenever he did) he (the lookout) could keep a watch on the café held by the men in uniform with whom they (the occupants of the cinema) exchanged from time to time not the odd bullet, not even insults, but scraps of conversation if not fraternal at least friendly enough for them to result on occasion, despite one man dead and another wounded in the shootings and bombings of the first day, in the sending of a dozen bottles of beer (the café seemed to have an inexhaustible supply of it) which was greeted with satisfaction because of course, as is the rule in any historic event, what the cinema's defenders were chiefly concerned about (apart from the lack of sleep and the boredom which he (the lookout) tried to overcome with reading

— not *The Missing Money-lender* this time, but a succession of Penguin Library titles) was food, drink and minimal comfort. However, none of the authors chosen by Penguin had apparently thought of writing a book (although some such must have existed) about this kind of situation, which might have enabled him to deal with the problem that faced him, that is to understand the whys and the wherefores of what he was doing there, sitting day after night and night after day (around noon the roofing baked by the sun became burning hot) listening to the racket, by turns increasing, decreasing, dying away, then breaking out again furiously, of an invisible battle (because, apart from the noise, nothing seemed to be happening and he never saw anything other than the rolling roofs, the pastry-like domes and the glittering sea merely changing from darkness to light, then from light to darkness, then again from darkness to light without anything else altering noticeably, so that after the 'bloody pantomime' which had lasted (which he had endured) the whole winter in the hills, there now followed what he later called a 'nightmare of noise without movement'), and (although it was said that in the working-class suburbs the men in uniform had been driven back), the question (or rather one of the questions) which still remained unanswered was who exactly was shooting at whom (unless one supposed that the home-made government had suddenly passed a law enabling itself to move to the stage of industrial — or, if you prefer, institution-alised — manufacture). In the end (and except for a night on the alert in which there was talk of attacking the occupants of the café from the roofs, which gave him the opportunity to check the pins on his bombs and the smooth functioning of the breech of his revolver, but in the event — perhaps in consideration of the bottles of beer — the attack was called off) he decided (in spite of the din and the ever-vigilant sniper posted at the window of the Youth League, the men in uniform had lifted off a few cane seats from the barricade of chairs and café tables which they had erected; these were now placed on the pavement and they were peaceably sitting on them, with their rifles simply across their knees, smoking little black cigars and gesturing from time to time in a peaceful, friendly way in the direction of the cinema), in the end, then, he decided that there was nothing to decide, that it was all simply absurd and, what is more, deadly boring, since, by virtue of the same principle expounded in the manual of trench warfare, there can be no genuine solution in street fighting, either, without the intervention of artillery (and quite obviously neither of the two (but perhaps there were more than two?) parties to the conflict could — or would — have recourse to it), so that in the end, if the whole business was pretty violent, the violence was balanced by inertia, the one counter-acting the other (he was later to realise that he had been wrong about that): now he had simply had enough of the whole business, even doubting (he was wrong about that too) whether it deserved to be called history with a capital H; clearly it no longer held his interest although (since he had begun) he could only remain sitting on the roof doing nothing except read the tedious Penguin volumes one after another. When it came to the point, if it had not been for his stomach, more or less empty except for a few bars of chocolate, complaining increasingly and racked by cramp, and the persistent sniper of the Youth League, it seemed less and less likely to him that he was taking part in a historic action: in any case, if action it was, it was appearing in the form — noisy, it is true, and loud — of non-action, unless it be admitted (which was possible after all, if scarcely uplifting) that History reveals itself through (is made up of) the accumulation of insignificant, even ludicrous details, such as those he recalled later, for example:

indifferent to the din and in the soft light of a fine morning in the soft springtime a fashionably-dressed woman walking a little dog on the deserted avenue:

a soberly-dressed, stiff-looking group of people (he supposed they were going to a funeral) were trying persistently to cross the square at the top of the avenue and were forced back each time by the no less persistent fire which burst forth each time from a machine gun perched on the top floor in the huge O of the sign of a requisitioned grand hotel

the appearance of newspapers (because they went on being printed and distributed, God knows how) so heavily censored that some of their pages (usually the front, with the editorial) were more or less completely blank

the dining room of the hotel where his wife was staying (he managed one evening, between two bouts of sentry duty, to reach it by slipping through the dark streets bristling with barricades), where the guests had taken refuge in the crowded back room (the windows of the one in front had been shattered by bullets and the shutters were closed), and where ceremonious waiters placed before each diner (they included newspaper correspondents, double — or treble — agents, lorry drivers and a few women, some journalists, some not, some pretty, some not) a single sardine, accompanied, it is true, on request, if one could afford the exhorbitant prices, by a vintage wine

one afternoon when there was a lull and suddenly the avenue, the streets, bathed in sunlight, having been deserted until then, and with no other sign of life than sporadic firing (unless, so far as he was concerned, he could call a sign of life the fact that he had spent, since the beginning of the affair three days before, about sixty hours (he worked it out) without sleep and more or less without eating), filled suddenly with pedestrians, with the shops open again, everyone hurrying in search of provisions, responding to a reflex more visceral than logical (the shops (at least those which sold food) having been (except those charging prohibitive prices) almost empty for some time), so that when one after another the steel shutters came down again with a metallic rumbling getting ever closer as the firing started up again and the streets emptied once more, it was hard to say whether the firing had only stopped to let people see for themselves that there was nothing to buy in the shops or whether the latter were shutting noisily to allow the shooting to start afresh, the lookout on the roof inclining more and more to the view that his ignorance or the inadequacy of his political (or philosophical) education was such that the practice (or how should it be designated: the exercise?) of politics (or of philosophy) caused him an indifference and a lassitude (if not a repulsion) growing from hour to hour from sleepless night to sleepless night and from day without food to day without food while apparently the men in uniform who occupied the café went short of neither, which no doubt determined their ultimate success not only on the ground where they gradually increased in number (those of the café, plus others again brought in as reinforcements by the government raised beyond any possible doubt now to the industrial level), but what is more (by reason of the eternal prestige attaching to a uniform, and of what it symbolises or rather materializes: good food and power) with the female population, another not negligible success: patrolling therefore at this time in the streets as if in conquered territory whilst the defenders posted behind barricades with desperately empty bellies were abandoning them one by one, then (the uniformed men) strolling peaceably, no longer in ranks or in groups but in twos or even singly (if that is the right expression, since each one carried henceforth, in addition to his well-polished cartridge-belts and his equally well-polished holster, a pretty girl hanging onto his arm), indifferent to the increasingly rare and increasingly detached bangs of a few shots fired by a few belated snipers, whilst another noise gained ground: that of the paving stones taken from the barricades and restored to their original purpose (one of the journalists — or double agents — staying in the hotel remarked facetiously that to save trouble in this town the paving stones should be numbered, which would allow the periodical building and demolition of the barricades to be carried out in a speedier and more rational manner): the trams moving again, the passers-by going about their usual business again (that is, chiefly, to stretch out in long queues in front of the doors of empty grocers' shops), the uniformed police (backed up as always by other defenders of the peace, in plain clothes this time, but no less active) carrying out their various tasks, some (those without uniform) drafting up proclamations, writing articles or delivering speeches (not censored, these) or else drawing up lists of names, the others (those dressed in elegant close-fitting uniforms) strolling with pretty girls hanging onto their arms and slowing them down, becoming prettier still, languid, their breasts heaving, amorously pressing their warm young flesh against the polished leathers and well-fed bodies, in front of the windows of the shops in fashionable districts permanently open again at last and offering their shelves tottering under delicatessen, sweets and multicoloured confectionery, candy pink, pistachio, candy green, cerise, candy yellow.

In his biography of Cardinal Manning, whose conversion to Roman Catholicism shook Victorian England, Lytton Strachey relates that two of the great man's contemporaries lost their faith during these upheavals, with this difference however that in the case of one of them the event turned out to be rather like the loss of a heavy portmanteau which one afterwards discovers to have been full of brickbats and old rags, whilst the other was made so uneasy by it that he went on looking for it everywhere as long as he lived. A brilliant Oxford graduate, the future Cardinal Manning belonged with Gladstone and Wilberforce to that category of young men for whom the world lay open, for, says Strachey, they were rich, well-connected and above all 'endowed with an infinite capacity for making speeches'. Among these speechifiers, Manning seems to have been won over by a theologian (or should he be called a theoretician?), Newman by name, who demonstrated that the Church of England was indeed the true Church, but that she had been under an eclipse since the reformation — that is, in fact, since she had begun to exist. The Christian Religion was still preserved intact by the English priesthood, but it was preserved, as it were, unconsciously — a priceless deposit, handed down blindly from generation to generation, and subsisting less by the will of man than through the ordinance of God as expressed in the mysterious virtue of the Sacraments. Christianity, in short, had become entangled in a series of unfortunate circumstances from which it was the plain duty of Newman and his friends to rescue it. They never ceased to wonder, Strachey goes on, that this task had been reserved for them; a small number of seventeenth-century divines had perhaps been vouchsafed, by divine favour, glimpses of the truth, but they were, it had to be admitted, glimpses and nothing more. No, the waters of the true Faith had dived underground at the Reformation, and they were waiting for the wand of Newman to strike the rock before they should burst forth once more in the light of day. The whole matter, no doubt, was Providential — what other explanation could there be?

Having returned to the front line towards the end of May 1937 after a short leave and a winter spent in the trenches on the Aragon front, O . . . is hit during a tour of inspection of the forward outposts by a bullet which goes clean through his neck. After receiving makeshift first aid on the spot and then treatment in various hospitals, he is finally invalided out and, with his discharge ticket in his pocket, returns to Barcelona where he arrives at the end of June to find himself immediately on the run from the police.

Later he will recall that what he felt when the bullet struck him was the sensation of being at the centre of an explosion, of hearing all round him what seemed like a loud bang, and of being blinded by a flash of light. He sees the sandbags of the parapet recede into an immense distance, and the next moment his head hits the ground with a violent bang. It does not hurt. He has only a numbed, dazed feeling. From this moment onwards, and apart from the few weeks during which he is transferred from hospital to hospital (that is when his seriously wounded condition excludes him to some extent from what is going on), he will, for various other reasons, go on living in that kind of daze which will not cease growing, in which he still finds himself when, back in England, he begins writing the book in which he goes back over what he has experienced from the moment he left there some seven months earlier to the moment when he again finds himself, more or less intact physically (except for the scar of the still-fresh wound to his neck) but reduced nervously to the condition of a man awoken with a start from a nightmare, bathed in sweat, still shaking with uncontrollable trembling, gazing in a kind of disbelief at the lush meadows the railway smothered in wild flowers, the horses in the meadows, with their shining coats, the idly meandering rivers bordered by willows, the gardens full of larkspur, the streets, the red buses, the cricketers, the passers-by in bowler hats, the pigeons in Trafalgar Square, the benign policemen dressed in blue, in the manner of someone who fails to convince himself that either what he is living through or what he has lived through is quite real.

Perhaps he hopes that in writing his adventure he will enable some coherent meaning to emerge from it. Firstly the fact that he will list in chronological order events which are inextricably mixed in his memory or reveal themselves in accordance with emotional criteria ought, in some measure, to explain them. He also thinks perhaps that within this first order the necessities of syntactic construction will bring out clearly the connections between cause and effect. There will however be gaps in his story, things left unclear, even contradictions. Either because he takes certain facts for granted (his past: the education he received in the aristocratic college of Eton, the five years he spends in the imperial police in the Indies, his sudden resignation, the àscetic life he inflicts upon himself afterwards, going to live in a depressed district in the East End, working as a dishwasher in Paris restaurants, his first literary efforts, his political opinions), or because, for one reason or another, he passes over his own motivations, in silence (for example the steps he takes on his first return from the front to join the faction to which he has up till then been opposed as soon as he realises that, being about to gain power, it is more likely to afford him better than any other the opportunity to achieve his aims, even if it means joining in against his former comrades in the repression of which he will himself be a victim). Indeed, as he writes his confusion will only get worse. In the end he reminds the reader of someone who undeterred by discouragement bleakly persists in going over again the instructions for use and assembly of an elaborate piece of machinery, unable to resign himself to the fact that the loose parts which he has been sold and which he keeps trying to put together, rejects in turn, takes up again, cannot be fitted together to make either the machine described by the directions in the catalogue or quite clearly any other machine, but only a grating set of gears with no other function but to destroy and kill, before falling to pieces and destroying itself.

To imagine him therefore, sitting at a table (he does not say where, except that it was once again England), the table perhaps placed before an open window, looking out on to the peaceful countryside, or moorland, or at the sea, or a street at the end of which he can again see cars stopping at the traffic light, pedestrians crossing, the cars moving off again, people going into shops, coming out again, buying newspapers, leading children by the hand, passing each other by without haste, the street lamps lighting up at nightfall, the traffic and the pedestrians gradually thinning out, then the untroubled night setting in completely in which the audience goes undisturbed to the cinema, returns untroubled from it without quickening its pace, taking refuge in a doorway only because a downpour is brewing or has burst and not because they have heard the sound of a motor-car engine, the car itself when it goes by carrying only people who are going home equally peacefully and not four or

210

five men ready to spring out holding a gun in their hands, the street soon almost completely deserted, the lighted windows going out one after the other, everyone tucked up in bed inside the houses, proud Victorian dwellings with shiny glossed peristyles, or trim cottages, or dark dripping rows of blackish brick, or even plain slums, but still nevertheless places in which one can sleep knowing that one will be dragged out of bed only by the ringing of the alarm clock and not by the sound of rifle or pistol butts banging savagely on the door, and the night fading little by little, the dawn breaking, and in the suburbs where washing hangs in narrow backyards, no body lies riddled with bullets in the gutter or on waste ground and the steel shutters and gates raised or drawn back in the morning by the shopkeepers, the grocer, the butcher, the baker, and the shops serving as proper shops and not as prisons in which those crammed into them have just about enough room to sit down, the other prisons being already full and not with pickpockets or burglars, but with people whose only offence is not to think in the same way as the ways of thinking which have been elevated to the status of laws by people with enough power to send out into the night men armed with rifles and revolvers who can stop and kill anyone they please without seeking the permission or even the advice of anyone else, and in any case not that of the half-dozen politicians looking like commercial travellers, with their airs of choirboys or overweight monks, their double or treble chins, their bass voices, their tortoise-shell glasses, the bags under their eyes, incapable of doing anything except bestowing ministerial titles on themselves, posing obligingly for photographers, conferring (endlessly) in an undertone in window embrasures, getting themselves cheered in political meetings by emphasising their words with their fists on the table, and turning aside with bent backs, spreading their arms wide to indicate helplessness when questioned about the cars at night, the prison-shops, the bodies found in gutters at daybreak, or the disappeared who were never seen again.

He tries to make all that comprehensible. Quite obviously he is writing (or rather speaking) with a particular audience in mind, an audience whose inclinations and opinions he knows and whose reactions he can foresee. On the one hand his upbringing (or his dignity — or his natural decency?) preserves

211

him from all boastfulness (he will even be inclined by a kind of affectation to describe his actions in the most critical circumstances in a way that is, if not ridiculous, at least somewhat ironical), on the other hand, in order to carry conviction, he tries (pretends?) to stick to facts (only later on will he try to write a commentary on them), livening his account with just enough local colour to prevent it from having the dryness of a straightforward report, giving it more persuasiveness, credibility, through several notations of those details, those eyewitness aspects, which every competent journalist knows constitute the best guarantees of authenticity of a piece of reporting, especially when they are inserted into a form of writing which presents itself as neutral (he has recourse to short sentences, he eschews wherever possible value-loaded adjectives and generally anything which might appear to give the appearance of a partisan or tendentious interpretation of events, for all the world as if he had not been closely involved in them but had been a dispassionate witness concerned only with gathering information).

Indeed, he is constantly attentive to the effect he is producing. Sitting there at his table, it will be as if he were talking to himself in the silence, interrupting himself perhaps from time to time to raise his hand to his neck, to touch the scar made by the bullet which has half sliced through his vocal chords, as if, to convince himself that he has not dreamt it all, then starting to write again, or rather to talk in his toneless, slightly husky voice, sounding like a gasp, with his attention very much turned to his invisible audience of the quick and the dead, at once incredulous and attentive, an audience made up of people who are with a few variations like so many faithful replicas of himself, cast in the same mould of that rigorous and puritan education, filling the colleges and ivy-coloured Gothic buildings of the old universities with lanky, bony young men with shaggy flaxen hair, slightly prominent teeth, lips always apart as if they had some difficulty in breathing as a result of badly treated adenoids or a blocked nostril from the blow of a hockey stick or the studs of a boot during one of those surreptitious knockabouts fought on or rather in waterlogged pitches, transformed by the rain into swamps in which the jerseys and shorts vanish under the blackish mud which also bespatters the exhausted, asphyxiated faces, lifted later under the scalding sprays of the showers, the abundant flow of which gradually reveals the chests and calves scored with blood gashes, the pink penises in their nests of reddish hair, the long milky bodies dotted with freckles, ghostly as in the clouds of stale steam, like some preraphaelite allegory of vulnerable, fragile flesh inhabited by a tough and inflexible determination. It was in December that he arrived in Barcelona, leaving behind him the country which he had slowly come to consider neither more nor less, he says, than a brigands' den, peopled with cynical tough guys, detestable old ladies busied with the ceremony of sipping with austere gravity in tearooms the contents of steaming cups (and on the other side of the glass the black, wet façades, the signs and windows of shops reflected in the wet asphalt, the wet passers-by, the buses with their high red shells moving slowly forward, swaying one after the other without making much progress down Oxford Street or Knightsbridge, the evening papers' placards with their tele-graphic style, the paper-sellers with their incomprehensible accents, the piles of damp newspapers, their news stories which, he will say later on, were nothing but lines of words, sequences of sounds yapped by husky, mechanical voices, gnomes with faces of wrinkled leather between their caps and their raised collars, their jackets with wringing wet, glistening shoulders, their leather palms blackened by printer's ink and metal coins, like a sort of robot fed with bronze, unreal creatures, minor deities at crossroads or tube station exits placed there to bellow out at the tops of their voices above the roar of the traffic their jarring cries, indefatigably intoning with the indifference characteristic of public announcers or blasé prophets their monotonous and daily litany of blood, murder and death, and he himself perhaps (O.) in one of those tearooms, or perhaps sitting aloof in one of those smoke-filled, noisy places stinking of warm beer, as indifferent to the old ladies as to the hubbub and the drunken singing, thrumming nervously a wet newspaper folded on the table or rolled into a cylinder in one of his hands, speaking in a hollow, determined voice to one of those girls (or rather young women) dressed in a trench coat shining with raindrops, with reddish or auburn hair, at once mannish and matronly, who is listening with knitted brows to what the Eton old boy is trying to explain to her, able still to hear outside the

213

mournful annunciators of disasters bawling in the rain and the night, their haunting voices arriving muffled like a noise in the background — or again, instead of the tea room and the loud cacophony of the drinkers, one of these bedsits with threadbare carpeting in which the gas fire turns cold without anyone noticing, and instead of the young woman three or four replicas of one and the same character, more or less identical whether they are twenty or thirty, that is identically dressed and speaking with the same studied casualness expressing themselves in solemn, thoughtful, laconic tones, taking pains to suppress as something obscene, unseemly, any show of emotion, capable of severity towards themselves in inverse proportion to their romanticism, their deceptive build and, their eternal student looks: their faces too pink or too pale, their paradoxical and threadlike physique of tireless long distance runners, their voices calm, phlegmatic and passionate raised turn and turn about, they themseves sitting in shabby leather armchairs, or on the floor, propped against the walls, their legs bent amid the shaky piles of Stravinsky records or of the sort of books and pamphlets which have short, neutral, educational titles, in drab stitched wrappers, with their pages covered in serried characters, their profusion of endless and painstaking diagrams, their appearance of textbooks written for night school students, to those practical guides which can be found in the do-it-yourself department at large stores, except that from their very inertia, from their utilitarian, greyish aspect, emanates that kind of concentrated violence peculiar to the packing materials round explosives, as if what they contained was something like nitroglycerine in the shape of printed paper, like what continued to be secreted from beyond the grave by the inert and formidable corpse of the prophet with imposing whiskers, respectably dressed in a lounge suit and starched shirt, at rest in a neighbouring cemetery with raked paths as one after the other on the stone which covers him the successive pious heaps of floral tributes decked with red ribbon wilt and fade.)

He has only recently married and the last book he wrote is still in the press when he suddenly leaves. What he has not foreseen is that in a few hours (the time it takes to jump into a train, then from the train into a boat, then from the boat into another train, to see on waking the vines, olive trees and stony hills gradually replacing the meadows and green slopes) he will find himself flung (he will fall) into something for which he will have been prepared neither by books, nor by what he has been able to learn on his own account during his successive experiences in the police service, then in the poverty-stricken districts of the East End, or again during the period in which he earned his living as a dishwasher, that is a world in which violence, predation and murder are permanent features, and not in a more or less sporadic, more or less hypocritical, relatively codified fashion, but free of all mask, all curb, without even those conventions which distinguish the underhand fisticuffs of the sports field from straightforward acts of butchery between neighbouring tribes, or rather from the savage oppression of the weakest by the strongest. He will look with the eye of indifference as, beyond the windows of his compartment, the monotonous rows of sooty brick houses with their parallel tiny front gardens, the parallel honeycombs of their backyards, pass by and finally disappear from view, and later, leaning on the ship's rail, deafened by the discordant screeching of the gulls, he will watch the proud wall of chalk cliffs fade and melt away in the mist. Borne long ago by the inert weight of the pamphlets and the politico-philosophical chatter by which he has been nurtured, he slips from the top to the bottom of the map of that narrow zone (that fringe, that thin edge — a remote island hanging above the extreme western cape of Asia — that last still-free space, still preserved, wedged between barbarism and ocean) without realising that as he goes southward he is journeying backwards in time, rushing through several centuries to be thrown into a world in which none of the notions, none of the words which make it up have any meaning, any more than it makes sense to compare a procession of more or less decently dressed, more or less decently fed people marching in good order behind placards, surrounded by collection-takers in armbands and escorted by unarmed policemen, with a ragged, starving mob fired on by machine guns as soon as their leaders appear round the corner of the street, hunted down murderously into their very homes because they have asked for what would just about keep a dog alive, and maintained indeed at the level of dogs, serfs, distracted by fiestas, by the recreation of slaves, going without food in order to crowd into arenas in

215

which wild men fight wild beasts, walking in procession behind bloodstained bejewelled idols in black veils, their hearts pierced with daggers, like symbols preserved intact not even from the past which others had repudiated at the same time as they cut off their kings' heads, but from something preceding even kings, as if at the extreme edge of a continent there hung a kind of withered and shrivelled fruit, forgotten by history and spurned, rejected by geography, like a receptacle, a kind of cesspool into which by the effect of gravity there had slipped, piled up, accrued what other countries over the centuries had slowly and painfully expelled, heaped there as if the bottom of a pocket, a cul-de-sac, blocked, evil-smelling and covered in flies.

And on the side of the pocket, spread out between its hills and the sea, this city or rather this yellowish, swollen expanse, bearing a name itself resembling a swelling, distended, puffed out, unfolding (slipping) from the initial double puffiness in sinuous convulsions of loops and downstrokes: like a monstrous proliferation which seemed to have swallowed by degrees around its cankered core, the old Gothic city, prickly, coloured in that almost black grey of dead tissue, with its narrow alleys, its stale cadaverous breath, hemmed in, stifled by one of those rather colonial agglomerations, of those megapolises erected in conquered, or rather subject territory, not shaped by time, by the gradual accretion and slow retouches made by successive periods of History, but feverishly, rapaciously constructed in a few decades by wealth, vanity, from sweat and plunder, according to a cursory, makeshift, geometrical plan, intersecting at right angles the long avenues lined with heavy, ostentatious architecture, the inflexible chequerwork crumbling under its own impetus, disarticulating itself so to speak, whilst the opulent stone buildings, the gentlemen's residences, the big houses paved in marble and surrounded by magnificent gardens, give way to plain concrete boxes, stone yielding to cement, the pebbledash flaking, the endless avenues wandering off, getting lost, their asphalt gradually scaling in patches, then, without transition, stopping, bluntly revealing the bare earth, pitted with potholes, furrowed, between façades no longer even pebbledashed, bare too, desolate, as if there were no middle point between the arrogance, ostentation and misappropriation of wealth, between savage, pitiless profit, and that from which it

216

is derived, the oppressive sprouting, the huge, monstrous cancer lying there, as if bathing in its own sweat, exuding a perpetual humidity summer and winter alike, secreting a kind of invisible pus, an invisible, unnameable cadaverous dejection (this then: the nagging posters of VD clinics, the sombre cloisters full of magnolias, the darkly sparkling foliage through which the sun's oblique, dusty rays shine, the dazzling white flowers against a dusky ground, the silence, the shrill cries of children reverberating under the arcades of a royal and dead square, the confused roar of the traffic, the dusty palm-trees, the bars as narrow as corridors, the omnipresent tepid smell of rancid oil, the displays of fish under arc lamps, blueish, metallic, lambent, pale pink, the windows filled with condoms the colour of mucous membrane, the shops painted in olive green or grey–blue gloss paint like urinals, the luxury hotels crowned with domes, scalloped cupolas, and tiaras, the pink posters against syphilis, the wheeling flights of pigeons, the pigeons' droppings on the bronze statues, the embossed architecture, the vertical waves of stone, the magnificent shiny cars driven by chauffeurs in black leather leggings, the sulphur-coloured posters against gonorrhoea, the lemon-coloured branches of the plane trees, in winter, against the blue sky, the clusters of legs, breasts, children's heads, arms and hands in wax hanging as votive offerings in the churches, the greyish waxen faces of the old prostitutes with false teeth in chrome steel, cheekbones smudged with rouge, the rusty freighters in the harbour, the luxurious windows on luxurious avenues, the steel sides of the freighters ringing under the syncopated blows of the hammers chipping away at the rust, the rattling noise of the lorries, the colonnades, the façades of granite banks, the smudged, taciturn faces of the stokers leaning on the sides of the freighters, dirty handkerchiefs knotted round their necks, the tops of the palm trees ruffled by the sea-breeze, the windows of the banks with wrought iron railings bristling with clusters of spikes, the liveried chauffeurs taking pekineses out for a walk on a lead, the luxurious brothels with black and gold baroque ornamentation, the pitiless faces highlighted with rouge of the old mummies with false teeth in gold for whom the chauffeurs in leggings open the doors of long black limousines, the parks with their exuberant vegetation of camelias, asclepias, mimosa and reseda, flamboyant bougainvillea, their wrought iron railings also bristling with spikes in clusters, the young, docile Murcian girls with oval faces in the luxury brothels, the flabby, shaggy, greyish genitals exhibited by the old whores lifting up torn lace petticoats, the black men on all fours, their knees protected by pieces cut from old tyres and tied with string, spreading the tar on the pavements in acrid, suffocating smoke, then the streets without sidewalks, the long yellow brick walls of factories in the suburbs, the huddled blocks of dwellings built (or poured out all at once, put down) straight onto the yellow uneven ground, with their dreary lines of washing hanging in faded garlands, the dark trousers stiff and flat like boards twisting and swaying in the languid breeze, the lofty plumes of dust spiralling up, scudding between the desolate façades, subsiding, rising, lifting again above the rutted, dusty roadways, on which meander in gluey runnels of black mud the effluent from continual pointless washing, discharged in short bursts from drainpipes, the blueish streams with their nauseating, stale smell of soap, of dirt (as if even when scrubbed and rinsed in plenty of water, poverty continued to stink), bestrewn with bubbles, with pustules drifting slowly along, forming clusters under the swarms of flies at the clogged mouths of the sewers, opaque, covered with a kind of coating, a film which stops them bursting, all that).

Then he will be there. That is to say the same city, the same palms, the same monuments, the same luxuriant gardens, the same vain, bombastic architecture, still standing, intact (except here and there a chipped cornice or garland of stone, the plate glass of the grand hotels starred by bullets, and only the black-walled churches gutted), but resembling now crustacean carapaces, those shells emptied of their contents, like those towns left untouched by the passage of some catastrophe, curiously protected by the very speed, violence and suddenness of a savage cataclysm, perhaps a hurricane or deluge of ash coming upon the inhabitants in the depths of sleep, then the hurricane gone already, the ash dispersed, leaving hardly any trace, at least nothing spectacular, and rediscovered centuries later with their houses and tables still laid, their rich mosaics, their monumental colossea, their priapic brothel-signs, except that neither old mummies with painted cheeks, nor pekinese on leads, nor liveried chuffeurs, nor owners of de luxe limousines were any longer to be seen, everything which resembled or was in any way connected with an old mummy, a pekinese or an owner of anything whatsoever had disappeared, those who had not had the time to escape having been killed without distinction of sex or kind, the former chauffeurs in livery and patent leggings dressed now in simple mechanics' overalls or in shirtsleeves driving at breakneck speed the limousines now dusty and dented, their sides daubed perfunctorily with bellicose acronyms, bristling with rifles, hurtling along the straight avenues, their tyres screeching as they turned into side streets without slowing down, crammed with men bearing the grim, naive look of illiterate labourers or peasants, at once resolute, sombre and alert, as if they could not bring themselves to trust in the reality of what they were living through, of the weapons from which they were never parted (as one wears next to one's skin miracle-working medals or talismans), using them with the sort of fanatical superstition of primitive people, that same conviction that they (the weapons) possessed some kind of purificatory exorcising power, like flame, like fire, and now vaguely frustrated, furious, not knowing what to do, because in the other half of the country the opposite had happened, and anyone with calloused hands wearing patched clothes had been slaughtered like so much butcher's meat, and there was now a war on, and if they had managed to capture a machine-gun nest at the corner of a street or an avenue they did not know how to tackle those dug in on a hill-top or so positioned as to sweep a bridge or a road with their fire, dully anxious, gnawed by that kind of curse which they had thought to have freed themselves from once and for all, to have eradicated from this bloated town, spying on each other from both sides of the luxurious avenues which now were theirs, from every flight of steps leading up to the grand hotels they had taken over, harbouring suspicions about each other with that touchy, deadly mistrust which characterises the weak, accusing each other of spinelessness, then of incompetence, then of treachery, at first *sotto voce*, then in veiled phrases, then, as if the heavy, yellowish cancer of stone built by and upon violence, at once stifling and flaccid, could secrete nothing but violence itself, beginning underhandedly to kill once more, and this time each other.

Perhaps he did not realise it at first. Or at least he does not say whether he realised it or not. Perhaps he did not see (did not wish to see) that this sort of baroque theatre, this kind of puffed out or rather puffed up decor, decked with victorious streamers, in which the stage-hands, still covered in black grease, now occupied both the stage and the rows of plush seats, and which probably represented for him, as it were, the exciting antithesis (or rather as with those photographic plates in which the gelatin has melted, slipped, the monuments wobbly, wavy, the figures twisted, stretched and pompous-looking) of the city of stilted architecture which he had left behind, black and white under its grey sky, marked like its inhabitants, with that stuffy respect-ability, symbolic of an order whose final destruction he was witnessing, even if, since the summer, the wind and rain had begun to tear and fade the festoons of triumphal bunting, even if the stage-hands were capable now only of looking at each other with sombre, murderous hostility in their eyes.

(He who continued to wear everywhere that invisible and stiff Eton collar, speaking always for that invisible audience whose stern questioning, doubtful looks he felt — as if he was again (or still) in one of those monastic study bedrooms, and around him three or four with girlish faces, milky-white or dotted with freckles, squatting on the floor or on the narrow bed, their legs pulled up to their knees, dressed or rather rigged out with studied untidiness in old, torn or stained woollens thrown carelessly round their shoulders, their sleeves tied across their chests, their shoelaces undone, and one of them perhaps still in a tracksuit, back from some ascetic and inhuman training session (those pale shapes that one sees looming suddenly in the glare of the headlights on winter evenings, running alone or in pairs on the roadside, or bursting out of a thicket, and once more swallowed up in darkness), their thighs bare, too pink under their bronze down, and in the austere cell plunged in semi-darkness (the functional reading lamp with metal shade and flexible metallic arm casting a cone of harsh light on the scattered papers, their faces lit up from below by the reflected light, flashing occasionally on the lenses of those who wear glasses) something like a smell of embrocation, camphor and whey, and sometimes one of them flushing suddenly, going red, his voice mumbling something indistinct, such as an excuse or a protest, demurely, a lanky body getting up, stretching, stepping

220

over the other bodies and the piles of books and leaving the room — or later around the traditional, icy and inexorable gas fire fed with one coin after another (as if time were measured against cold, as if time and cold had to be paid for at set intervals, like a tithe, a toll exacted regularly — and not infrequently they overlooked it, noticed suddenly that for a while already they had been shivering without realising it, one or other getting up, taking a handful of change from his pocket, taking a coin from it, pushing it into the slot, and then time, the bitter cold drawing back for a fresh instalment not of heat but of mild warmth during which they could again forget it), conversing with studied nonchalance, without ever raising their voices, in their elegantly articulated, slightly precious Oxford English, with carefully distinct syllables and measured intonation: impersonal, cold, examining the contingencies, possibilities and likelihood of error as if they were mere academic hypotheses, accidental shortcomings of a theory always admitting of correction or amendment so long as one took care to use moderate, polished, temperate language: hardly changed, then, although a few of them have now traded their slovenly jackets with leather elbow-patches and their baggy flannel trousers for bland, anonymous, anonymously pressed suits such as teachers or civil servants wear, certain among them having perhaps attained the promising rank of something like the briefcase or overcoat carrier to a minister, until the day when the newspapers will publish on their front page the photo of one or other of them, his hair soberly parted on one side of his head, a little thicker around the waist, but still wearing an impeccable tie, when leaving no address he disappears between two conferences or two planes without forgetting however to take with him either the minister's briefcase or his address-book containing private telephone numbers).

Perhaps certain things seemed to him a matter of course. Or perhaps it seemed to him now that they were not really a matter of course and he avoided speaking about them as if he feared that a member of his audience might make a remark about it or raise an objection. He does not spell out the reasons for proceeding to the barracks of a particular militia, or what he did, or the places he went to on first getting off the train, or which people he saw or met before proceeding to that barracks (or no doubt before even leaving England) who pointed out the way to him or gave him the address. He says only (as if it was the only one in the town, or as if it was so named simply to distinguish it from the others, as in garrison towns in which several regiments are stationed) that it was placed under the auspices of the bald personage with slightly slanting eyes, slightly prominent cheekbones and short goatee whose name, what is more, as in certain mnemonic systems or as is the case with those makes of lift produced by double-barrelled manufacturers, was in a way the unavoidable complement to that of the heavily bearded prophet claimed as patron — or guide — by the occupants of one of the other barracks their two faces stencilled within purple halos (or meticulously painted, or in the form of busts, or sometimes linked in profile, like the founders of some cult or the dual incarnations of some double-headed divinity) offered to the passers-by on both sides of the central reservation in the avenue leading down to the harbour, for the same reason as the portraits of the first combatants fallen to machine-gun fire, amidst that profusion of fancy-goods, souvenirs, medals, badges, headgear, votive offerings, flasks and scarves which seems through a sort of spontaneous generation to be produced by any gathering of crowds, by sporting events or by pilgrimages, gazing with their stern eyes, opaque or with hollowed-out pupils, upon the kind of confused and unceasing deambulation of men and women, armed or unarmed, going uphill or downhill, meeting, as if at once busy and aimless, like Sunday crowds drawn to city centres emptied of their usual inhabitants, wandering at a loose end, vaguely out of coun- tenance, worn out and ill at ease. The autumn was drawing to a close then, marked by that melancholy which the season brings in those countries in which it follows the excessive heat, the excessive and noisy exuberance of summer: its delicate light, at once purged and exhausted, its days shorter and shorter, its sly and fleecy dusks drawing down a little earlier each evening, the night shrouding the city under its hesitant shades, laden with menace, with a yellowish oily black in the niggardly light of its streetlamps in fluted cast-iron, dotted here and there with red splashes, the bombastic streamers, faded now, strung from balconies, waving feebly, feebly phosphorescent in the darkness above the avenues with their russet trees whose last leaves were

222

falling, used on certain days (or rather filled to overflowing) under the grey sky by long funeral processions for some hero or other shot in the back during an engagement or found dead in the early hours on waste ground, followed by silent crowds with tired, worn, impenetrable, suspicious faces beneath unfurled, rippling calico banners, repeating the same distrustful, insistent questioning, as if (like those cloud-shaped balloons which cartoonists use to convey the thoughts of their characters) a palpitation of shrouds or bandages, bloodstained like the wrappings of a corpse, of some gory, stinking phantom crying vengeance and to all appearances falling apart, was floating, suspended, ectoplasmic and erratic above the crowded heads, with its unanswered inverted question-marks, its impotent rage inscribed in letters of scarlet. In the dreary barrack squares, a light wind, as if itself tired out, piled up and then scattered (in turn) with a rustling sound the last dead, withered, shrivelled leaves. He recalled the buglers' wrong notes, the horsey smell of urine and rotten oats, the filth, the crunching sound of hobnailed boots tramping through the dust down long corridors with ringing vaulted ceilings, the disorder, those puzzling heaps of broken furniture and other objects which seem to constitute the inevitable dejecta secreted by every company of men suddenly freed from habitual constraints and habitual responsibilities by the act of donning an anonymous uniform (if, that is, such a name could be given to the incongruous outfits which the volunteers were supplied with) and of carrying a weapon (although these, obsolete and practically unserviceable, were only issued to them once they were in the trenches), vested, if only potentially, with a power of life and death normally reserved to gods, even at the risk of their own lives, their own deaths, and no matter how.

Apart from the fact that he did not mention the parades, nor the insiduously murderous newspaper headlines, nor the rivalry between different barracks with different sponsors, he spoke of everything else in the same dreamy, thoughtful, would-be neutral tone, taking care to conceal under a detached, mildly humorous air what was touching about his adventure, saying that he had attributed to war the dreary, sinister atmosphere of the town (those were the words he used), the appalling filth, dreadful mess and fearful waste which prevailed there and which, at the time, he understood as the outward signs, the confirmation of a world at last and in every respect the opposite of the one he had left, repudiated, spewed out. He does say however, without considering it necessary to specify which, that certain things seemed to him incomprehensible, and even displeased him, writing (or rather talking) with as it were one corner of his mouth pulled down, tugged to one side by a grin at once mocking and nervous: the same embarrassed — or, rather, pained — grin, the same slight, hesitant wink, that in describing this first character, this apparition who seemed to have sprung straight out of a novel by someone like Fenimore Cooper, who appeared suddenly before him on his arrival at the barracks the day before he joined, for all the world as if he were the incarnation of his ideal and of his dreams as well as foreshadowing things to come: a symbol, one of those allegorical figures which can be seen on the covers of books or on propaganda posters, or embellishing commemorative monuments, decked in attributes, and surrounded by objects themselves symbolic and loaded with meanings: the ordnance map which the militiaman was gazing at, quite obviously incapable of reading it, the shabby uniform, the peaked leather cap pulled over one eye above a face of which he says that it was the face of someone who was as capable of committing murder as throwing away his life for a friend, a face with both candour and ferocity in it, so that, he goes on to say, he knew that if he wished to retain his first impression of him and keep the liking for the man which had spontaneously brought them into contact, he must never see him again.

And yet he went and did precisely the opposite. That is to say instead of obeying his instincts, instead of running as fast as his legs could carry him to the station and jumping into the first train back to the place whence he had come from, he joined up. And in the very same barracks in which he had seen rise before him, like a vision warning of disasters to come, this prophetically allegorical character (unless he created it later as he got deeper into his story: not entirely made up, exactly — he must actually have met him, or at least one like him (since they were more or less all built on the same pattern) — but described in such a way as to maintain his self-esteem, as much in his own eyes as in those of the public, insinuating that he had not been taken in, was not so naive, in spite of the romantic and dusty quality of the clichés with which he peppered his account, emphasising even, with a sort of bitter perversity, their romantic, dusty aspect, through a kind of bravado, of defiance, going so far as to speak of enemies of the revolution who, disguised as its fiercest supporters, were there only the better to work for its destruction, in just the same way as those who hunted him down later with that indifferent casual ferocity, that pitiless serenity of men as convinced as himself of their proper appraisal of the situation and events were to say of him). He had only come to Spain with some notion of writing newspaper articles and yet, almost immediately, joining up seemed to him the only conceivable thing to do. Later, he said that by this time the revolutionary phase was probably drawing to a close but that for someone who, like him, had come straight from England it was hard to realise it. He says nothing more about what took place in his mind during the twenty-four hours he gave himself to make up his mind, that is the twenty-four hours during which he must no doubt have weighed the pros and cons between, on the one hand, nothing less than his life (or rather his death — although he was quite unable at the time to imagine the way in which that death would be required of him), on the other hand what pleasant and unpleasant things he had seen since his arrival. The fact remains that without further delay (or perhaps without allowing himself to delay any further) he made his way back to that barracks and there signed his enlistment papers.

Years later there could still be seen, drawn in charcoal on the wall of one of the side chapels of Lerida cathedral still in ruins, a diagram showing the principles of ballistics by means of the straight dotted line which goes from one eye, passes through the sight and bead to reach the target where it meets the arc representing the real trajectory of the projectile rising on leaving the barrel then falling again under the influence of gravity, the head of the marksman (no doubt to make the drawing more attractive) being that of a woman, recognisable from her generously curved, roughly outlined bust and from the abundant frizzy hair flowing from underneath her forage hat and represented by a mass of tangled lines twisting back on themselves. A pile of debris from the fallen vault rose in a slope at the foot of the wall. Another hand had written a little above the forage cap, crowning it with a sort of halo, the word PUTA in large capitals scored with a sharp point (knife? bayonet?), the word dragged out by its own weight as it were, leaning from left to right, the final A (one of the branches of which almost touched the confused tangle of hair) tilted at about forty-five degrees, the slightly bluish rendering (as in those chapels dedicated to the Virgin) chipped unevenly on either side of the furrows made by the point and thus edged with tiny hairy patches or sandy, ochre notches. Apart from the insulting inscription added afterwards, it was to such kinds of drawings that more or less the whole military training of those joining the militias amounted. He also related that: the week or so he spent in the barracks where, although because of his abilities he had been offered to be let off it, he made a point of following the instruction received by the other volunteers, consisting for the most part of boys of fifteen to seventeen of which, he said, a certain percentage were good-for-nothings, only drawn to it by the lure of the pay, sharing in their efforts until they were at last made to form up in threes, stand to attention, keep in step, do a right turn and a left turn, and, owing to a lack of weapons for them to learn how to use, nothing else, he (O.) forcing himself to repress as betraying heredity or shameful habits his instinctive aversion to the muddle, slovenliness, indiscipline prevalent there, perhaps even feeling, deep down inside, a sort of secret and perverse delight in the practice of those in some way spiritual exercises, sleeping on the rotten straw of the empty horseboxes, eating out of a greasy pannikin, sharing, too, his food and his cigarettes with the primitive beings around him, becoming acquainted at the lowest level with one of those communities of the most rudimentary sort, that is entirely organised around instincts and urgent needs like sleeping, eating and fighting. And always in that same ghostly, toneless, husky voice which he was now able to coax from what remained of his vocal cords, he described their departure: the bustle, the marshalling in the barrack square, the uproar, the excitement, the rolling red flags flapping in the torchlight, the political commissar's speech, the theatrical march-past, the rhythmic tramp of boots, the interminable route they were made to follow to show them to the whole town, the band, the women on the balconies, the shouting, the crowds thronging the pavement whilst he marched, lost in that sort of apotheosis, blind and deaf to everything except what he perceived immediately around him, supplied like his comrades simply and solely with a thin blanket, rolled bandolier-wise across the shoulder, a knapsack and empty cartridge-pouches, passing without seeing them (in any case he did not mention it — or perhaps they were part and parcel, with the mythical apparition which had assumed material form before him on his arrival at the barracks, of those things which he had decided once and for all no longer to see) in front of the dark, uncommunicative characters with the heads of eagles or tubercular stokers, equipped and rigged out like walking arsenals (or rather as if, suddenly, a rifle or an automatic pistol had taken human shape: inert in some way, the colour of burnished steel, as inexpressive, dangerous and lethal as firearms can be when primed ready for use), sitting silently on café terraces or else rocking back in cane armchairs next to the well-oiled machine-gun which defended the entrances of requisitioned buildings at the windows of which sometimes, perhaps, the clamour, the flickering torch lights, the band, the measured tramping led to a curtain being pulled aside to reveal half of one of those heavy, tired faces whose slightly slanting eyes above broad cheekbones would gaze for some moments thoughtfully (not anxiously or angrily, just thoughtfully) at the boisterous parade, then (because people of that sort have little time to waste and work late into the night) disappearing behind the curtain feebly lit by the glow of some desk lamp or other reflected by a pile of coded dispatches, reports, lists ticked in red or marked with tiny crosses.

But he did not mention that either. Perhaps because he restrained himself from looking up at windows lit late into the night. Or because he had decided to say nothing about it, at least at this stage in his narrative. Not that he knew nothing at the time about the presence of such kinds of people. He knew they existed somewhere, that is as one knows (but is not acquainted with) something learned through newspaper articles or in books, without forming a clear idea of their reality, as of abstractions, or mistakes, those by-products or temporary defects of History which it will put right of its own accord. He had doubtless even discussed it together with other academic hypotheses in the narrow student bedrooms in which the

227

steady, sober, slightly precious voices answered each other, calmly raised in the bluish whorls of pipe smoke and, later, around ashtrays overflowing with cork-tipped cigarettes barely lit before being absentmindedly stubbed out. He knew enough about it, though, to tell himself that a revolution is not an invitation to tea (besides no one had invited him) and that what was happening in this country at this time could not be carried out without the inevitable contradictions and inevitable blemishes inherent in this sort of thing. But apparently the sole eventuality which he had not foreseen was that he could suddenly be set upon and hunted down, he who had come only to write articles, had preferred not to write them, had chosen on the contrary to go and fight without wishing for more. And not being hunted as an intruder, a foreigner, being told to mind his own business and go back home, but as a rabbit, or rather a rat, a cockroach is chased, with the deliberate intention of destroying it, and that those who gave the order to do it were likely to be the same: people who except for what was contained in the suitcase which they had brought with them, that is a change of underwear and two ties (they were just about the only men who wore a tie then in that part of the country), had no personal possessions, not even a name, not even an individual description (they were hardly ever to be seen, always discreet, unobtrusive, occasionally saying a few words at some meeting or other after the fat and sweating politicians, the commercial traveller types with triple chins and the grim, empassioned orators who hammered out their words with their fists, rarely getting involved, as unobtrusive as ever, in the confabulations held in the shelter of window embrasures, one of them sometimes sending his name up, waiting placidly on the sofa of an anteroom before being shown into the office whose occupant watched him draw near and take a seat with dejected and helpless disquiet, waiting again until the usher had carefully shut the padded doors behind him, saying then what he had to say, in a calm, courteous tone of voice, after which, still without haste, he went back inside some consulate or some luxury hotel emptied of its millionaires and got down to work again), having nothing on them (or rather not on them: in them) but power, or rather something which was like the very essence of power, holding it and wielding it not in the same way as he (O.) had

228

believed up till then it was taken and wielded, that is through or for the possession of wealth, by obliging those who possessed nothing to work for them, or by stripping rivals of their wealth, but a power without restraint, without those impediments, those limitations encountered by owners of land or machinery competing with other owners of land or machinery, because however much land or machinery one owns, it is impossible to own everything and so attain that total power which is conferred by the clear conscience of making no one work for one's own benefit, and now there, invisible behind the windows of buildings with doors protected by machine guns, steel shields or piles of café tables, moving about discreetly in cars with drawn curtains: not cruel, bloodthirsty: merely sober, pragmatic, each one provided with several surnames, several passports, to the extent doubtless of no longer being sure themselves, of perhaps having forgotten (and in any case they lost no sleep over it) their real identity, had indeed for some time had no longer any identity, in much the same way as identity is not an attribute of machines prepared and programmed by means of punched cards on which were transposed in coded language a few formulae drawn from a mixture of philosophical precepts and police tricks, the first as elementary (and as effective) as the second (something, in short, like a philosophy of the police or a police of philosophy), so that his adventure (or rather the adventure which he (O.) was now trying to relate) resembled one of those novels in which the narrator leading the investigation turned out to be not the murderer, as in certain sophisticated versions, but the dead man himself, overwhelming the reader with a mass of irrelevant details, the accumulation of which enables him to conceal the hidden link in the chain, the missing piece of information, History itself attending to the rest, outdoing in its mischievous perversity those authors who amuse themselves by plunging the reader into confusion by attributing several names to the same character or, conversely, the same name to different protagonists, and, as always, acting (History) with its alarming lack of moderation, its incredible, ponderous humour: the same inexpressive face, a little heavy, a shade broad, and behind, in several copies, the same imperturbable personage known sometimes under the name of Grigoriev, at another under that of Grigorievich or even Goriev (and, in actual fact it was neither Grigoriev nor Grigorievich, nor Goriev, but Berzine — and, in reality — it was neither Grigoriev, nor Grigorievich, nor Goriev, nor Berzine, but Stern) and another Codovila, or Medina, and another (and always the same interchangeable face, the same interchangeable build, rigid, massive, the same somewhat formal bearing, the same stare, at once meditative, composed and lifeless) Ercoli or Alfredo, and Pedro or Gerö, and Douglas or Smuchkievich, and Vidali or Contreras or Carlos, as if instead of names they had been assigned simple combinations of letters, sometimes with slight variations, at other times without any connection, hung on some thing (not individuals, distinct beings: some thing) vaguely fictitious, without genuine existence, even when the thing decided that the time had come to act in earnest, to do away once and for all with everything which however closely or remotely seemed to him rightly or wrongly to impede his progress, seemed not to behave or simply not to think properly, whether that thought emerged from the twists and turns of the brain of a peasant, of an illiterate labourer, or of subtle minds schooled on the cricket fields or the campuses of Anglo-Saxon or other universities.

The fact remains that he left all that behind him: the nocturnal toilers in the bedrooms of luxury hotels, the adipose and garrulous politicians, the taciturn riflemen (or rather men-rifles) with wooden faces, always impassive, who, some mornings, without even a wink, passed over to each other the newspapers (including those edited by the occupants of the hotels in front of which they mounted guard) whose enormous headlines framed by tiresome exclamation marks reported the discovery of some new Patroclus (occasionally one of the orators who seethed at meetings) found at daybreak smeared in dried blood on an abandoned building site, or in open country, or else who simply vanished without trace, led away, as the expression had it, to 'take a little walk', and whose tumultuous funeral procession they watched tramp along under its futile, vengeful banners, as it passed slowly by, with the same indifferent stare as they did the boisterous warrior battalions, getting up, saluting with their fists or presenting their once more well-greased arms to the jolting heap of floral tributes swathed in red (or red and black) under which the coffin disappeared, he

(O.) also leaving behind him the accredited correspondents perched on their bar stools, busily writing for the organs of the liberal foreign press the articles which he was later to devour on his return with the dejected amazement, the dejected indignation that a survivor of a shipwreck would feel on reading in black and white that there had been neither storm nor shipwreck, or at the very least that the ship's captain after being inconvenienced for a while by engine room problems had shown sufficient presence of mind to save his cargo and passengers by getting rid in time of a few saboteurs, a few greasers or stokers taken on board with false certificates, he (O.) interrupting himself, pausing in his story (alone in the peaceful night, sitting at his table, and the sheet half blackened by his writing, pale and unrelenting under the harsh light of the lamp, with at his back, leaning over his shoulder, the unquiet ghosts of those who had not been lucky enough to escape the nocturnal motorists), in order to stoop down, pick up one of the newspapers scattered around him on the carpet or the floor, reread once again what he could not manage to believe was written there, one of those articles hardly a few months old which seemed to him already to date from several years previously (but he knew them all by heart, perhaps only needed to convince himself that he had really read it all, to touch the paper with his hands, to gaze at the printed columns), then dropping it among the others which were strewn about on the ground, in unsteady piles or just as they had slipped from his hands, that is half opened out, crumpled, sagging like a kind of bird with greyish, broken wings, inert beneath his gaze marked by that meditative incredulity (although then it was of a different nature) which he had felt, crouching in the mud, sheltering after a fashion behind a parapet of sandbags themselves stacked more or less properly around a fortified post, contemplating the rifle with the split butt and rusty bolt which had been assigned to him, as derisory, as unusable in the situation in which he now found himself as the entire philosophical contents of the suitcase so long humped around: it was a desolate landscape, not because of the war (as on the classic photographs showing the pustulary expanses of shell holes encroaching on each other, with here and there the eloquent carcass of a shattered tree) but in itself, such as millions of years beforehand it had

231

been formed by the slow contractions and the slow pleating on the surface of a ball of mud or of molten lava, hostile (the spot) to all life and remaining that way (except perhaps, in as much as such a thing is possible, that it had reached an even more absolute degree of desolation, ravaged by the rains, the inclement weather, the alternation of frosts and blazing summers which had succeeded each other for centuries and had even more completely stripped, scored and polished it), uninhabitable and uninhabited, except for a few sparse populations which had themselves remained in a savage, primitive state, driven or kept there by some curse or other, as if only such phenomena of a cosmic order, so to speak, as invasions, famines, wars or revolutions could force human creatures to cling to these stony hills, dotted with stunted vegetation forcing its way with difficulty between the limestone rocks sticking out of the ground here and there like bones between which ran trenches of a sort: an empty landscape, without birds or other sign of life except that characteristic smell of war which he noticed there for the first time and which, he says, was the smell of an extraordinary quantity of excrement and of decaying food. It was only the lower foothills of the real mountains, and the region seemed to be the domain of rain and fog, a cold, penetrating fog which blurred the lines of the crests, lingered in the hollows, saturated clothes permanently, and against which blankets (if they had an extra supply) nor even camp fires were of any avail. He says that the cold was one of the things which had most scared him in advance, thinking about it with terror during the nights which preceded his departure for the front, imagining the ominous dawns, the long hours of sentry duty with a frosty rifle in his hands, the icy mud in which he would flounder. And similarly he would write later of the filth, the lice, weapons which exploded in the faces of their users, the absurd orders, the attacks or rather the forays (he said it was not exactly a real war) stupidly ordered and stupidly carried out, the exasperating halfwittedness of the boastful urchins around him whose recreation consisted, in order to prove their virility, in blazing away, using up cartridges more or less at random, disabling themselves with their own weapons and playfully rolling hand-grenades into the fire on which their mess-tins were being heated. He told all that, still in the same

232

even, unconcerned tone, sometimes barely marked by slight irritation, but without revolt or anger, as if such things had happened to someone else or he were drafting for some parliamentary commission or some philanthropic committee one of those reports, those memoranda on the condition of the poor or the bad state of the hospices, recommending in notes ways of putting things right, proudly mindful never to evoke pity, even less admiration. It was war, and even if it were being badly conducted he 'had no fundamental reason to rebel. Moreover, he knew enough about it (had read enough about it — since, when all is said and done, until he left for Spain and apart from his experiences in the imperial police, in East End districts or as a dishwasher, the derisory nature of which was now clear to him, the bulk of his knowledge had been inculcated in him by books) not to be unaware of the fact that war is a dirty business, represents a fearful waste of both human lives and material, and that all and sundry are encountered there. He says that in fact the question which overshadowed all others there was that of firewood. In those bare hills, practically bereft of vegetation, overwhelmed the whole winter in fog and icy rain, nothing else mattered except the search for it, not even the bursts of enemy machine gun fire which fell, fortunately not very accurately, onto the wood gatherers. In other words, the dilemma he faced was no longer the choice between death and liberty, but between death and firewood, or rather, as he says jokingly still, between violent death from bullets or explosives and death by pneumonia. So the winter passed, hardly disturbed by those raids or occasional patrols resulting in nothing more, it seems, than in an orgy of bullets fired haphazardly in the darkness and in the experience of things, like fear or danger, much less important than the nagging concern to gather whatever was likely to catch fire and give off a little warmth. And whilst he was retelling all that, his tone gradually altered without his realising it. Although he was still careful to say nothing which might arouse admiration or pity, he spoke differently, had ceased to twist his mouth down at the corner and to overdo the winks. He was no longer concerned with approval or disapproval, good or evil, any more than during those days when he had reached a sort of degree zero of thought as it were, sleeping on the nights he was not on guard duty in a

233

niche hollowed out above the mud of a dugout, living by day in a trench gluey with excrement and littered with empty tin cans, shivering in his increasingly ragged and increasingly dirty clothes, his feet frozen in his boots with their soles getting progressively thinner, his whole being absorbed in the paradisiacal dream of a nirvana of firewood, having reached the sort of total destitution, at once material and moral, in which valour, courage no longer even counted (he only related the episode of the raid for so to speak documentary, anecdotal reasons, more like a windfall, an exciting interlude which occurred happily to interrupt the everyday monotony), but rather patient obstinacy to resolve the elementary problems of survival, his mind occupied exclusively with the necessity of struggling without respite against filth, cold, vermin, of sheltering from the rain or from the fire of a machine gun, of cleaning his weapon, of mending his rags, impregnated with those heady odours which reduced everything to common organic or chemical denominators: those of dirt, of the mud in which he lay flat, of the ammoniacal sweat sticking down the hairs on the flanks of the donkeys which he unloaded, of things coming out of or extracted from the earth only to be absorbed by it once again, to return to it in the shape of excrements, of rusty metals, of sulphur and carbon exploding with that savage and innocent violence of matter in contact with which he now lived in a kind of symbiosis, whether it was inanimate or living, raw, like those animals, the inhabitants of those wild hills who drove their mules with kicks in the testicles, the sparse, wild vegetation, the rats which he heard paddling in the water of the ditch, he with his invisible and impeccable tie, his invisible top hat and his impeccable Eton collar now replaced with a grubby cap with earflaps and a muffler in holes, washing in the mess-tin he used to eat from, squatting in the refuse, with his hands, their nails broken, swollen with abscesses, their benumbed fingers clumsily gripping his gun while he was quietly shivering with cold at a fire-slit, watching the stars going out one by one, the sky growing pale, the coming of dawns of steel grey or of dazzling soft colours, periwinkle blue, jonquil yellow, iridescent with amethyst, coral, purples, so much so that, later on, he had to lay down his pen once again, pause a moment there in front of his sheet of paper, thoughtful and wary, his brows knit, his face

234

slightly distorted, not because of the memory of what he was trying to relate, but of the difficulty of relating it, of making it also believable, hesitant, like someone speaking in a dull, dreamy voice, staring before him into the void and stopping suddenly (a man describing the passion which he felt for a woman and which, as he is well aware, is incomprehensible to anyone but himself, anticipating the stifled jump, the polite, amazed acquiescence of the confidant to whom he is going to show the photograph), and in the end taking the plunge, letting out the word which was so hard to get accepted but which was the only one that translated the untranslatable, shaping one by one on the sheet, slowly, the letters which made it up, writing that this period had possessed the quality of 'magic' . . .

So that everything suddenly exploded in his face, just like the red balloon which a boy is blowing up until he is out of breath, marvelling at seeing it inflate, swell up, holding it away from his mouth, gazing at it ecstatically, feeling it, fascinated by the glossiness and tautness of its skin, listening to it squeak beneath his fingers, then starting to blow again until the thin elastic membrane tears, the compressed air suddenly released with a deafening noise, a nasty sharp bang, then nothing left, the air absorbed into air, into the void, and nothing left either in his hands but a few limp shreds of crumpled rubber, drab, shapeless and unusable. When they were relieved, the scanty shrubs which grew in the stony soil of the hills were slowly putting out buds, then leaves, the wild rose-bushes were becoming flecked with petals, and now the sun had taken over from the cold and rain, burning the bare shoulders of the men carrying sandbags for the parapets, making the rocks white hot, turning foetid the permanent smells of excrement, rubbish and rotting things left lying about above the barbed wire entanglements and dugouts like the clinging efflux emitted by some corpse or other which had not been properly buried in the autumn, had been preserved by the winter frost, and which, with the return of the heat, began now to decompose. Although what struck him most forcibly when he got back to Barcelona was not so much a stench of corpse as something like those suffocating smells of formalin and of powerful disinfectants which seem to impregnate the shiny painted walls and linoleum flooring of those cold, silent buildings in which bodies are kept

235

in numbered drawers, finding himself there once again with amazement, dirty, in tattered clothes and boots of which not much more than the uppers remained, in that town which had seemed to him in the autumn like a crucible of molten metal and which had been transformed in his absence, had now become, he said, more like a health resort, in somewhat straitened circumstances, perhaps, but nevertheless clean, neat and even smart, with, once again, restaurants with deferential, skilled waiters, shops in which those who had money could buy any expensive item, luxury brothels, beggars, pedestrians in elegant summer suits, officers in well-cut, close-fitting uniforms, in wonderfully shiny boots, like dummies seen in shop-windows, and wearing hanging from their Sam Browne belts automatic pistols like those which had been in such short supply for fighting in the hills, the poorest section of the population no longer preoccupied with war nor even with revolution but only with getting in return for endless waiting in endless queues the bare minimum needed for subsistence. No doubt, although in less abundance, the red or red and black flags still floated here and there, but with something anachronistic, unusual about them now, something at once outmoded and suspect (or something perhaps too new, too innocently smart, or rather flashy, too clean), in the same way as if one had renewed some of those bunting pennants with their triumphal inscriptions slung from one balcony to another, it was, it might have been said, like the piously arranged flowers are renewed in front of those altars on which are kept behind glass, enshrined with veneration, some yellowed piece of bone belonging to the saintly hospitaller who presides over the activities of those establishments with meticulously raked courtyards, geometrical avenues of lime trees pruned in a dead straight line, with trim flower beds between the freshly-painted buildings, euphemistically known as rest homes, with in its niche above the entrance some statue or other, its gentle face touched up with pink, dressed in blue, with a halo of multicoloured bulbs framing its head, and spreading its arms in a gesture of welcome, smiling and chalky in the disturbing silence, the kindly, terrifying peace which surrounds like an impenetrable mantle what in ordinary parlance is called simply (that was the term which he used later) a madhouse.

And yet that too he admitted. He did indeed say that right from the beginning it still seemed to him that something was going wrong, or rather was going on in such a way as he began seriously to wonder whether the cause for which he was there was not a completely lost cause. He did not at once make the connection between what he now saw and the discreet establishments placed under the protection of Marian saints crowned with electric bulbs. Or perhaps he had found another subject to interest him, the cold, the lice and everything he had undergone during the previous four months had perhaps given him access to another scale of values than those which he had discussed during the innumerable nocturnal discussions between the brilliant adolescents (then the brilliant young men) endowed with that infinite capacity for making speeches which was accompanied in his case by an infinite capacity for enduring suffering. What is more, he had been taught since childhood not to admit defeat until the referee has blown his final whistle and even to redouble his frenzied efforts as defeat began to look increasingly possible, to let himself be trampled on by studded boots, to get up again without even needing to hear the snarls of his coach running along the touchline whilst with the back of his hand he wiped away the blood streaming from his nose or his split lip, got trampled on again, picked himself up once more, was yet again trampled, and so on. The only mistake he had made, he now realised, had been to select the wrong barracks on arrival, to rely on people who had been able to send him to brave only cold and lice with precious few opportunities for fighting, so that since it was becoming more and more obvious that power was in the process of changing hands (that is power strong enough to send him with near-certainty onto a sector of the front from which he would be very unlikely ever to return) all that he was left free to do was to throw in his lot with it. And he was endeavouring to do just that when History (or destiny — or what else?: the internal logic of matter? its relentless mechanisms?) decided matters differently.

Naturally, whether it was from pride or from modesty, he did not relate things quite like that, no doubt did not acknowledge them to himself in those terms. Later, he embarked upon complicated and so to speak technical explanations, studded with acronyms, with the initials of parties, of trade unions, of factions, of police organisations, of leagues or of associations, like those chemical symbols which are comprehensible only to the initiated and which, depending on the way in which they are mixed and measured, can be combined almost to infinity to make up fertilisers or detergents just as readily as explosives. He still never spoke boastfully but always in a tone of voice which had become neutral, detached, as if he were talking about someone other than himself and about things which were a matter of course, reflecting that sort of candour, that kind of subtle mixture of disingenuousness and naturalness which is the rule in confrontations that centre around a ball from one end to the other of the muddy fields in which all is permitted provided one chooses the moment when the referee is looking the other way. He admitted that if he had been successful in his attempts to join up in the barracks which he now considered as the most suited to further his object, he would probably have found himself sooner or later in the unpleasant situation of having to fire on his former comrades. He does not say what he would then have done, except that he would have been in an impossible position. As (good? or bad?) luck would have it, events were to let him off from having to debate afresh this new problem, for hardly had he had time to shake off the dirt of the trenches, to sleep a few nights by the side of the woman who had come out to join him, to gorge himself until he felt sick with every-thing that could be purchased in the way of food and alcohol, to contact his new friends, order himself a new pair of boots and negotiate the purchase of a hand gun, when he again found himself, armed with two bombs and a rifle, stretched out on the roof of a cinema and engaged in keeping an eye on the uniformed occupants of a café situated on the other side of the avenue onto which the cinema gave, whilst he could hear the deafening racket of the bursts from automatic weapons and of the explosions which brutally shook the smart health resort with its heavily ornate domes, its heavy pastries in stone, its rococo buildings, its avenues of palms, its miniature skyscrapers, its gothic church towers, its gardens planted with magnolia and its proud requisi-tioned luxury hotels, the machine guns of which now fired on everything which passed within range and even (for good measure, to show that they were plentifully supplied with those munitions stingily meted out at the front) beyond their range.

238

He related that no one seemed to have acquired a very clear idea of what was going on and that he himself did not immediately get one either. He was content simply to say that it was chance, almost a question of the hour of the clock, of the time required by the boot-maker to deliver the boots he had ordered. However that may be, the truth is that he found himself on a particular day at the right place and at the right time which meant that his destiny changed irremediably at that moment, precipitating him into the hideous, appalling mess which would leave him no recourse other than flight, and not only out of that town, as he had done on an earlier occasion, but rather from the country, and more than from the country: expelled from himself in a sense, forced to recant, prevented even from taking the honourable way out he had thought he could use, because if those or that (but who or what then?: the heavily-bearded prophet? the likes of Smuchkievich? the laws of matter?) for whom or for which he was risking his life or rather his death accepted it, they still required that such a death should take place in a manner agreeable to themselves, that is not as he may have thought a death if not glorious at least clean, straightforward, but on the contrary ignominious, derisory, preceded and accompanied by a ceremonial itself ignominious, degrading, so that it might serve as an example, discouraging for ever in future all those who, whatever their origins or their capacity for making speeches, might take it into their heads to come and query the quality or the shade of red with which the only authentically red flag was dyed, and therefore this: at about three or four o'clock in the afternoon, when he was about half-way along the avenue which runs down to the sea (going or coming back from buying himself cigarettes, or a bottle of whisky, or trying on his new pair of boots), and suddenly the shots, the people breaking into a run or taking shelter behind the trees, the shopkeepers hurriedly lowering their steel shutters, the clatter of unrolled metal sheeting getting nearer and nearer, the snapping noise they made mingling with that of the bullets, with the muffled explosions of bombs, the lorries bristling with rifles suddenly bursting into view as if materialised out of nothing, hurtling along at top speed with their cargoes of armed men swaying at every corner, clinging to the rails, stretched out on the bonnets or mudguards, watchful, their

239

fingers on the triggers of their rifles or pistols, with the sort of sallow faces which one had believed forgotten, ravaged, dark, inhabited by that kind of taciturn, blind violence which in their dusty and yellow suburbs, or else in the mean districts near the harbour, had already flung them less than a year earlier from their slums or their factories, already running, finishing dressing or putting on their equipment without ceasing to run, made them pack into the lorries, the lorries setting off without even waiting until the last had managed to clamber aboard, racing ahead with their overhanging clusters of clinging bodies, their rings of legs thrashing around in the void, converging, engines racing, as if guided by some instinct, some ancestral reflex towards those avenues, those luxury hotels from the balconies of which still hung the last vestiges of the victorious banners, those barracks once again carefully swept, at the gates of which the guard was now mounted by sentries strapped in shining leather dressed in those uniforms which for them (the inhabitants of the sordid suburbs, of the cheerless blocks of bricks and cement) represented that against which they nourished a hereditarily transmitted hatred, as symbols can be hated, the living personifications of something which, for centuries past, from father to son and from mother to daughter, had stood for suffering, humiliation and loss, even if at present the triple-chinned politicians tried to make them see that nothing can be achieved without order or blacked boots, even if the elegant window-dummies waved a piece of paper signed by one of those whom they had cheered in the meetings or at the parades (indeed such people did little else now but sign, watch the usher showing in one or other of the Grigorieviches or the Smuchkieviches who, moving towards them, courteous, inscrutable, would hold out to them the piece of paper (the decree, the decision which had been drafted thousands of miles away, transmitted in code, decoded, then translated and typed with just enough blank space left for the signature), sit down, open a packet of tipped cigarettes, offer them one always with the same impervious courtesy, and wait politely (and between the two men — both equally exhausted, their eyes reddened from lack of sleep, their features haggard or unhealthily bloated — between the two men, then, it was as if the caller had first of all drawn his revolver without haste, then laid the revolver on the

240

table between himself and his host, the barrel pointing in the right direction, the face of the office's occupant flushing, crimson with annoyance, his hands, his lips, his chops and his triple chin quivering with indignation, the caller still sitting patiently, looking out of the window at the spring sky, the flocks of pigeons, the still tender leaves of the plane trees, drawing calmly all the while on his cigarette until the man sitting on the other side of the desk stops protesting, then stops haggling, then stops entreating, then stops talking altogether, bows his back, sinks his head into his shoulders, takes a pen and writes his signature at the spot set aside and marked in pencil with a cross, the caller rising then, taking the piece of paper, checking the signature, folding the sheet in four, putting it in his pocket, expressing his thanks and leaving the room), he (O.) then, perhaps taking cover now with a few other passers-by behind the trunk of a plane tree or a newspaper kiosk, then someone suddenly looming up, he too as it were from nowhere, spontaneously assuming human shape (he did not even seem to know his name, he says merely that he was an American, a doctor, and that he had met him somewhere at the front, and nothing further, neither before nor after this moment, like a sort of mythical apparition, those characters without real existence made up of invisible deleterious particles, materialising and vanishing in the next instant), then both of them (the man grabbing him by the arm, hauling him along, and he himself) running too — and he did not know that from that moment he would not stop again, that is not stop running, even after the man had let go of him, after they had rushed into that hotel (it was not the Ritz, only a hotel in which he himself had stayed, where friends of his — those friends he was preparing to repudiate — were still staying, although at that moment he could see no familiar faces in the confusion), recrossing the street, still running (he said that the American — the doctor — had disappeared by then), reaching another building (a sort of headquarters, he explained, normally occupied by his friends) in which a man whom he had never seen either (a tall, pale, rather handsome man of about thirty in civilian clothes) was handing out rifles to people as they arrived, turned him away at first, then (he had after all found someone he knew, another Englishman, who apparently knew the man with the rifles)

241

changed his mind and gave him one, then (he related that there too it was the same confusion, the same disorder, with women, babies, boys, foreigners and passers-by fleeing in for protection) once more without a rifle (one of the boys hanging about there had stolen it from him), then armed with two of those bombs which were about as dangerous for the person carrying them as for those against whom they were thrown, then sleeping fitfully, wrapped in a torn stage curtain, amidst the wailing of babies in tears, and even asleep he went on running, the bombs clipped to his belt digging into his sides, expecting any moment to be blown to pieces by them or by some other bomb thrown through the door or tossed into the corridor, struggling cautiously so to speak in that sort of half-sleep from which it seemed to him he would not manage to wake again, interrupting his writing once more to peer at the invisible listeners whom he was addressing and who were watching him, shaking their heads sceptically, avoiding his eyes, exchanging brief furtive glances concealed behind their glasses in slender frames, listening to him with that indulgent commiseration reserved for fanatics and mad people, a little upset, somewhat embarrassed, giving off a smell of embrocation and damp woollens, with their long scarves (and later their ties) in the colours of colleges and universities with prestigious names, as one stands round the bed of an invalid, watching him count up on his fingers, in order to be certain of having forgotten nothing, of having made no mistake, each episode from the moment he had entered the barracks seven or eight months earlier right up to the days which he was now describing: the town ripped apart, the barricades, the people crossing the street brandishing a white handkerchief, the long hours of sentry duty on the roof of a cinema opposite the café MOKA (one of those in front of which he had marched in procession one evening to the light of torches and the sounds of a military band) not occupied either by those taciturn louts with black and red kerchiefs tied around their necks but by their opposites so to speak (although they had the same faces the colour of wood or earth, bony, with sharp angles, shrivelled, or rather as if mummified, savage and indifferent, burned, tanned, worn it seemed from before their birth by the sun and the labour of the fields: a race sired by remote cross-breeding between Visigoths, Saracens and Indian

242

slaves to produce something in between the mule, the cutlass and firearms, except that the leather faces were now to be found under patent leather cocked hats and over uniforms buttoned in the prescribed manner), the lookouts sitting on the cinema roof swapping with them, depending on the moment, insults, consoling remarks, bottles of beer or, now and then, a few shots: but it was of no importance any longer: everything seemed so remote, unreal, so completely devoid of meaning: simply he (O.) was running: it was as if he were in motion, pulled or rather sucked into a kind of tunnel, continuing mechanically to move his legs underneath him, caught up and outpaced by the deafening hurricane of an express train, tossed to one side by the blast, the rapid lights of the carriages searching him out a second time, revealing him once more in one of the successive positions of a man in the act of running, as in those kaleidoscopes in which the tiny fragmented images of an athlete can be seen immobilised in the discrete attitudes of a foot race, the only difference being that the cylinder would be turning in reverse, so that he seemed as it were to advance backwards: once more en route for the front, then once more in the same desolate hills, once more fighting against lice and rain, once more volunteering for patrols (there was no longer any question after what had just occurred of his choosing one sector rather than another, nor a regiment either, or a division, and the divisions now did not bear the name of the bald one or the bearded one any more than that of any thinker, bald, bearded or not, but, as in every army in the world, merely a number), and from time to time he learned that one of his own sort, a Thompson or a Smillie, had been arrested, or were being sought, or had vanished without trace, he continuing to move as if in a void, like a sort of automaton carrying out the tasks for which he was detailed, or rather, which he had assigned himself, until, stupidly (at least he said that it was stupidly), he found himself one quiet morning in the trajectory of that bullet which by chance again or mischance struck him a fraction of an inch to one side of the right spot, laying him out in a heady smell of chloroform, of bandages and antiseptics, from which with the sickening taste of ether still in his mouth, his vocal cords severed and one arm out of action, he emerged to find out suddenly that beyond the shiny painted walls, the peaceful garden with

243

geometric lime trees and a goldfish pond, in the clumps of magnolia or behind the merciful statues in painted plaster, there was waiting for him, on the lookout for him, like the sturdy male nurses responsible for maintaining order in the quiet rest homes, a pack of organised killers who, as soon as he had passed through the iron gates, hurled themselves in his pursuit, running him to earth, hemming him in whilst he was no longer running any more now for any other reason than to flee, panic-stricken, through the streets of that town in which, the previous autumn, he thought he had caught a glimpse of the image of a new world, sleeping at night on waste ground, in gutted churches, derelict building sites, hunted like an animal, a stinking, terrified animal — and for months afterwards he was still running, although he was sitting in a quiet bedroom, enveloped in the peaceful English night, with, before him, that suitcase the handle of which had stayed in his hand, its shoddy locks torn off, its sides gaping, its derisory intestines of rubbish and old newspapers with yellowed paper, which he laboured again to gather up, put away in their imitation leather coffin, shutting the lid, closing up the tears as well as possible and replacing the missing handle and the faulty locks with innumerable interlaced pieces of old string so that it (the suitcase) now resembled those to be seen in stations and airports, carried on one shoulder by one or other of those emigrants floating in their threadbare garments, with their identical fevered, worn faces, their identical exhausted gaze, their identical mauve-clocked socks and their thin down-at-heel shoes, indiscriminantly assimilated (or rejected) in that im-precise family (or ethnic group) with hollow cheeks, greyish skin, vagrants chased from port to port, from station to station and from slum to slum by one relentless curse, they themselves, their swarming children, their heavy prolific women trotting along with lowered eyes, excised and enveloped in veils, their cardboard baggage counted and recounted at every change of train or boat, opened on the platforms, revealing their poignant contents — the togs, alarm-clocks, incense-burners, Swiss cuckoo-clocks and gilded Eiffel towers — sorted through by customs officers or policemen prodding them with their shoes, gathered up, rewrapped, redistributed anew piece by piece in the cardboard boxes, strengthened or rather hooped and bound by lengths of frayed string with that meticulousness, that undaunted fervour and that infinite patience so characteristic of the poor.

V

And he (he, the former captain of Bombardiers, the ex-Mountain deputy, the kingslayer, the Year II general, the ex-ambassador, the former Excellency) for one more year, like something tossed on the scrap heap, left on the shelf, discarded (since they had not managed (he had not managed) to destroy him (to destroy himself) — at least by means available to men: cannon, grapeshot, gunmen, judges, hangman or firing-squad, so that they (men) had given up, had left it to the laws of nature, knowing full well that somewhere, after all, in the mountain of flesh and bone, some tired, worn organ would in the end give out: sentenced then to this slow death, this betrayal, the desertion by this body killed under him, so to speak, with as little consideration as a war horse, a mount spurred to the point of exhaustion): one year more, then, and no other enemy to contend with other than this humiliating physical decay, staving off boredom or rather filling in, occupying as best he could the time he had left to live, deluding himself, calling for the barouche in order to drive around the pathetic domain of a couple of hundred acres (he who had ridden the length and breadth of Europe), the fields which he had over the years ploughed and reaped in his head, giving his orders now in person to her whom he had for so long bullied in letters, still through force of habit getting up at dawn or, when he really began to sink, having himself woken then at least, and going to sit (or having himself carried) onto the terrace which was nearing completion under his supervision, set down or rather tipped out by two farm workers on sunny days weather permitting, just as women get rid of a child they are suckling to go and see to the housework, scrub the floor, light the fire, do the washing-up, put things away, going from time to time (Batti) as far as the doorstep to take a look, not to make sure that he is still there but that he is still breathing, that a bird is not using him as a perch and that she will not in the evening have to clean off his shoulders a whitish layer of accumulated birdshit into the bargain: a spring, a summer, an autumn and the first days of winter, the positioning of the armchair changing by degrees as the day wore on and according to the season: fully exposed at first to the sun, turned three-quarters round nonetheless to shield his eyes, the downy buds barely sprouting on the plane tree, then the miniature leaves clinging to the branches tossing stiffly, bumping into each other in the bitter April wind, perhaps at that moment wearing a threadbare army greatcoat with fraying bands of tarnished gold, the raised collar making him appear to peep out of a turret, locks of his snowy mane sticking out from under his forage cap like ragged hemp, his old varicose-veined legs wrapped in a blanket, and that dead woman under the headstone in the valley bottom, the lips, the neck, the delicate breasts, the moist tender slit into which he had so often plunged, now so thoroughly decaying, tatters of rottenness hanging still from a few bones, from a jaw grinning rodent-like, teeth bared, the tomb, the mausoleum in austere classical style with its melancholy epitaph (and already invaded by moss, the black velvety patches almost hiding the chiselled letters, the marble names: Sparta, Greece . . .), not visible from the terrace where he too was now rotting alive, feeling day after day something like worms already hard at it, working surreptitiously towards his destruction, able to see over the elm walk, lower than the meadow where the graceful, dainty ghosts of dead colts trotted, the silvery tops of the poplars planted around the tomb, the endless flickering of pale leaves, catching their soft rustling, like ruffled silk, like an endless shudder, a muted, shivery, glum protest, and every so often this watchful, thoughtful glance shot at him, the sound of sweeping suspended, the figure in the doorway (but he did not move or turn his head), the tall woman with gaunt features under her flounced cap, not of the same blood but suckled at the same breast, who now, wizened and indestructible, fed him, put him to bed, helped him to get up, to dress, had his armchair moved as the days got longer, levelled out, then grew shorter again, bringing him sometimes, laying open on his lap, the register in which, as he slowly turned the pages, he stared with runny eyes at the much crossed out list of his stallions and mares with their Arab names (Harais, Nemena, Zeraide, Abdelmelec . . .) sired by the thoroughbred brought back from Africa or else acquired after a victory in conquered territory, sent home under military

250

escort, covered and crossed methodically afterwards and by correspondence as it were from Milan, Pomerania or Spain, dying without being replaced any more, the survivors harnessed less grandly, to ploughs or carts, the old wrinkled, freckled hand taking the pen which she (Batti) held out to it, crossing out in brown ink in a succession of oblique strokes, flat and slightly curved in the shape of an S, yet another of those descriptions in which, opposite the name written in the margin, the height, coat, markings, stockings and pedigree were meticulously set down: three or four lines which the deletions seemed to envelop in spirals like spiky sheaves of bones wrapped in rust or bituminous strips: mummies, the skeletons of chargers entrusted with escorting into the next world some pharaoh or satrap surrounded by his dogs, by his falcons, by his guards, the soldiers whose names he also kept lists of entered in other registers together with the record of their wounds and feats of arms, the volunteers who, under him, had taken the place of the cut-throats, village idiots and drunkards enlisted before by a recruiting sergeant on market days, in an inn corner for the price of a drink, dressed like clockwork toys or performing monkeys in brightly-coloured uniforms, leather straps and blancoed gaiters, whipped, broken on the wheel alive, or hanged for the slightest of offences, before the massed companies and squadrons of the regiments of the time, with their silk standards of pink, ivory, emerald green, sky blue, scarlet, saffron yellow, bearing the emblazoned names of the fiefs, the provinces, owned (regiments, horses, idiots, cannon, drunks, fifes, drums, waggons, gun carriages) like a sow, a cow, a donkey, exchanged, lent, purchased, or received in dowry (at the same time as towns, abbeys, valleys, forests, with their inhabitants, their stags, their beggars, their wild boars, their syndics, their partridges, their harvests, their does, their fir-plantations, their spinning-girls, their woodcutters, their oaks), thrown indiscriminately together as wedding presents, between damask sheets which gave off the ammonia smell of children's clumsy semen: Artois, Rohan, Soubise, Royal Allemand and the Toul Artillery which had seen him arrive at fifteen, his brand-new commission in his pocket, lugging about, with a sabre too large for anyone of his age, a stock of algebraic formulae and Latin authors no doubt also dinned into him by generous use of

251

the cane and the belt, bawling his head off in his just barely broken voice, manoeuvring louts some of whom were old enough to be his father, bringing guns into action, aiming the heavy bronze pieces with their chimera or dragon's mouths, starting to cast upon the world about him . . .

There is also, in this eastern garrison where he does his military service, an artillery regiment: at the far end of the parade ground they can see them bringing guns into action, the gun crews leaping off at full gallop, disconnecting the pieces of ordnance, swivelling them around, putting them in a firing position, the barrels raised quickly and made ready to fire, the tiny figures then ceasing to move, standing frozen to attention, every man at his post, whilst still galloping the teams sweep around the parade ground in a huge circle which eventually brings them back to the ordnance, the little figures in action again, running, bustling about, the first piece already hitched up and some way off already as the last team halts beside the last piece, so that the whole thing seems to be in perpetual motion, so that at no point do the horses seem to have stopped galloping, the commands and swearing of the NCOs coming from far away through the frosty air, the distant, flat little figures, men, guns, horses, bluish–grey, like lead soldiers, in the lemon, or pink, slightly misty light of winter days, their own NCOs briefly distracted too by the sight pulling themselves together again, yelling orders once more as to how to wield the sabre which they will never need to use, thrust to the front and to the left, thrust at an enemy on the ground, the sabre getting heavier all the time, the pain and weariness spreading out like tentacles from their shoulders, creeping round the shoulder blade into their back muscles, their sweat cooling instantly and making their stiff shirts stick to their skin.

. . . starting to cast upon the world about him that young giant's gaze, marked by a shrewd, patient serenity, his intellect maturing too, growing stronger all the time, while the silks of the quartered, emblazoned or fleur-de-lys standards frayed, ripped, fell in tatters at last, the dukes and princes whose names the regiments bore taking flight, or being chased away, plain numbers soon being given to the units, the half-brigades which were to replace the old mosaic of kingdoms, electorates and bishoprics with a new geography, the twin pages of the register divided into seven columns, the names and dates of birth of the men he had under his command, the communes and departments they came from in France, their service records, the comments (*dependable, has ability but lacks motivation, needs a sedentary post, particularly as his wound troubles him whenever the wind changes*) set down in the painstaking hand of the secretary leaving out or putting in capital letters at random, campaigns and feats of arms listed as in history textbooks, with the names of towns, fortresses or rivers standing out, like the pivots, epicentres or lines of force of some subterranean convulsion, the colossal upheaval of a whole continent (and of more than a continent: a millennia-old state of affairs condemned and swept away . . .), the wrinkled hands turning the leaves one after another, the sunken eyes in the puffy face all gone to fat glancing down the columns whenever a request or recommendation arrived, or a testimonial was asked for, for a post as gamekeeper, footman or janitor . . .

louis Cahagne, 35, Evrecy, dep^t of Calvados — veteran of all the Revolutionary campaigns: campaign of 1792 and 93 in the army of the north, id. those of years 2 and 3 in the army of the high alps, served in the blockade of Mantua and the siege of Valenciennes where he was wounded in the left cheek by a shell splinter in 1793, made a prisoner of war at the citadel of ferrara.

françois-simon Esselin, 34, Parroy, dep^t of the Meurthe — veteran of the Revolutionary campaigns in the armies of the Rhine, switzerland and Italy, he served at the siege of the city and fort of Manheim, at the blockade of Mainz and at the siege of Kehl; in the latter unspiked 10 pieces of campaign ordnance with the help of sergeant Breton of the same company and of the drum major of the 67th ½ brigade which had been spiked by the austrians.

françois Peutet, 47, Auxonne, dep^t of the Côte d'Or — served at the sieges of calvi, Mantua and perrugia, id. at the crossing of the mincio, at the battles of lodi and arcol where he kept on firing with a single piece of ordnance for a whole hour while the troops rallied.

pierre Amiel, 34, Saintegabelle, dep^t of the haute garonne — veteran of the campaigns of years 2 and 3 in the pirenees, of the ones following in Italy, received two bullet wounds with the 1st army, underwent the blockade of genoa in year 8, and . . .

. . . his tired arms finally letting go of the heavy register, dropping it on to his lap snugly wrapped in a blanket, the corners of the leaves curling in the same breeze that was making the shivering tops bend on the poplars at the bottom of the valley, a puff of wind perhaps lifting the pages, brutally flattening several of them with a worried sound of crumpled paper, a succession of tiny, sharp flapping sounds, the heavy grey-haired head drooping sideways, or thrown backwards, its eyes closed, the sun playing on the bloodshot eyelids and stretching, dividing, reassembling once more vaguely patterned shapes, incandescent, purple, jade, garnet, turquoise . . .

Or perhaps not: with his eyes open wide, staring unseeing straight at the drive with its elms, the meadow for the foals, the orchard, the facing slope of the dell, and on his lap (or perhaps on the table which he would get brought out, or else, on rainy days, in the library in the tower with its wooden panelling in which later the idiot was to store his heaps of seed potatoes) one of those plain unbound notebooks made up of leaves roughly sewn together by hand on the first pages of which he would write: 'Report on my embassy in Naples', or 'Travels in Barbary', or 'Recollections', his handwriting slack now, as if tabetic, resulting no doubt from his irregular heartbeat, the letters too large, sometimes almost skimped, scrawled, as if he lacked the strength, the first pages blackened in a kind of fury, of senile energy, the lines then becoming distended, divergent, with the corrections, deletions and insertions growing more numerous . . .

the french government was able to see only through the eyes of its agents who themselves could only see through the eyes of their passions so that with the best of intentions the government could be only the plaything of others' passions. It was this situation which at the court of naples led to an audacity which nothing could justify, they could not see the precipice towards which their ambition was precipitating them dragging them they hoped that the combined forces of austria and of england and of the two Sicilies were going to drive the french back over the alps they hoped perhaps that italy's discontent would break out in new sicilian vespers but republicans know that kings never forgive when danger struck they reunited to fight, the naples court was mistaken how could the neapolitan Gov^t be confident of success was it with troops raised hastily and half willingly half forcibly? was it with badly paid troops led by the stick that they hoped to defeat seasoned veterans of six or 7 campaigns, troops who had defeated those who passed for the best in Europe our republican phalanxes in a word in which every soldier knows that he is fighting on his own behalf and so becomes a hero; was it not the height of folly to wish to confront them with inexperienced soldiers recruits led by a general whose talents were proclaimed in the gazettes but who had not yet been seen in a line command? I tried to point out all these things to Mr de Gallo but it was in vain, I went to see both portici and pompeya in the one day; pompeya and herculanum were two cities of the roman empire they were engulfed in an eruption of Vesuvius in A.D. 79 the first of these two cities was by ash the second by lava the first was covered by a thin crust the fecond was buried more than 60 feet deep the latter city was destroyed by thick lava formed by fusion which resulted in a verie hard stone which formed one with the houses, the two cities were discovered by chance . . ,

. . . the erasures increasing in number as if in the old poorly-irrigated brain everything was getting mixed up, one thing on top of another, dissolving in a sort of indistinct jumble, men, countries, old scores: the thin notebooks abandoned almost at once, with a few leaves barely covered, as if in haste, as if he knew that his days were numbered, in that handwriting at first impetuous, violent, scarcely under control, becoming gradually disjointed, unsteady, the text stopping suddenly in the middle of a sentence, sometimes at the top of a page which was hardly begun . . .

. . . it is truly fatal as far as the prosperity of states is concerned that members of governments attach so little importance to the public-spirited actions of the agents they employ their carelefs attitude almost always betokens weaknefs and decay I had received the most flattering letter of thanks from the directory of liguria and the five directors of france my former colleagues had hardly any inkling of what I had done, one of them said as I entered his house and it was Reübel *ah so it's you? yes C^{zen} director you have been in Barbary? yes C^{zen} director were you made a eunuch? C^{zen} director you would furely not expect me to own up to it in front of these ladies another was* threillard *he received me in a most dignified fashion but did not ask me anything about my mission* Barras *gave me a friendly welcome but with the lack of attention of a man worn down by pleasure and lacking all interest in affairs of state, as for* merlin *and* larevellière *in spite of leaving my card 4 times at their residence their door was always closed to me the unassuming* larevellière *was always in the middle of the botanical gardens and* merlin *just like pigmalion kinge of egypt he saw in his palace only people he wanted to bribe or the legislators he was afraid of*

we were approaching the time of the partial renewal of the directory the priest Siéyès *a man always behind the scenes in the great events of the revolution although he was no stranger to any of them after having through cowardice refused the directory on principle had seen by their results that directors' posts were not to be sneezed at and might enable him to replace the tithes the loss of which was a matter of some regret to him while still obfcure and metaphifical he had founded a kind of fanatical fect and had profellites who only spoke when it was likely to procure him some advantage he operated at a considerable remove from the directory he affected never to see it but he had Ch . . . 1 and a few other henchmen who fomented plots of which he was the hidden instigator he longed in fpite of being reelected by the people to be ambassador in prussia he got his way he was the sure that from then on . . .*

the page in front of him hardly touched, his arm hanging down, his fingers still gripping the pen, the writer motionless, as if that huge carcass treated roughly for years despite its protestations, its wounds, its infirmities, humped about from battlefield to bivouac, from one siege to another, from election meeting to speaker's platform, dragged from torrid regions to frozen plains, worn out and broken, was giving in, giving up, as if the heap of old flesh and bone at the mercy now of a blood-vessel, now of a small vein threatening at any moment to burst, was refusing even to go on writing down words on a sheet of paper, remaining there then, without movement, in that more or less vegetative state deep into which no sounds reached him other than the tiny ones of the countryside. He had forgotten those sounds: it was as if he were rediscovering everything, his ears buzzing, his head still full of shouting, voices, abuse, bugle calls, cannonades, as he emerged from the long tumult which had begun (which he had entered, thrown himself into) twenty-two years earlier and which, since then, had never ceased, this whirlwind, this storm which had tossed him, raised him, lowered him, raised him again, borne him to the highest offices as if to cut him down the more effectively thereafter, hardly allowing him (between two campaigns, two missions, two commands or two elections) to as it were dismount, pass through the chateau gates, jump down in front of the steps from a carriage or a broken horse, bound up the stairs four at a time: barely enough respite to gaze upon the body of a dead young woman, to bury her, to kiss a child, pat the withers of the horses in the stable, get a fence raised and put back or a gap in a hedge mended, gone again already, already riding once more the rutted lanes, as if without even unbuckling his spurs, leaving hanging in the air behind him the smells of encampments, crowds, gunpowder and the stuffiness of assembly-rooms, he had merely crossed this landscape without stopping, these fields, these hills, this valley, these thickets which throughout all those years had existed for him only as things not quite real, with no substance other than the immateriality of memory, abstractly represented on the plan which he carried everywhere with him, unfolded every time he found an opportunity to do so under a tent, in a requisitioned palace or in a billet, and which he would pour over with knitted brow between two reports, two drafts of a speech or two army projects, would annotate, correct, embellish, furrow and plant by proxy, using not ploughs and harrows but that brown, rust-coloured ink, on the grainy paper of the innumerable letters sent to Batti, entrusted to unreliable mails or to a courier who happened to be going in that direction . . .

Then as if suddenly deaf — or what must have seemed to him at first like deafness, an additional affliction, an additional blemish, that is for the first time in twenty-two years, hearing (being able, being allowed to hear) the silence or rather the minute manifestations of silence in the rustling of grasses, leaves, the invisible movement of insects, the confused murmur of tiny hummings and flutterings: for years he had not heard (not heard that he was hearing) a bird sing, or felt (had not let himself feel) the cold, the heat: his old, worn-out body sensing now the warmth of the winter sun, the ozone fragrance of the icy air, the thin crackling of the frost, the sweet-smelling freshness of spring nights, the song of the nightingale, the scent of mown hay, of decaying autumn leaves, of burnt stubble, the cuckoo's call echoing in the woods; and during the long afternoons gilded rays playing amidst the leaves, dappling them with a lemon transparency, two sparrows sweeping down into one of the orchard trees, chirping, chasing each other and squabbling, invisible in the sharply rustling, shuddering boughs, while they flit here and there, hopping and toppling each other unexpectedly from one branch to another, twitching their tail feathers, taking flight, *the light gradually changing, fading, the faint barking of the dog that herded the cows straggling in the meadow, on the side of the hill, on the other side of the little valley, the pale, cumbersome shapes galloping stiffly, wavering back and forth, harried by the inexhaustible red-haired ball darting to and fro, descending, climbing, the suddenly-enhanced scent of the meadows, rising as the evening dew forms,*

257

the first vocal flourishes of the blackbird, below, somewhere in the poplars, the first attempts, hesitant, questioning, three notes, then silence, then three more notes, the valley slopes, the still woods, fathomless, reverberating the silence, then the double triplet, a burst of sound, coiling swiftly around itself, uncoiling itself, looping backwards, deviating, falling, breaking off sharply on a high note, unexpectedly, and silence again, the distant barking, the distant tinkling of cowbells, heard from the hill after an interval of time, as if in order to reach the ears of the old man-mountain seated upon the terrace the sounds had to penetrate dense walls of silence (and maybe it was not tiredness that had stilled his hand, leaving three-quarters of the page untouched: simply the cuckoo, the blackbird, the smell of the meadows . . .), as if he who was near to death was already separated from this world of many rustlings, of tiny echoes, by a window, one of those thick panes of glass which in aquariums define the boundaries between one element's empire and the next, *a long cloud in the shape of a fish hanging motionless floating above the darkened hilltop, pale at first, then salmon-pink in the periwinkle-blue sky, turquoise*, the birds falling silent one by one, he, still there, massive, more and more indistinct, as he, too, is enveloped in the gloom, and all of a sudden, behind him, a flickering light, coming and going, then the thin, dim shape of Batti standing out sharply against the lighted doorway (the old beast of burden, preserved or rather mummified, as if she had been faster than he, had overtaken him, while still alive had already entered a sort of immortality, a sort of final and definitive state which made her like one of those mythical creatures, one of those servant deities who must accompany the shades, help them across that last interval during which matter, sustained by momentum already gathered, lives on for a while yet, wearing itself out little by little, until the moment when it will stop forever), and almost immediately the sound of her footsteps on the terrace, a rustling of cloth, then her voice very near, mumbling while she gathered up the scattered papers, took the writing case, the blanket under her arm, then the two of them returning slowly towards the house, he leaning on her, she dressed in one of those hard-wearing loose blouses, one of those hard-wearing skirts cut from a piece of cloth that he had perhaps sent her years earlier, from Flanders or somewhere else, he in his old cape, his old soldier's greatcoat, and perhaps, before crossing the threshold, turning round one last time, looking at *the hillside now dark, the faintly phosphorescent spot where the cows were herded together for the night, the long fish-shaped cloud now completely black, floating or rather as though painted on glass, with its dorsal fin ruffled, coral in colour, like sparks, the cloud as though lightly brushed on, lit up by the reflection of a fire, set alight, blazing, then, suddenly, guttering, grey.*

And this dead person, Marianne, or rather this thing now, this pulpy mess (what?: scraps of shrivelled (or sticky?) cardboard, cavities, gaping holes — and perhaps brownish or yellow, if there had been any light, but all uniformly black in the black of the tomb) under the ton of rock, the neoclassical mausoleum in this, the bottom of the small valley, the spongy, permanently damp ground, the water which in winter over-flowed from the watercress bed seeping in through the joints of the tomb, through the rotten planks of the coffin, like nothing doubtless so much as an unmentionably foul mess floating damply in a black, putrid liquid, the long and imputrescible hair swaying, unwinding in lazy curls around the face with its empty eye-sockets, its tongueless mouth lipless, the incisors sticking out under the eaten-away nose, the empty breasts, like the flat black dugs of a monkey, like thick sticky slurries of bitumen covered with a viscous film as they cooled, with a leathery skin wrinkling under its own weight, the stomach (it was probably there that she had started to rot, that the worms had attacked) ripped apart by the gases, or rather torn to shreds, collapsed, and no more pubis, no more vulva apart from this wrinkled crack, retracted, creased like a mouth sucked in from the inside, gathered in, a few sparse, clinging hairs stuck on like a beard, a goatee beard, glued together, hanging under a prominent bone, the entire body (the thing) like one of those goatskin tents, eaten by mites and full of holes, with their ineradicable woolgrease stench, deserted, fallen in, still sup-ported here and there by shapeless debris, splinters, pegs leaning crookedly or broken: a carcass, remains . . .

And the other one, his second wife, the royalist, this Adelaide or rather this Omphale, whom he had snatched from the guillotine at the height of the Terror, married three days after the Tenth of Thermidor, and who left him now, a semi-invalid, to a lonely death in that godforsaken chateau, no longer writing to him except to ask for money, getting ready to betray him as soon

259

as he was cold, to denounce him, sully his name by giving it back the noble *de* which he had disdainfully dropped: this romance (or this abduction): he having just returned or rather escaped from Corsica . . .

The pompous language of the speech for the defence printed by courtesy of the barrister which seemed (with the same letters carved and cast by hand, the same typography) to be a ludicrous riposte to the Declaration of Opinion which twenty years earlier he whose effects she was now contesting had drafted and presented to an assembly so that his memory would remain indissolubly linked to what in his eyes was not simply a speech for the prosecution of a man but the proclamation of the end of one world and the advent of another:

ABSTRACT

FOR the defendant, Madame Adelaide Micoux, resident in Paris, widow of M. Jean-Pierre L. St M . . .
Major-General; Inspector
General of Artillery; Grand Offi-
cer of the Legion of Honour; Knight
of the Iron Cross;
AGAINST the plaintiff M. Eugène L. St M . . ., landowner residing at St M . . . de V . . .
For having concealed as heir an immense sum of money and several items of valuable jewellery thereby causing the loss to the widow, legatee of one quarter of her husband's estate
Providence has clearly protected the defence of Madame de St M . . .
God, who sees all crime, has brought into the light of day the mysterious disappearance of an immense sum of money and various jewels, made all the more precious due to the glorious circumstances to which General de St M . . . owed their acquisition.
The breaking of several seals, the escalade, forcible entry, theft . . .

this romance, then, or this abduction (although one may ask oneself which of the two — the man or the woman — had abducted the other): he just back from the island where for over a year he and a handful of men had stood up to a wild, insurgent population supported by two naval squadrons, escaping the ambushes, the assassins hired by the foreign power, eluding by night the watch of the English fleet in a small, plain boat, managing to reach Genoa, and from there Paris, then almost straight after Dunkirk, as if having left his cannon simply to rush to other ordnance, to command once more the battery formation, to coordinate the firing, as if having left the fight for a moment simply to gallop over France from south to north, holding his nose as he swept like a whirlwind through the town which gave off the stench of corpses, uncaring, disdainful of everything other than defending this thing for which he had left everything, risked everything, spilled his blood, too busy to linger, to take an interest in the quarrels, the intrigues, the blind struggles for power, ducking so to speak, without stopping in his gallop, to snatch up the woman with one arm, plucking her from the ground, hoisting her up behind him and carrying on, still galloping, running once more towards the cannon: a pause, a brief no not rest but change of scenery, of decor, between two battles, finding himself, his clothes still stiffened by sea salt, still lame perhaps from the shot received at Saint Florent, his trousers more or less repaired at the point where the bullet had ripped them, in Paris again, the city he had left fifteen months earlier, suddenly choked by something that was almost the opposite of the smells of gunpowder, of cordite, the fragrance of earth, of sea spray, that remained embedded in the folds of his clothes: as if, having barely crossed the barriers between the houses with their harsh outlines and heavy columns ringed by cubes, with the frieze of dancers in their flimsy short tunics, he had suddenly entered not a town but a sort of enclosed field, a sort of festering tip where, in a stench of stagnant blood, men were now clashing with each other, killing each other or rather completing the job of killing each other, exhausted, furious, aged by ten years, reduced to a state of parodical ghosts, caricatures of themselves, the last representatives of what had formerly constituted a sort of club, a closed circle whose rules for entry were based not on wealth or birth but on intelligence, magnanimity, courage, the unrecognizable survivors (men nearly all of whom he knew by their first names, with whom he was on familiar terms), fewer every day, caught in a trap, prisoners of a sort of labyrinth whose exits someone (some employee within the circle, some cruel and facetious usher, the attendant at the turkish baths perhaps) had supposedly locked, unsteady, haggard, like people under the influence of drink, leaning upon the oozing walls, paralysed with fear, with exhaustion, jumping at a footfall, at the shadow of a shadow, blindly battering each other to death, each trying to get in the first blow, joining forces like vagabonds or castaways in a group of ten in order to strangle the eleventh, then in a group of nine to strangle one of the ten, then eight, then seven, as if during his absence History had diverged, had, unseen, split, continuing on the one hand in broad daylight, openly, with cannon fire, on the other hand forced to make itself up, disregarding all known rules, groping along, faltering, slipping, suddenly losing its footing and thus losing its head, hurrying, running free, runaway even, veering towards parody, towards the farcical: one of those speeded-up films, with its feverish crowds, its jerky characters, their gestures incoherent, incomplete — or completed too soon — the invisible director in a hurry to finish it, overwhelmed by the retakes of a sequence acted out a hundred times before, barely allowing the actors time to reply, already beckoning to the next, tyrants, despots, for a month, a week, a day, dead the following evening, following on from one another, old actors worn out by thirty, jostling each other for the privilege of showing themselves off one last time, to exchange their life against the opportunity of delivering a monologue, a tirade, and more often than not, not even the entire tirade, no more than the first line, the first words, some actors insisting stubbornly, protesting, pushed off stage to the booing, the laughter, the jeering, others already cold, icy, as though prepared for a final ceremony, stiff, their jabots fluted with a small iron, spreading round them at the same time both a smell of starch and the stench of a tomb, affected, stilted, as if by one last challenge, a burst of arrogance and pride before death, they had straightened their clothing, tightened their cravats, standing stiffly, their necks cramped, their tail-coats over their stockinged calves, like some kind of wader, jerking their heads round, climbing the steps of the platform, watched by terrified eyes, placing before them the pages that had been corrected, altered all night, casting a final glance, filling their lungs, raising their heads, opening their mouths, interrupted, questioned almost immediately, and then standing there in silence, haughty, cold, indifferent, the useless pages still spread out, with their crossed-out words, their alterations added excitedly that very morning, at the last moment, already pushed back into the past, condemned, History already moving away, abandoning their truncated corpses, the headless monster in a never-finished death, the sun rising every morning over the muggy city, bathed in sweat, one day following another in paradoxical monotony, with their series of dull and devious police conspiracies, tedious plots all hatched, discovered and thwarted in one night on the same corner of a table by a few hard up prosecutors, clerks and judges clad in black, their shoes, stockings, breeches, their expressions and feathered hats all completely soaked in a bath of ink, like the embodiments of darkness, the officiating priests at pernickety, fussy rituals, scrupulously following the order of some liturgical calendar with the names of places and festivals printed in red, Carmel, Abbey, Bishopric, Mother of God, Saint Ammaranthus, time both static and runaway, History beginning to spin on the spot, without moving forward, with sudden flashbacks, unforeseeable detours, wandering aimlessly, sweeping away everything within reach of this kind of whirlpool, snatching himself on the way, by surprise, casting him (or hurling him) into the very centre of the maelstrom (perhaps to use him in a decorative sort of way, as a character witness, a guarantor, like those retired and doddering generals who are cleverly made to sit on the boards of bankrupt companies), keeping him well in sight, in his dusty and crumpled uniform, his breeches mended over the wound which would never heal up, at the very foot of this platform at the top of which a handful of half-mad men were threatening each other, anathematizing each other, vowing to send each other to the guillotine, listening to them, watching them, more impassive than ever, entrenched in or behind that monumental mass of calm, contenting himself with casting his eyes around him cautiously and expectantly like a man of the soil, a look inherited from his ancestors, the long line of local squires whose coats of arms had lost their shine, living like peasants in their chateaux with rickety furniture and threadbare carpets, and from whom he had inherited that inscrutable horsetrader's face, that ability to detect at a glance an animal that was sick or had been tampered with, the gift of suppressing, snuffing out their piercing light, the brightness which sometimes streamed from under the thick folds of his eyelids, just as he had learned on the battlefields to judge, assess in an instant the extent of a disaster, accept it, quickly work out what could be saved, rescued, and then reacting, moving into action, regaining his self control, wriggling out of the trap (unless he had only accepted the post, that hazardous job as secretary in an assembly of the living dead, as a better way of escape), using the weight, the prestige of his new title to force doors open, to penetrate the offices whose occupants with their sleepwalker's stare would on his entrance stop checking letters of denunciation, stop going over lists of people condemned to death, would gaze at him in amazement, like something come back from prehistoric times, listening to him without fully understanding, letting him exhort a signature, an order of mission, rummaging in the files to oblige him, in deference to some old friendship perhaps, or some service rendered (or perhaps simply these people, now no longer moved by anything, were trying to redeem their own past through him), pulling out a prisoners' register, or a list of suspects, making him repeat the name, raising their eyebrows in surprise, and in the end scribbling out a pass, a chit for a team of horses, a carriage, an escort maybe, and while the sound of his boots was fading away down the corridor, scratching their heads for a moment, picking another name at random and putting it in the place of the one they had just crossed out to make up the numbers, he, already in his carriage, crossing the barriers this time in the opposite direction, the precious piece of paper held at arm's length under the guards' noses, his cocked hat with its tricolour feathers filling the doorway, hiding from the armed men's sight the woman huddled up in the shadows, the future Omphale (met where? when? how? perhaps glimpsed or recognised between two guards in a corridor, in a court-clerk's antechamber, in one of the inky prosecutors', she pale, trembling, beseeching the monumental warrior through her tears, her plea granted with a shrug of the shoulders as a favour, a reward, booty?), already disguised perhaps by his huge dark greatcoat, its hood masking her face as if she were a Julie or a Briséis, a ribbon accentuating her bust, her hair done in the Greek style, as in the miniature which later (she was then bedecked with diamonds, decorative, demanding and tiresome, followed by a small black page in a brocade turban) a painter was to paint in grisaille of her neoclassical profile, but at this moment she was crouched in the back of the carriage, the cabriolet with the hood lowered (the berlin? the postchaise?)

inside which the jolts were throwing them roughly against each other, the closed, dark, suspended box jumping and bouncing in the ruts (and perhaps possessing her just there, without further ado, or rather mounting her, biting her mouth, her breasts, his herculean hand fumbling about under her long skirt, lifting it up, tearing it perhaps in his haste, uncovering her white thighs, her belly, her dense pubic hair, sitting her on top of him, both of them still brutally shaken by the jolts, she leaning forward, her hair disarranged, undone, hanging in front of her face, clinging as best she could to the supports of the hood or the door, whilst he groped, searching in the curly hair for the thin, narrow crack, the silky moistness, thrusting blindly the stallion's penis sticking out of him, muscular, erect, she still savagely thrown from one side of the gloomy box to the other, one hand still held out searching for something to get a grip on, the other guiding him, inserting between two jolts this stake, this impaling post, Leda, Io, Pasiphae, heaving a long sigh, starting to pant, her loins, her buttocks coming and going, lifting and falling, then jumping, then crashing, in a sort of fury or frenzy, both grunting loudly in the darkness (and perhaps through gaps in the foliage sweeping past the carriage a quick, furtive ray of moonlight appearing and disappearing, penetrating inside, and revealing bluish, marble-like thighs, muddled folds of cloth, an arched back, the cameo face now raised, contorted in a cry, now both shouting, or rather roaring, the general of Year II and the prisoner delivered from the dungeons of the Terror clinging fast to each other in a confusion of jolts, jerks, raucous noises: not love, not even pleasure, but animal rutting, satisfaction, deliverance, whinnying, plunging . . .) whilst, as the endless northern plains flew past under the wheels, the putridness became more distant, the evil-smelling maze of stones and streets, of empty palaces and of prisons, under its foul cover reeking of stagnant blood and badly-limed corpses, ceased gradually to poison the air — then he was there again: again cannon echoing majestically, the familiar, reassuring smell of gunpowder, of flint, of wad still smoking, he standing again on some escarpment or other, some dune, whipped up by the saline air, with again in the disc of his eye-glass, ramparts, smoke-shrouded ships, the sea oyster-coloured now, lowlands, phantasmagorical mountain ranges of motionless clouds, banked up over a flat horizon, distant steeples, limbered cannon still red hot, swept off at a gallop, unhitched, unlimbered, the battery thundering again, shaking the air, marking the beat with their solemn pounding (the captive, plaintive and grasping Briséis following with the baggage train, married between two cannonades, between the forcing of two breaches, the act drawn up, the contract drafted between two maps spread out, countersigned (as requisition, provision and revictualling orders are countersigned) between two commands to march and attack, by four general officers: the horses pawing impatiently outside, held by the orderlies, the four cocked hats with their rosettes, the four red, white and blue plumes bowing in turn, moving forward, swaying, then rising, continuing to rock for a moment, then stabilising, each of the four faces, weather-beaten, stern, expressionless, bending one after the other over the open register, the sound briefly heard of a quill pen scratching, of a signature being written, and afterwards the four faces, not smiling (they (the general officers) did not know (or knew no longer) how it was done exactly) but their features stretching horizontally, their eyes with fan-like wrinkles in the corners (the skin paler in the clefts of the folds, wan, almost tender) lingering momentarily over the bared bosom, the naked shoulders, and perhaps the brief ringing sound of clinked crystal (or of plain kitchen glasses), the brief sparkle of wine in the glasses (and maybe — as news of what had occurred three days earlier in Paris had just reached them — perhaps, in a forgotten (or repressed) reflex suddenly resurfacing after four years, the four waving, sumptuous plumes bending a second time, the four rough, leathery faces bowing again, each in turn, to kiss a woman's hand), then, like a metallic echo to the sound of glasses clinking, the four pairs of heels clicking, the four silvery ringing sounds of spurs, and that must have been about it), the maps spread out under the tents, or in the open windy air, soaked by the rain, on the trestle tables, with two or three stones, or a pistol, or a mud-stained sword stopping them from blowing away, or sheltered in a porchway, a farmyard barn, a market hall, or under the vaulted ceilings of a rathaus belonging to a fawning burgomaster, then (this time the carriage surrounded by hussars, the guards at the barriers doing the honours, the timorous Briséis no longer concealed fearfully in the shadow of the hood, but showing herself proudly at the door, wearing a low-cut dress despite the cold, adorned and bold) recalled, the return to the city which was still shaking, not properly roused from its nightmare, in a daze, at the start of a bleak and hard winter, which it was entering in a state of exhaustion, ruined, famished, while converging on her were the armies of an entire continent, kings thirsty for revenge, emperors momentarily terrified, attacking from without and within, from behind, by land and sea, already preparing their troops' victorious entry, with the names of the men who had made them tremble (or at least of those who were left) inscribed on lists of people to be executed or exiled, and then, behind a door guarded by an armed sentry, this: one of those scenes, those gaudy cheap pictures naively coloured in red and blue, like those life-sized portraits of people and period costumes which can be seen in waxwork museums where the hordes of visitors gaze with horror at an emaciated child surrounded by rats and sitting against the wall of a dungeon, watched over by a grim-faced warder, then gaze with admiration at a room with bee-motif wall-hangings, full of women wearing long dresses and diadem tiaras, bustling round a small podgy man wearing a grey–green frock coat, whose small hands stir a cup of coffee, and between the two (between the gloomy cell and the richly decorated room) a room with walls and tables covered in maps (and not of a delta, or polders, or a province this time, but of the entire course of a river, a section, an entire slice of Europe), the people not made of wax, rigid, but moving, speaking, the faint murmur of the calm, steady voices of men accustomed to giving orders and to being obeyed without needing to raise their voices, coming, going, sitting down, passing along some missive or other, getting engrossed in confabulations, reflecting, standing up, walking, alone or in pairs, up and down, not through nervousness but because of the simple bodily reflex for which movement, exercise, physical fatigue are necessities, and enclosed there, taken away from their tents, their camps, their bivouacs, made to think war, that is to say, to think sectors, strengths, dispatches from ambassadors, reports from spies, from the police, transactions, dismissals, sectors, proclama-tions, means of subsistence, grain, rest stops, coin, horses, mules, forges, epidemics, powder, cannonballs, saltpetre, shredded linen bandages, nails . . ., and sometimes, outside, distant at first, vague, indistinct, then getting clearer, a humming sound, then a rumbling, then, coming to strike the walls, a surge, turmoil, clamour, raised fists, jeering, death cries, one of the people in the room, perhaps he (his massive back bent over a table, his ruffled shock of hair framing his proconsular mask), or someone else (to be present no longer meant to rule, to impose the law, but simply, for four months, for each of them in turn to get through the work), so one of them, lifting his head again, with knitted brows (not worried, not alarmed, just irritated) saying without raising his voice: 'What is it?,' not expecting any reply, not even expecting the man to turn who had walked towards the window, drawn back the curtains, glanced down at the sea of upturned, protesting, half-starved faces contorted with anger, saying in the same calm, steady voice: 'Bread? Yes. Of course,' saying again as he bent over once more, his head once more bowed, industriously scribbling something in the margin of a letter, a dispatch: 'What are the guards waiting for?,' reading through and perhaps crossing out or correcting what he has just written, saying in the voice of one doing (or thinking) two things at once: 'Those fake notes they print in London, it shouldn't really be that difficult to find them . . .,' saying: 'Those in the front,' taking up his pen again, thinking for a moment, saying again: 'No: behind the women,' then, forgetting the shouting, getting up, turning his back on the commotion, the furious clamour of the human mass that was backing away from the whips, the bayonets and the thrusting horses, signalling to the others (the other gold-braided uniforms — but not much braid: he was still only a brigadier himself, and some of them were not even professional soldiers — though they had led charges, armed simply with a plumed hat, a scarf and a sword, seized trenchworks, batteries, withstood the charge of the Croatian horse, marching at the head of battalions of ill-trained recruits, not even turning round to see if the rest were following), going over to one or other of the maps spread out on the tables or pinned to the wall, the little group of men stopping there, pensive, consulting each other in hushed tones, exchanging brief remarks, contemplating the meandering course of rivers, of coasts, the empty expanses of paper, examining and comparing their notes, counting and

268

recounting the brigades, the divisions, the armies halved in size, reassessing yet again the contents of depots and arsenals and magazines all three-quarters empty, attempting to calculate marches in terms of empty stomachs, unshod feet, lame horses, rereading ambassadors' dispatches, spies' reports, prisoners' statements, glancing once more at the outline of the besieged citadel a thousand kilometres long and as much across, dusk falling, orderlies and ushers carrying in the lamps, the hours passing, night slipping by, the candlesticks and candles gradually burning down, flickering, collapsing, while a winter dawn was breaking behind the windows, with their panes, dirty or white with frost, and eventually the last of them (the three or four with or without braid) parting, leaving him alone amidst the spread-out maps, the torn-up drafts of orders, starting to dictate to the secretary the halting, clumsy, harsh and ludicrous sentences, giving orders to retreating troops to attack, to manhandle the guns, to seize provisions from the enemy, the regular thud of his heels, the creaking of the floor under his tremendous weight accompanying in the silence the faint scratching of the pen on the paper, faltering, breaking off while he would look with astonishment (or perhaps with implicit approval for self-control, order, meticulousness) over his secretary's shoulder at the delicate, fine hand which had never grasped the hilt or butt of a weapon (unless the secretary happened to be an old disabled sergeant-major, inflexible over the flourishes and regulation embellishments), scrupulously adorning with loops and complicated elegant astragals those orders at the foot of which he would quickly make, crushing the pen as if were a seal, the unyielding mark of authority, a scrawl, some sort of ball of tangled string instantly recognisable to the recipients of the missives feverishly torn open, unfolded, read with a curse, crumpled furiously into a ball, perhaps stamped upon in rage by desperate generals, the messengers galloping off with the sealed dispatches, terse, menacing assemblages of words which using nothing more than a little pink ink on a scrap of paper managed to get exhausted armies to advance and conquer, which emphasised the stubborn determination of the shaky power, itself in an equally desperate predicament, the secretary helping him on at last with the huge greatcoat which he would draw around himself like a toga . . .

269

17 Germinal Year 3. From the Committee of Public Safety to the People's Representatives with the Armies of the North, Sambre and Meuse, Moselle and Rhine, Alps and Italy, Eastern Pyrenees, Western Pyrenees, Brest and Cherbourg Coasts:

Dear Colleagues, We hereby inform you that the enemy's hopes have once more been dashed. For some time now all bulletins from abroad have been giving warning of impending insurrection in Paris. The false food shortage was the pretext, Royalism audaciously raised its head, but the National Convention, firm at its post, bided its time to strike back at the instigators, yesterday seizing the opportunity. Yesterday a number of sections came to the bar to present a petition concerning provisions. The Convention believing itself amongst brothers received these citizens without regard to their numbers, when in contempt of the law and the respect due to the National Representatives, the seat of its deliberations was violated, but at the call to rally, at the summons to arms, the good citizens came in a body and surrounded the Convention, peace was restored in the seat of deliberations and public order was upheld in Paris.

The four People's Representatives, whose trial had been a matter of dispute for some time, were sentenced to be deported. The National Convention has ordered People's Representatives Choudieu, Foussedaire, Huguet, Leonard Bourdon, Ducamps and Châlier to be held at the chateau of Ham.

Amar and Ducheur have been arrested.

Keep order within your armies, there has been no disturbance here. The staunch attitude of the National Convention has imposed respect on all those wishing it ill, all instigators of Royalism and Terrorism will be assid-uously sought out, and the Constituted Authorities will be cleansed of them.

We are sending you the Laws passed on this matter and the Decree which has been issued about it. Watch closely the movements of the Armies in front of you, we have reason to believe that it was a planned move and it could be that the enemy sought to coordinate external actions with internal ones. The whole plan has collapsed, we have thwarted the former and we rely on you to deal with the latter.

The National Convention congratulates you on not having forgotten that the laurels which you have won must be a constant reminder of your triumphs and of your obligations. You have not shed so much blood, braved so many dangers and endured so many hardships just to stand by and watch the motherland torn apart by factions and anarchists and to see yourselves bowing again beneath the yoke of the monarchy which you helped to destroy.

Bring to completion what you have started so well, lay our external enemies low, whilst the steadfast and courageous National Convention will avenge your motherland on agitators and trouble makers.

General in Chief Pichegru has been appointed Commander of the Armed Forces in Paris for the duration of the present insurgency. In a few days' time he will go to the Army of the Rhine.

Please put this letter on general orders. Fraternally Yours.

. . . the huge greatcoat which he would draw around himself like a toga, with a flap thrown over his shoulder, walking already, stopping, retracing his steps, perhaps stopping again in front of a map, the secretary catching up with him, talking rapidly to him, the head already wearing the plumed cocked hat nodding in agreement, and as he was walking away, leaving the room, the secretary coming back to sit at the table, taking another sheet, the pen running again over the paper . . .

The Committee of Public Safety resolves that the Weapons and Gunpowder Commission of the republic supply a fine hussar sabre with belt to War Commissioner Lierval employed in the service of the Committee of Public Safety to replace the one he lost while defending the National Convention. He will also be given two fine pistols.

. . . the footfalls dying away in the long corridors, the giant saluting the sentry absent-mindedly, climbing, exhausted, into his carriage, waiting to drive him back in the growing dawn through the city streets still strewn perhaps with debris, those mounds of wreckage which riots leave behind them, to the rue du Hasard whose name was seemingly chosen by fate itself, stopping in front of a house where he ponderously climbed the stairs, pushing a door open, standing on the threshold gazing at the untidy drawing-room, still warm (the Briséis, the Omphale now no longer humped along with the baggage in a waggon but settled amidst mahogany furniture, spending her days reclining artistically on one elbow on a Pompei-style couch, or sitting at a spinet, or a harp, surrounded by other Omphales, other Julies, by dandies with hair done like the coat of a wet dog, silk cravats, kid boots), casting his eye over the leftovers of supper, the half-empty glasses, scattered packs of cards, a music score still open on the keyboard: not bitter, mocking rather (with barely, perhaps, on one side of his mouth, a slight pull or curl of the lips), as if he were gazing at himself — either his destiny, or History, futility, fatality — blocked inside the colossal im-

271

passivity which allowed him to face up to setbacks and disasters, whether they were the result of the fortunes of war, of men, of a woman, of intrigue: as if absent, as if the hundredweight of muscle and bone were concealing . . .

breaking of several seals, the escalade, forcible entry, theft, with the help of several persons, in an inhabited house, the removal of seven hundred thousand francs in cash, more than six hundred and fifty thousand of which in gold: the criminal hand which received the stolen money; everything is known, everything is sworn.

The certainty of these facts has become a matter of common knowledge.

This Abstract has no other object than to give the details and to apply to them the laws which assure Madame de St M . . . of the recovery of the effects stolen from her in her husband's estate.

FACTS

On 1st September 1806, *General de St M . . . made his will in his own hand: it was recorded and deposited with M. Grélet, solicitor in* Paris, *on* 10 February *last.*

The testator declares Eugène-Maurice-Henri L . . . St M . . . *his* son, *his* SOLE *heir.*

I give to Adelaide Micoux *my dear wife, the quarter of my goods in full ownership: plus a quarter to be enjoyed during her lifetime only.*

Since I do not want any dividing up and sharing out *of the* real estate, *the entire property at* St M . . . de V . . . *will go to my son, and* Bauchamp *to my wife.*

I suppose that they will both sufficiently *respect* my wishes, *whose sole aim is to avoid any arguments between my wife and my son, to take the two built properties, one of which I assess at a quarter of the value of the other, without repeat of added value, given that I estimate* Bauchamp *at only twenty-five thousand francs, because it is almost all laid out as unproductive pleasure garden, and is burdened with the maintenance of the surrounding walls.*

I estimate St M . . . de V . . . *at* one hundred thousand *francs.*

Should the parties concerned however not wish to accept my estimate, the two built properties would not be any the less indivisible, *and each would belong to the person to whom I give it under the present clauses, with the exception of the one who will have too much, to transfer it to the other in the dividing-out.*

The contracts and notes *will be shared out in the proportion which I have above established.*

The personal effects, furniture *and* everything *which will be at* St M . . . *at the testator's death will go to the testator's son, who will have sole possession,* without exception or division, *and likewise the horses,* dogs *and ploughing gear.*

In the same way, *my wife will have* sole ownership of everything *to be found in* Paris *and* at Bauchamp, *furniture, linen, her personal jewellery, for her own use,* without valuation.

My personal wardrobe *will go to my son. Regarding* the silver, *this will be shared out in the above proportion, with the exception of a small silver soup tureen which I gave my wife as a birthday present and is hers by right already.*

The small coffee-pot with three cups will go to my son, since it came from his paternal grandfather.

It is obvious that, in his will, General de St M . . . forbade the dividing up *and* sharing out of his real estate.

Like Mithridates, *he arranged with a word for the sharing out of his possessions.*

St M . . . *to my son; to my wife,* Bauchamp.

For you, Pontus: *for you,* Colchos: Racine.

General de St M . . . *died* with this intention on 27 January last, at seven o'clock in the evening.

Everything indicates that he suffered a stroke: he was in an armchair by the fire: he wanted to change places: as he was being turned round, he died.

In the morning of the day of his death, the General had washed and dressed very early.

He had gone up to his terrace: he had spoken to the workmen who were building it: he had been to see a plasterer in one room, and a decorator in another.

He sent a groom to take a horse to his son in Toulouse.

That same day he died, the general wrote to his wife, Madame de St M . ., *in Paris: he charged Mr Fabre, the local mayor, with posting the letter in St A . . ., which is the nearest post office.*

This letter will be too influential in the case: it is too important for the truth, for it not to be copied out in its entirety here: its contents are as follows:

St M . . . *the evening of the 27th, 1812*

TO MY WIFE,

I have just had a violent attack, and I cannot see my son arriving: I am

273

very worried about what may have happened to him. *I may lose consciousness*; I alert you *therefore to the fact that I leave here* in a water jug twenty-four thousand Napoleons: *plus*, six thousand in my writing desk. Louis, *the mayor*, knows about it. *There are in addition a roll of* louis, *and a few bags of crowns*, which I am relying on to pay for the diamonds.

M. Lacombe (Joseph) *will show you what I have on the* Toulouse *stock-market: that amounts to some thirty thousand francs. I have one more property which he knows about: you will tell* Eugène *about the money with* Solages *and at* Pontoise. *I am convinced that you will live in harmony together:* Le Bugnet *owes me twelve thousand francs. Farewell, dear children; if I die, love one another.*

Yours affectionately, J.P. L . . . St M . . . — *signed thus in his usual signature.*

This letter reached Madame de St M . . . *in Paris by the same post as the news of her husband's death.*

The property of the estate began to be removed on the very day he died.

Shortly before, the general had given his cook, Marie-Anne Dubos, the key to his study to look after.

In this study was the bureau which the general refers to as his writing desk, *in the letter which . . .*

. . . as if the hundred weight of muscle and bone were concealing, were hiding something impossible to kill, as imperturbable at the sight as of one of his ruined batteries, among the overturned guns, the dead men, the horses thrashing in their entrails, as in the middle of an assembly of yelling madmen, or else bombarded with dispatches, with appeals for reinforcements, examining bare, empty maps, then later, when the tide ebbed, swept along but still standing in the eddies, the confusion, held up to ridicule, booed by the very same people who had pushed him forward, retreating from an attacking, vengeful rabble made up of notables, wig makers and priests, and then coming up again, displaying once more in some council or at another meeting (and then in a foreign court, then in captivity, and later in some new form of disgrace, and later surmounting ever more heavily braided uniforms), the Roman senator's features, gradually thickening out, becoming blotchy, his flesh sagging, framed by grey wisps of hair and topped with the old forage cap, firmly clamping up on his secret, with that slight grin which perhaps played upon his lips, the huge old collection of maltreated organs, pipes, tubes, intestines, membranes, all sitting heavily on the terrace, his eyes staring, vacant, looking every evening at the shadows that crept slowly over the meadows, invaded the little valley, shrouded the woods and hedges one by one, gradually darkened the silhouette of the hill that stood out movingly against the sky, made the shadow under the foliage of the elm walk more dense, spreading like a black cloak the nostalgic and silent dusk punctured here and there in the distance by the faint barking of a dog.

And the brother! . . . The younger one, the Chevalier, the ghost, now nothing but a decaying corpse, like she who lay under the poplars at the bottom of the valley, that part of himself which, for him, had begun to rot even during his lifetime, right from the moment when he had torn it out of himself, stripped himself of it by an act of terrible mutilation, as if he were tearing his eyes out or chopping off a gangrenous limb, or to obey some biblical commandment, not only refusing to recognize him, but blotting him from his memory, never writing that name (Jean-Marie) which somehow comple-mented his own (Jean-Pierre), the two only distinguished by the female addition, as if at their baptism it had been intended to join the two boys in one bicephalous being, speaking of him, when he had to, with the apparent indifference he would have shown a neighbour or stranger in a dispute over boundaries or a disagreement over a right of way, referring to him then not by his first name, those syllables, that familiar collection of sounds almost exactly like his own, but rather by calling him 'my brother', not only in his dealings with other people, not only with his own family, his mother or his sisters (spending in any case years separated from them — as if in return they had expelled him from their universe, cut him off, flung him from them with horror), but even with Batti, charging her laconically on his decisions, writing to her: 'You will tell my mother and my sisters that the deal they are offering me over my brother's inheritance is worthy of an imbecile, and I am not one,' or: 'As you know, my brother . . .,' or again: 'My brother's share . . .,' and nothing further.

To Batti! To her! . . . She who was, so to speak, like another

275

brother, that is, more than a sister — not of the same blood but of the same milk as they, with whom they had been as one: fed, grown up in their shadow, all three of them with the same bare, hard-skinned feet, the same grazed knees, the same lips stained with blackberry juice, the same torn clothes (and she probably knocked over, mounted — as they could observe the bull or the stallion doing — by one or the other, or by each in turn: in the hay, in a corner of the barn, or in a meadow, behind a hedge, in the shelter of a thicket, forced by the threat of a clip over the ears, tripped and thrown on the ground, choking back her sobs, sniffing back her snot, rewarded (her smile showing through her tears) with a captive cricket, birds taken from a nest: she standing full of alarm at the foot of the tree, her head thrown back, one hand pressed tightly over her lips, watching them disappear in the highest branches: the screeching parents' frantic circling above the sun-riddled canopy, the downy grey balls, their tragic sightless heads, with wide open oversized beaks, yellow, avid, protesting, stuck on top of stringy, purple necks — and the freshwater crayfish, the snared rabbits, the sharp juice of stolen apples, the sledge in winter on the shiny black ice of the steep road, the same punishments, the same birchings, the same, not tutor but parish priest, the same who had taught her to read and write alongside them, as a sort of fee, a due, a payment in return for the milk they had sucked . . .

Then suddenly she was left alone. Or rather, in the first stage, left alone together: no longer three but two: she and the younger one for one year more — but it was already over: as if she could not separate them, conceive (in the double meaning of the word, that is in her mind and in her being as a woman) of the one without the other, widowed (soon twice over) at an age when girls do not even know yet how boys are made, knowing (when they returned, reappearing for a few days, with their three-cornered hats, their curled wigs, their boots, their swords, their brutish ways of brutalised young lads, trained brutally to obey and to command) that she could expect nothing more from them than the passing stroke which might be given to a bitch, to the old mare they had been first lifted on to, one of them perhaps whistling softly to her, the gun already under his arm, giving her a wink on the way through the kitchen, making the agreed sign, a silent lip movement, towards the woods, the cover, the shed, and making an excuse, she getting away, running along the muddy lanes or those concealed by weeds, joining him, breathless, passionate, mad not with pleasure received but with the pleasure she gave, not expecting more, not imagining even that she could be jealous, taking the sheets from the cupboard, removing the lavender sachets, unfolding them, supervising personally the preparation of the bedroom, perhaps putting a bouquet of wild flowers in a vase, then waiting on the steps for the carriage which finally arriving, coming to a halt, tilting sideways under the weight of the giant getting out, who turning then helped out in her turn the delicate foreigner (the Dutch woman) whom he led up the steps: passing the male staff, the cook, the cowherd, then the female staff, introducing them one after the other, and introducing her last of all (perhaps in a slightly different way, saying for example: 'And this is Batti . . .,' or maybe not, maybe just: 'Leon, François, Louis, Albert, Batti . . .').

Then transferring on to the newcomer (since she had been chosen by one of them, she was by virtue of that fact a part of him — and later, when she was dead, on to the child, the son who if he was not the product of her womb had been given her as it were by proxy), transferring then to the newcomer that fidelity, that animal devotion, and perhaps, between the two women (the one, the blond delicate Huguenot snatched from her mists and canals, from the gleaming interiors of cloth merchants or diamond dealers, exiled in this chateau which was in fact nothing more than a big farmhouse flanked by towers and inhabited by half-savage creatures barring the door of their wretched church to her as to animals — the other, the peasant, with her face burned by the summers, the winters, an impassioned, inscrutable face, treated herself with scant regard as little better than a beast), perhaps then, between the two of them (they who had both experienced the weight of the same body, the same muscular thrusts, the same savage, weighty bull's discharge) a sort of connivance, a kind of complicity, throughout those years when he appeared only now and again, thanks to a bit of leave, for a few days, soon going off again, leaving them alone, coming back, abandoning them once more (now, when he turned up, there was no longer, hanging about him, that indelible wild animal scent, those sharp odours of

277

sweat, of rotten straw, of gun grease, of leather equipment, but of something different: the dense smells of public meetings, of assembled crowds, an effervescence, an excitement . . .), and she again (still she: a little bonier perhaps, with that impassive wooden face typical of a country woman close on forty) choosing with care the finest linen, wrapping up the young woman's corpse in it, pulling the end of the flap over her waxen features (as she was to do for him twenty-two years later), and after that the child all for herself alone: not a triumph, not getting her own back: she had no doubt always considered that he belonged to her, like those lawful but barren wives in the Bible or in primitive tribes astride whose bodies a pregnant Circassian or Numidian slave comes to give birth, squatting, twisted with pain, flooding them with her blood and her waters, giving them in this way the child which will be their own, all for herself now, then, without even any of those brief appearances any more . . .

in this study was the bureau which the general refers to as his writing desk, *in the letter which has just been transcribed: the same in which were the* six thousand Napoleons, *the roll of gold louis and the bags of crown pieces mentioned in his letter to Madame de* St M . . .

The woman Batti, chief servant or housekeeper in the household came the same evening to ask the cook for the key to this room.

The cook was unwilling to entrust her with it: without showing either mistrust, or suspicion, she chose instead to accompany Batti to the study.

She saw that in crossing the general's bedroom, Batti *opened the drawer of a chiffonier*, and that she took from it two golden snuff-boxes: *one with the picture of the viceroy* of Italy; *the other larger, oval in shape and chequered.* Batti *took* both of them *away.*

She walked round the study with the writing-desk, peeping here and there, and left in possession of the two snuff-boxes: Batti *placed them in a cupboard in the bedroom over the kitchen, to the left of the fireplace: this cupboard was* for Batti's exclusive use.

The next morning, the 28th of the same month, at very first light, Batti, *who slept in the cook's bedroom, rose before she did, and asked her again for the key to the study with the writing desk.*

The cook replied that this key was in her pockets, hanging on a chair beside her bed.

Batti *rummaged in these pockets*, took the key, *and left alone, while the cook was still in bed.*

Batti, *accompanied by* Joseph Pequet, *manservant, and by* Blanchard, *groom, went up to the general's study*; going to the writing desk, she showed them a lady's leather elbow-glove, long in form, filled with gold.

Batti took part of this gold from the glove, *saying that she would share it with them* (Pequet *and* Blanchard), *if Master* Eugène *failed to return.*

Batti also found, in the writing-desk, rolls which she opened, which she checked, and which also contained gold coins. (*Everything which is in Roman in this Abstract expresses a fact known for certain, or the text of a law.*)

As Batti *checked these rolls, she put them in the leather glove*, until the said glove was full once more; *then she tied it up again, and gave it to* Blanchard: *she charged him, and* Pequet, to put it in a place where it would be safe.

Both men went straight to their bedroom: Blanchard, *in* Pequet's *presence, put the glove* filled with gold under their mattress, on a plank of their bed.

As they went out of the study to go to hide the glove filled with gold, *the manservant and* Blanchard *left* Batti alone in the study in front of the writing desk in which there were other rolls, after the glove had been opened, filled, and closed again.

There were also in the writing-desk full bags, *similar to money-bags, which were not opened in the presence of the manservant, or of* Blanchard; *and finally a gold snuff-box which* . . .

. . . without even any of those brief appearances any more, the sudden cracking of whips, the sudden crunching of gravel under the wheels of a carriage, the hooves of a weary horse, the sudden intrusion of the booted, mud-bespattered giant striding across the hall, going straight up to the child's bedroom, inquiring after his health, then disappearing again. Nor the other (the other giant): neither had the time now to come (too many things were happening then, too quickly, too far away: things too remote from the world around her: things one only learned on market days, in town, or from a pedlar, or a passing traveller, a notice put up or trumpeted by the town crier . . .), she just about got news of them from letters: those which arrived from Strasbourg with monotonous regularity (and more than monotony: she could feel his presence, even though she did not read them, only stood there after handing them to the old lady

279

who opened them, read them, saying simply at the end: 'My son' (or perhaps 'Jean-Marie') 'sends his greetings' (or perhaps 'sends his love'), then fell silent, absorbed in thought, dismissed her, with unmoving gaze, fiddling with the folded sheet in her hand) — and the others (the other letters, the first of the innumerable missives which were to follow one another for twenty years, addressed first of all to Mademoiselle Batti, then to Citizeness Batti, then once more to Mademoiselle Batti), sent, the letters, from Paris, Soissons, Toulon, Savoy and again from Paris (and later from all the corners of Europe), scribbled in haste, sometimes under a tent, or by means of a postal relay, in the evening at an overnight stop, devoted more or less entirely to instructions about sowing, wood-cutting, planting or bottling, but which seemed, in an indefinable way too, to bring with them something of that ceaseless movement, those tumultuous comings and goings under whose auspices they were written —and she for a moment lost in thought, trying to understand, suspecting with a vague anguish, an obscure foreboding of trouble, what was different, what was grimly incompatible between the letters sent from Strasbourg and the others, reflecting, then preferring not to reflect, shutting her eyes, blotting everything out: the child was there: she asked for nothing more: it was as if everything were beginning again: the same places, the same games, the same grazed knees, the same crayfish in the stream, the same crickets, the same birds plucked from the nest, the same frozen scent of lilac in spring, the same insistent song of the nightingale reverberating on May nights, the same flocks of starlings in autumn, the same . . .

Then he was taken from her. That is to say she got a letter (not from Strasbourg: it was a long time now since one had reached her from there any more, since she had last heard the old lady say as she folded up the opened letter: 'Jean-Marie sends his greetings' . . .) telling her to get the boy's clothes and his linen ready, and informing her that he would be fetched or that she had to take him to a place where he too would be taught differential calculus, the existence of irrational numbers, Latin, and the way a cannon is fired.

And then, almost at once, the other returned. As if somewhere in the wings someone was seeing to it that the stage was needful, or rather what was never left empty, that she (Batti) never lacked for long what was needful for her. For assuredly it was her that he came to find, instinctively, naturally, without even thinking that he had a mother, sisters as well, sisters: on the lookout for her, knowing her habits, the jobs she did, the paths she took: lurking behind a hedge in his ragged clothes, whistling softly as she passed by, and she giving a start, halting, making him out suddenly, shuddering, biting her fist so as not to cry out, looking at him (her eyes wide with fear, with pity, and filling with tears): a wolf, a wild beast: emaciated, his cheeks covered with beard, whilst he emerged from the bushes, casting furtive glances to right and left, beckoning to her, drawing her into the undergrowth, and the two of them now, the two animals, the beast preyed upon and the beast of burden face to face, staring at each other (she hardly seeing him, glimpsing through a misty blur the exhausted, feverish, bristly face, which seemed to liquify, to melt, to slither as it dissolved in her tears), both of them (in one of these same paths, at the corner of one of these same woods) worn, aged, beyond their actual number of years, she who ever since she had been able to dress herself had got up every day before dawn, had slept all her life in an unheated hovel, broken the ice in the pitcher, in winter, to wash, who had helped the cows to calve, had ruled over the servants, kept vigil over the dead, had never owned more than one spare garment, for whom . . .

As she gave them the glove, Batti told them that if Master Eugène came back, the glove would be returned to him; if not its contents *would be shared between* Batti, *the manservant and* Blanchard.

These acts of purloining must have taken some time, because the cook was still in bed when Batti *took the key to the study; and when she returned to hand it back, the cook was already in her kitchen.*

Batti told her that she had taken money from the writing-desk to run the household; that if Master *Eugène* did not turn up, they must not get into difficulties; that if Master *Eugène* did not come back, the money would be shared amongst the four of them.

Back in the kitchen, Batti *asked* Blanchard *and* Pequet, *in front of the cook, if they had locked their room; when they said no,* Batti *told them that they ought to have remembered* what it contained.

It is appropriate to set down here, without getting dates confused, something which happened earlier; it helps to give an idea of the value of the rolls.

In the very month of his death, *this general wrote asking M. Hugonet, his friend, to bring to him at St M . . . M. Rigale, one of the most famous surgeons in the district, and as distinguished by his learning and his services to the community as by the rewards heaped on him by government on several occasions.*

The general sent a relay from St M . . . to meet them half-way . . .

M. Rigale, on arrival, attended to the general's case and lavished upon him the comfort and counsel which his state of health required. As a result, the general was able, by taking care, to prolong his career yet further.

He presented M. Rigale with a hundred francs as the fee for his visit; he asked M. Hugonet if that amount sufficed; he added that he was about to make a much more considerable outlay, which he had to take from there, pointing to the writing-desk and tapping on it, twenty-four or twenty-five thousand francs *for his future daughter-in-law's diamonds.*

Indeed, M. Hugonet saw on the writing-desk a green silk purse, full of cash; with gold pieces beside it, and rolls of coin wrapped in paper.

The same day 28 January, they started putting the seals on; some *say at ten in the morning, others at one o'clock* in the afternoon.

It makes no difference; prudent Batti *had already succeeded in diverting a considerable part of the gold, silver and jewellery.*

Master Eugène St M . . . *arrived the same evening, after his father's interment.*

He has just declared quite recently that on his arrival, Batti *handed him part of the purloined items, that is, two golden snuff boxes and eight thousand francs.*

M. Eugène St M . . . *received also from* Mr Joseph Lacombe *twenty-four thousand francs in* gold Napoleons, *kept in a water jug.*

When the seals had been put on, the magistrate took away the keys of the locks on which the seals had been placed.

Batti too had duplicate keys; *in this way*, she could open and close the cupboards as she liked.

She removed the seal bands with the blade of a knife, softening with a candle the wax which held them in place.

As soon as she had opened the cupboards, Batti took from them what she considered appropriate, closed them, and reinstated the seals, softening the stamps again with a candle-flame, applying

282

her thumb onto the wax as the only imprint.

This breaking of the seals thus accomplished having been clumsily reinstated, *one* Venton *noticed it*; Batti gave him some linen in return for his silence.

Some persons in the household having pointed out to Batti *that she was compromising herself* in breaking the seals, *she excused herself on two grounds.*

Firstly, that she was looking for papers needed for the marriage of M. Eugène St M . . .;

Secondly, that she was trying to find a pot filled with gold *which M. Eugène* St M . . . *was asking for, as having been referred to in a letter of his father's.*

Batti *added that moreover* she did not care a fig.

She gave, in gold, two double louis to the cook, four double louis to Joseph Pequet, and four double louis to *Blanchard*: she strongly advised all three not to breathe a word about it.

Everything points to the fact that Batti was in collusion with M. Eugène St M . . .

After breaking these various seals they had left only a cupboard hidden by hangings in the privy in the north tower.

M. Eugène St M . . . *sent for* Dourdon *the carpenter, who worked in the chateau: he enquired of him what means of access there were to this privy from the general's quarters, the door of which was under seal.*

After having devised ways and means and given his opinion to M. Eugène St M . . ., Dourdon fetched a ladder: *he fitted it on to the privy pipe:* he removed the plank *which served as the seat, and entered the room.*

Blanchard *followed him in: he climbed into the cupboard above the privy-recess; he found nothing.*

Dourdon *went in after him: the first thing that struck him was the water-jug* filled with gold.

It was antique in shape: its handle was broken: its liquid capacity was a litre and a fifth, or three uchaux *in the old regional measures of* Gaillac.

Dourdon *gave the pot to* Blanchard, *who, although* he held it in both arms, *had* much difficulty in carrying it.

Dourdon *replaced the plank in the privy: he* sealed it with plaster and mortar, *so that it would not appear to have been disturbed.*

Blanchard *handed the water-jug* filled with gold *to M.* Eugène St M. . . . *in the parquet room: it was* emptied onto the table, *and* the coins counted.

The result of this count has not been ascertained: but the sum is known for certain from the general's letter, in which he himself sets it at twenty-four thousand gold Napoleons.

To these divers abstractions may be added, with the same degree of truth, a large number of others which merit no less Madame de St M . . .*'s laying claim to them.*

Principally a case containing one dozen silver forks and spoons and one large silver spoon, brand new: the general collected them in Paris *the last time he left there to come to* St M . . ., *where he died.*

Passing through Toulouse, *this case was left in a chest of drawers* at the Rising Sun. *Madame* Daumont, *who runs this hotel, sent the case at once to the general, by express messenger at full gallop, who returned it to him a short distance away.*

There were at St M . . ., *at this same period, one dozen silver-gilt coffee spoons, and a large silver-gilt ordinary everyday fork and spoon, which the general used daily at lunch.*

What has happened, too, to his gold buckles, large and small, and his two repeater watches, the one gold, the other silver?

And all the fine linen which the general had brought and sent to St M . . ., *on his return from* Venice, Genoa, Italy, Spain *and* Barcelona.

His red morocco wallet, and a tin box with a padlock closure, *in which the general kept his diary-journal and his papers, seen in his bedroom at* St M . . . *shortly before his death.*

Not a trace of so many precious effects in the inventory made in the presence of M. Eugène St M . . . *on his representations, and his declarations.*

It will not be believed that of all these pecuniary values, all that was found under seal was TWENTY-FOUR FRANCS TEN SOUS.

Why, at the closure of the inventory, did M. Eugène St M . . . *perjure himself in replying, with his accomplices, to the magistrate's* peremptory question, that he knows only what is entered in the present inventory?

Why did he hide from this magistrate the fact that as soon as he arrived, *he had received from* Batti *two gold snuff-boxes, and eight thousand francs,* mostly in gold, *and from* M. Joseph Lacombe *twenty-four thousand francs in* gold Napoleons, *kept in a* water-jug?

Why, above all, did he not declare to the magistrate that Pequet, *manservant and* Blanchard, *groom, had handed him shortly afterwards, and* long before the inventory, *a water-jug* full of gold, *which* Blanchard, *a strong, sturdy man, carried*, with much difficulty, in both arms?

Will it be believed that after all these deliberate *misrepresentations and omissions, M.* Eugène St M . . . *had the effrontery to come,* A YEAR LATER, *and say* brazenly *that he* took the first opportunity to make this revelation to the officers of the law?

Why did he not make during the magistrate's investigations, either in the course of the inventory, or during the conciliation procedure, or somewhere in the writs, summons, subpoena, pleas *served on Madame de* St M . . ..

These facts speak for themselves: there is no need to strengthen the colours to make them more repulsive and more serious.

They appeared so criminal in the eyes of the public prosecutor, that at his request the imperial procurator proceeded with the prosecution.

Writs have been issued against four accused who are still at large.

. . . she who had never owned more than one spare garment, for whom the furthest point of the known world fell within a radius of fifteen to eighteen miles (the distance one could go and come back in a day, on foot or bumping along in the cart drawn by the old mare, she herself with the face of a horse, a mule or a goat, a passively repulsive countenance which weariness and age had gradually fashioned for her), and he, the younger brother, the Chevalier (if these words really still meant anything when applied to a lean old wolf at bay, from whose face had been wiped all vestige of youth, of any hint even of having been youthful once — except perhaps for that still untamed look he had — this outlaw who roamed the woods like a poacher, who did not even own a horse, and of whom no trace later was to remain, not a medallion, not a letter, not a document testifying to his existence (except these two simple words: my brother, when it was a question of dividing up his possessions, or that poster, those three printed columns which only vouched for his existence by the judgement which deprived him of it), he whose very name could no longer be mentioned (except sometimes, perhaps, by the women in low tones amongst themselves, in the evening around the fire), and suddenly there, back again, as if sprung from nowhere, from that vague beyond in which for her (Batti) the names of cities, of countries, of continents (when she was able later on to read the judgement, the interrogation — if, indeed, she was ever made aware of it, was informed other than by a laconic sentence in a letter sent from Turin or Milan) meant no more than those of some small market-town or other, of a wood, a meadow, a pond . . .

. . . questioned as to his profession before the Revolution? replied was Captain in an artillery regiment at Strasbourg. Asked since when he had left his unit? Replied since the month of August seventeen hundred and ninety-two. Asked where he had moved to? Replied had embarked at Bordeaux for Pointe-à-Pitre and had returned in seventeen hundred and ninety-three. Asked where he had been then? Replied at home . . .

of a meadow, a pond, asking him nothing — he would probably in any case have told her nothing (speaking to her in a rapid, staccato voice — not hard, but beyond hardness: as a wolf speaks in its own language, no doubt — about precise things: food, traps, places to sleep): neither how he had gone, nor how he had come back, whether he had been taken care of and handed on by some clandestine network or other, the secret brotherhood of conspirators, of crazy diehards, wigmakers, English spies, marchionesses, priests carrying under their skirts, instead of rosaries or breviaries, a dagger or a pair of pistols; or whether he had crossed alone, and on foot, the whole of south-western France, disguised perhaps as a journeyman, or as a pedlar, ready at any moment to grab the weapon concealed beneath the lace, the ribbons and the elixir bottles, making wide detours to avoid towns, the smallest hamlet, to elude the vigilance of guard posts, sections, committees (spending hours at the edge of a wood, at the skirt of a thicket, keeping watch on a farm, calculating the distance yard by yard, weighing up the possibilities of retreat, lengthily scrutinizing every silhouette, trying to make out from a long way off anything that looked like a gendarme, a soldier, an informer, keeping his eye, too, on the faces of those he showed his shoddy goods to, the laces and the gaudy pictures coloured blue, red, yellow, full of flames and smoke, representing, illustrating perhaps feats of arms, victories, events, each of which bore a name that was for his party a defeat, a setback, a sentence), mistrustful, packing up and making off at the least suspicion (and suspecting everything: a too winning smile, a too insistent look, a frown, protracted haggling, a refusal, indifference, interest . . .) serving little by little, every inch of the two hundred miles of vines, hills, meadows and woods, his apprenticeship as a wild animal, as game, all his senses awake or rather permanently on the alert, on the qui-vive, like a hare, a fox — *and once he plunged into a bog without realising it, the ground in a clearing (or rather what he took to be a clearing) getting spongier and spongier without his noticing it (he had already crossed waterlogged meadows and woods), the sucking noise of the water under the tall grasses louder and louder at every step until he had to make an effort to lift his feet, to pull them off the ground, to tear them from a kind of sucker which seemed to grip his soles and refuse to let them go, then suddenly sinking in up to the ankle, the water striking cold as it filled his shoe (and he still thinking that it was nothing, nothing but a flooded hollow), then he was in it up to his calves, suddenly, just like that, as if he had gone down an invisible underground step, hastily beating a retreat then, or at least trying to get back onto the solid firm ground where he had been standing a moment earlier, and then, just where his foot had been a short while before (at least where he thought it had), sinking now up to the knee: and not water, that is liquid with underneath a bottom, even a muddy one: it was uniformly soft, both on the surface and deeper down, the grass merely shorter, without water or a sheen being anywhere visible: nothing but a brownish mud in which a few bubbles rose and burst where his leg had been, both limbs imprisoned now up to the knee, and then reflecting, trying to get his bearings and not to panic, noting the sun's position, the edge of the forest which surrounded the clearing, the place he had left, much further than he would have thought, nearer on the left it seemed, managing after several attempts to extricate one of his legs, to turn ninety degrees, his left foot, when after raising it high he put it down, meeting something solid, leaning on it then with all his weight, tossing his kit far from him, leaning with both hands on the ground, flexing his muscles, pushing and pulling his right leg with all his might, feeling it slipping little by little, freeing itself, and suddenly something yielding, the left foot and the two hands sinking in at the same time, the two arms up to the elbow, the right leg not completely freed, and then blind panic, breathing faster, looking over his shoulder at the trees (they were pines), the foliage slashed by sunbeams, two white butterflies chasing each other, fluttering above the clearing, moving from sunshine to shadow, at one moment bluish, at another lemon-coloured, and somewhere the song of a bird, and through the vertical trunks, on the right, in another clearing, the roof of a farm house (but he could not shout for help, could not bring upon himself a danger greater still perhaps than the one he was confronting, shuddering, quivering, quaking at the thought that a child, a dog, could come upon him unawares, stuck there on all fours, held up to his elbows and knees in this cold, inert substance (it only moved if he did, was content merely to cling to him, to swallow him up a bit more if he shifted his weight from one limb to another), panting now, deafened by his own heavy breathing, not daring to make the slightest movement, until at last it occurred to him to lie down, to let himself go, rolling gradually over to his side, and in this position, when he had managed to free his limbs one after the other, slowly, with infinite care, starting to crawl (no longer even an animal — at least the sort you see running or swimming: something like one of those organisms half-way between fish, reptile and mammal, which at the dawn of time, before the land rose up from the sea, crawled through the mud using things themselves half-way between two definitions: fins already no longer, but not yet limbs), and at last, exhausted, taking a long while to get his breath back, once again in the shelter of the tall ferns, gazing at the innocent and treacherous clearing over which the shadows of the trees were beginning to lengthen, the same two white butterflies still rising and falling in the sunshine and the dazzling dragonflies, poised on their metallic wings, horizontal, motionless, changing height all of a sudden, then once more still in the still air, and he noticing rise up within him a sort of overwhelming, savage joy, a sense of triumph, a feeling of peace —* and later, whilst he slipped along a hedge, hailed suddenly, and not turning his head, hastening his step, deaf to the shouts of those following him, watching out of the corner of his eye, casting a glance over his shoulder, at the silhouette running to head him off, running himself too now (the shouts louder, nearer) then the other (either because he knew the lie of the land better, or because he was sturdier) cutting him off, suddenly there in front of him, panting as well, his hand already placed on the handle of the weapon concealed under his rags, the other stopping, speaking quickly, very quickly, without taking his eyes off the place where the hand has disappeared, opening his arms wide, showing his own hands unclenched, empty, still speaking ever more quickly (and all he hears are the words hunger, eat, hide), reiterating the words and gestures of peace, of invitation, moving forward, walking on, turning round, making with his carved arm over and over again the gesture urging him on, as you would a stray dog, moving on, turning round again every few yards to make sure that he is still behind, and he moving forward just like a dog, cautiously, guardedly, keeping close to the hedge, stopping short in sight of the farm (the handle of the weapon warm now in his palm as he has not let go of it), then at

288

the door, then at the entrance to the main room, turning his head rapidly from right to left, darting his gaze into every nook and cranny before going inside, taking a seat so as to be able to keep an eye on both doors, then, with one hand (the other still clutching the handle of the pistol under the table), putting in his mouth, chewing, swallowing ravenously, like a dog still (with the same intent, watchful look which hungry dogs have), whatever the fearful woman placed in front of him, assenting with brief nods of the head, but without paying attention, to the story she was telling him: her husband, her brother, her son, the parish priest (what did it matter? one or the other: so many people were dying . . .) arrested, convicted, executed — what did it matter?, all his attention concentrated now not on the two doors, the window, a suspicious movement, nor any longer on the things which he barely took time to chew without noticing their taste before swallowing them, washing them down with a glass of wine and filling his mouth again (it was only his eyes, his jaws, his teeth, his tongue, muscles, the animal part of him which functioned, stood ready, too, to get his finger to squeeze the pistol trigger, to tear his body from the bench, to make it leap over the table in one bound, and to hurl it through the nearest exit: simple reflexes like those an animal already has at birth, that makes a cat or dog thrown in the water start instinctively to swim), his attention, then, concentrated solely (whilst in between gulping down glassfuls of wine he grunted inattentively in reply to the woman's tearful plaint) upon that strange thing which had little by little taken root within him as the days had gone by and now had taken complete possession of him: that intoxicating feeling of jaunty triumph, of invulner-ability, of a pure state of violence, of absolute liberty, the kind of state of grace that is attained by those who have deliberately placed themselves in a state of lawlessness or of madness (and perhaps he was, perhaps he embodied, both at the same time, either because a sort of irrationality, an inbuilt tendency to rebel, to transgress, had led him to flout the law, or the opposite), *the world at present turned inside out like a glove, a garment as it were, shown wrong side up, or rather perverted in the sense that nothing in it had the same meaning any more, if any meaning at all, that the woman herself, her tears, her lamentations, the lad who had brought him there, the two little girls watching him bolt down in a few minutes what a*

normal man takes a week to absorb, were as foreign to him (by the simple
fact that they were living in a fixed place, under a roof topped by a chimney
with smoke coming out of it) as a domestic animal would be to a wild one:
he was elsewhere, he had passed without noticing it, without realising the
precise moment, to the other side (against the shady background of the pines
the two dragonflies hover motionless, finely tooled in the sun, resting on the
quivering action of their metallic horizontal wings, sometimes changing
position, or gaining height, by a swift action of displacement, then hovering
motionless once more — and suddenly, following a linear, slightly oblique
trajectory, one of them takes up position above the other, the two weightless,
exactly similar shapes superposed, until the long, slim abdomen of the male
slowly droops, fits together with the female's, the two glittering pairs of mica
wings still quivering with the same lightening rapidity, and now a single
body, welded together, a single elegant, elaborate jewel, the bird in the pines
(a woodpecker? a hoopoe? a cuckoo?) still regularly repeating its call in the
silence: the same silence, the same peace as a little earlier, when this cold,
inert thing grabbed him by the legs, closed over him, the same two white
butterflies flitting lightly, jerkily, ramblingly about, rising, turning,
dropping, climbing again, the shafts of sunlight merely slanting a little more
now (tomorrow, at the same hour, they would slant in exactly the same way
again, and the next day, and the next year, and the next and the next), the
precious gem, the delicate masterpiece of jewellery with the double abdomen
wrapped in its quivering silver wobbling a moment, sliding still in one piece
to one side, climbing suddenly in a disordered, winding trajectory, as if
shaken by something thunderous (but what, in the elaborate, ephemeral and
fragile grouping of organs, the wing-sheaths, the corselets, the rings made of
apparently insensate substances (horn, shell, silk): pleasure? orgasm?
release? fulfilment?) thrown off balance, wild, swept away in frenzied
flight, the metallic blaze fading, vanishing in the shadows, then, almost at
once, a single dragonfly hovering motionless once again in the sunshine over
the spongy clearing, and a few seconds later the other one, a couple of yards
to the right and a little higher up, motionless too (and somewhere under the
rings, the corselets (in the middle of the sort of yellowish or pale green, sticky
purée which spurts out, with the barely audible sound of a bag bursting,
from crushed insects, from grasshoppers, from crickets with soft bellies under
a thin carapace), something alerted, something new, something infinitely
small, infinitely fragile, which was beginning already to feed itself, take
shape, grow . . .) and he already embarked on the opposite
process, already filled perhaps with the premonition that
nothing of himself would survive, not even a name on a stele, a

cross, with no stone covering his remains, having already arrived at or rather settled into a sort of beyond, a world apart, whilst he (at least his jaws, his tongue, his throat), was crunching, chewing and swallowing the nutriments with the same untamed, lordly indifference which was later to dictate his insolent replies to the court, if this term really applies to a summary commission of seven men (six officers and a quartermaster sergeant) hastily convened not to deliver a judgement (that is to say to weigh, to determine the circumstances and motives of an offence) but to act as witnesses to a swift identity check . . .

It was Uncle Charles who found the letter: at the old lady's death, in the double bottom of her black metal jewel casket with the copper edgings and the lid fitted with a little metal handle, naively concealed under a pile of the sort of underclothes old ladies wear, permeated despite frequent washes and lavender sachets with an odour of old worn flesh, continuing to exist (something which is to flesh as obstinacy is to the will), and which she only took out (the casket) from its shroud of petticoats and camisoles, only opened for special occasions to choose from it an antique jewel, to make a gift of for one or other of her daughters or granddaughters, for a first communion or a wedding, (the casket) with its tiny key hanging on a yellowed ribbon which, when she had turned it in the lock, revealed as the lid was raised a tray, black too, with three metal compartments, in which lay the garnet crosses and the brooches with their old fashioned settings saved from ruin and wrapped in beds of cotton-wool: and it was there that it was kept: more timorously and secretly held than the jewellery, hidden under the tray, as if shielded, protected by the mineral gleam of the precious stones which seemed to stand guard like so many fiery-eyed dragons: a sheet of yellowed paper folded in four on which was simply written in pencil, in a hand which was not the old lady's: 'Letter from Jean-Pierre L.S.M. to the lieutenant of gendarmerie at Caylus on the subject of the arrest of his brother Jean-Marie'—: Yes, their police was well organised. Only they did not arrest him at once. I mean when the other got back from Tunis via a detour to the chateau to bring back the stallion. Perhaps they missed him that time, or perhaps they did it on purpose, perhaps they only left him at large, went on leaving him at large, so as to have a better hold on the elder. No doubt they found that the elder was becoming too much of a nuisance. His name was being mentioned at that time in connection with the ministry for foreign affairs. In times of revolution, families can always be turned to account in valuable ways. At any rate the dates seem to tally: it was after that that

291

Reubell and Barras made him feel unwelcome in that boorish manner. But he was still too much of a big shot to be chucked overboard just like that. So they sent him to Strasbourg to take command of a sector covering a mere couple of hundred miles. So I think you can twig now why they chose Strasbourg . . .

And then perhaps this encounter: the final meeting (or the final confrontation) between the two men, the two brothers who were never to see each other again after that: the sudden arrival, unexpected as always, of the giant who had once again traversed the pitfalls of destiny intact: hunted, evicted, contrary to all decent practice, by the treachery of an enemy court, the hatred of the sister of the queen whom he had cut down, practically handed over to pirates, taken captive, released, hunted once again by other pirates, half drowned in a storm, and, landing at last at Genoa, he was led straight (guided, warned by what instinct, what premonition?) to the place where, in the middle of some fields and woodland lay not just a heap of old stones but the most secret, the innermost part of himself. It would probably only take a glance for him to understand immediately: he wouldn't need to ask any questions (no doubt he would even avoid asking any), or to see any more than Batti's face, her bearing, her eyes, letting nothing show, and perhaps that very evening, that very night, watching in the silence, listening for the furtive sound of footsteps, of someone running away, then tearing down the steps four at a time, slipping through the door which had only just been closed, entering the darkness and the shadows in his turn, blind at first, listening for an instant, advancing a few steps, stopping, listening again: then no sound, the night, silence, the cry of the nightjar, waiting till his eyes got used to the darkness, going on again, moving down the avenue of elm trees, suddenly making out the faint sound of the clink of a gun being cocked, stopping, saying only in a low calm voice 'It's me,' and then nothing again, the never ending blackness, the night, the silent breathing of the two men in the shadows, the gentle sighing of the wind in the branches, the muted echo of a shoe scraping the stable wall, and this invisible gun pointed at him, both of them standing still, breathing silently until at last he utters the name, saying: 'Jean-Marie?', and not a sound more after that, but knowing, being able to make out the movement of the gun being lowered . . .

And What? What words, what talk passed between the two, between the outlaw and he who was the law itself, who had drawn it up, or if not drawn it up then voted it, promulgated it and enforced it, making out now in the darkness, not even hidden any more by the trunk of the tree, in front of the dense laurel, this wolf at bay. No words passed between them (not through prudence, not because either of them feared to waken a valet or a servant girl (however careful Batti was, the others also all knew how to count the eggs, the rashers of bacon and the loaves of bread) but because both of them now knew too much and had seen too much blood flow to think of groping for words as well): the silence then, after the brief murmur, the brief recognition, the two giants — the one, monumental and placid — the other (who by the addition of the second, female christian name was in a way both male and female) like a sunk-carved replica of the first, gifted, in inverse order, with the same stubbornness, the same obstinacy which had let the first through years of storms and upheaval, but it was as if this obstinacy, this pig-headed perseverence were subordinated in his case to something fantastical, something capricious: there was an insolence, a casualness, an arrogance which in that moment (the two dark figures still standing facing each other at the corner of the avenue of elm trees, staring at each other (their eyes gradually getting used to the darkness) with the same avidity, the same inexpiable hostility, the same overwhelming fondness) seemed to reverse the roles: the rebel, the refractory one, he who was now living like a hunted animal, starting at the slightest alarm, his arm constantly extended by this pistol as naturally as if it had constituted a sort of organ, an additional appendage (like those one-armed people fitted with a hook in place of their missing hand: it was such a swift, lightning-fast movement, that it was as if the gun had jumped of its own accord from the pocket or the belt into the palm, like a sort of conjuring trick, those objects or those spheres suddenly materialised between the fingers which seem to snatch, to draw them out of nothing, out of the very air) — the wolf at bay, then, with his wildcat arrogance, untamed, his thin, nervous body all muscle beneath his patched clothes, personifying at that moment something more powerful than power (not because he was still holding the gun, whose barrel was now pointing towards the ground, forgotten, but solely by virtue of the insubordination which he represented): wild, haughty, with something worse than hatred or contempt in his expression: defiance, mockery, perhaps even pity for the older one, this double scarcely older than himself, and who (during those six years when he (the younger) had hidden himself by day in attics and cowsheds, hurrying at night from one conspirators' meeting to another, living like a highwayman, with a price on his head, at the mercy of a sacked manservant, a too garrulous chambermaid, or a child, and resorting perhaps to looting on occasion) had (the elder) taken his seat in assemblies and committees, tried a king, relieved generals of their command and conducted wars — and suddenly a quiet kind of nervous laugh, as if he, the gambler, the dare-devil who was practically dead already, had simply dropped the brief question: 'Well then?' — and nothing else, nothing but these two statues face to face, the silence, the darkness, the cry of the nightjar once again, the long faint quivering of the poplar leaves at the bottom of the little valley, and perhaps one of the dogs, knowing that something was going on, coming running, the bright blurred shape hurtling down the steps, bounding along the avenue of elms with a startled, distressing howl, stopping dead (perhaps because one of the two men — without moving or turning their heads — had simply murmured 'Mirza!' or 'Pipo!' . . .), the wriggling dog now rubbing itself against their legs, wagging his tail, making quick, faint whimpering sounds, both men still motionless, listening to the chorus of awoken dogs answering each other from farm to farm, hill to hill, doleful, restless (and Batti perhaps roused too, half hidden by the curtain of her window which she holds to her, tightly, her bosom rising and falling rapidly, peering into the shadows below her, finally making out (perhaps because of the movements of the dog, or the restless sooty shape) the two dark silhouettes standing near the laurel outlined against the milky background of the gravel path, her hand gripping the curtain even more tightly, her withered breasts rising and falling quickly, and something like a tidal wave rising within her, overwhelming her, her thin shoulders and her whole chest shaken with convulsive jerks, two thin silvery lines shining in the darkness, working their way down her cheeks, her lips twitching silently and very quickly (so quickly that it is more like a trembling; a spasmodic nervous tugging), shaping mechanically the same syllables like a prayer, a supplication — and how long? and in the end what? for an instant the two silhouettes perhaps indistinguishable (an embrace?), for three, four, perhaps five seconds (how could she tell through the darkness and tears?), the vague pale shape of the dog continuing to twist around them, brushing against them with soft, muffled, doleful yelps, Batti's hands crumpling up the edge of the curtain in front of her mouth, making it into a ball which she stuffs between her lips and gnaws, sobbing, her body shaken with hiccups, and now only one of the two silhouettes standing motionless, colossal, pathetic in his heaviness, the dog motionless too on all fours and tense, as if making a dead set, looking despairingly somewhere into the darkness, the night, the empty shadows . . .

And he quite alone now standing rooted to the spot, wrapped in the coat (or blanket) thrown hastily around his shoulders by the woman (the royalist), hampering him, clinging to him, trying perhaps to hold him back, alarmed (although she had never seen his brother, although for her he was to some extent a legendary figure) or perhaps cherishing a secret and vengeful passion for the rebellious one who had remained faithful to the king: the cold pale light of the night already sculpting as in marble, obliterating the colours, hollowing out the reliefs, the monumental statue still turned towards the place where, with a short laugh, a part of himself had just vanished along with his double, was going away from him forever, whilst at that very instant, sanctioned by that sarcastic 'Well then?', the period of History was coming to an end which had seized him, sublimated him as it were, carried him above himself during the time when it needed him (as if he for his part needed these upheavals, this turmoil in order to exist, to feel alive), as if somewhere someone had, in advance, divided his life into two symmetrical periods, separated by the dazzling gleam of lightning, of a thunderstorm, only taking him out of the greyness in a fleeting blaze of glory to plunge him back into it again immediately afterwards (the doors closing suddenly before him: but it would not be so much Barras, or Reubell, not so much the doors of salons and antechambers: simply that History was going to turn aside, to follow a course where there

295

would no longer be any room for people of his kind), weighed down by an excess of gold braid on the uniform with its red, rigid collar, which would hide his stouter frame, his wounds scarcely closed and soon other disabilities, commanding in the field for a while still, then rejected, confined to honorary duties, employed on inspections or desk chores, then called up again to help ford a river or lead a siege, wounded again (as if History did him the kindness, the favour of always considering him good enough for that), then sent back to tedious staff jobs, deteriorating little by little, gritting his teeth and stifling a groan each time he hoisted himself up into the saddle, a blotchy, apoplectic and taciturn Excellency, keeping a weary eye on the sordid intrigues of policemen and shady generals, held up by the siege not of some proud fortified town, of one of those legendary crossroads like Mainz or Verona whose surrender decided the fate of a province or a kingdom, but of a quite minor place, a village held by peasants armed with scapulars and blunderbusses, and eventually brought back, decrepit and finally beaten, to die a slow death on this terrace from the foot of which ran the avenue of elms where he and his brother had stood face to face in the grounds at night, confronting each other like two incarnations of the same congenital spirit (or need) of revolt, that is the younger rebelling against the power, the authority which the elder himself derived from an act of rebellion, both of them to some extent outlaws, both of them avidly watched no doubt from another dark window by the woman with dry eyes, a dry face and a cold beauty, as if History was taking pleasure in making three destinies intersect at that point, destinies which had been decided by the solemn sound of cannon fire on the tenth of August several years earlier, triggering off three complicated mechanisms which were to lead them briefly to this nocturnal meeting place only to separate them and make their paths diverge with the same pitiless brutality: three beings which everything brought into conflict and yet who had everything in common at the same time, each of them equally passionate, bold, unyielding and hard: the Jacobin, the impassioned royalist who was capable (and she was to take advantage of this later on in order to claim a state pension) of walking through the middle of a struggle, between violent men killing each other, shooting each other at point blank range, of people whose throats were being cut, in order to slip a note to the deposed monarch who was taking refuge in the Assembly, which, at that very instant, was issuing the decree making her future husband one of the twelve messengers responsible for announcing this dethronement to the four corners of what was now (had become in the space of a few hours) no longer a kingdom, a piece of private property, but the nation from which the third person (the outlaw) was going to cut himself off, to expel himself of his own volition, with a sort of fratricidal rage and cold hatred, on mere presentation (or perhaps it was read in front of the assembled officers of the garrison?) of this signed and sealed act, which carried at the bottom of the first page, among the names of its executants (or perhaps he thought of them as its instigators?), his own name, that of his elder brother now standing before him, as he, peering into the darkness, noticed under the romantically untidy hair which was beginning to go grey, the face, suddenly aged, pitted with shadowy holes: and so perhaps no embrace, not even a fleeting moment of weakness, not even a word; only the scornful cruel laugh echoing in the silent night, awakening with a start the mother who would subsequently leave the chateau to take refuge with one of her daughters, who would curse the first-fruit of her womb, focusing on him her condemnation as upon an amputated part of her body, refusing to see him for years, only contacting him about business matters through intermediaries, Batti or solicitors, and only on the eve of her death reconciling herself with the man whom she considered an assassin . . .

And eventually, one day, not a single one of these rolls remained in the store, for they were used up gradually as the wall paper, softened and decayed by humidity, was torn off the walls of the staircase. That was a long time after the death of the old lady: she (or whoever had built up the stock) had apparently planned on a large scale, as for a long time still, once she was gone, whether out of habit too, or out of respect for the memory of the woman whom he had seen throughout his life attending with fanatical care to the preservation of the same decor, Uncle Charles went on (doing it himself at first, then, when he was too old, he got in the painter who complied with bad grace) cutting out and with varying degrees of success matching up, to the tracery of the foliage the rectangles or trapezia taken from the store, the supply gradually dwindling, being reduced to three, then two, and then one last roll itself getting slimmer, soon no thicker than a small stick, then it was reduced to a light cylinder, then a flute tied up with piece of string, and then nothing.

And so the time came when a decision really had to be made. And it was then (in a sickening smell of steam, of Turkish baths, and of hot old glue, the layers of overlapping wallpaper (there were two other papers, one with an olive pattern, in imitation of Cordoba leather, and the other mustard, under interlacing reddish foliage) coming off in long hanging tongues, showing the plaster underneath, which was also so rotten that in places great sandy grey slabs crumbled and came off with the paper) that they discovered it: halfway up between the ground floor and the landing of the first floor, the concealed door of the cupboard which had been passed up and down hundreds of times for a century perhaps by family, visitors, domestic staff, guests and children, and behind it a mass of documents, registers, manuscripts (letters, reports, marching orders, provision dockets, jewellers' bills, troop movements, speeches, decrees of the Convention, domestics' accounts, reports on battery inspections and fortified towns, estimates of fire power, states of garrisons, supplies of victuals and munitions, orders for silk stockings, plans showing the lie of the land, the strength of the enemy, possibilities for manoeuvre, for attack, for resistance, instructions to Batti, police reports, speeches to the Convention, advice on growing potatoes and the upkeep of hedges, addresses to the Emperor, remedies for dysentry and typhus, promissory notes, recommendations for promotion and for medals, accounts of journeys, personal notes, inventories for probate, various testimonials, plans for gun carriages, arsenals, and armies, with a complete list of the number of cannon, rifles, swabs, cartridges and fuses, recapitulations of wounds, campaigns, complaints, requests, orders, counter-orders, corrections, requisitions, instructions), and between the piles of notebooks, of sheets with dog-eared edges lay, folded in four, this sentence, the public notice with its official heading above an oval scroll surmounted by a Phrygean cap, surrounded by rays and decorated with laurel leaves, on which were written the simple words THE LAW. *Then this:*

JUDGEMENT
delivered
by the Military Commission of the 20th Military Division
WHICH condemns to death the prisoner L.S.M.
Artillery Officer, Émigré,
Dated tenth Prairial, year seven
of the French Republic, one and indivisible
IN THE NAME OF THE FRENCH PEOPLE

We Luce, Head of the 15th Squadron of the National Gendarmerie; Savanié, Captain, Aide-de-Camp to Major-General Chalbos; Bonnaire, Captain, Assistant to the Adjutants-General; Riboulet, Captain of the National Gendarmerie at the Périgueux residence; Valette, Lieutenant of the National Gendarmerie, same residence; Thomasson, Lieutenant, first Battalion, 70th half-Brigade; Pelat, Quartermaster-Sergeant, same Battalion: appointed and convened today tenth Prairial year seven, at eight o'clock in the morning, by Major-General Chalbos, commander-in-chief, 20th Military Division, to form a Military Commission to try the prisoner Jean-Marie-Eugène L.S.M., charged with emigrating.

The Military Commission having taken its seats in one of the rooms of the Central Administration of the Department of the Dordogne, and its members having sworn individually an oath of *hatred towards royalty and anarchy, of loyal devotion to the Republic and to the Constitution of year III*, the President read out eight letters from the Ministers of war, justice and police concerning Military Commissions, the whole brought to our attention by General Chalbos. The laws of nineteenth Fructidor year five and twenty-fifth Brumaire year three, were laid on the table, with the general list of émigrés. The guard were commanded to bring up the prisoner, who appeared free and unfettered, accompanied by his appointed Defence Counsel.

Asked for his names, forenames, age, address, place of birth and profession; gave answer, was called *Jean-Marie-Eugène L.S.M.*, aged forty-five, born at St M . . ., canton of V . . ., department of the Tarn, occupation none. He was read forthwith the report of and the reasons for his arrest, together with a letter from the Central Administration of the Department of the Tarn dated twenty-ninth Floréal last, and addressed to Gendarmerie Lieutenant Cledel.

Asked what his occupation had been before the Revolution? gave answer, was Captain in a regiment of artillery. It being asked, since when had he left his unit? gave answer, since the month of August seventeen hundred and ninety-two. It being asked, what reasons he had for leaving his unit? gave answer that he was tired of the army.

Asked whether he had not taken any documents or affidavits confirming his resignation and his service record? gave answer, that he had taken none. It being asked, in what place had he gone to live? gave answer, that he had embarked at Bordeaux, to sail to Pointe à Pitre, and had returned in seventeen hundred and ninety-three. It being asked, where he had been after that? gave answer, at home.

Asked whether he had had a passport? gave answer, that he had never had one. Asked whether he had made his residence known to the proper authorities? gave answer, no. It being asked, where he had lived? gave answer, sometimes in one house, sometimes in another, either in the Department of the Tarn, or in that of the Aveyron; and being never able to tell us the names of the people he had stayed with.

Asked why he changed his address so often? gave answer that he had a taste for it. The objection being put to him that it is very surprising that, travelling very frequently and moving from one Department to another, he had never taken out passports, and had never presented himself to the official authorities?

Gave answer that he had never had passports, and had never made himself known to the official authorities.

Asked why he was armed with a double-barrelled gun and two pistols, having on his person a belt containing thirteen bullet-cartridges and chucks, powder, bullet-moulds, pistol-locks and extraction worm? Gave answer that it was to defend himself against brigands.

The prisoner *Jean-Marie-Eugène L.S.M.* having been given the opportunity to reply on every point of his defence, both on his own and through his Defence Counsel, and both of them having declared that they had nothing to add, the guard was ordered to take the said person charged with emigration to the gaol.

The spectators having left and the doors having been closed, the members of the Military Commission read once again all the documents relating to the said L.S.M., looked again through the general list of émigrés, made sure they were thoroughly familiar with the law of nineteenth Fructidor year five and that of twenty-fifth Brumaire year three, of the letters of instruction from the Ministers of war, justice and police, and after mature and serious deliberation, the President put the following question:

The prisoner *Jean-Marie-Eugène L.S.M.* is he the same as the

300

one entered on the general list of émigrés under the following heading: *L.S.M., Artillery Officer* (*Bas-Rhin*, Strasbourg), *thirteenth August seventeen ninety-two?*

The votes having been cast, starting with the lowest ranking member, it was declared, by a majority of six votes out of seven, that *Jean-Marie-Eugène L.S.M.*, is truly the same as L.S.M., entered on the list of émigrés; in consequence, and in the light of article XVI of the law of 19 Fructidor year 5 and of article II, heading IV, of the law of 25 Brumaire year 3, dealing with émigrés, the Military Commission rules that the said L.S.M. shall be put to death.

Calls upon the Commander of the Périgueux fortress, in state of siege, to carry out, in all its particulars, the present Judgement, and that, within twenty-four hours.

Copies of this Judgement will be sent by the President, to the Ministers of war, justice and police, to Major-General Chalbos, to the Central Administration of the Department of the Tarn, and to the commander of the Périgueux fortress, in state of siege.

Signed, sealed and delivered, at noon, in Périgueux, tenth Prairial, seventh republican year.

Signed *Pelat, Thomasson, Valette, Riboulet, Bonnaire, Savanié, Luce*.

AT PÉRIGUEUX

From the Press of the Republican DUPONT, printer
to the Department

Uncle Charles slowly folding up the sheet of thick grained paper, scarcely yellowed at the edges, and setting it down on his desk, saying 'The Law. Passed by the older brother himself. The first time in ninety-three and the second at the time when he was sitting on the Council of Elders. Perhaps even when he was its president. The dates would need to be checked. But what difference would it make?: he had in any case passed it, if not put it forward, as he had voted, even called for the death of the king, the first vote entailing the second. Perhaps he even saw it as a duty. Just as he would not have hesitated to have the other fired on, or to fire on him himself, had they found themselves face to face in a battle. Besides, perhaps he did not know where he who bore the same name as himself was at that moment, perhaps he thought him dead already . . . In any case the law was quite explicit, automatically imposing the death sentence on every émigré who returned to France and was arrested carrying a weapon. And the other brother was just as unyielding, just as obstinate as he was. Because he was one of the last:

301

five months later, it was Brumaire . . .' There were some on the side of his desk (the thick register-size notebooks with their scuffed boards in faded blue, with spines and corners in vellum, and hand-sewn sheets, and letters, some of which still bore traces of yellow sealing-wax), his own papers, the analyses of musts, calculations of degrees of alcohol, craftsmen's invoices and wine-merchants' contracts pushed aside to make room for them, the registers' boards not exactly dusty (except in places, on the sections (tiny triangles) which had stuck out of the pile and on which, in the darkness of the cupboard, sandy fragments of mouldy plaster had crumbled over the years) but impregnated with or rather exhaling a fusty smell of the past about to re-emerge, if not intact at least palpable, irrescusable, like the marble monumental bust itself, the voice of Uncle Charles saying: . . . 'They are at your disposal, if that interests you. Perhaps you may still be too young, but later on . . . when you are old yourself. I mean when you are capable not of understanding but of feeling certain things, because you will have experienced them yourself . . . It is both tedious and fascinating. Because for the most part it consists of troop movements, estimations of strengths and inventories of equipment. As in great theatrical productions, or even pocket ones, there must be months of tedious rehearsal and tons of stage machinery with the sole purpose of allowing the tenor or the tubercular heroine to launch with grace into a supreme grand finale, the last sublime climax before collapsing and dying. As if History were above all an accountants' affair with long additions of figures where the balance-sheet is summed up in a few moments of commotion and murder. But, after all, he was an organisation man, an artilleryman, a specialist in alloys, in the manufacture of gunpowder and in differential calculus. That is probably even the reason why Napoleon never gave him the galloon (or the star, or the epaulette or the coil of additional gold braid — I don't know what distinguishing marks they wore in those days . . .) which he had every right to expect and which he considered himself to have earned not just by his wounds and his campaigns, but to an even greater extent by the fifteen hours' work which he got through each day. Because he (Napoleon, that is) mistrusted them. I mean: in a general way: the artillery. This body of men who were too well educated, too argumentative. Without taking into account the fact that this one had had the bad taste to be a regicide into the bargain. An autocrat, even if he owes his own throne to that initial operation, cannot allow himself to forget that fact. In any case you two have something in common: you have waged war yourself on a horse. Or rather, from what you've told me, been subjected to it . . . Like wild game, wasn't that what you said? Since our peace-loving politicians had carried obligingness to the point where they sent you to serve as moving targets so that the Germans could check the perfection of their aircraft and their bombs . . . Horses . . . along with the 'Social Contract' and Virgil, it seems they were one of his passions. Basically, as with all country gentry, in spite of his knowledge of mathematics, he was a peasant. Which explains the constancy with which he attended, by means of letters, to his several hectares of land, and the way he used the same style quite naturally to order Jourdan to guard the Rhine crossings and Batti to see to it that the field gates were kept properly shut. All those letters during all those years . . . A real handbook of agriculture. It was just as cyclic, just as regular as the hands of a watch returning to pass over the same figures on its face, month after month, season after season, while he hurried about in all directions from one end of Europe to the other with his cannon, his range tables and his interminable records of equipment. Although, if you think about it, the two things are not really that different. I mean as regards the qualities required. What I am getting at is this eternal renewal, this tireless patience or, no doubt, passion, which makes it possible to return every so often to the same places in order to carry out the same tasks: the same meadows, the same fields, the same vines, the same hedges needing replanting, the same fences to check, the same towns to besiege, the same rivers to cross or defend, the same trenches periodically opened up under the same ramparts: Koblenz, Pavia, Namur, the Meuse, Mantua, the Ijsel, Antwerp, the Adige, Verona, Peschiera, Mainz . . . Taken, crossed, lost, retaken, re-lost, re-conquered once more, lost yet again, tirelessly, without end or hope of an end, the sole variations being the foreseeable contingencies of successive coalitions of rain, frost or drought.' He (Uncle Charles) was silent, put the judgement away in one of the registers which bore on its spine, written in round hand, the ink half obliterated: 'Private correspondence of General L.S.M., from 24 Germinal Year VII to 15 Pluviôse Year VIII', absentmindedly thumbing through the pages with their pencil notes in the margin, covered from top to bottom in the same rust-coloured ink, the name of the recipient in the margin, each copy of a letter carefully separated from the next by a horizontal line drawn with a ruler, the places they were sent from and the date immediately below them, then closing it again, putting it down on the cluttered table, saying: 'And so, I suppose, you can see now why your grandmother always hid it. She who had borne the name, had written it on the flyleaves of her books when she was a girl, had, as grandfather, the son of a man whom she considered to be his brother's murderer. Why they had sold the chateau, left the village where everyone knew. The same blood which had flowed at Saint-Florent and at the crossing of the Adige pouring from the

303

chest of a condemned man stuck in front of a firing-squad and shot as a
traitor. And why he himself, in none of his letters ...

Yes. Never alluding to him. Never talking about him. Never
writing the christian name, no doubt forbidding it even to be
mentioned in his presence, including by Batti during the long
tête-à-tête in that year they spent together at the chateau, she
and he, at the chateau whilst he gradually neared his end: the
rest of a winter, a spring, a summer, an autumn, the beginning
of another winter, as if he were granted as a kind of last favour
the chance of following other than on a blue, pink or yellow
coloured plan the eternally repeated cycle of the seasons, of
ploughing and sowing, of cutting the corn and picking the
grapes, ordering the carriage to be harnessed on fine days to two
of the last horses still left in the stable, getting himself driven
from one field, from one wood to another, pointing out to Batti
with his stick the hole in a hedge, the trees to be felled, a fence
needing mending, coming back to take his seat on the terrace
whose construction he urged forward as if aware that his old
arteries were becoming less and less supple, harder and harder,
ready from one moment to the next to burst somewhere in this
brain which still functioned, this body which death itself was not
to leave in peace, doomed not only to be harshly snatched from
its grave by a mechanical digger (as if nothing were to remain of
the two brothers: the skeleton of the one mixed up with those of
other executed men in an unmarked grave, the bones of the
other scattered to the four winds), but also to be profaned,
mutilated, while still barely cold, as if not content with having
destroyed him piecemeal, condemned him to die ingloriously
in an armchair, fate had a last upset in store for the colossal
carcase: his aide-de-camp, the Le Bugnet who had followed him
everywhere, who had stood shoulder to shoulder with him on
every battlefield, coming running over at the news of his death,
getting the still fresh grave opened up again, the coffin, the
monumental marble-grey corpse exhumed now, laid on a
kitchen table (or in the open air because of the smell), the gold-
embroidered tunic unbuttoned (or snipped open: no doubt he
was beginning to swell), the chest with its greying hairs cut into
by a local surgeon or vet (or perhaps the butcher used to carving
up bullocks?), the people standing around holding knotted
handkerchiefs to their noses, the sound of the ribs being sawn

304

into, and then the heart, the muscular, purplish–blue mass, with its crown of veins and arteries sliced through any old how, hauled out, hastily dropped in a jamjar filled with alcohol and straight away covered with a sheet of parchment ties with string, the gaping chest sewn up again with big cross-stitching like a shoelace, the tunic clumsily put back in place, haphazardly rebuttoned, the body stuffed back one more into its coffin, the coffin nailed up again, lowered back into the grave, the grave refilled once more, the bystanders breathing freely again, the surgeon (butcher) washing his implements in a bucket whilst the aide-de-camp set off again, carrying away the jamjar in which the bloody mass wobbled in the colourless liquid, just like a huge prune, holding it in both hands on his knees in the carriage bumping in the ruts, then no doubt shelving it in a store-room or cupboard (coming from time to time perhaps to have a look at this sort of huge inert ball, narrowing towards its base like a strawberry, red, enveloped in yellow fat, surrounded by a network of jade-coloured veins, floating weightlessly, distorted by the magnifying curvature of the glass walls), until in reply to his there came from Paris a letter signed with a scrawl by some functionary or other with an illegible name at the foot of a few lines drafted in the administrative, dry, military language which he (the dead man) used to employ himself, with the added particular, underlined in an annoyed fashion: 'not senior officers: only supreme commanders' (or perhaps not a letter at all: the war office had other worries at the time than generals who had died in their beds, being busy with counting up everything which, from the general to the ordinary infantryman, could mount a horse, march, handle a sword, fire a rifle or a cannon, and send it to freeze to death at the other end of Europe), and then what?: coming back (the aide-de-camp), going over the same ground again in the reverse direction with the jamjar in his lap, having the grave opened up again? (surely not the coffin: too afraid no doubt of what he might not find in it), putting the jar in it? or burying it in his garden? or keeping it reverently in the cupboard until at his death his children find it, in amazement, nonplussed, and throw it out with the rubbish, higgledy-piggledy with chicken offal, bluish intestines and other refuse? . . .

As if he were being vindictively pursued beyond the grave by a triumphant, mocking curse, inventively determined to crown (punish?) his stormy existence with revolting medics' pranks, to engineer revolting, sordid vaudeville plots, pitting his heirs one against the other, so that they wrangled bitterly, through long years of legal action, lawsuits, and trial judgements, over what he left behind him: the widow who rushed over from her property at Montmorency and who had hardly stepped out of her carriage before she threw herself on the cupboards, the writing-desks, opening the drawers one after the other, crossly closing them once more, fuming, threatening, hurrying off again furiously to the nearest lawyer, she who some years later . . .

the first part of this summary is complete: the facts are established beyond reasonable doubt.

It only remains to recall the provision of the laws which condemn such actions, and which ordain that the heir convicted of unlawful possession shall make restitution to Madame de St M . . . *of the effects purloined, to her detriment, from her husband's estate.*

There is, on the subject of thefts and concealments, a principle which is attested by every author and which is enshrined in four articles of the civil code.

The principle is that the heir or surviving spouse who purloins or conceals effects from the estate, must hand them over in full without being able to have any share in them: everything belongs to the heir or to the spouse to whose detriment the objects were misappropriated, or concealed.

Count **Merlin**, *Councillor of State, member of the Institute of France, grand officer of the Legion of Honour, has written the best treatise on jurisprudence there is: he puts it as follows:*

'The penalty for unlawful possession lies in the convicted party being required not only to add to the inventory the items concealed, but also to forego the share which he might have had in them.'

But when the law speaks, what need is there of other authority, however eminent?

The civil code *has four articles bearing on this subject: 792, 801, 1460 and 1477.*

The first and last are so clear, that it is impossible to resist the temptation to quote their words.

The heirs who are shown to have misappropriated or concealed the effects of an estate, may take no share in the misappropriated or concealed effects. Civil code, article 792.

The husband or wife who is shown to have misappropriated or concealed any effects from the joint estate, shall forego his or her share of the said effects. Civil code, art. 1477.

Thus fact and law join forces in overwhelming Mr Eugène St M . . . with shame and in compelling him to hand over what, to the detriment of his father's widow, he has concealed.

Will it be objected that the acts of concealment are proven, but that the value of the items concealed is not?

It is proven massively *by the letter his father wrote shortly before his death, while still in possession of the most sound intelligence and of his most lucid* reason.

An essential part of the value is proven also by the witnesses who saw the groom Blanchard, *a sturdy and athletic man, carrying* with great difficulty, although holding it in both hands, *a water jug* filled to the brim with gold, *to M^r* Eugène St M . . ., *in the parquet room.*

If this water-jug had contained only twenty-four thousand francs in gold Napoleons, *this sum would have weighed only* fourteen pounds two groats; *how then can such a light weight be reconciled with the need for the efforts and the two arms of a man as strong as* Blanchard?

The value could also be proved in a third manner, if the General's diary *had not been made off with, since it contained all his effects detailed in the clearest order.*

This diary was in the padlocked *tin box: this was at* St M . . . *at the time of his death, as was his wallet.*

If they had not been purloined or destroyed, a faithful picture of the General's fortune would be revealed.

Fortunately Providence which, like time itself, uncovers the truth, has remedied the theft of the journal and has replaced it with notes written in the General's hand. Uno avulso, non deficit alter.

He took the precaution of preparing on loose sheets, sometimes on the back of letters, in notebooks, the jottings which he later wrote out in a fair hand in his big record book.

He was seen to write, write unceasingly: Voltaire.

He transferred every day to his diary the results of these calculations.

It is to this praiseworthy habit on the General's part that Madame de St M . . . *owes her knowledge of the state of her husband's capital, and the state of his annual income.*

If any one of the facts set out in this Abstract is denied, proof of it has been offered to Mr Eugène St M . . .: it will be done in the most compleat fashion, as the law requires.

Such is the Lawsuit pending before the Court of the first district of the Tarn.

TOULOUSE, *13 January 1813.*

SALAMON, *sometime Magistrate, briefed for the defence of Madame de St M . . . by his Excellency the High Judge and Minister of Justice.*

. . . she who some years later was to repudiate him, writing in the petitions she addressed to the sovereign hoisted on to the throne by those armies against which, all his life, the dead man had fought: 'to remove the prejudicial associations attached to the name I bear', just as she had abandoned him, left him to die by entrusting him to the care of a servant woman as soon as it was obvious that he could be of no further use to her (he who, as she herself admitted, had saved her from the executioner ('without him I was lost'), had married her daughter to a general, had made of her one of the queens of a Milan which at the time dazzled with festivities, with balls, with lavish hospitality, and in which, at the theatre, in the palaces, she took precedence over countesses and kept in her service two lady's maids, a chef, a coachman, a gardener, footmen and a little negro dressed in brocade) except to go on paying her debts, her dresses, the landscaping of woodland and the siting of pavilions in the park of the property which he had bought for her, Omphale taking for granted the . . . what? good nature, weariness? a giant's meekness? or the hold that she still perhaps had over him?, the memory of that beauty which had mastered him to the point of leading him to compromise himself, put his credit, his very life, at risk, to get her out of prison at a time when in the space of a few hours people were arrested, tried and executed on a mere rumour, a mere nod of the head from an informer (or for nothing at all: just to round out a list, make up a cartload, a full batch) — unless what still united them, even in old age, was the feeling of being rejected, assigned to the fringes, of belonging to that kind of freemasonry of boldness, of courage, which makes two foes respect each other, both possessed by the same impetuosity, the same daring which had enabled this woman to get to the royal presence on the evening of the Tenth of August and later (she was to make a point of that too), at the Temple prison, to hand him gold coins hidden in her headgear (disguised? in the costume of a baker's girl? of a laundry-maid? carrying a basket of pasties or of clothes? distracting the guards' attention with a yawning blouse, a slipping shawl?), she, with her cameo profile, her Greek-style chignon, her powdered breasts which she no doubt still went on showing off in the sort of bodices which looked like baskets, making as her only concession to her condition as a general's widow the sub-stitution of transparent muslin by satins, by velvets, choosing the colours as well (plum, hazel, olive) which suited her state as a plundered spouse, stealing a march on the provincial barrister with the turgid style, no doubt pestering him with letters as she pestered the dead man, pouring out her woes, clamouring for justice, dancing attendance, knocking on doors, wiping away innumerable tears, with red eyes, imploring, histrionic, whilst at the back of some cupboard or store-room the old worn-out heart, with its coating of rancid fat, its burst veins, its strained fibres, coloured whitish and purple, cut out with a butcher's knife, shrivelled slowly in its liquid alcohol grave.

And that son, born of the Dutch woman, brought up by women, moving almost straight from their hands to those of the quarter-masters of the training ship, and whom, in all his life, the father cannot have seen for much more than a few days, between two assignments, two postings for both of them, the lazy lieutenant-commander on whose behalf he wrote endlessly to ministers, to former friends, soliciting a promotion, protection, a favour for him (that is to say — he could conceive of no other — the first place when danger threatenend, the command or the service where he could, as he put it, 'have the opportunity to distinguish himself'), getting a miniaturist to do the portrait which adorned the cover of his tortoise-shell snuff-box, gazing thoughtfully no doubt at the flabby, surly young face with its heavy, round chin, with its sullen pout, its delicately rouged cheeks, mounted on the plinth of a gold-braided uniform collar as stiff as a stovepipe, with that blond hair, curled with tongs and ending in sailor's sideburns which looked like false whiskers, as if he were a dressed-up, spoilt child, as if here too a cruel fate had been at work, mocking him in what remained most dear to him, making of this only child, this sole fruit of his seed, of the womb in whose softness he had been engulfed, a kind of rosy-cheeked, babyish, sulky caricature, a colossus not effeminate but as it were feminised, faint-hearted, slothful, as if the blood which had flowed vigorously in the veins of the two brothers circulated here now only at a slower rate, watered-down, faded, strength now changed to heaviness, firmness of purpose to obstinacy, love of life to world-weariness: posing then for the painter, stiff, done up and chubby-cheeked, a curiously childish image of starchy propriety and of respectability, in that uniform or rather that disguise put on with a bad grace, waiting only for the death of his nuisance of a father to slough it off, to repudiate once and for all his father's world by giving up his service career, as if suddenly the sum of those stormy years lived through, cheerfully borne by one generation, weighed unbearably heavily on the shoulders of its sons, freeing himself, throwing on the rubbish heap with his stripes everything which, for better or for worse, had governed his father's life, the rashness, the transports of the heart, the ambition, the fondness for risk-taking, finding now enough strength, enough daring only to squabble wretchedly with the ageing Directory beauty over the gold louis, the coffee spoons, the earrings and the tea services.

Though he took good care to appear as little as possible, to preserve that stiff respectability which he wore like a corset, leaving again immediately after the funeral, driving four-in-hand in some gig or other harnessed to one of Moustapha's sons (perhaps the one his father had sent to fetch him the morning of his last stroke), sporting already instead of the hated uniform an elegant olive or snuff-coloured frock-coat over the embroidered waistcoat, together with silk tie, suede gloves, elegant supple top-boots, and postilion's hat cocked rakishly over one ear, as if he were outside, in total ignorance, alien to the whole business: the breaking of the seals, the furtive gleams which lit up first one window, then another, in the chateau at night, the snap of forced locks, the prised-up floorboards, the heavy tread of bearers stumbling on the stairs (as if some parodic ceremony or other was taking place under cover of darkness: as if they were removing a second time in bits and pieces that nuisance of a corpse, and in the shape not of saddle-pistols, spurs or short-sword but of Venetian glass, silver cutlery and rolls of gold coin moved out illicitly in a procession back and forth of hump-backed shadows which stretched out eerily on the walls in the light of a candle whose flame was being shielded more or less from the icy draughts by the old wrinkled hand with its yellow, chapped, horny skin, as hard and as dry as the leg of a chicken).

For he (the son) had inherited her too, along with the woods, the meadows, the vineyards, the geese, the pigs, the stallions, the mares, the hinnies, the mules: she, the old beast of burden, whom the lawyer accused of being at the bottom of it all, the survivor who had seen the foreign woman, then the younger brother, die one after the other, who had just opened up once again the linen-press in which the grave sheets were stored, selected one, wrapped it round the corpse dressed in its gold-braided uniform and folded back the flaps over the set features, her features (an old mule's or an old goat's) set too, her eyes dry or (but how could one tell? swollen and pinkish with conjunctivitis for so long) rheumy, leaking all the time without her noticing that something which was shiny and slimy, barely salty, not even tears any more, sliding over the skin (the papery leather) which framed the wings of the nose, descending towards the crumpled corners of the mouth, drying as it went or wiped away occasionally, mechanically, with the back of her hand, grim, like a sort of keeper, a kind of divinity not from an underworld kingdom but deputed by the very earth she trod without ceasing, the woods, fields and tracks, an aged ossified sovereign in her earth-coloured clothes reigning over an empire of dead men, stallions, crammed geese, and ghosts.

Or rather no. The opposite. That is to say it was she who had inherited him. They had taken the two others away from her, they had snatched this one from her ten years earlier to send him far away, into the vague beyond, without clearly-defined shape or limits, which began a day's march or cart-ride from the place where she had been born, where her whole life had been spent, and which made up, so far as she was concerned, the totality of the known world, surrounded (as on those old maps where geographers used to encircle lands which had been explored with a liquid ring peopled with monsters) by reefs and whirlpools which swallowed up those who ventured near them, or who, at best, came back transformed by some witch or other

311

into wild beasts, or were thrown away like trash, worn out, drained, at the end of their tether, just about able to hang on for a few months longer in an armchair, before collapsing suddenly and giving up the ghost.

But that one, at least, was returned to her. And not yet knackered: not hounded, run to earth, in hiding, posed to commit murder, but respected, prosperous, and not half-crippled, breathing his last, but fresh, pink, whole. And then pressing him, urging him on herself perhaps to throw off that uniform, to reject everything which, in her eyes, recalled, symbolised in one way or another that violence, that curse which had swooped down on the family like a plague, a taint, had ravaged and scattered it, had devoured, consumed the two brothers, had consumed her herself, destroyed her slowly in their shadow, reduced her to wearing mourning for them while they were still alive: perhaps, with his girlish complexion, his insipid looks, he seemed to her to personify an insolent denial of fate, a triumphal revenge, the reward of years spent not only in counting and recounting the sacks of grain or the casks of wine, checking the fences, restocking the hedges and supervising the tree-felling, but also in waiting, alone and in silence, slowly desiccating, watching grimly over those animals, those meadows, this deposit or rather this burden which she was at last going to be able to free herself of by handing it over to him in order to have, at last, the right to die herself, to take a rest, now that all was over, that the last shovelful of earth had fallen back on the coffin of the last survivor of the two brothers, to whom it only remained, as the last duty she would be called upon to perform, to become a thief on behalf of his son, at a pinch even (assuming the lawyer was right) against his will, rebelling for the first time against him who all his life had tyrannised her, speaking to him now as an equal (since she herself was soon going to die), the two old people (or rather the dead man — the monumental corpse slit open like a mattress, emptied neatly and sewn up again by the mattress-maker — and she who was not much more than a mummy) continuing not in the grave but as it were through the tombstone the conversation carried on for years through hundreds of letters which converged from all over Europe on the same point and the replies which went back from there, the sheets covered with her clumsy, painstaking handwriting in

312

which she made pathetic efforts, her face screwed up, to turn into words meadows, ditches, young seedlings, foals, ploughed fields, woods, the hours of walking, roads, getting a few weeks later from one of the places whose names she laboriously copied out (Turin, Milan, Hanover, Mittelhagen, Barcelona) the letters sealed with wax which she opened, deciphered or rather decoded, trying to see in what he called the blue division, the green division, the pink division, those poplars, acacias, fields, vineyards despatched in a way by post on square pieces of paper covered with little signs on the basis of which (after the fashion of those microscopic Japanese flowers which, when dipped into water, swell up and fan out into unsuspected whorls of petals) there took shape once more the exacting soil, the hills, the valleys green, russet, parched or muddy by turns under the changing skies, the slowly drifting clouds, the dew, the storms, the frosts, in the unchanging alternation of the unchanging seasons.

She then: her yellow body, her shapeless clothes, the same skirt, the same loose jacket apparently impossible to wear out, worn winter and summer buttoned up to the chin, the too-wide, gaping collar revealing, like the mouth of a shell, a tortoise neck with bulging sinews sticking out, more and more emaciated and scraggier as the years went by, up the first, last to bed, grabbing a bite standing up, like a horse, the bread and the cheese in one hand, the knife in the other, gazing straight in front of her, setting off again before having even swallowed the last mouthful, hustling along the farmhands and maidservants, counting out the wages, presiding in person like a sort of female eunuch over the matings which she kept detailed accounts of, wrote up in the evening by candlelight in a notebook with pages covered in deletions, columns added up again and again, making mistakes, starting afresh, stopping to think, counting on her fingers, crossing out the sums she got wrong, getting up at night to attend to a horse with colic, to help a foal to be born, month after month, year after year, bringing home every fortnight with unfailing regularity the same letters at once tyrannical, patient and meddlesome which she held at first at arms' length for a moment, her head and shoulders thrown back, screwing up her eyes to make out her name, the address, with each time the same puzzlement, the same apprehension, before going up to her room, groping in a drawer for the case against whose clasp her broken fingernails scrabbled clumsily until she managed to get it open, taking from the threadbare velvet padding one of those steel-rimmed pairs of glasses whose bridge was fitted with a scrap of yellowed cambric wound up with black thread, opening them out, fitting the sides carefully behind her ears, closing the case again, making up her mind at last (resigning herself) to prise off the wax seal, going up to the window, her lips moving silently whilst between her flabby eyelids her pupils moved slowly from left to right, returned quickly to the left before moving off once more, her brow knitted, her lips continuing to mould the words one after the other, then, her reading done, standing without moving, still facing the window, her head raised, gazing into space, both hands holding the letter now like an apron in front of her stomach (like the members of a chorus waiting patiently, expressionlessly, for the conductor to point his baton in their direction, the score dangling at the end of their arms), then reading it through once more, as if she were trying to learn it by heart, going back over a sentence, a name, rereading several times the closing formula, always more or less the same: 'My son is well, my wife sends her regards, yours affectionately,' or: 'Madame and Eugène are well and send their regards, yours affectionately,' or: 'Madame sends her regards to you and Blanchard, I have no news of my son. Yours affectionately', making up her mind at last to fold the letter up as carefully as a laundress, paying heed to tuck in each fold precisely, smoothing them down, undoing three buttons on her jacket, slipping the letter inside, putting away her glasses, her gaze still absent, thoughtful, whilst over and over in her head ran the words, the sentences, the orders, the advice, the reproofs, as if she could hear the familiar voice itself, obstinate, authoritarian, stamped with that quiet harshness, that unbending calm which he seemed to have elevated into a rule whatever the circumstances, dictating to successive secretaries who copied out with equal unconcern, in successive registers bound in faded blue boards, battle-plans as well as instructions about seed time, letters to ministers as well as directions about potato growing, and proposals for promotions and decorations as well as reports of service missions: *I think that what was left of the stubble in the plum-*

314

tree division has been ploughed in for some time now with the big plough, in case it has not been done you will see to it at once so that the frost can get at the soil and so that once May is out there shall be no land lying fallow but all shall be under cultivation,' 'It is necessary, citizens, to send large calibre cannon balls to Flessingen. You can check whether any were sent to Dunkirk when I was in charge of the expedition to that island. Political reasons dictate that you should always maintain an imposing strength on Vanheren island to defend the mouth of the Scheldt on which Flessingen stands, you must know that the english will make the greatest efforts to seize it and so long as we are not in control of a river which can rival the Thames . . .,' 'You will see to the cutting and faggoting of the portion of the big wood which I had felled two years ago and which I decided to leave on the ground to protect the undergrowth: I thought that the branches would make it harder for the animals to get in; you will set aside every log which is six foot long or more, is straight and able to be squared, the rest should be roped up, you will let me know the quantity,' 'All my efforts to keep peace having been in vain I was expecting war between France and Naples to be declared any day by one or other of the two powers when on 27 frimaire I received a letter from Mr de Gallo which informed me of the intention of the King of the Two Sicilies to break off all friendly relations with the French Republic, he added that a dispaccio would be issued the next day by H.M. which would order all french people to leave his dominions within forty-eight hours under pain of being treated as spies; I resolved therefore to charter a genoese vessel La madona del porto salvo displaying the flag of truce, and to announce to the french that we would take aboard as many of them as it would carry . . ,' 'Dear Batti, I have received the letter in which you announce Jean's arrival; care must be taken to exercise those mares every day so that their legs do not swell; it would be even better to get them to do some harrowing. If the ground is not too soft do not neglect to do that. You complain that I scold you, but I must when you do the wrong thing: for example you should . . .,' 'We particularly enjoin you, Citizen General, to station a strong garrison on Belisle, you must sense that once the equinox is past the english will try to harry our coasts, and it is a question they must be giving particular attention to, our confidence in your abilities is entire and we are fully persuaded . . ,' 'You will get the gardener to thoroughly work all the acacias in the wood, all the little horse-chestnut and sweet-chestnut trees planted near the big poplar cave, you will get him to weed the maze of my North house, all that done and done properly and inspected by you, you will give me an account of,' 'On 21 frimaire about eight o'clock in the morning, finding ourselves off the Roman beaches to the north of Monte Circeo, we

315

espied 3 vessels appearing to take the same course as ourselves, about 10 o'clock we joined up with them being called to submission by one of them: I myself went on board the latter in a small boat despite a heavy swell, taking along passports given me by Admiral Nelson and by Mr Hamilton the English ambassdor, but . . .,' 'Tell Louis Fabre to get building stone quarried, preferably in the old hemp field; there are several lucerns which are on the surface and that will do the field good; I need plenty of building stone. I hope the gardener has already replaced the hedges and dead trees, as well as thoroughly restocked the banks of the . . .,' 'The movements of the Austrians on the Adige, said to number 70,000 by units, make me wait impatiently for the 400 horses which should arrive next month in Novara: having here only from 10 to 12,000 infantrymen, 25 to 30 cannons would be needed to defend the positions and to avoid being overrun in an instant; if we are attacked, I will take all measures in my power to have this number of cannons in the battery, I will mix horse and foot artillery, both French and Italian, and as I shall have many unemployed gunners, until I can supply them with cannon, I will lead them myself into the line . . .,' 'As soon as the Poux field is well ploughed, manure it. Once the soil is ready you will get it sown with big vetch and with rye, but dose the rye extremely thinly, you will have alfalfa put in at the same time good and thick, that is to say in two sowings, but you will have this done with the big plough in furrows 8 to 10 hands wide to allow the water to drain off, you will leave . . .,' 'the bey has one of the handsomest faces I have seen in my life, he has a penetrating gaze, he is 40 years old fairly dark-skinned without being black, fine colours fine beard starting to go white, he was on a sofa, sitting in the oriental manner; he made me sit beside him and had coffee served. It will perhaps be curious to establish a comparison between the Bey of Tunis and the King of Naples and Francis the second, it will perhaps be piquant to make the contrast between a prince whom Europeans call a barbarian and that crowd of princes who rule in Europe, some of whom take pleasure in coursing rabbits in their apartments whilst others indulge in hunting and sex and surrender one of the most beautiful countries in the world to the whims and dislikes of a princess who listening only to the voice of the spirit of vengeance . . .,' 'The damage which you tell me was done in the garden and in the meadow by the floods of 18th 7ber must be repaired at once. But I had clearly told the gardener that he had to plant there a good double hedge which does not stop the water but does stop the brushwood it carries. Give me a full account of when the repairs were carried out and of the way they were carried out,' 'I do not see that any of the preliminary measures have been taken: the plan is to use sand moulds, but while waiting to go about it it seems to me that it would have been a wise precaution to have the means of making castings according to the old method as a standby: however I am sure that no chill-mould has been put into working order, although there exists in the arsenal at Turin a great quantity of bronze ordnance of different calibres, it was made in the days of the King of Sardinia; in my capacity as General Commander in Chief of the artillery in Italy, I have the right to complain about the unconcern shown by the Deputy-Director of the ironworks; when the government has set up . . .,' 'I am pleased to learn that this year's colts are fine-looking: it is impossible with an Arab stallion and with thoroughbred mares not to get good results. It is pretty difficult for the grain of seed to get lost in the soil through drought, unless the animals eat it; I suppose if as a result of the solstice it is raining there as it is here the potatoes will be . . .,' 'I have every reason to believe that my son will be made lieutenant-commander at the next promotion board, if he was not last time it is because he has not shown much zeal for the service; he has asked me several times if he can leave it; when he came back from America and disembarked from La Badine, instead of asking to serve again straightaway, he quickly asked if he could return to Toulon, what business had he there? The whole Navy has asked to serve in the Channel, it was at the time the most brilliant posting, but did he ask for it? When at his age one fails to show . . .,' 'You will get the plot which I bought near the river sown with little millet, vetch and maslin; I don't want my pigeons to starve. You will tell the gardener if he is there, the servant if he is not, to have plenty of willows planted below the path by the river which ends at the bridge, in the old bed of the stream and adjoining the path at the spot where no grass grows, a large number of willows should be planted well separated from each other, tell Blanchard not to forget to break in my fillies and the little mule, he . . .,' 'I had designated the sites of eight batteries on the Adriatic coast, they have been working on them for five or six months now, and as the work of earth-piling was to be done by peasants for payment, I now learn that the whole month has been allowed to go by without their being paid and that instead of getting wages they have been subjected to punishment, I learn that the gunners who were only supposed to supervise the work and load the batteries and to whom ten French sous a day had been awarded work the whole day in the mud and that they get only ten Milanese sous: you can appreciate, General, that I will not put up with such abuses, as soon as I found out about them . . .,' 'as soon as you get my letter stop letting either La Superbe or Saléma go to pasture, get them well fed in the stable but without oats, get them to do every day half a league or a league so that the road does not come as a surprise to them: if they have not been shod they

317

must be shod. As soon as the second crop of hay has been cut by the river you will turn the first, the Redon meadow, over to pasture; when it has been well grazed you will get the ordinary plough passed over it once and not too deeply . . .,' 'Citizen General, when you passed through Piacenza I had the honour of seeing you for a minute only, but you led me to hope that on your return you will be able to grant me a few moments more. I passed on your message to Mme Scuti, she was grateful to be reminded of you so respectfully, but she added that when one knew Gen. Murat, the ladies especially were not content simply with kind remembrances and that she still wished to see you, she is looking forward to your return, and I only wish, General, that it can be another reason for . . .,' 'Take good care that the horses do not go grazing in the cherry-tree division, coloured blue, the lucern and the clover which are there not having been cut yet being tenderer than the others could not be grazed without damage,' 'I have the honour to inform Your Excellency that arrangements have been put in hand at the foundry to do a casting in H.I.M.'s presence in Pavia; as firing must begin 16 or seventeen hours before casting, I would be grateful, My Lord Marshal, if you would let me know if His Majesty intends that it be carried out in his presence and what is the hour that would suit him. I need to know this in order to fix the time when the fire has to be lit. If H.M. wishes to see the various artillery establishments, I have the honour of alerting Your Excellency to the fact that the workmen come on duty at 6 o'clock in the morning and that if His Majesty wished to see them earlier, it would help if I could be told beforehand so as to get them in earlier, always assuming that H.M. would wish to see the workshops in full operation. I have the honour to be, Your Excellency, Your Excellency's most obedient servant,' 'Get ivy planted round the fountain wall as well as round the poplar opposite, see to it that it is planted carefully because nothing takes so easily as ivy does and if it does not take I shall know that you have been remiss, do not forget to check whether the . . .,' 'It rankles with me, General, that you told me the other day that I had made excessive demands after the siege of Stralsund, but I only asked for favours in respect of six individuals, i.e. four crosses and two promotions; His Ex. Marshal Brune to whom I submitted the list finds it insufficient, not only for the french but he tells me that I was forgetting the foreigners and that I must not lose sight of the fact that I had 4,000 artillerymen under my command, not only frenchmen but italians, spaniards, bavarians, wurtembergers, hessians and dutchmen. Still, among the requests I made I did reward two horse Artillery companies for the siege of Kolberg, particularly one captain who had five horses killed under him, as for the foreign officers I saw them at work and it is there that they must be judged and particularly on 17 April when we fought for 17 hours . . .,' 'Take good care to have weighed a cart of 10 hundredweight of hay and make them all the same, give me a full account of the number of carts returning, by meadow and by numeral; tell me the quantity of bundles I got both from the Strébole mowing and from the orchard above the avenue. Is the corn looking good? Does the clover in the green division yield plenty of fodder? Has the big walnut-tree division been mown yet? How many cartloads were there? Are the potatoes good? Is the corn high? Will there be some straw? Go round and check all the climbing vines, look into . . .,' the handwriting of successive secretaries changing, at one point ornate with elegant flourishes, paraphs, calligraphed endings, at another whimsical, uninhibited, at another again dry, regulation-style so to speak, the lines stretching out monotonously one after the other as if the indefatigable marble voice carrying on dictating was becoming more monochord in tone, revealing nothing yet however, although here and there moments of slight weakness could be felt, with one year heaped on top of the next, frailty on top of injury, exhaustion on top of fatigue, as if the gigantic statue was starting just noticeably to split, to crack, the tone changing sometimes too, becoming less self-assured: *'. . . as for my future plans, I have not yet made any. H.I.M. has twice promised me the Senate and I am sure I will end up by getting it, but I am forced to follow events; I firmly intend to avoid active service in future, two gunshot wounds which I received, a double hydrocele which tires me greatly on horseback no longer allow me that activity which must constantly be deployed, I was officially recommended to H.M. to take command of the Artillery of the Armies in Spain, but he replied 'He must rest', I would have found it really tiring chasing all over Spain without any hope of glory since not a shot will be fired . . .,'* the cracks getting stealthily larger, the assemblage of flesh and bone, of pipes, of worn-out muscles, giving in, letting him down for the first time, fighting shy, put to work again nevertheless in spite of its protests, the humiliations, in Toulouse, now, rather than in Milan, in Perpignan rather than in Mantua, then, as they still needed old horses, tireless nags, kept happy with a new decoration, a knick-knack, as a dog is thrown a bone, sent (dragged) grumbling, stiff in his joints, to the country where no glory awaited him, the monumental and apoplectic Excellency striding one more up and down on the floorboards or flagstones of some official residence where, in the courtyard, the couriers' horses were pawing the ground,

319

listlessly dictating routine orders, casting a weary eye over the dispatches, the victory bulletins, Lerida, Mequinenza, reading for the nth time in twenty years reports which had also become routine: '*18 days of siege, 6 days of open trenches, 4 days of fire, 10 thousand cannon-shots, breach, prisoners . . .,*' handing the dispatch to the secretary or the staff-officer inured to the formulae of congratulation, registration and transmission, signing without bothering to read over, the old blotchy mask whose flesh was starting to sag, to sink, to slip over the embroidered collar of the uniform, rigid most often (not severe, hostile: simply rigid), whilst day after day with an empty stare he went on dictating the same reports, the same arsenal inventories, the same complaints, the same summaries of goods, fodder and gunpowder available, apathetic, far away, only brightening up, every week, at the same time, once the day's business had been dealt with (and then leaning over the secretary's shoulder, attentive, watchful — and only, in the silence, the pen scratching as it ran over the thick paper, the shoes of a restive horse clattering from time to time on the paving-stones outside — and perhaps somewhere in the room too the invisible sniggering ghost, its body peppered with bullets) in order to dictate with an old man's stubborn, bitter relentlessness the instructions repeated a thousand times, the questions asked and asked again a thousand times, the painstaking suggestions about sowing, covering, bottling, until gradually the worn-out voice begins to lose its strength too, to drop, until the monotonous rows of signs written in rust-coloured ink repeat only bitter recriminations, a monotonous rehashing of grievances, of reproaches, and at the end, giving vent dismally, gloomily, interminably to one long moan: '*I do not see the point of paying a gardener for the whole year and then when I come to St M . . . finding nothing in my garden it is outrageous that I spend 6 to 700 francs a year on food and all and still have, three-quarters of the time, to buy the onions and garlics and all the big crops that keep: I have no need of melons and fine crops since I am not there: I need lots of onions, peas, lots of garlic, lettuces, chicories, cabbages of all kinds, leeks, turnips, lots of sorrel, spinach, artichokes and I have not yet eaten any at St M . . .; you can tell the gardener that I am not pleased with my garden, that he takes very little interest in it, that provided that his days are paid it does not matter to him if the garden produces things or not, and that does not suit me, I do not mind the money if there is some return on it* but everything that was spent on my garden has been wasted as if I had thrown it out of the window, you do not tell me whether you have had the foot of the hanging vines hoed and manured, both at the wood by the track and at the North house, you do not tell me whether you got the acacias which I planted in the wood seen to, you do not tell me if you have had the nurseries by the tomb bank worked over, you tell me that you have made thirty-five ells of tow and twelve of linen, that is a very small amount, so much linen is needed in a house, I am not pleased that you only make so little, a hundred ells of each kind need to be produced each year, all the hemp must be put to it, have it spun either for cash if spinning is cheap, or by part exchange if spinning is dear, I do not mind paying to have it done, since you have been there I should have had my cupboards full of linen and I have very little, have all the dead hedges and small trees been replaced? I see to my chagrin that you have not bottled my white wine, you know very well I get my white wine bottled every spring, if you haven't any bottles you should write to me in advance, I would have some sent to you, you must realise that I have too much on my mind to go bothering myself how many bottles I have at St M . . .: see though how your carelessness deprives me of a particular enjoyment: when I go home it is to drink or eat what belongs to me, the best available, but white wine cannot be made to sparkle if it is not drawn at the full of the March moon, so if there is still time when you get this letter see that some of it is drawn, be it only 20 or 30 bottles so that I can taste it when I arrive; this is how you can get bottles, the bottles of blackcurrent wine must be emptied into a keg, this ageing wine has seemed to me to be going off, you will fill a certain number of bottles the day after you get my letter and you will take care to write down the date when you do it, you can also put some into demijohns, you will put two or three grains of barley into each bottle and two crossed threads over the cork, in spite of which I can tell you that the results will be poor because the wine will not be the colour it should be, I cannot, however good-willed I feel, praise you for your carelessness any more than for remembering to have the hedge which divides me from the Marshal's wood checked only at the end of March whereas in the wet weather during the months of 9ber and Xber a hedge which today will not take could have been replaced successfully, that makes a whole year wasted then, so you imagine that I have many years left to throw out of the window? When you only have 5 or 6 years to live you have to be a bit thrifty with your time, I would have preferred you to have made me run up debts of a hundred crowns than to have lost me a year as you have done, because with a hundred crowns I will not get back the enjoyment I would have had drinking good wine from my own estate, wine whose quality depends on *being bottled at the full of the March moon which only lasts eight days, that's how through carelessness when I get back home, I find neither garden produce, although for two years now I have paid the gardener for the whole year, nor fruit because nobody takes the trouble to preserve them, although my father was a very good fruit-preserver, that's how I find neither lentils, peas nor beans, even through they grow well on my land, simply because nobody takes the trouble to do it; and then you will say that nothing pleases me, but once again do you think I have so many years to throw out of the window? . . . '*